THE BEAUTY

™

VOLUME ONE

CAUTION   BIOHAZARD   CAUTION   BIOHAZARD

IMAGE COMICS, INC.

ROBERT KIRKMAN Chief Operating Officer • ERIK LARSEN Chief Financial Officer • TODD McFARLANE President
MARC SILVESTRI Chief Executive Officer • JIM VALENTINO Vice-President • ERIC STEPHENSON Publisher
COREY MURPHY Director of Sales • JEFF BOISON Director of Publishing Planning & Book Trade Sales
JEREMY SULLIVAN Director of Digital Sales • KAT SALAZAR Director of PR & Marketing • EMILY MILLER Director of Operations
BRANWYN BIGGLESTONE Senior Accounts Manager • SARAH MELLO Accounts Manager • DREW GILL Art Director
JONATHAN CHAN Production Manager • MEREDITH WALLACE Print Manager • BRIAH SKELLY Publicity Assistant
SASHA HEAD Sales & Marketing Production Designer • RANDY OKAMURA Digital Production Designer
DAVID BROTHERS Branding Manager • ALLY POWER Content Manager • ADDISON DUKE Production Artist
VINCENT KUKUA Production Artist • TRICIA RAMOS Production Artist • JEFF STANG Direct Market Sales Representative
EMILIO BAUTISTA Digital Sales Associate • LEANNA CAUNTER Accounting Assistant • CHLOE RAMOS-PETERSON Administrative Assistant

www.imagecomics.com

THE BEAUTY, VOL. 1. First printing. March 2016. Copyright © 2016 John Layman. All rights reserved. Published by Image Comics, Inc. Office of publication: 2001
Center Street, Sixth Floor, Berkeley, CA 94704. Originally published in single magazine form as THE BEAUTY #1–6, by Image Comics. THE BEAUTY, its logos, and
the likenesses of all characters herein are trademarks of Jeremy Haun & Jason A. Hurley, unless otherwise noted. IMAGE and the Image Comics logos are registered
trademarks of Image Comics, Inc. No part of this publication may be reproduced or transmitted, in any form or by any means (except for short excerpts for journalistic
or review purposes), without the express written permission of Jeremy Haun & Jason A. Hurley or Image Comics, Inc. All names, characters, events, and locales in this
publication are entirely fictional. Any resemblance to actual persons (living or dead), events, or places, without satiric intent, is coincidental. Printed in the USA. For information
regarding the CPSIA on this printed material call: 203-595-3636 and provide reference #RICH–669196. For international rights, contact: foreignlicensing@imagecomics.com.
ISBN 978-1-63215-550-4. Comic Cave variant ISBN 978-1-63215-789-8. Hurley's Heroes variant ISBN 978-1-63215-808-6. 6ixth City variant ISBN 978-1-63215-810-9.

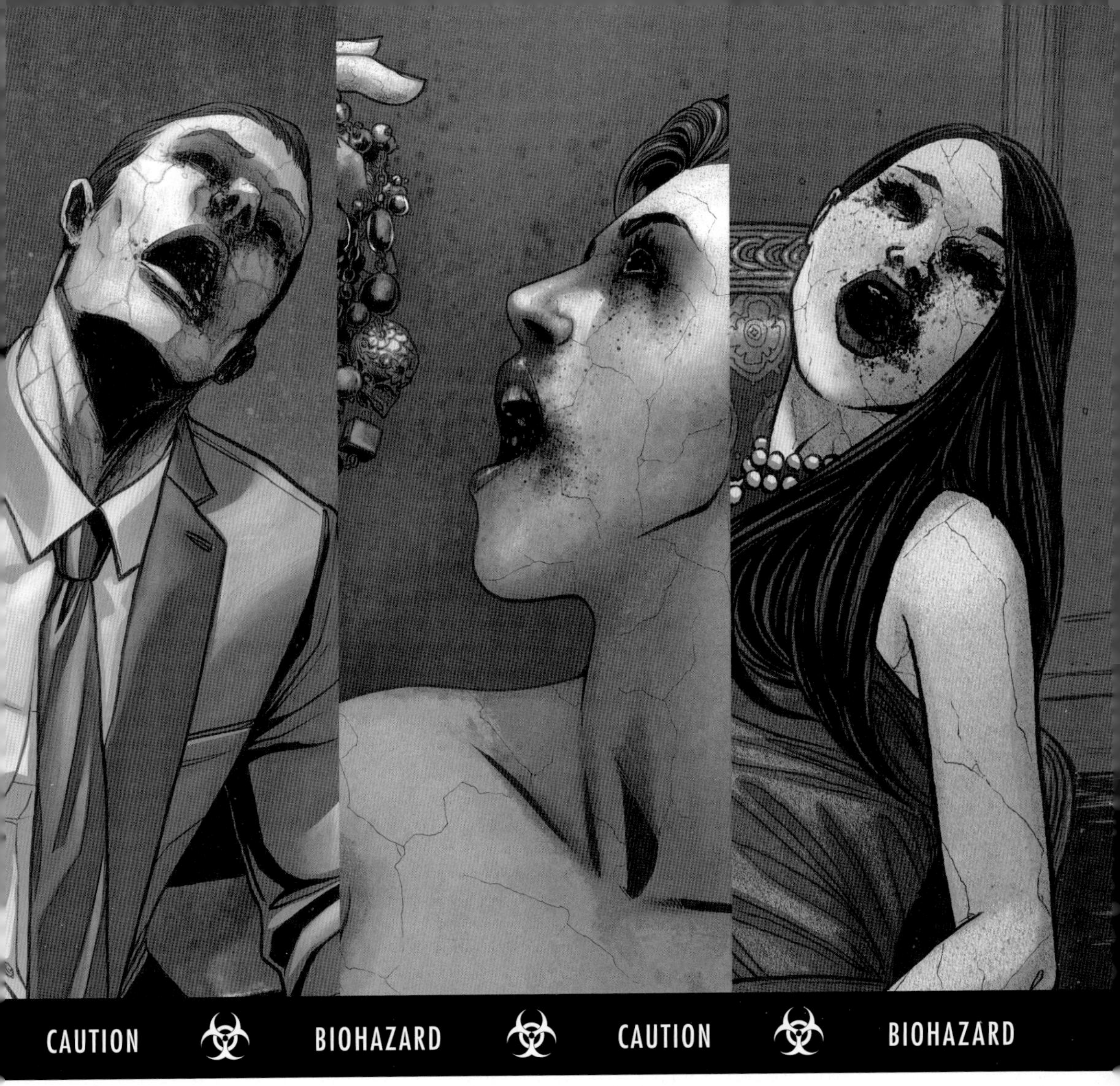
CAUTION
BIOHAZARD
CAUTION
BIOHAZARD

JEREMY HAUN
JASON A. HURLEY
story

JEREMY HAUN
art

JOHN RAUCH
color

FONOGRAFIKS
lettering & design

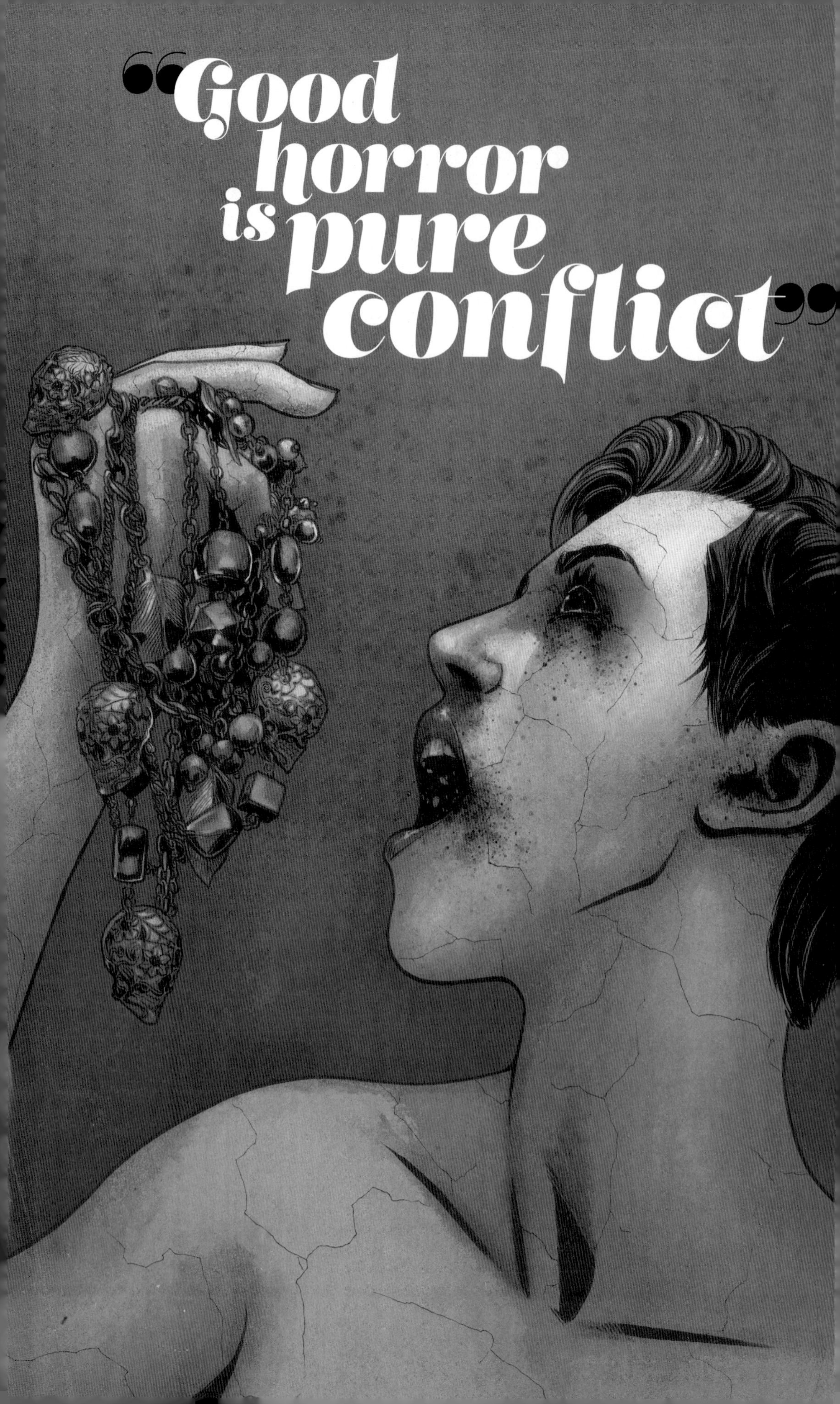
"Good horror is pure conflict"

INTRODUCTION

I HAVE ALWAYS BEEN A HORROR BUFF. The first novel that ever really caught me was a horror tome. I was about nine and I was away at sleep away camp for the first time. The camp was intensely focused on sports, and me, being a D&D kid... needless to say I felt a bit out of place and lonely. I had a couple pals, fellow geeks, and we'd volunteer for arts and crafts every chance we could to trade comics our parents had sent in the mail or run campaigns. (An aside, but my handwriting, should you ever see it, STILL bears traces of my dungeon master script in its 'y's and 'a's). But it was a rough summer. There was a good deal of bullying, of stronger kids winning out, and so on. I was looking forward to getting home, and that was it.

So I didn't think much of it when the counselor in our bunk told us he was going to make a ritual of reading to us every night. He had a book he wanted us to hear. He'd measured the length and if he did it right, he could start the book on the first night and end on the last. The book was Stephen King's *Eyes of the Dragon*. At first, I was too wrapped up in my own worries to listen much, but within days, the story—with its wonderfully twisted mythology and rich, complicated character work—had caught me. The evil Flagg. The unfortunate Roland. The highlight of the day for me quickly became the coming of night, when King's world would open to me again.

Now, as an adult, I've re-read the book a couple times. And what I've realized is that the things that caught me about the story weren't the things I assumed were catching me back then—the suspense and scares and the gruesome ends (though no one does better gruesome ends than King). The things that caught me about the book had to do with the way in which it used its monsters and heroes to hold up a kind of mirror to the reader. This was the '80s

and as a kid I was deeply scared of nuclear war, of things falling apart because of political dealings I didn't understand, and here was a villain—Flagg—who plotted and schemed to destroy the kingdom from the inside. It spoke to me personally, character after character; here was a boy who let his own brother be imprisoned because of his insecurities. Here was a son imprisoned in a place from which there was no escape, but who refused to lose hope and wove himself an escape rope from a toy loom.

I'm digressing, but my point is this: I fell in love with horror because what the best horror does is make us look at the most frightening aspects of ourselves. The monsters are reflections of our fears about the world we've made or about ourselves.

Good horror is pure conflict, and it's hard to find.

But when Jeremy first sent me THE BEAUTY, I knew this series was just that: good horror. The best.

The book has one of the best high concepts I've come across in a long time—what if there was a disease that made its hosts beautiful? It's the kind of premise that immediately offers scares in the best way. And from that first death on the train, the story will grab you. Not because it's horrific (though it is), but because it speaks to something deeply scary about human nature. The whole book does. Its characters are fantastic, Vaughn and Foster are rich and layered creations. The plot is gripping and expertly designed. I could go on and on but I don't want to ruin this one for you. Just know that you're in for a wonderful, twisted treat.

In the end, THE BEAUTY is the kind of book I look forward to reading at night after a long day, not to escape what's scaring me, but to look it in its ugly, beautiful face.

Scott Snyder
February 2016

CHAPTER

1

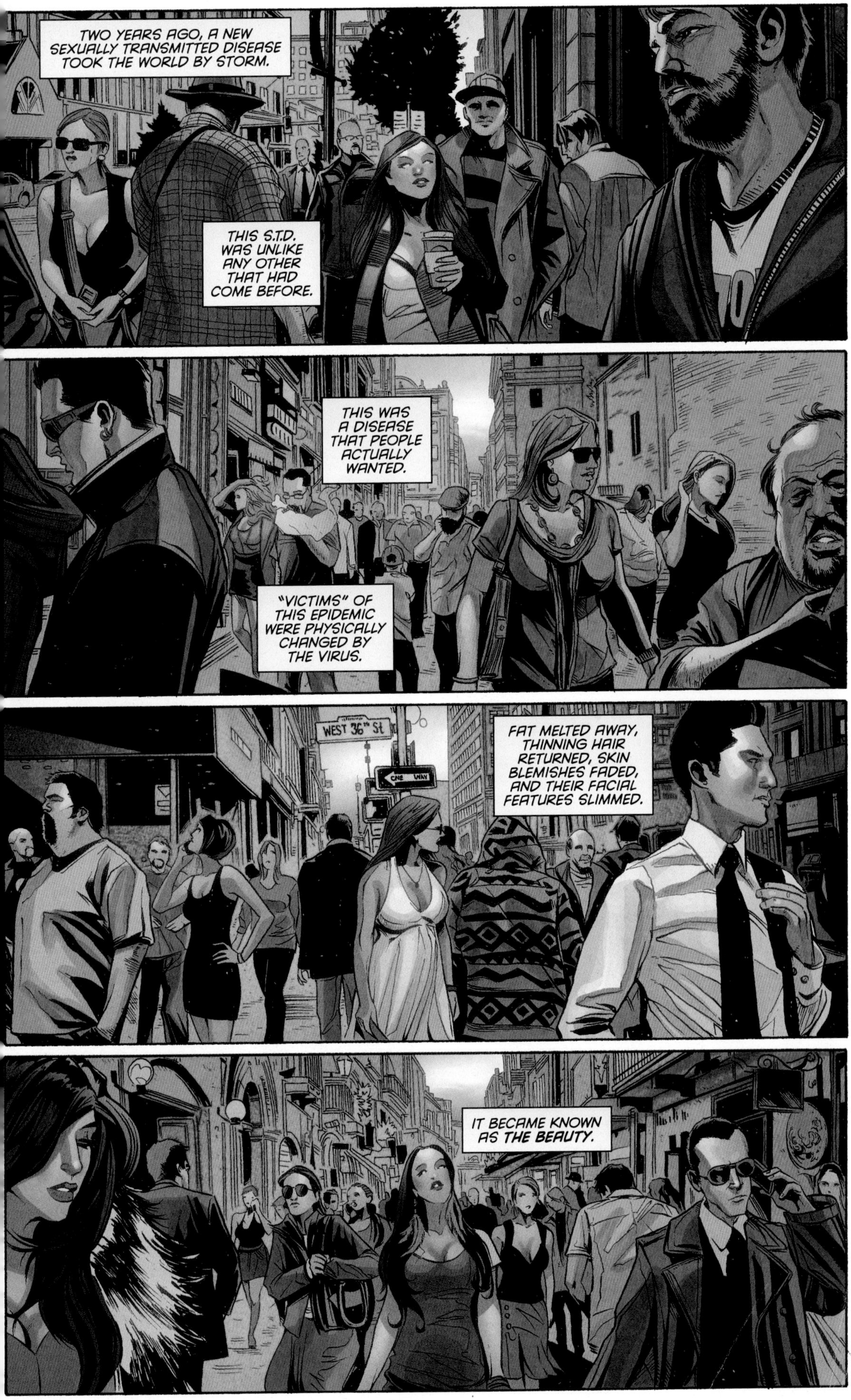
TWO YEARS AGO, A NEW SEXUALLY TRANSMITTED DISEASE TOOK THE WORLD BY STORM.
THIS S.T.D. WAS UNLIKE ANY OTHER THAT HAD COME BEFORE.
THIS WAS A DISEASE THAT PEOPLE ACTUALLY WANTED.
"VICTIMS" OF THIS EPIDEMIC WERE PHYSICALLY CHANGED BY THE VIRUS.
WEST 36th St
ONE WAY
FAT MELTED AWAY, THINNING HAIR RETURNED, SKIN BLEMISHES FADED, AND THEIR FACIAL FEATURES SLIMMED.
IT BECAME KNOWN AS THE BEAUTY.

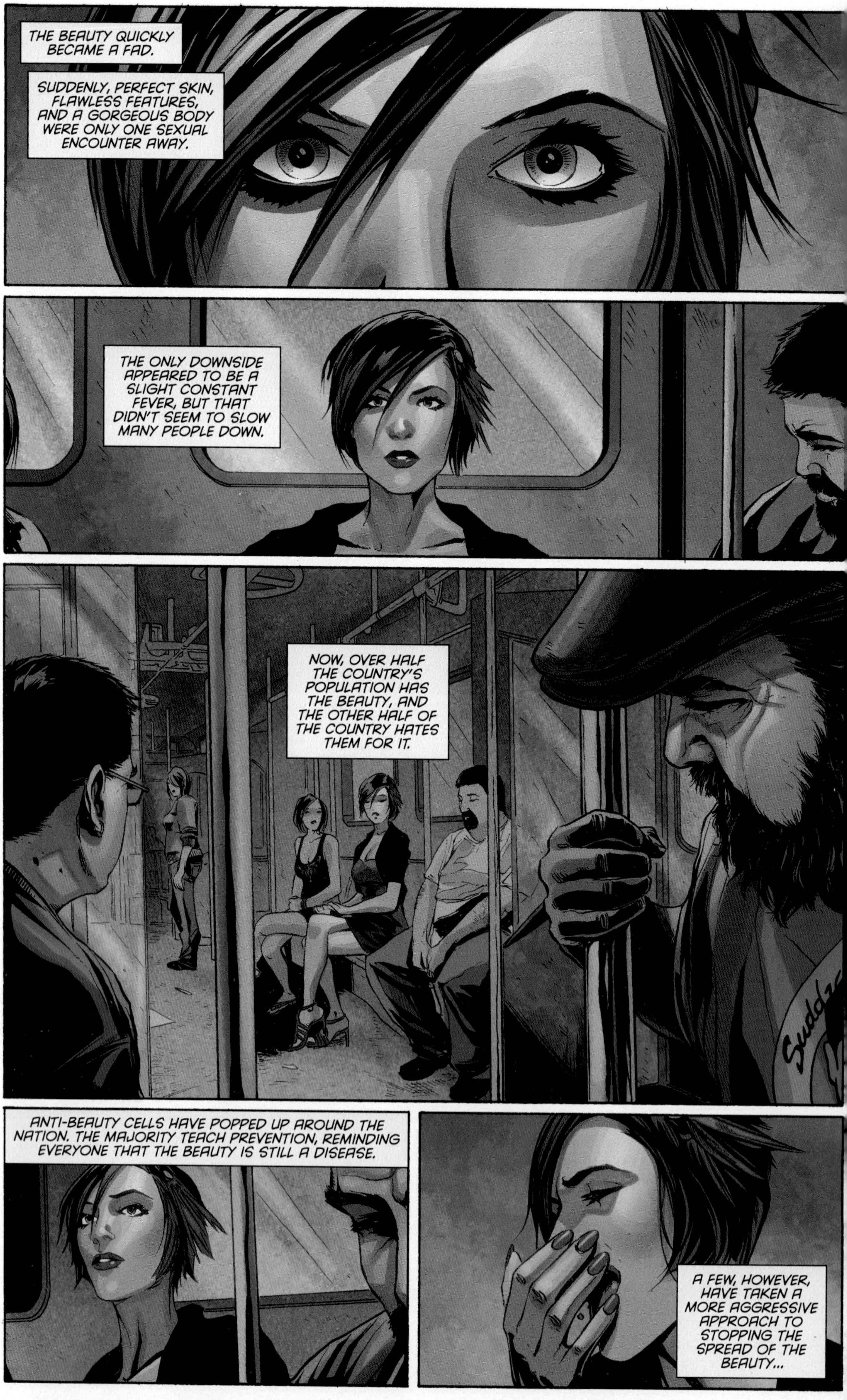
THE BEAUTY QUICKLY BECAME A FAD.
SUDDENLY, PERFECT SKIN, FLAWLESS FEATURES, AND A GORGEOUS BODY WERE ONLY ONE SEXUAL ENCOUNTER AWAY.
THE ONLY DOWNSIDE APPEARED TO BE A SLIGHT CONSTANT FEVER, BUT THAT DIDN'T SEEM TO SLOW MANY PEOPLE DOWN.
NOW, OVER HALF THE COUNTRY'S POPULATION HAS THE BEAUTY, AND THE OTHER HALF OF THE COUNTRY HATES THEM FOR IT.
ANTI-BEAUTY CELLS HAVE POPPED UP AROUND THE NATION. THE MAJORITY TEACH PREVENTION, REMINDING EVERYONE THAT THE BEAUTY IS STILL A DISEASE.
A FEW, HOWEVER, HAVE TAKEN A MORE AGGRESSIVE APPROACH TO STOPPING THE SPREAD OF THE BEAUTY...

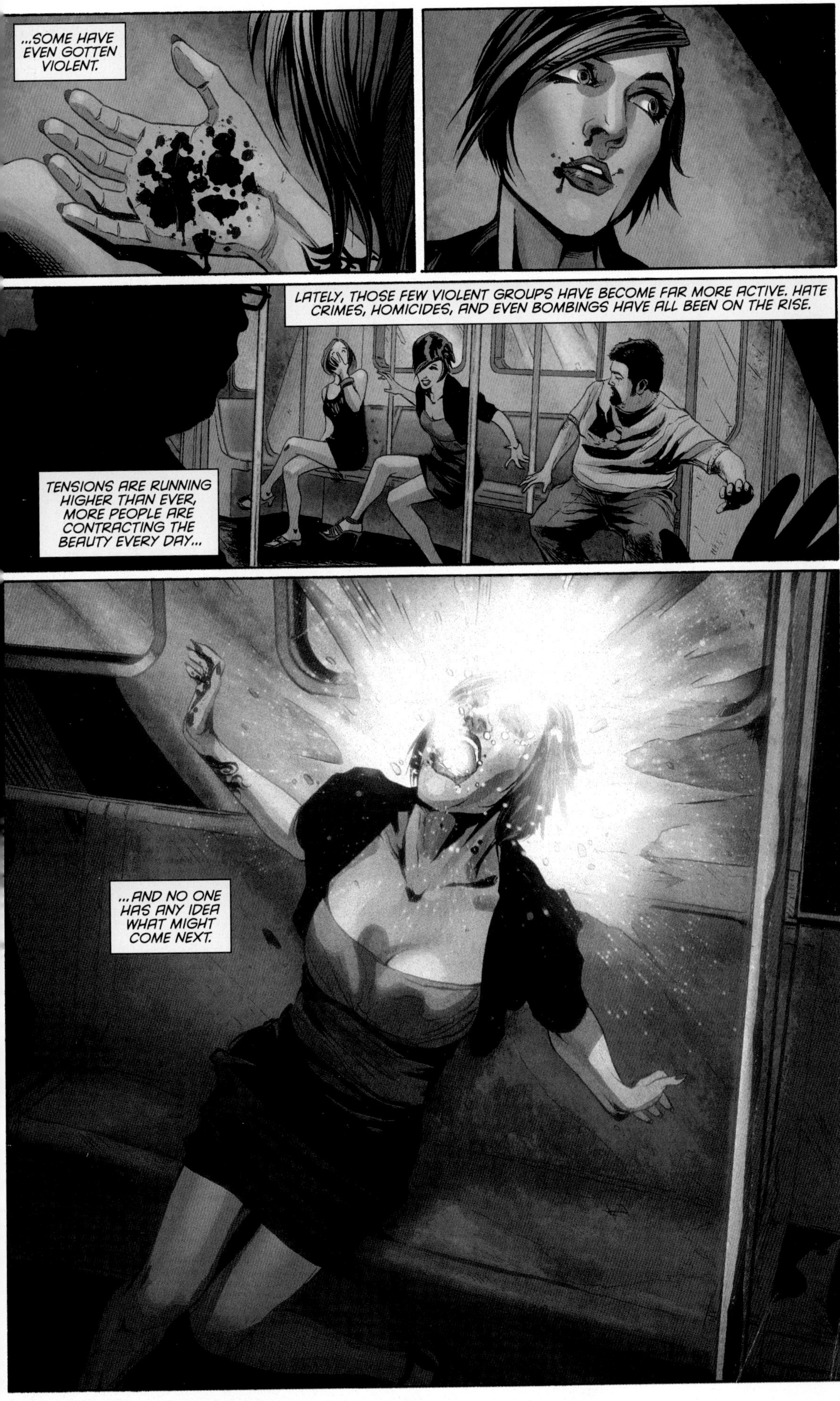
...SOME HAVE EVEN GOTTEN VIOLENT.
LATELY, THOSE FEW VIOLENT GROUPS HAVE BECOME FAR MORE ACTIVE. HATE CRIMES, HOMICIDES, AND EVEN BOMBINGS HAVE ALL BEEN ON THE RISE.
TENSIONS ARE RUNNING HIGHER THAN EVER, MORE PEOPLE ARE CONTRACTING THE BEAUTY EVERY DAY...
...AND NO ONE HAS ANY IDEA WHAT MIGHT COME NEXT.

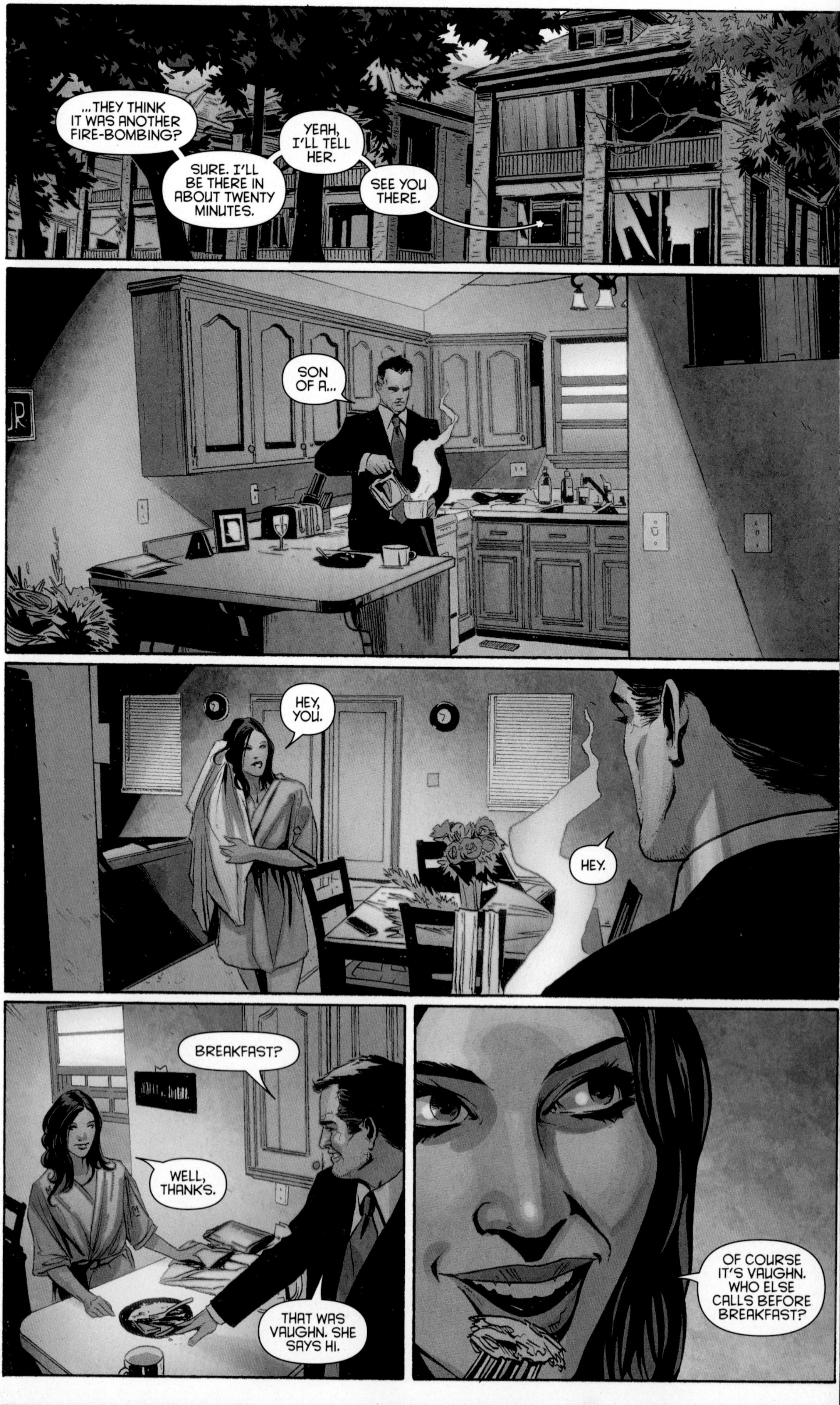
...THEY THINK IT WAS ANOTHER FIRE-BOMBING?
SURE. I'LL BE THERE IN ABOUT TWENTY MINUTES.
YEAH, I'LL TELL HER.
SEE YOU THERE.
SON OF A...
HEY, YOU.
HEY.
BREAKFAST?
WELL, THANKS.
THAT WAS VAUGHN. SHE SAYS HI.
OF COURSE IT'S VAUGHN. WHO ELSE CALLS BEFORE BREAKFAST?

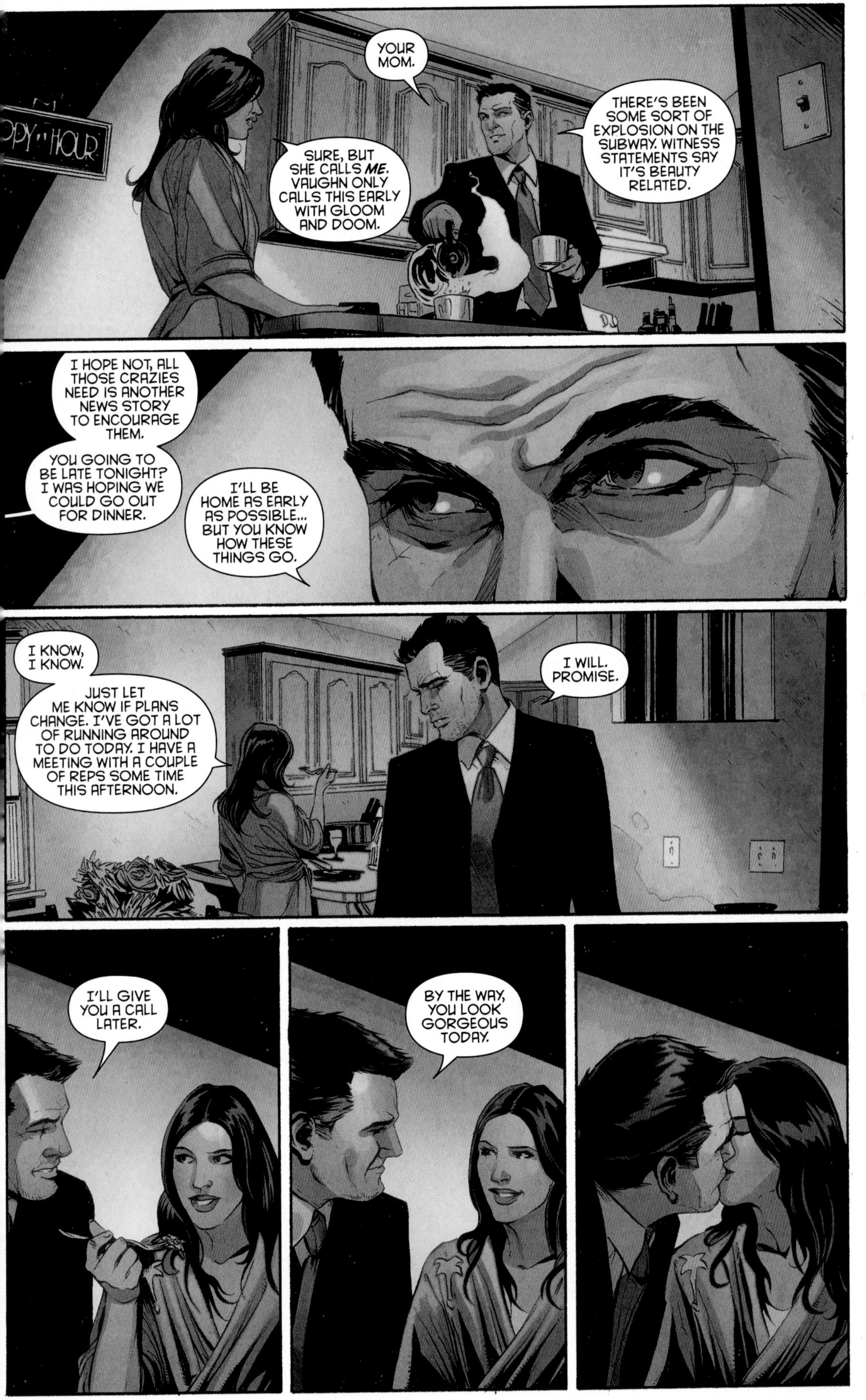

PPY HOUR
YOUR MOM.
SURE, BUT SHE CALLS ME. VAUGHN ONLY CALLS THIS EARLY WITH GLOOM AND DOOM.
THERE'S BEEN SOME SORT OF EXPLOSION ON THE SUBWAY. WITNESS STATEMENTS SAY IT'S BEAUTY RELATED.
I HOPE NOT, ALL THOSE CRAZIES NEED IS ANOTHER NEWS STORY TO ENCOURAGE THEM.
YOU GOING TO BE LATE TONIGHT? I WAS HOPING WE COULD GO OUT FOR DINNER.
I'LL BE HOME AS EARLY AS POSSIBLE... BUT YOU KNOW HOW THESE THINGS GO.
I KNOW, I KNOW.
JUST LET ME KNOW IF PLANS CHANGE. I'VE GOT A LOT OF RUNNING AROUND TO DO TODAY. I HAVE A MEETING WITH A COUPLE OF REPS SOME TIME THIS AFTERNOON.
I WILL. PROMISE.
I'LL GIVE YOU A CALL LATER.
BY THE WAY, YOU LOOK GORGEOUS TODAY.

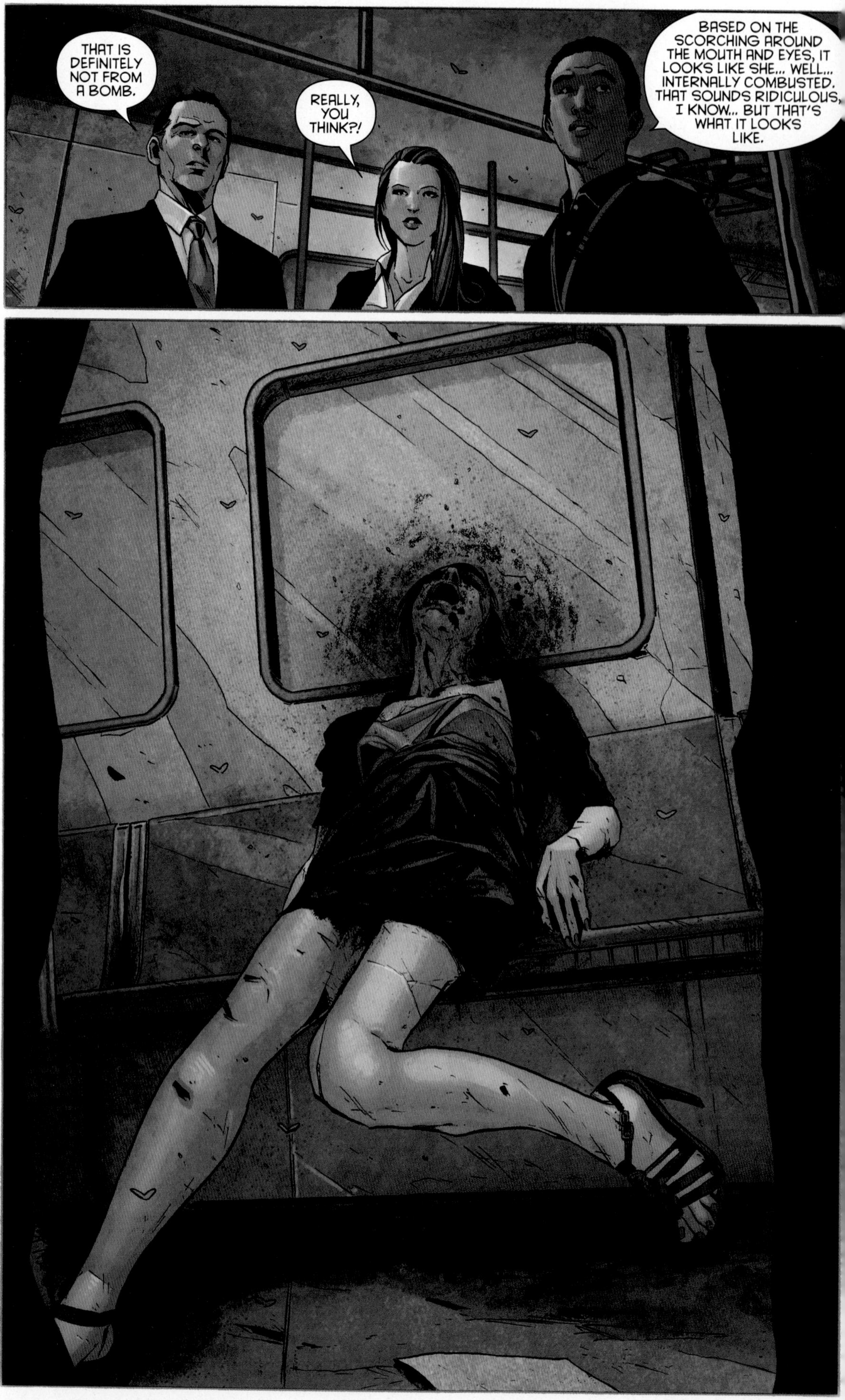
THAT IS DEFINITELY NOT FROM A BOMB.
REALLY, YOU THINK?!
BASED ON THE SCORCHING AROUND THE MOUTH AND EYES, IT LOOKS LIKE SHE... WELL... INTERNALLY COMBUSTED. THAT SOUNDS RIDICULOUS, I KNOW... BUT THAT'S WHAT IT LOOKS LIKE.

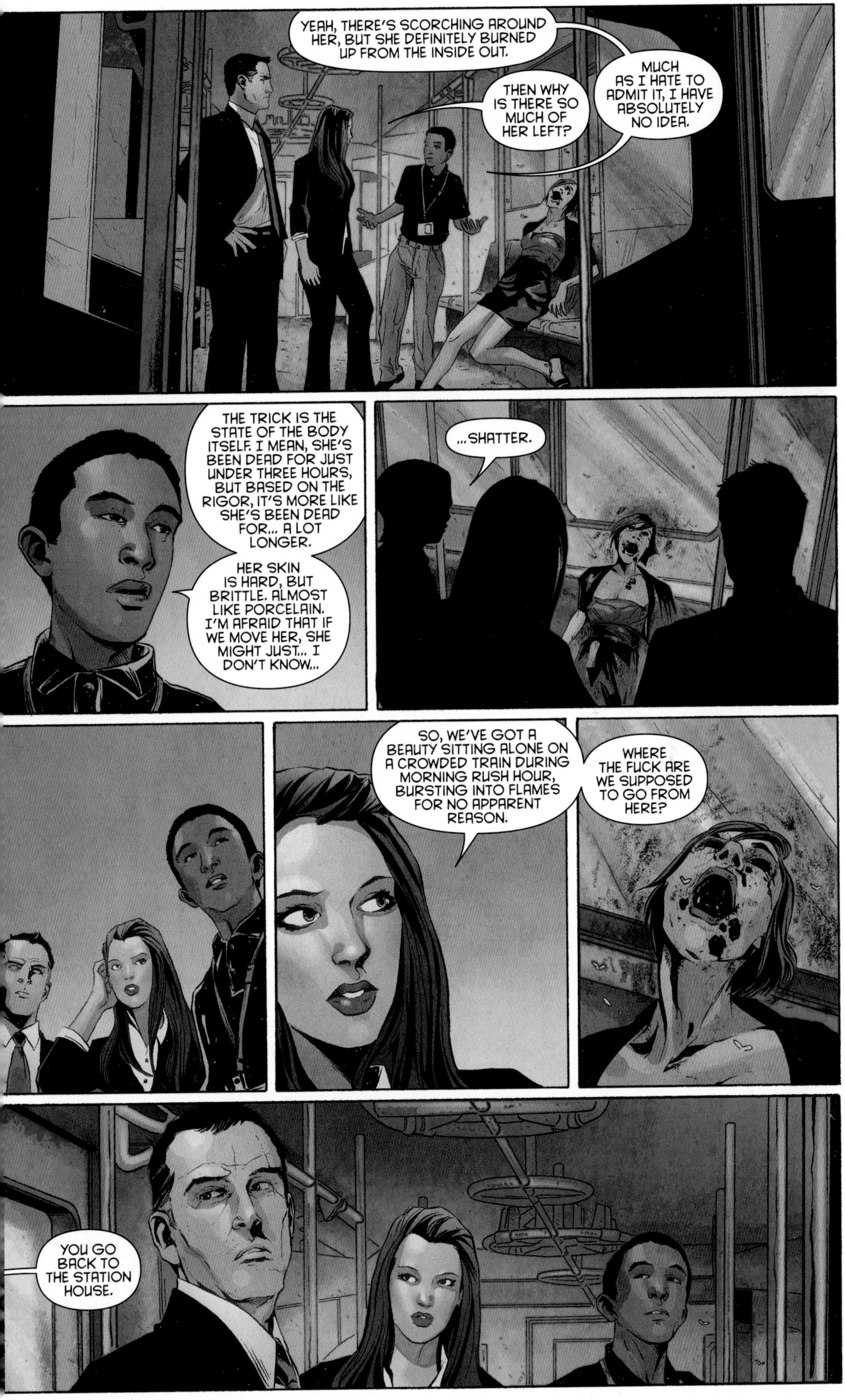

YEAH, THERE'S SCORCHING AROUND HER, BUT SHE DEFINITELY BURNED UP FROM THE INSIDE OUT.
THEN WHY IS THERE SO MUCH OF HER LEFT?
MUCH AS I HATE TO ADMIT IT, I HAVE ABSOLUTELY NO IDEA.
THE TRICK IS THE STATE OF THE BODY ITSELF. I MEAN, SHE'S BEEN DEAD FOR JUST UNDER THREE HOURS, BUT BASED ON THE RIGOR, IT'S MORE LIKE SHE'S BEEN DEAD FOR... A LOT LONGER.
HER SKIN IS HARD, BUT BRITTLE. ALMOST LIKE PORCELAIN. I'M AFRAID THAT IF WE MOVE HER, SHE MIGHT JUST... I DON'T KNOW...
...SHATTER.
SO, WE'VE GOT A BEAUTY SITTING ALONE ON A CROWDED TRAIN DURING MORNING RUSH HOUR, BURSTING INTO FLAMES FOR NO APPARENT REASON.
WHERE THE FUCK ARE WE SUPPOSED TO GO FROM HERE?
YOU GO BACK TO THE STATION HOUSE.

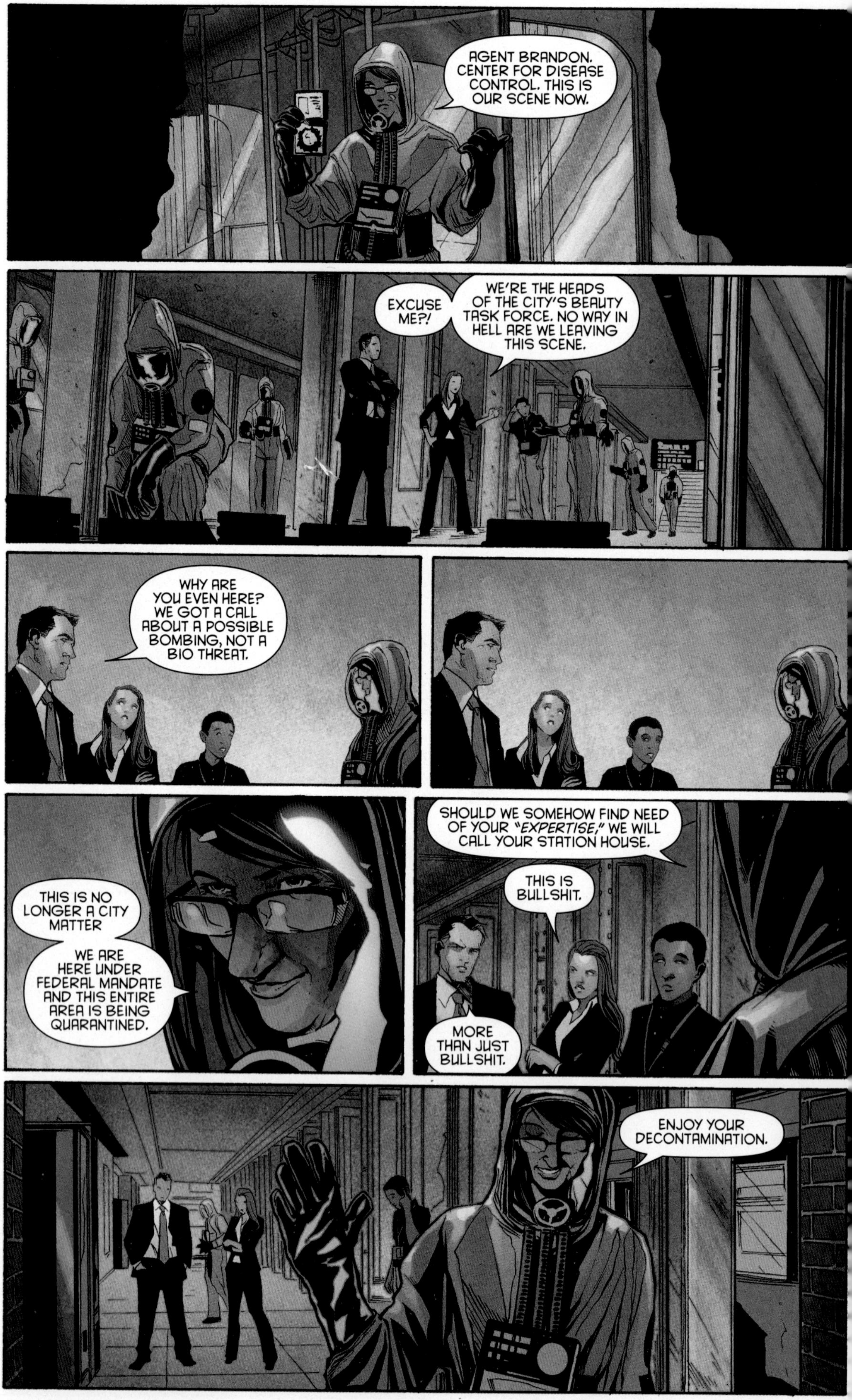
AGENT BRANDON. CENTER FOR DISEASE CONTROL. THIS IS OUR SCENE NOW.
EXCUSE ME?!
WE'RE THE HEADS OF THE CITY'S BEAUTY TASK FORCE. NO WAY IN HELL ARE WE LEAVING THIS SCENE.
WHY ARE YOU EVEN HERE? WE GOT A CALL ABOUT A POSSIBLE BOMBING, NOT A BIO THREAT.
THIS IS NO LONGER A CITY MATTER
WE ARE HERE UNDER FEDERAL MANDATE AND THIS ENTIRE AREA IS BEING QUARANTINED.
SHOULD WE SOMEHOW FIND NEED OF YOUR "EXPERTISE," WE WILL CALL YOUR STATION HOUSE.
THIS IS BULLSHIT.
MORE THAN JUST BULLSHIT.
ENJOY YOUR DECONTAMINATION.

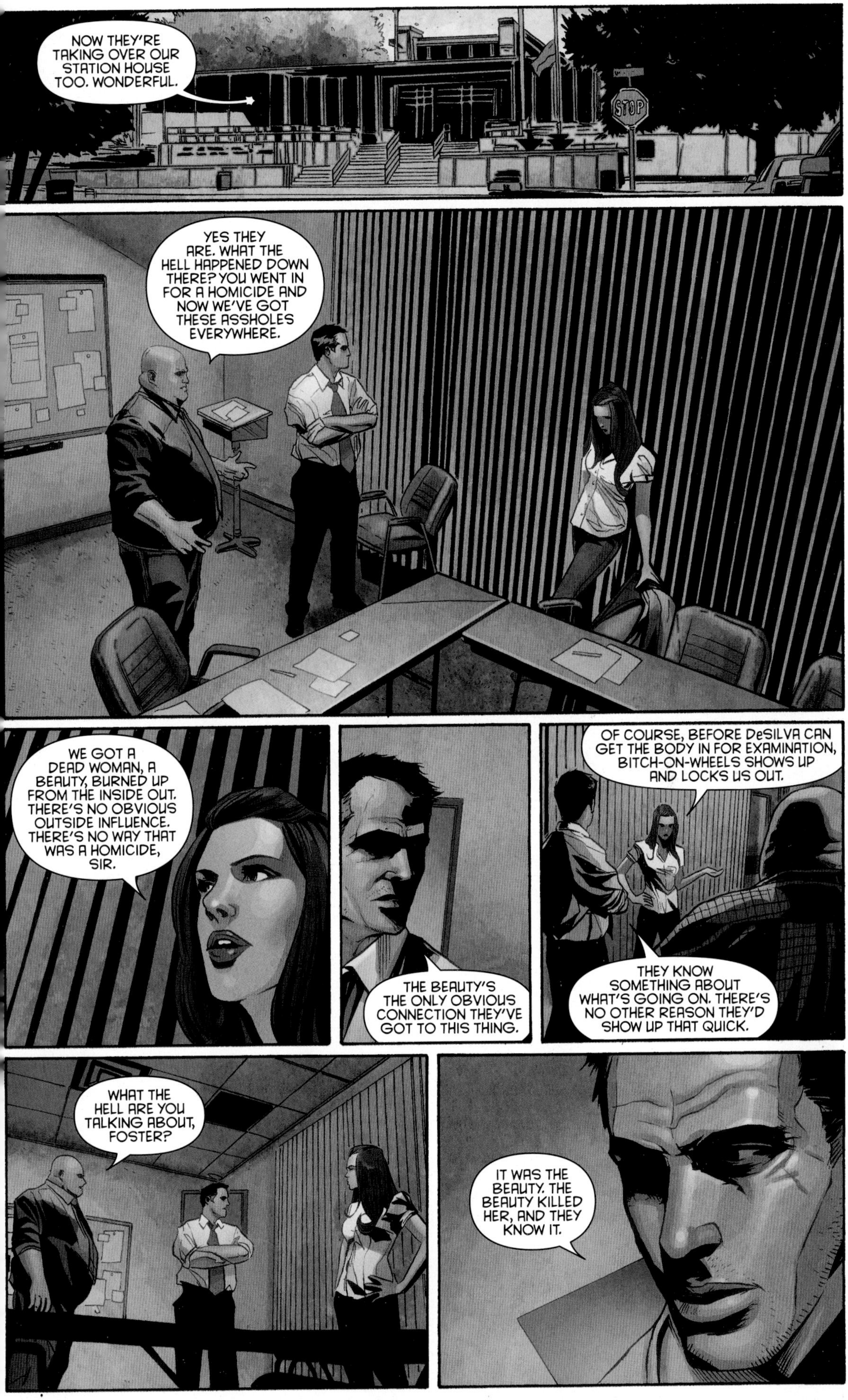
NOW THEY'RE TAKING OVER OUR STATION HOUSE TOO. WONDERFUL.
STOP
YES THEY ARE. WHAT THE HELL HAPPENED DOWN THERE? YOU WENT IN FOR A HOMICIDE AND NOW WE'VE GOT THESE ASSHOLES EVERYWHERE.
WE GOT A DEAD WOMAN, A BEAUTY, BURNED UP FROM THE INSIDE OUT. THERE'S NO OBVIOUS OUTSIDE INFLUENCE. THERE'S NO WAY THAT WAS A HOMICIDE, SIR.
THE BEAUTY'S THE ONLY OBVIOUS CONNECTION THEY'VE GOT TO THIS THING.
OF COURSE, BEFORE DeSILVA CAN GET THE BODY IN FOR EXAMINATION, BITCH-ON-WHEELS SHOWS UP AND LOCKS US OUT.
THEY KNOW SOMETHING ABOUT WHAT'S GOING ON. THERE'S NO OTHER REASON THEY'D SHOW UP THAT QUICK.
WHAT THE HELL ARE YOU TALKING ABOUT, FOSTER?
IT WAS THE BEAUTY. THE BEAUTY KILLED HER, AND THEY KNOW IT.

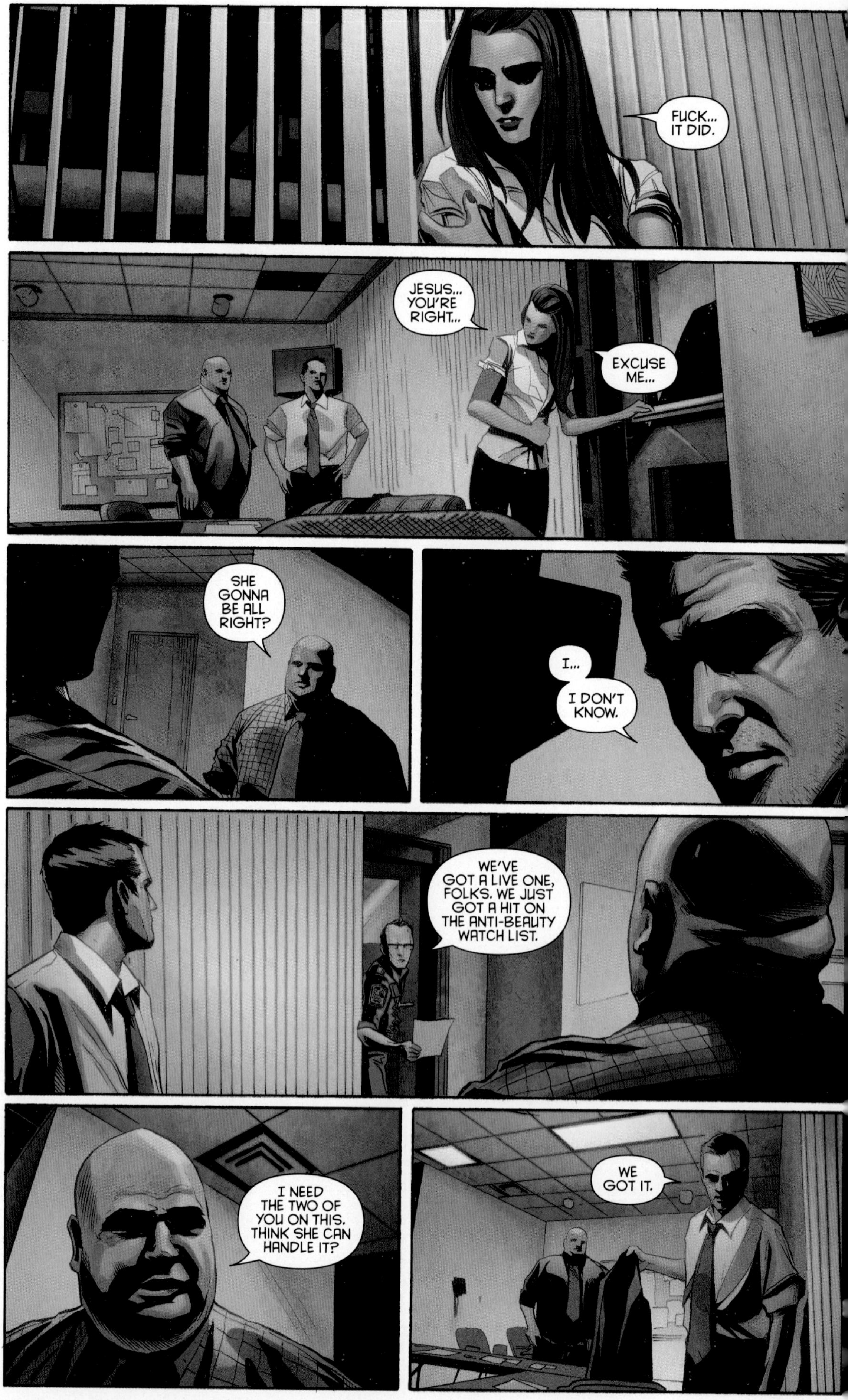
FUCK... IT DID.
JESUS... YOU'RE RIGHT...
EXCUSE ME...
SHE GONNA BE ALL RIGHT?
I...
I DON'T KNOW.
WE'VE GOT A LIVE ONE, FOLKS. WE JUST GOT A HIT ON THE ANTI-BEAUTY WATCH LIST.
I NEED THE TWO OF YOU ON THIS. THINK SHE CAN HANDLE IT?
WE GOT IT.

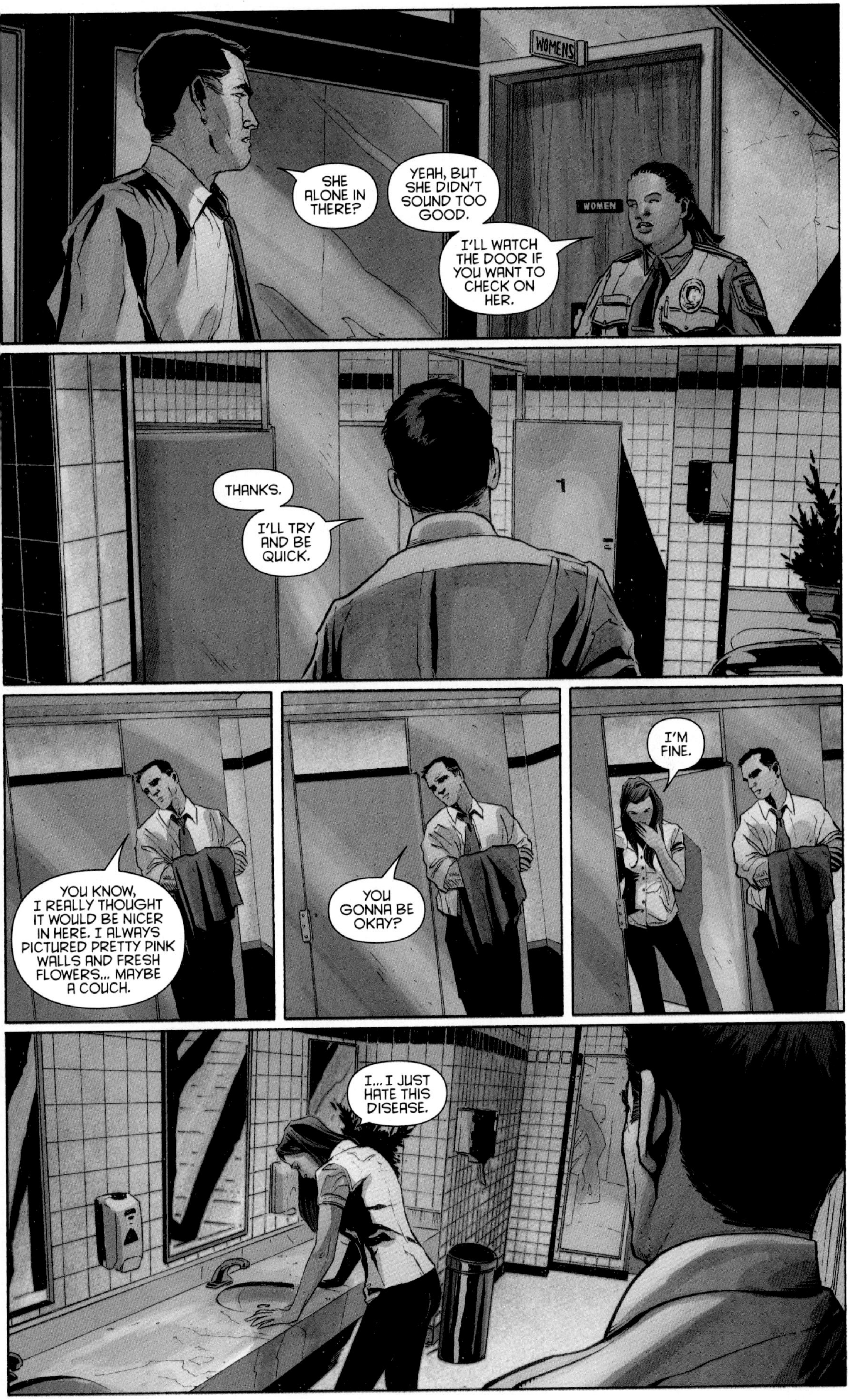
WOMENS
SHE ALONE IN THERE?
YEAH, BUT SHE DIDN'T SOUND TOO GOOD.
I'LL WATCH THE DOOR IF YOU WANT TO CHECK ON HER.
WOMEN
THANKS.
I'LL TRY AND BE QUICK.
YOU KNOW, I REALLY THOUGHT IT WOULD BE NICER IN HERE. I ALWAYS PICTURED PRETTY PINK WALLS AND FRESH FLOWERS... MAYBE A COUCH.
YOU GONNA BE OKAY?
I'M FINE.
I... I JUST HATE THIS DISEASE.

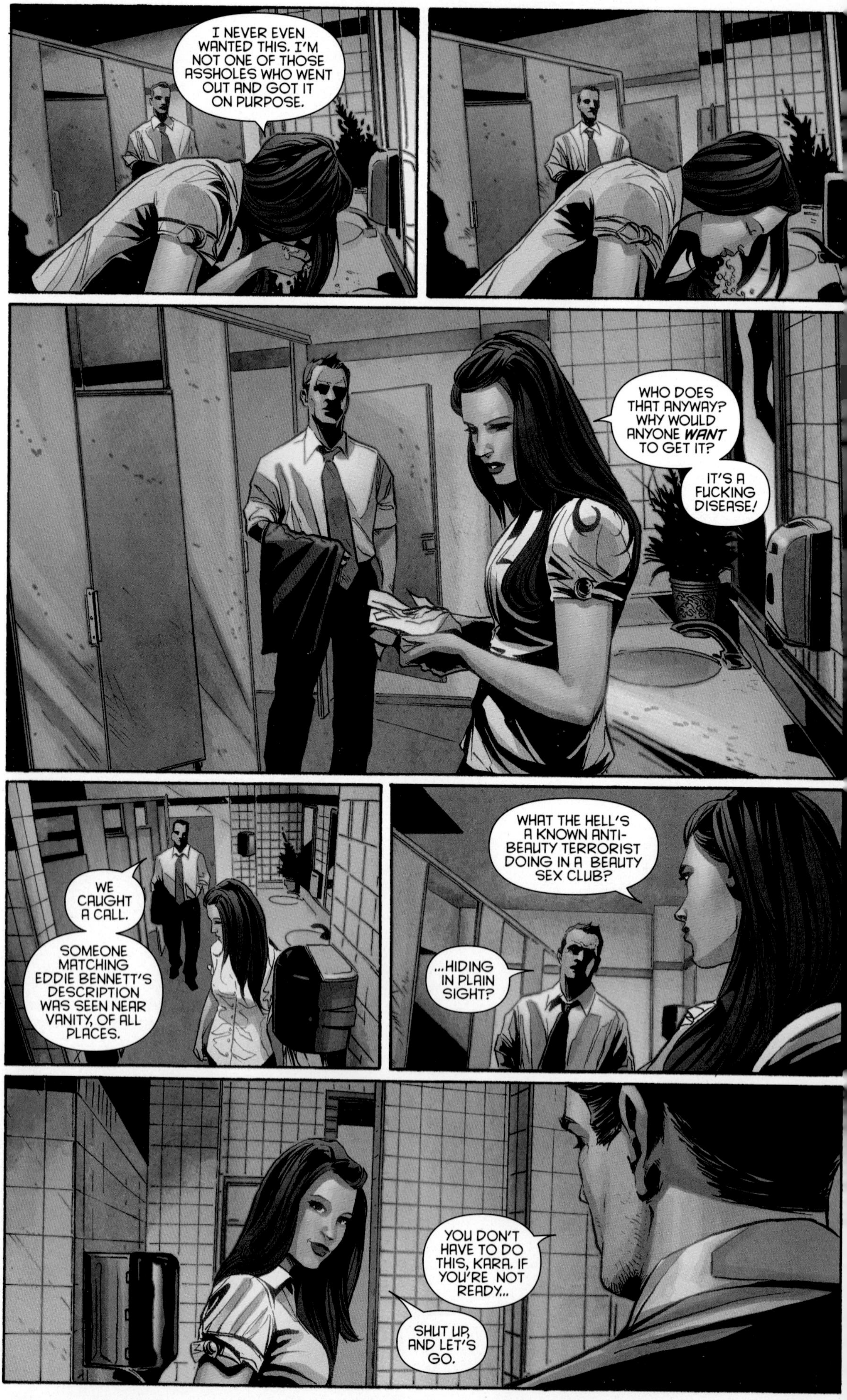
I NEVER EVEN WANTED THIS. I'M NOT ONE OF THOSE ASSHOLES WHO WENT OUT AND GOT IT ON PURPOSE.
WHO DOES THAT ANYWAY? WHY WOULD ANYONE *WANT* TO GET IT?
IT'S A FUCKING DISEASE!
WE CAUGHT A CALL.
SOMEONE MATCHING EDDIE BENNETT'S DESCRIPTION WAS SEEN NEAR VANITY, OF ALL PLACES.
WHAT THE HELL'S A KNOWN ANTI-BEAUTY TERRORIST DOING IN A BEAUTY SEX CLUB?
...HIDING IN PLAIN SIGHT?
YOU DON'T HAVE TO DO THIS, KARA. IF YOU'RE NOT READY...
SHUT UP, AND LET'S GO.

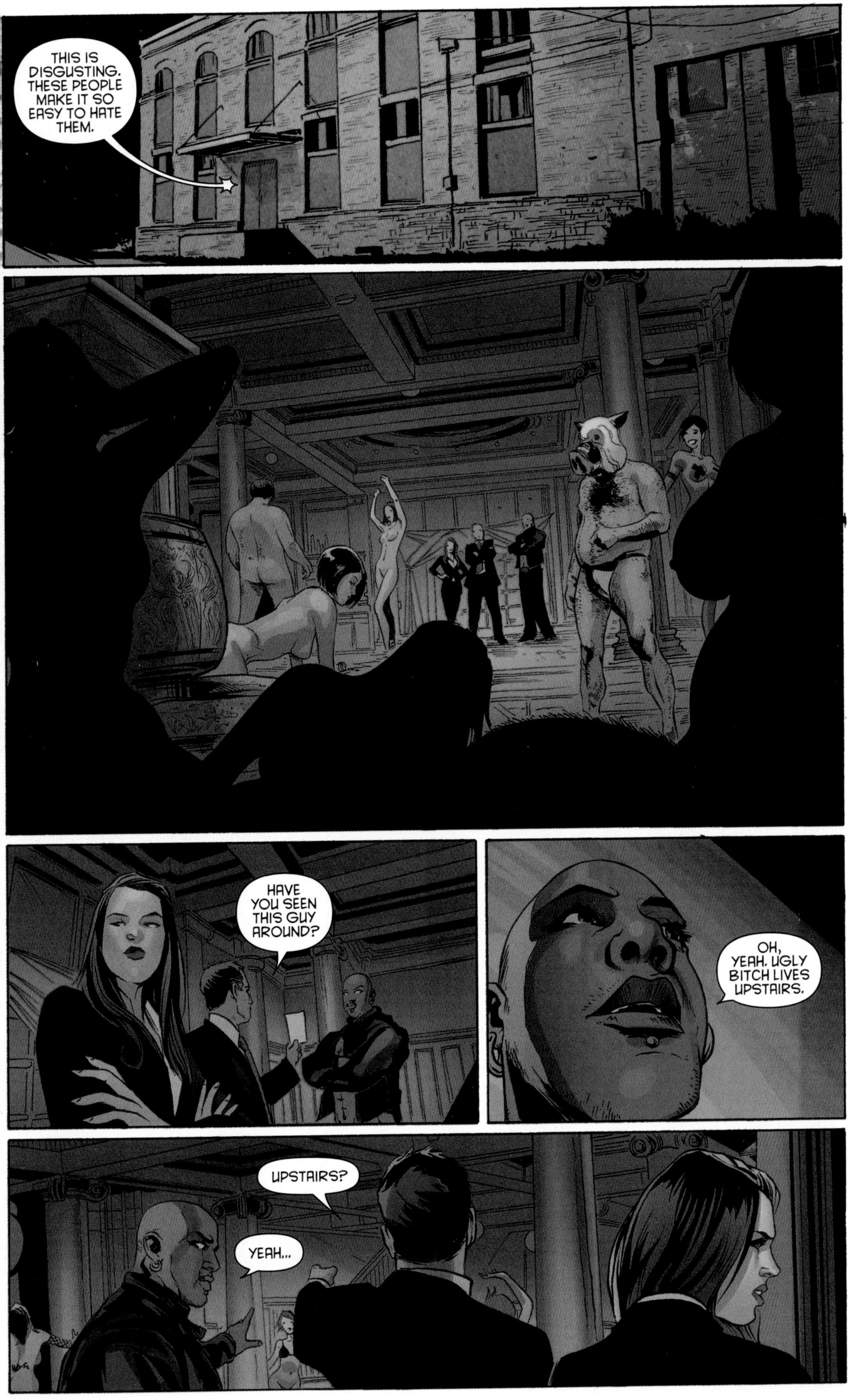
THIS IS DISGUSTING. THESE PEOPLE MAKE IT SO EASY TO HATE THEM.
HAVE YOU SEEN THIS GUY AROUND?
OH, YEAH. UGLY BITCH LIVES UPSTAIRS.
UPSTAIRS?
YEAH...

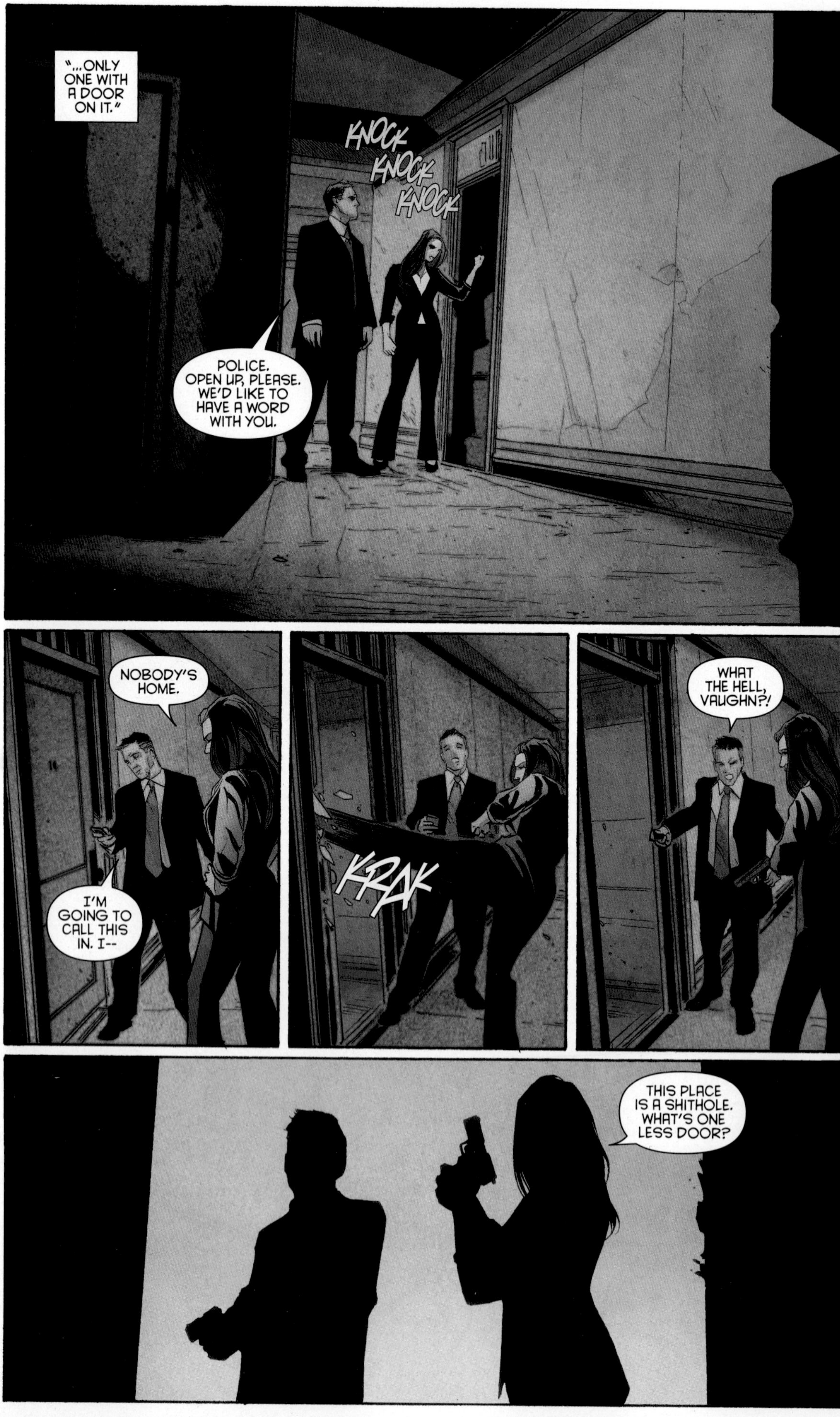
"...ONLY ONE WITH A DOOR ON IT."
KNOCK KNOCK KNOCK
POLICE. OPEN UP, PLEASE. WE'D LIKE TO HAVE A WORD WITH YOU.
NOBODY'S HOME.
I'M GOING TO CALL THIS IN. I--
KRAK
WHAT THE HELL, VAUGHN?!
THIS PLACE IS A SHITHOLE. WHAT'S ONE LESS DOOR?

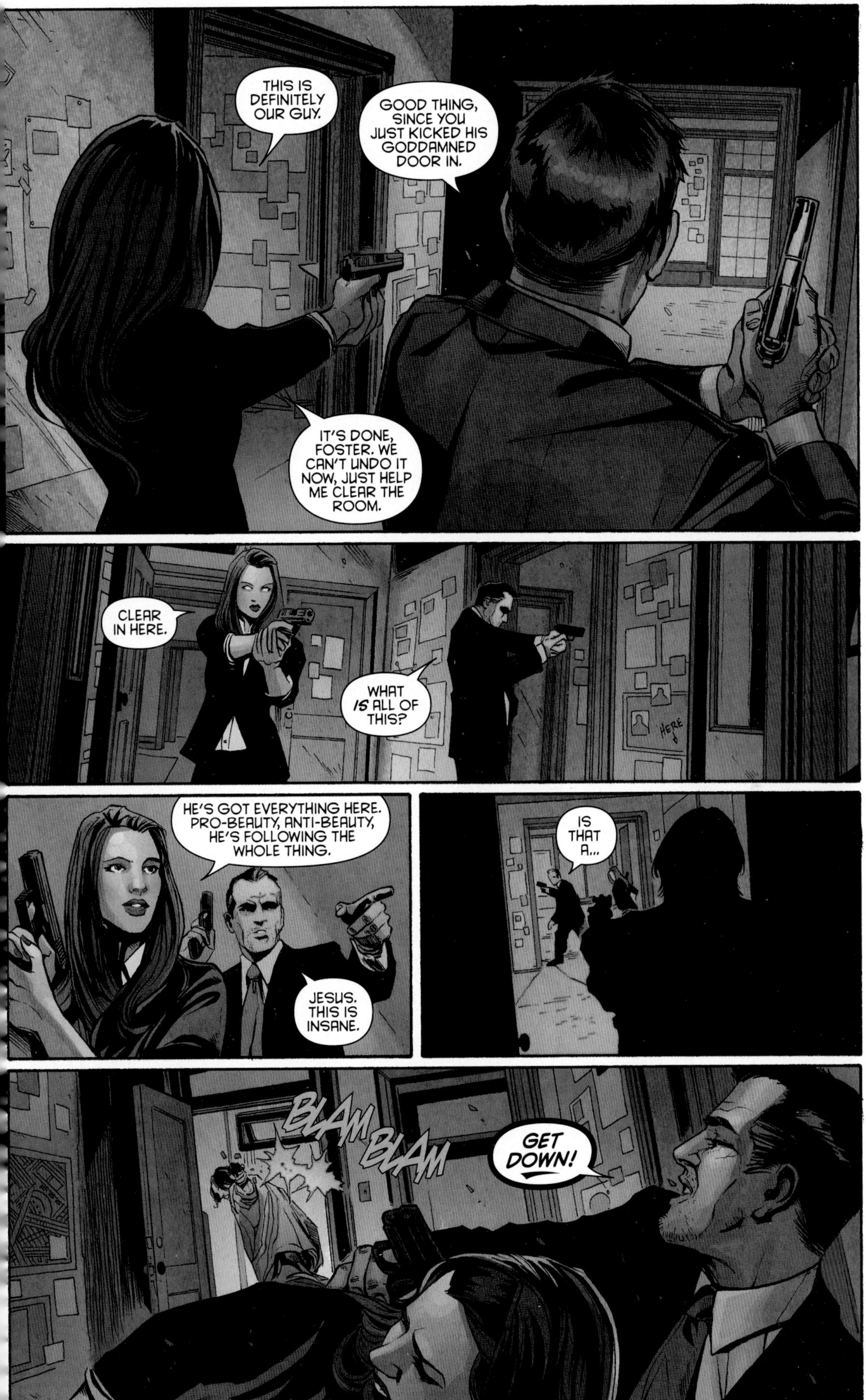
THIS IS DEFINITELY OUR GUY.
GOOD THING, SINCE YOU JUST KICKED HIS GODDAMNED DOOR IN.
IT'S DONE, FOSTER. WE CAN'T UNDO IT NOW, JUST HELP ME CLEAR THE ROOM.
CLEAR IN HERE.
WHAT *IS* ALL OF THIS?
HERE
HE'S GOT EVERYTHING HERE. PRO-BEAUTY, ANTI-BEAUTY, HE'S FOLLOWING THE WHOLE THING.
JESUS. THIS IS INSANE.
IS THAT A...
BLAM
BLAM
GET DOWN!

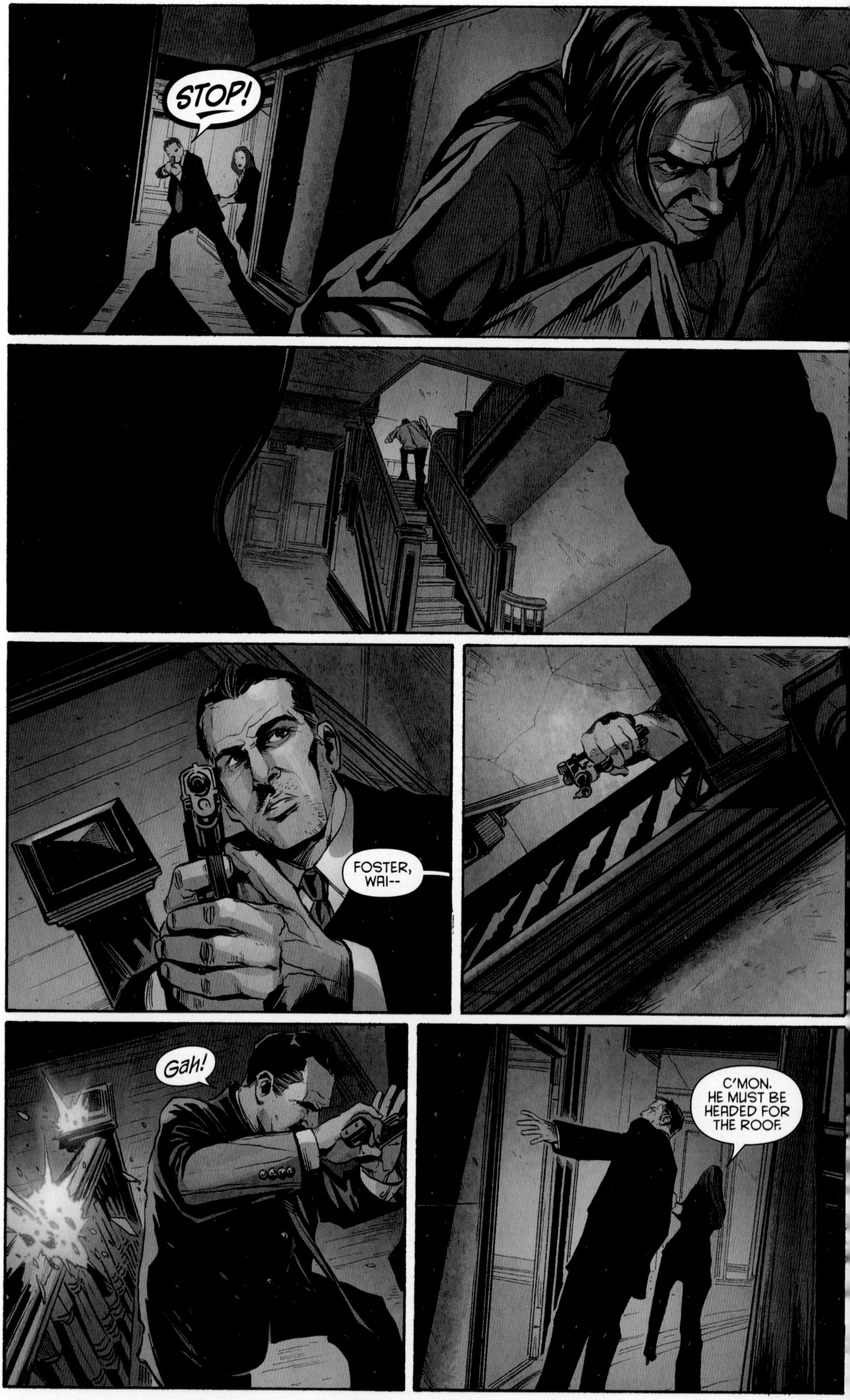
STOP!
FOSTER, WAI--
Gah!
C'MON. HE MUST BE HEADED FOR THE ROOF.

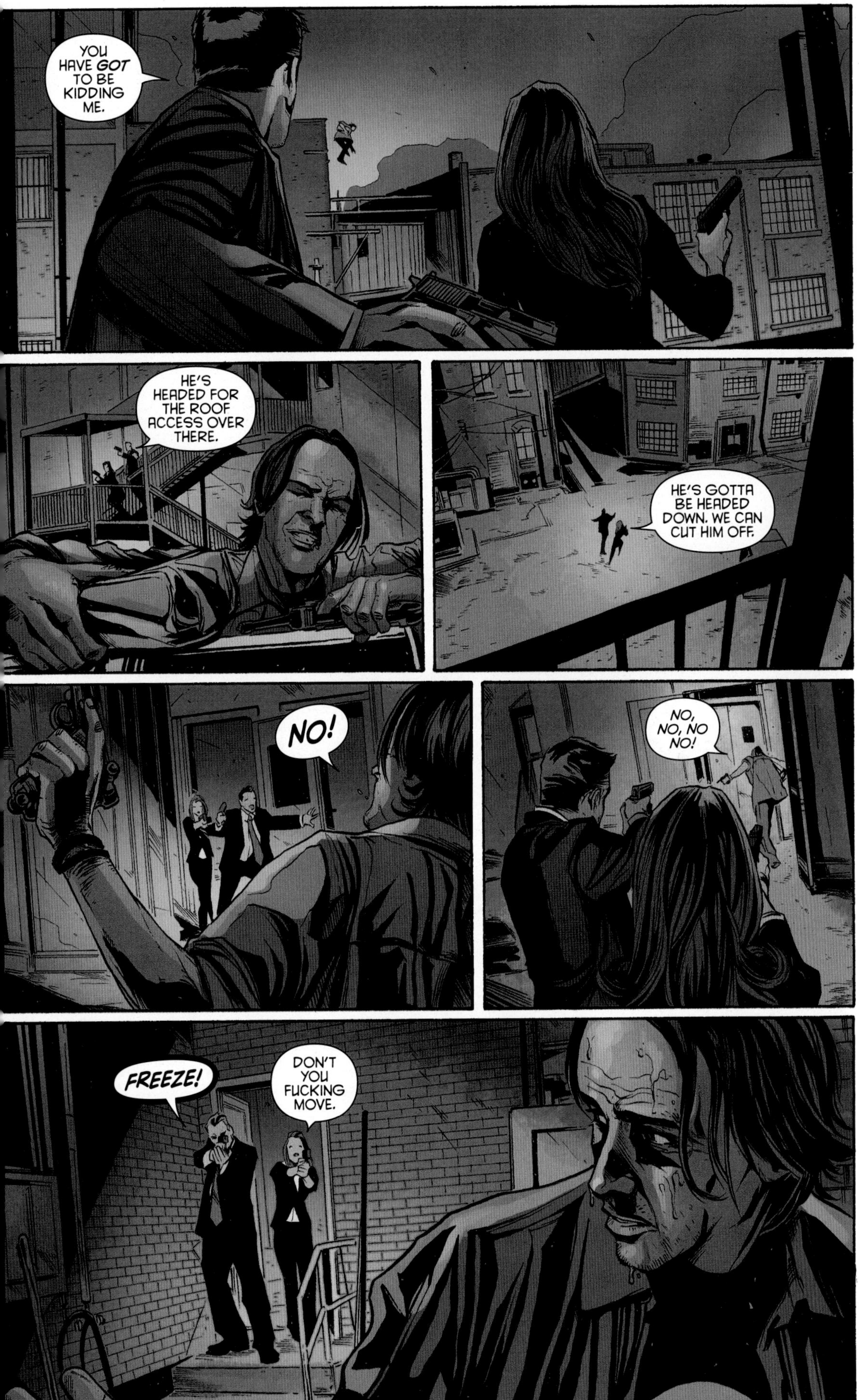
YOU HAVE GOT TO BE KIDDING ME.
HE'S HEADED FOR THE ROOF ACCESS OVER THERE.
HE'S GOTTA BE HEADED DOWN. WE CAN CUT HIM OFF.
NO!
NO, NO, NO NO!
FREEZE!
DON'T YOU FUCKING MOVE.

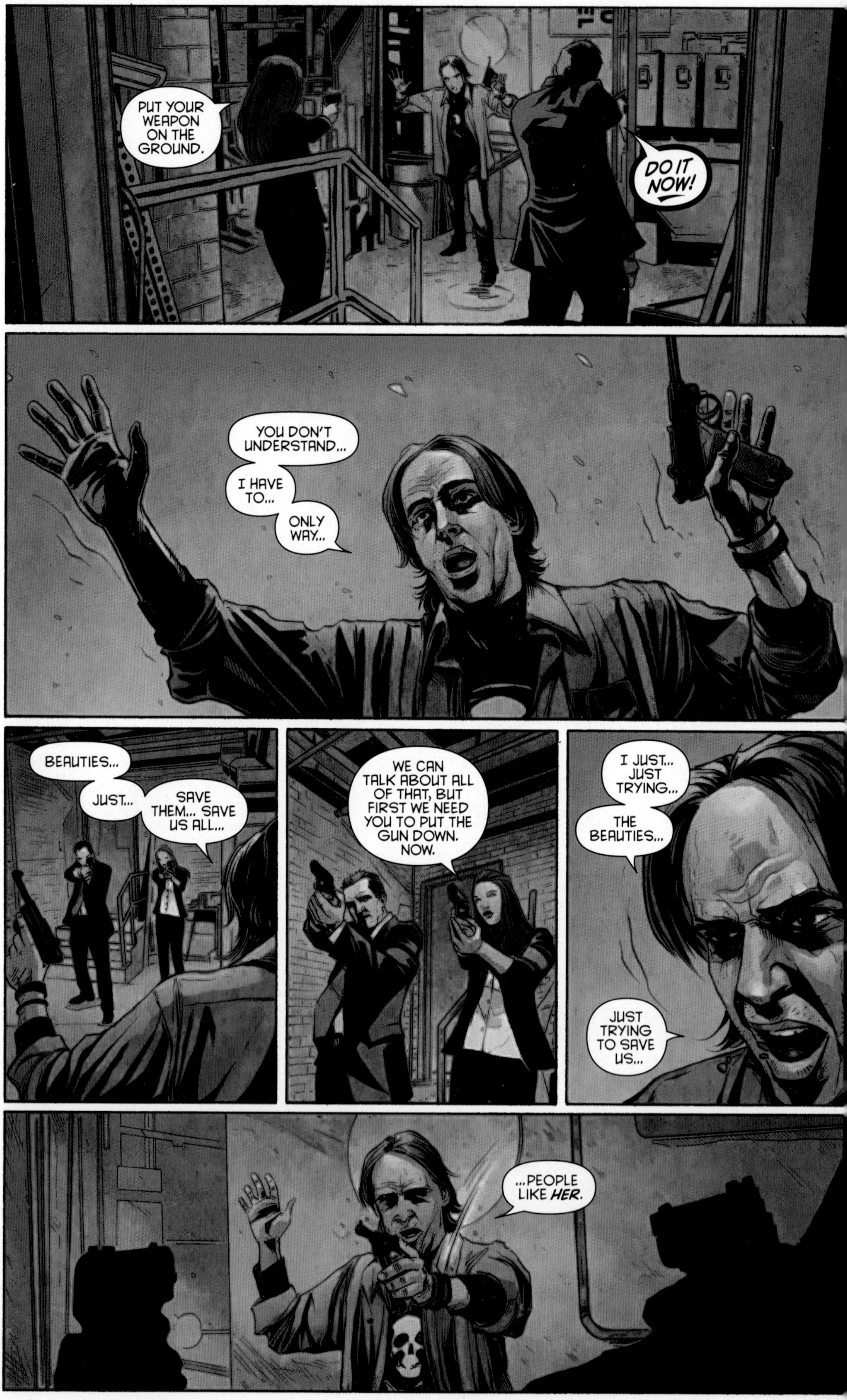
PUT YOUR WEAPON ON THE GROUND.
DO IT NOW!
YOU DON'T UNDERSTAND...
I HAVE TO...
ONLY WAY...
BEAUTIES...
JUST...
SAVE THEM... SAVE US ALL...
WE CAN TALK ABOUT ALL OF THAT, BUT FIRST WE NEED YOU TO PUT THE GUN DOWN. NOW.
I JUST... JUST TRYING...
THE BEAUTIES...
JUST TRYING TO SAVE US...
...PEOPLE LIKE HER.

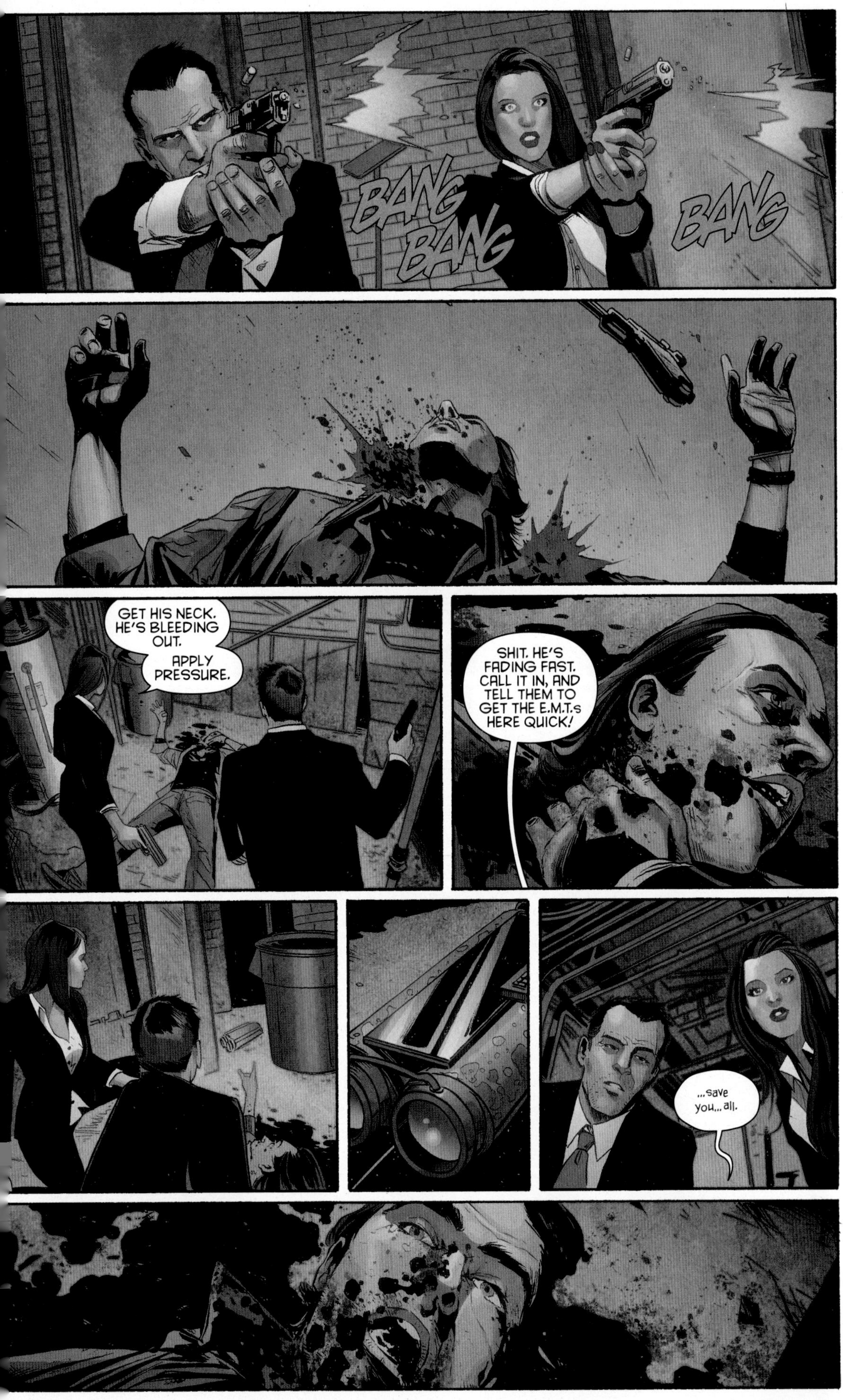
BANG
BANG
BANG
GET HIS NECK. HE'S BLEEDING OUT.
APPLY PRESSURE.
SHIT. HE'S FADING FAST. CALL IT IN, AND TELL THEM TO GET THE E.M.T.s HERE QUICK!
...save you... all.

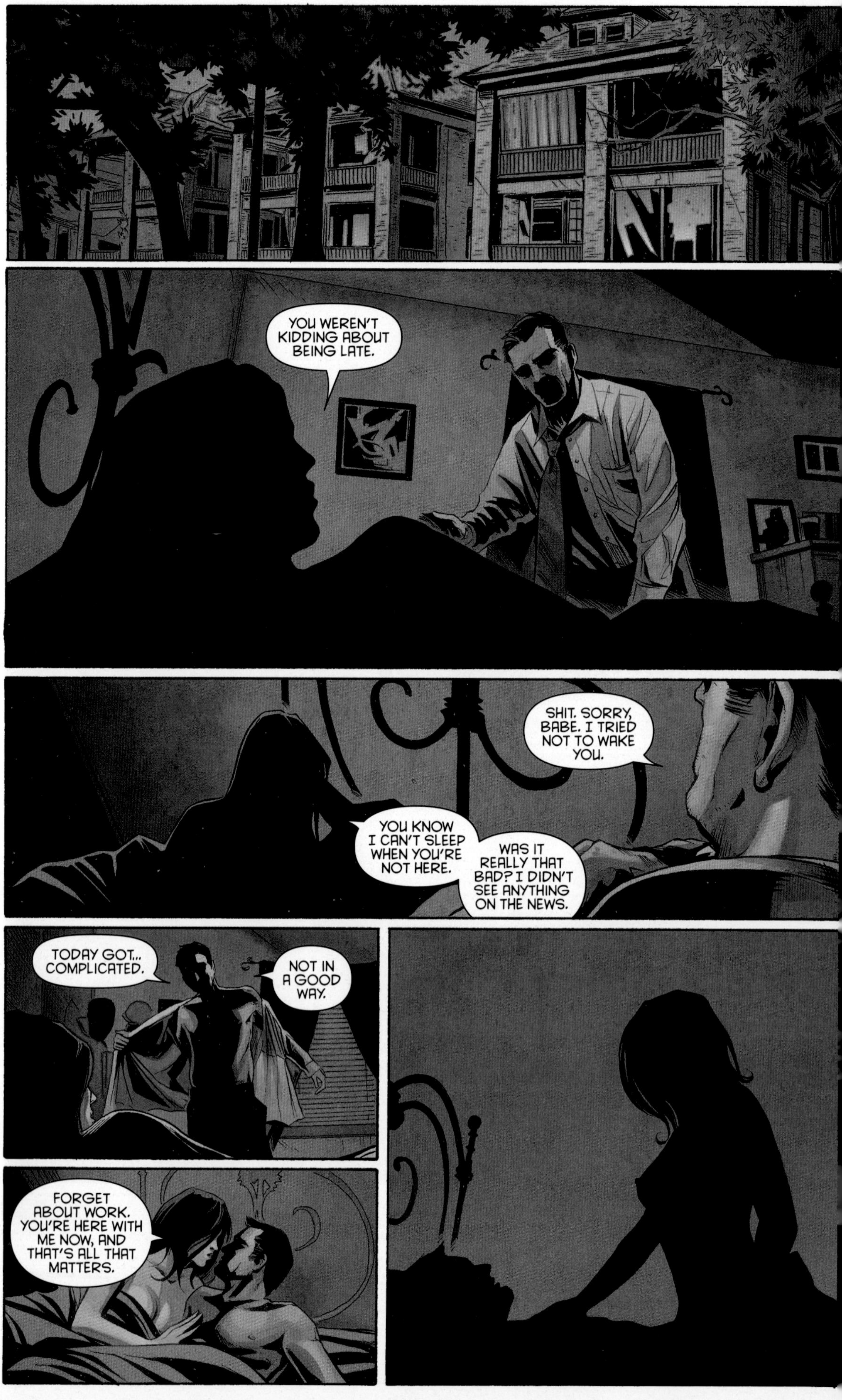
YOU WEREN'T KIDDING ABOUT BEING LATE.
SHIT. SORRY, BABE. I TRIED NOT TO WAKE YOU.
YOU KNOW I CAN'T SLEEP WHEN YOU'RE NOT HERE.
WAS IT REALLY THAT BAD? I DIDN'T SEE ANYTHING ON THE NEWS.
TODAY GOT... COMPLICATED.
NOT IN A GOOD WAY.
FORGET ABOUT WORK. YOU'RE HERE WITH ME NOW, AND THAT'S ALL THAT MATTERS.

BZZZz
BZZZz

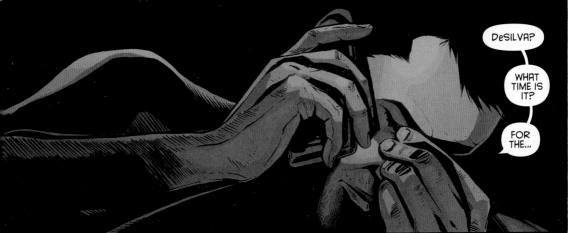

DeSILVA?

WHAT TIME IS IT?

FOR THE...

HOLD ON A SECOND. I DON'T WANT TO WAKE UP MY WIFE.

SO WAIT, IF IT'S NOT A BOMB, THEN WHAT IS IT?

BUT YOU DON'T KNOW WHAT'S IN THERE?

ALL RIGHT. I'LL BE IN AS QUICK AS I CAN. TRY AND HAVE SOMETHING FOR ME BY THE TIME I GET THERE.

CLICK

OH...

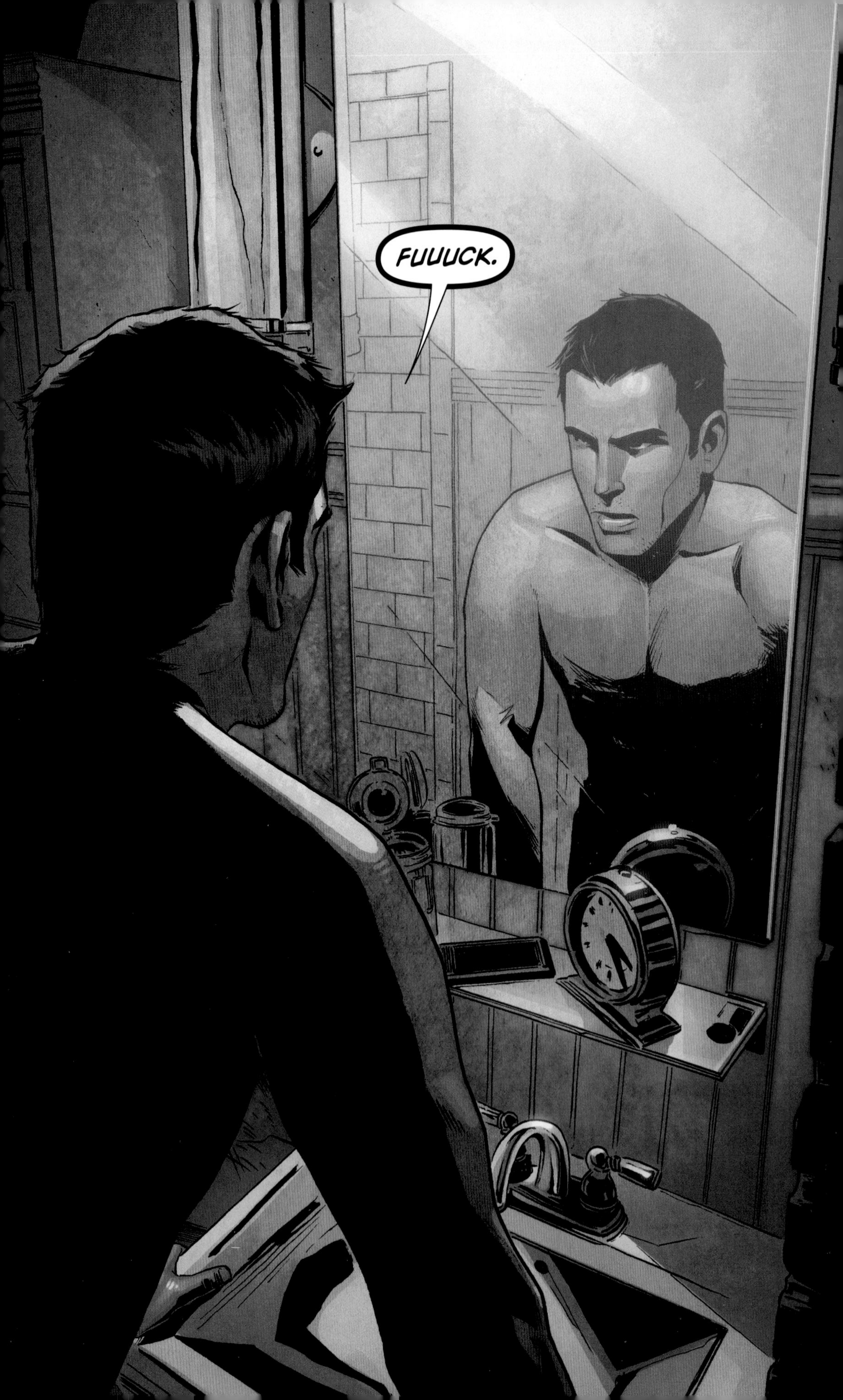
FUUUCK.

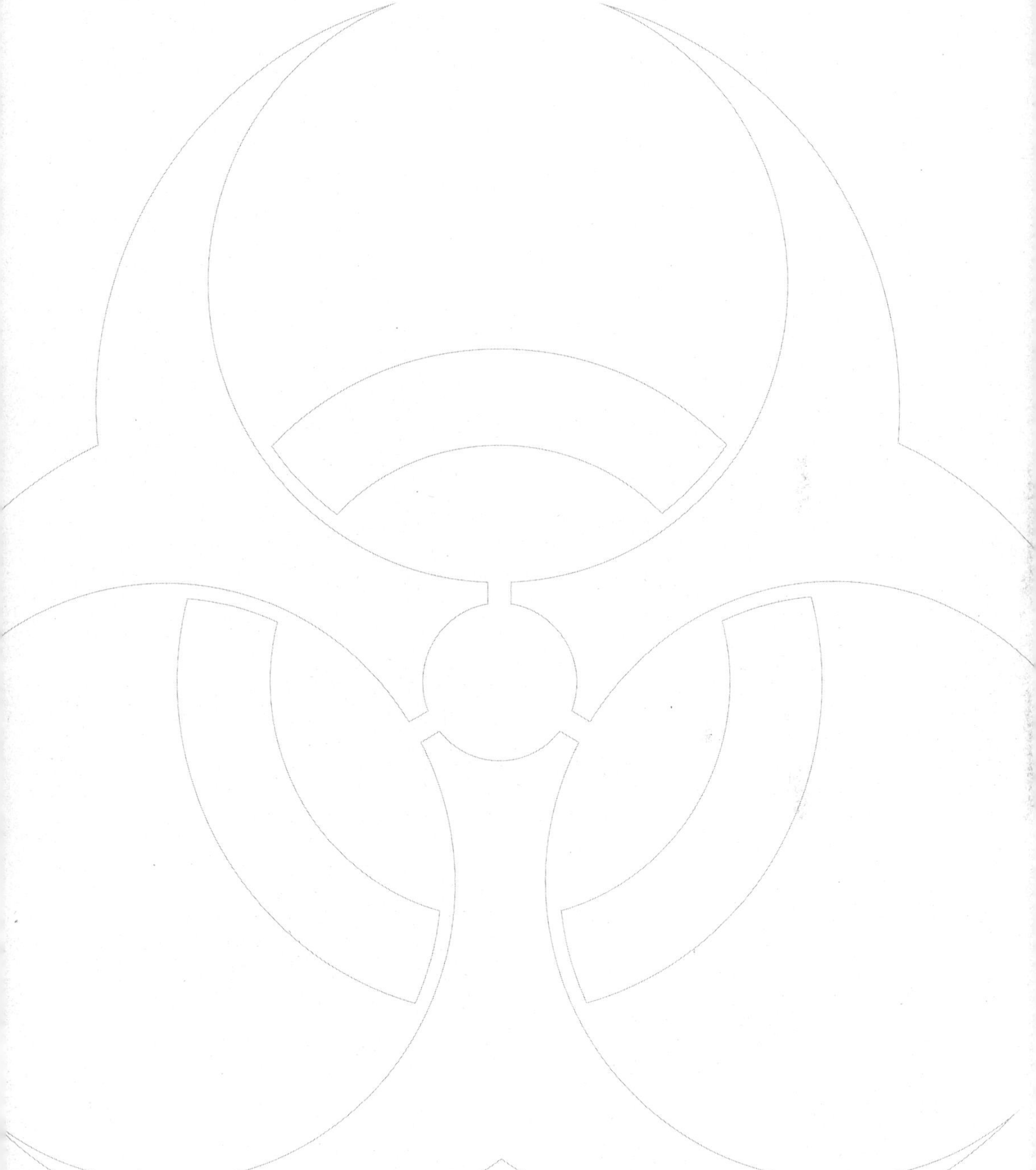

CHAPTER 2

BEAUTY

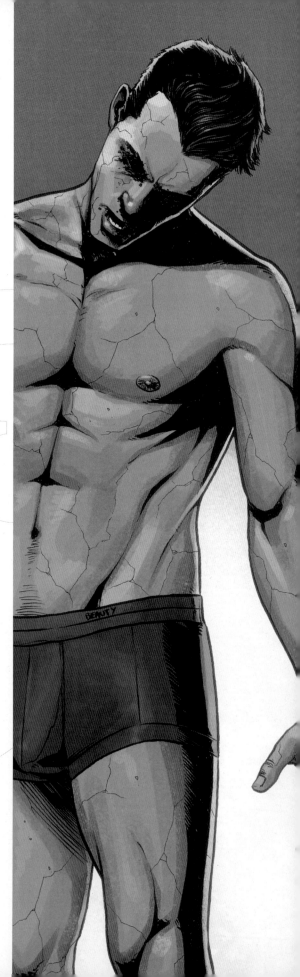

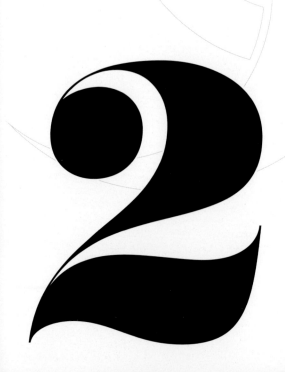

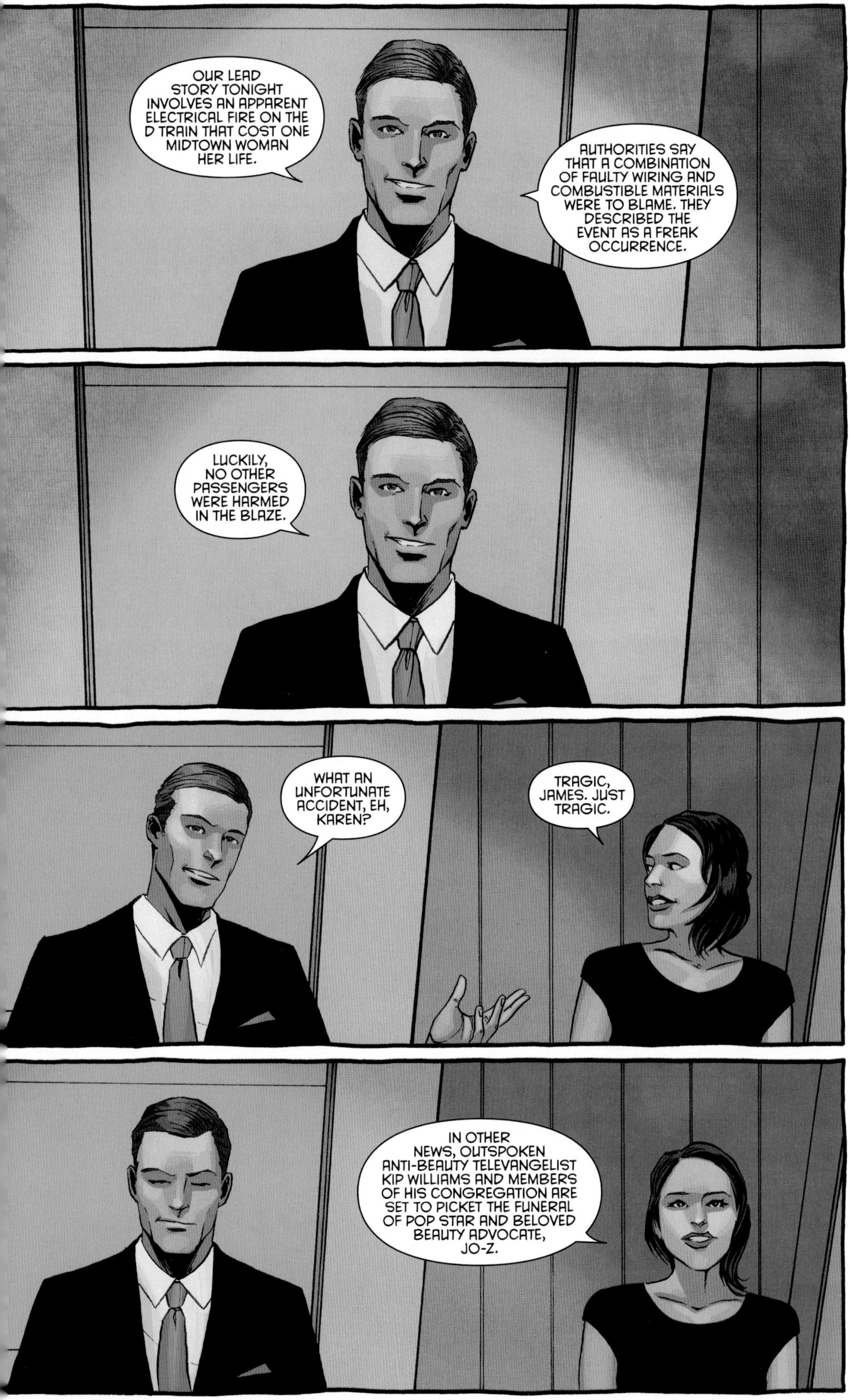
OUR LEAD STORY TONIGHT INVOLVES AN APPARENT ELECTRICAL FIRE ON THE D TRAIN THAT COST ONE MIDTOWN WOMAN HER LIFE.
AUTHORITIES SAY THAT A COMBINATION OF FAULTY WIRING AND COMBUSTIBLE MATERIALS WERE TO BLAME. THEY DESCRIBED THE EVENT AS A FREAK OCCURRENCE.
LUCKILY, NO OTHER PASSENGERS WERE HARMED IN THE BLAZE.
WHAT AN UNFORTUNATE ACCIDENT, EH, KAREN?
TRAGIC, JAMES. JUST TRAGIC.
IN OTHER NEWS, OUTSPOKEN ANTI-BEAUTY TELEVANGELIST KIP WILLIAMS AND MEMBERS OF HIS CONGREGATION ARE SET TO PICKET THE FUNERAL OF POP STAR AND BELOVED BEAUTY ADVOCATE, JO-Z.

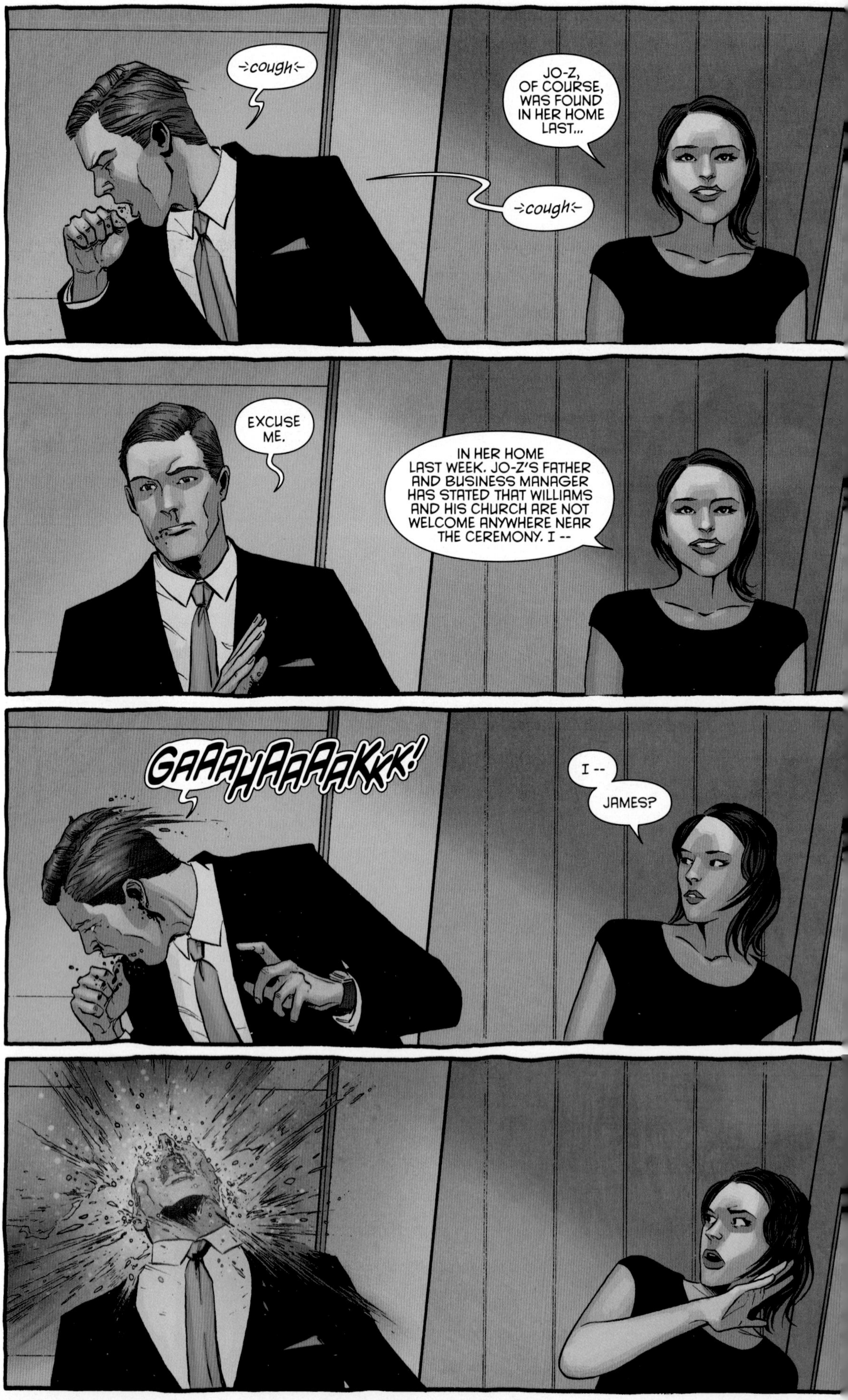

-cough-
JO-Z, OF COURSE, WAS FOUND IN HER HOME LAST...
-cough-
EXCUSE ME.
IN HER HOME LAST WEEK. JO-Z'S FATHER AND BUSINESS MANAGER HAS STATED THAT WILLIAMS AND HIS CHURCH ARE NOT WELCOME ANYWHERE NEAR THE CEREMONY. I --
GAAAHAAAAKKK!
I --
JAMES?

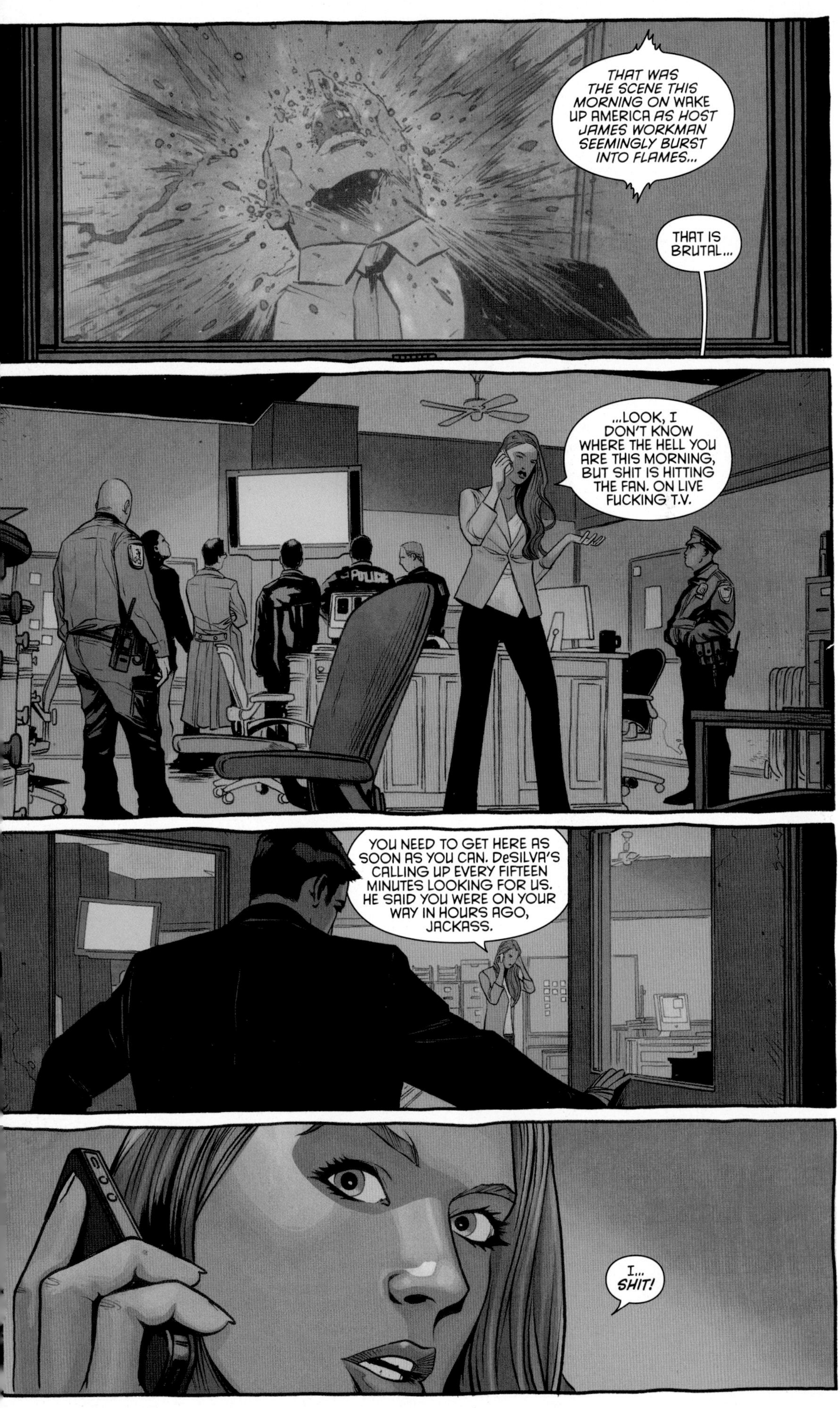
THAT WAS THE SCENE THIS MORNING ON WAKE UP AMERICA AS HOST JAMES WORKMAN SEEMINGLY BURST INTO FLAMES...
THAT IS BRUTAL...
...LOOK, I DON'T KNOW WHERE THE HELL YOU ARE THIS MORNING, BUT SHIT IS HITTING THE FAN. ON LIVE FUCKING T.V.
POLICE
YOU NEED TO GET HERE AS SOON AS YOU CAN. DeSILVA'S CALLING UP EVERY FIFTEEN MINUTES LOOKING FOR US. HE SAID YOU WERE ON YOUR WAY IN HOURS AGO, JACKASS.
I... SHIT!

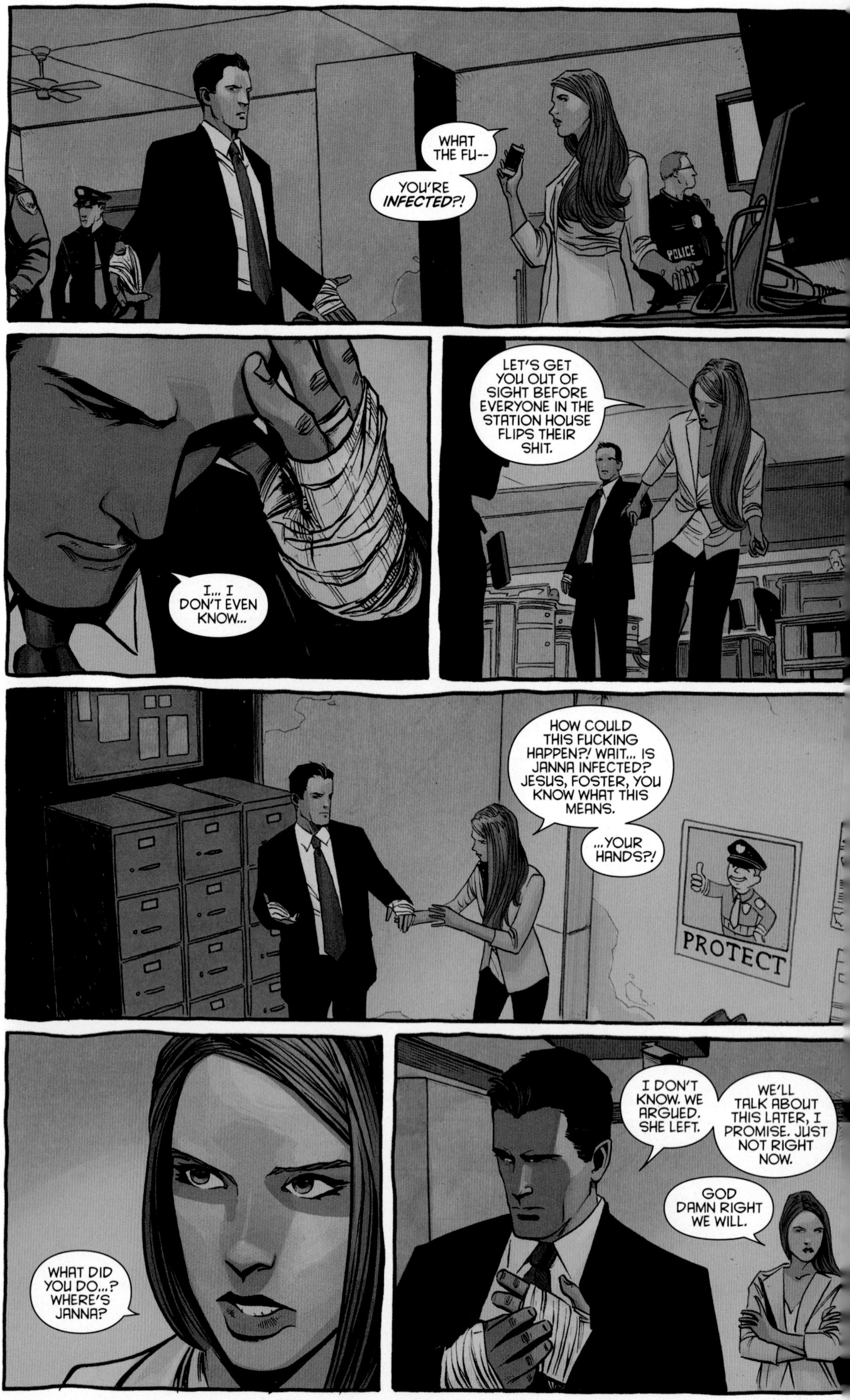
WHAT THE FU--
YOU'RE *INFECTED?!*
I... I DON'T EVEN KNOW...
LET'S GET YOU OUT OF SIGHT BEFORE EVERYONE IN THE STATION HOUSE FLIPS THEIR SHIT.
POLICE
HOW COULD THIS FUCKING HAPPEN?! WAIT... IS JANNA INFECTED? JESUS, FOSTER, YOU KNOW WHAT THIS MEANS.
...YOUR HANDS?!
PROTECT
WHAT DID YOU DO...? WHERE'S JANNA?
I DON'T KNOW. WE ARGUED. SHE LEFT.
WE'LL TALK ABOUT THIS LATER, I PROMISE. JUST NOT RIGHT NOW.
GOD DAMN RIGHT WE WILL.

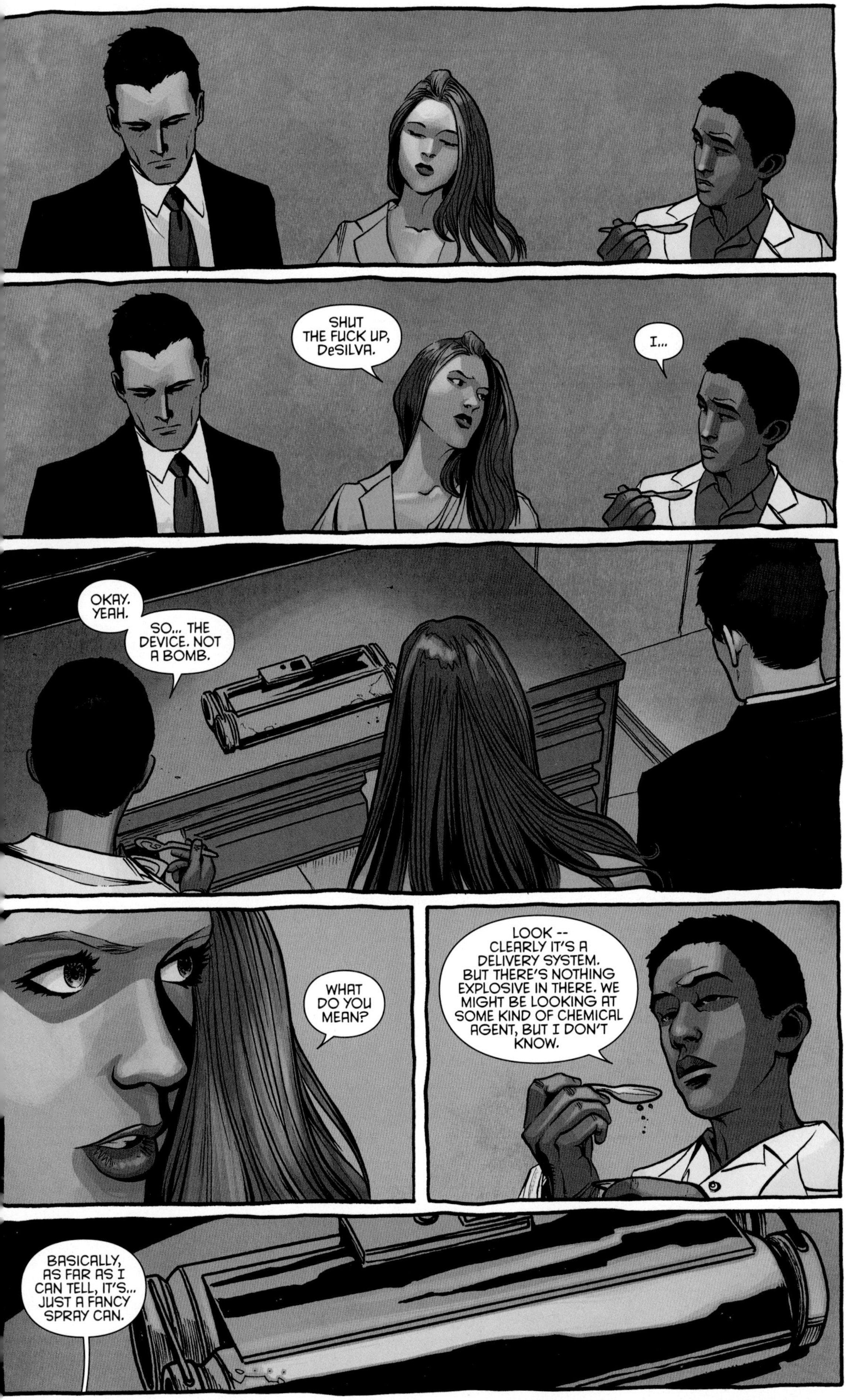
SHUT THE FUCK UP, DeSILVA.
I...
OKAY. YEAH.
SO... THE DEVICE. NOT A BOMB.
WHAT DO YOU MEAN?
LOOK -- CLEARLY IT'S A DELIVERY SYSTEM. BUT THERE'S NOTHING EXPLOSIVE IN THERE. WE MIGHT BE LOOKING AT SOME KIND OF CHEMICAL AGENT, BUT I DON'T KNOW.
BASICALLY, AS FAR AS I CAN TELL, IT'S... JUST A FANCY SPRAY CAN.

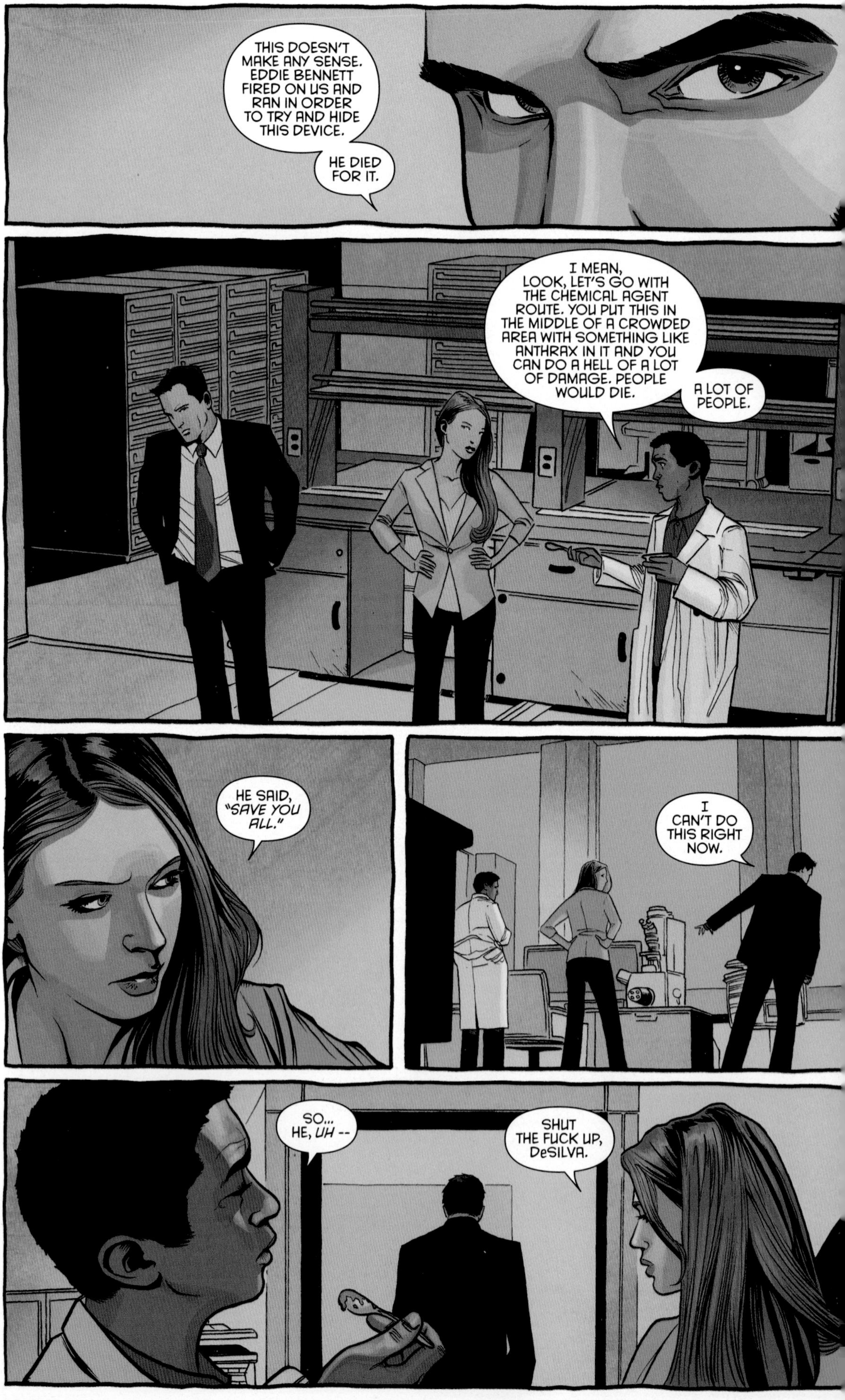

THIS DOESN'T MAKE ANY SENSE. EDDIE BENNETT FIRED ON US AND RAN IN ORDER TO TRY AND HIDE THIS DEVICE.
HE DIED FOR IT.
I MEAN, LOOK, LET'S GO WITH THE CHEMICAL AGENT ROUTE. YOU PUT THIS IN THE MIDDLE OF A CROWDED AREA WITH SOMETHING LIKE ANTHRAX IN IT AND YOU CAN DO A HELL OF A LOT OF DAMAGE. PEOPLE WOULD DIE.
A LOT OF PEOPLE.
HE SAID, "SAVE YOU ALL."
I CAN'T DO THIS RIGHT NOW.
SO... HE, UH --
SHUT THE FUCK UP, DeSILVA.

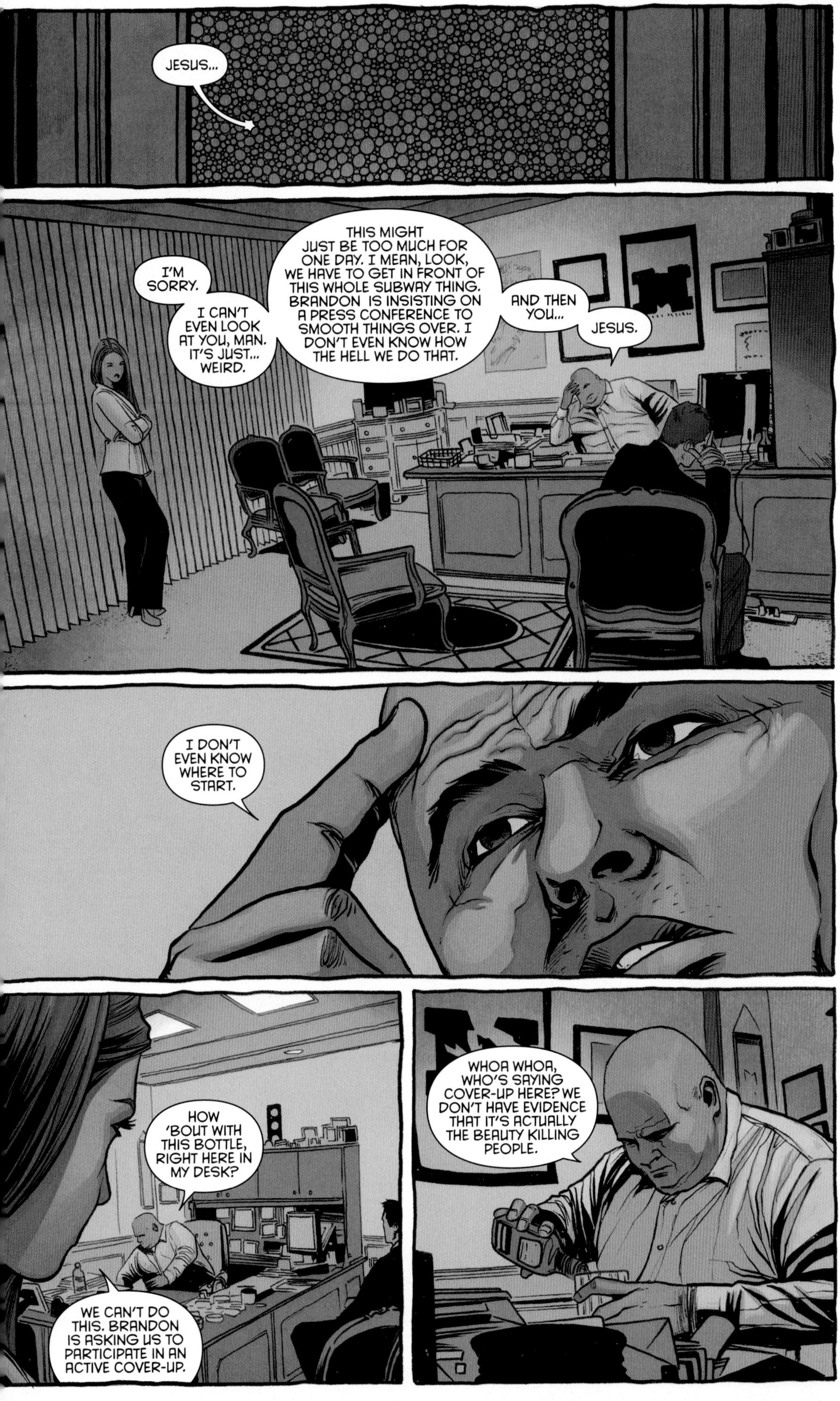
JESUS...
I'M SORRY.
I CAN'T EVEN LOOK AT YOU, MAN. IT'S JUST... WEIRD.
THIS MIGHT JUST BE TOO MUCH FOR ONE DAY. I MEAN, LOOK, WE HAVE TO GET IN FRONT OF THIS WHOLE SUBWAY THING. BRANDON IS INSISTING ON A PRESS CONFERENCE TO SMOOTH THINGS OVER. I DON'T EVEN KNOW HOW THE HELL WE DO THAT.
AND THEN YOU...
JESUS.
I DON'T EVEN KNOW WHERE TO START.
HOW 'BOUT WITH THIS BOTTLE, RIGHT HERE IN MY DESK?
WE CAN'T DO THIS. BRANDON IS ASKING US TO PARTICIPATE IN AN ACTIVE COVER-UP.
WHOA WHOA, WHO'S SAYING COVER-UP HERE? WE DON'T HAVE EVIDENCE THAT IT'S ACTUALLY THE BEAUTY KILLING PEOPLE.

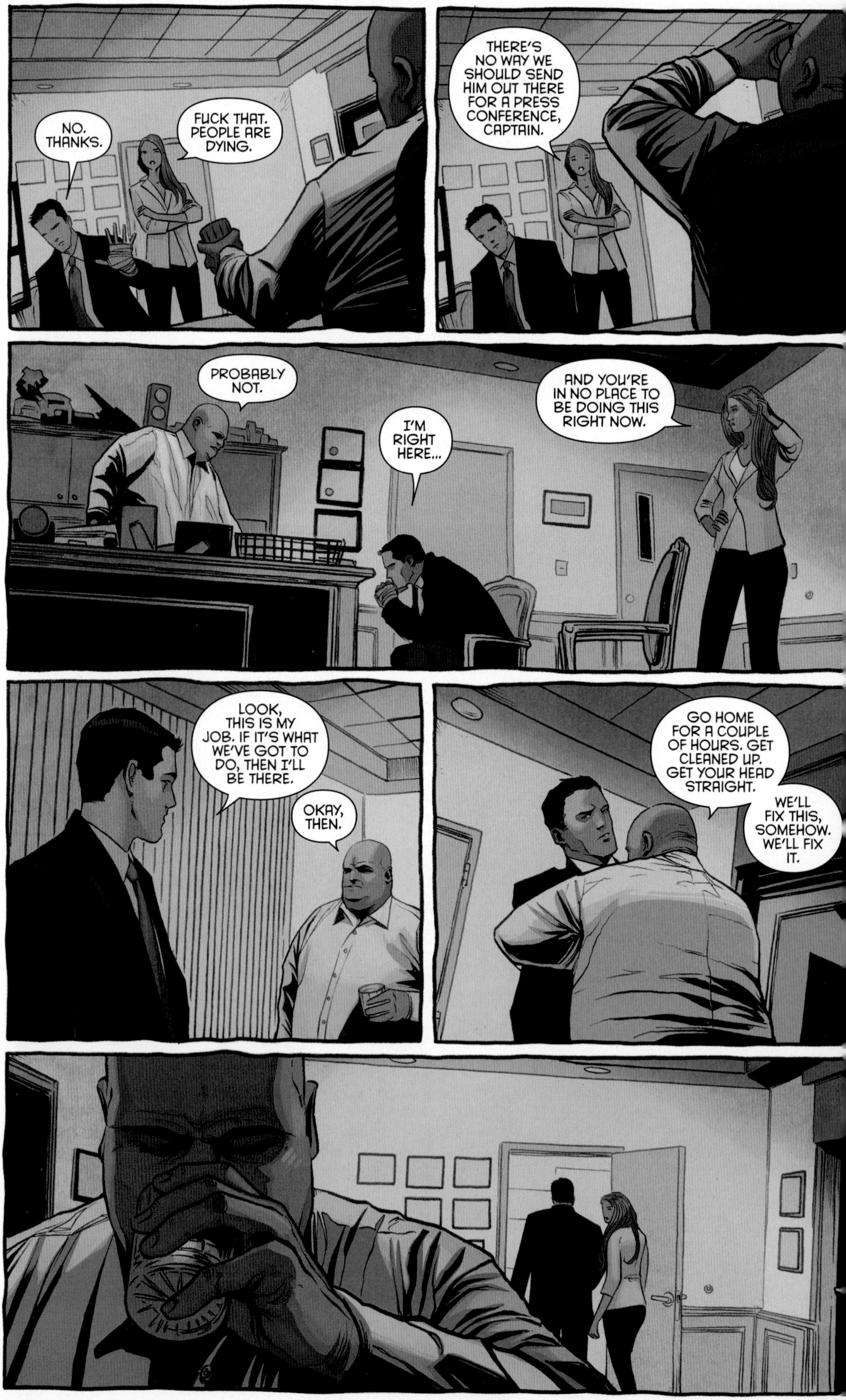
NO. THANKS.
FUCK THAT. PEOPLE ARE DYING.
THERE'S NO WAY WE SHOULD SEND HIM OUT THERE FOR A PRESS CONFERENCE, CAPTAIN.
PROBABLY NOT.
I'M RIGHT HERE...
AND YOU'RE IN NO PLACE TO BE DOING THIS RIGHT NOW.
LOOK, THIS IS MY JOB. IF IT'S WHAT WE'VE GOT TO DO, THEN I'LL BE THERE.
OKAY, THEN.
GO HOME FOR A COUPLE OF HOURS. GET CLEANED UP. GET YOUR HEAD STRAIGHT.
WE'LL FIX THIS, SOMEHOW. WE'LL FIX IT.

I WAS STANDING THERE LOOKING IN THE MIRROR AND I DIDN'T EVEN RECOGNIZE MYSELF.

IT WAS ONLY AFTER THAT THAT I RECOGNIZED IT IN HER.

I NEVER THOUGHT SHE COULD BE MORE BEAUTIFUL, SO I DIDN'T EVEN NOTICE WHEN SHE WAS.

I DIDN'T WANT TO NOTICE.

BUT THERE SHE WAS, BEAUTIFUL, PERFECT...

...AND RUINED.

I SAW ALL OF THAT BEAUTY, AND ALL I WANTED TO DO WAS SMASH IT.

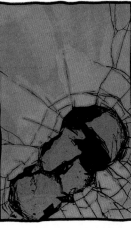

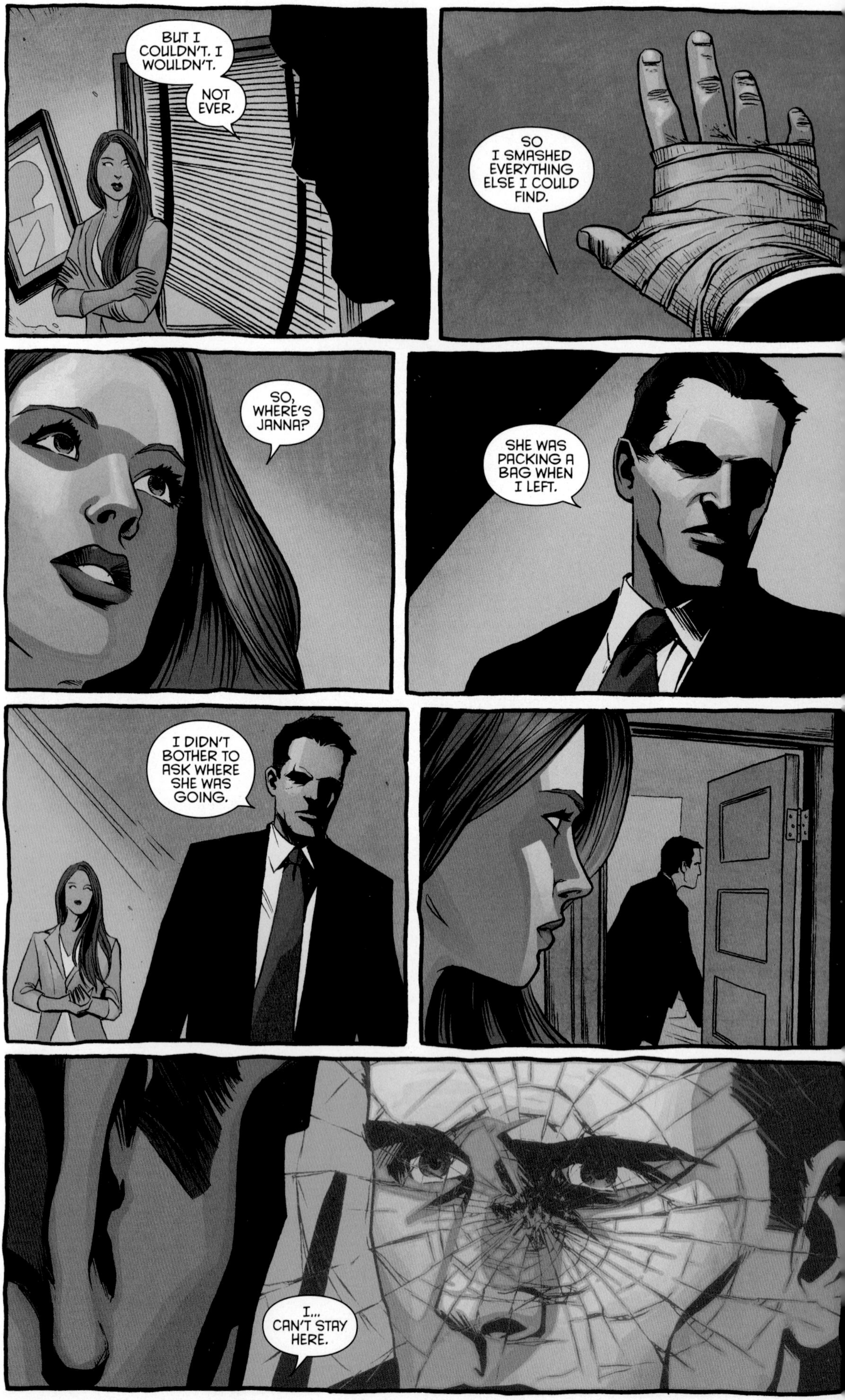
BUT I COULDN'T. I WOULDN'T.
NOT EVER.
SO I SMASHED EVERYTHING ELSE I COULD FIND.
SO, WHERE'S JANNA?
SHE WAS PACKING A BAG WHEN I LEFT.
I DIDN'T BOTHER TO ASK WHERE SHE WAS GOING.
I... CAN'T STAY HERE.

AND YOU SHOULDN'T.

LET'S GET YOU TO A HOTEL FOR THE NIGHT, GET THROUGH THIS STUPID FUCKING PRESS CONFERENCE, AND WE'LL WORRY ABOUT EVERYTHING HERE TOMORROW.

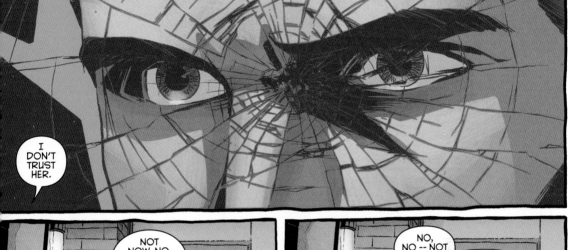

I DON'T TRUST HER.

NOT NOW, NO. YOU'LL GET BACK THERE THOUGH. JUST GIVE IT TIME.

NO, NO -- NOT JANNA.

BRANDON.

SHE'S THE ONLY ONE THAT KNOWS WHAT THE HELL IS HAPPENING TO US.

...WHAT'S HAPPENING TO JANNA.

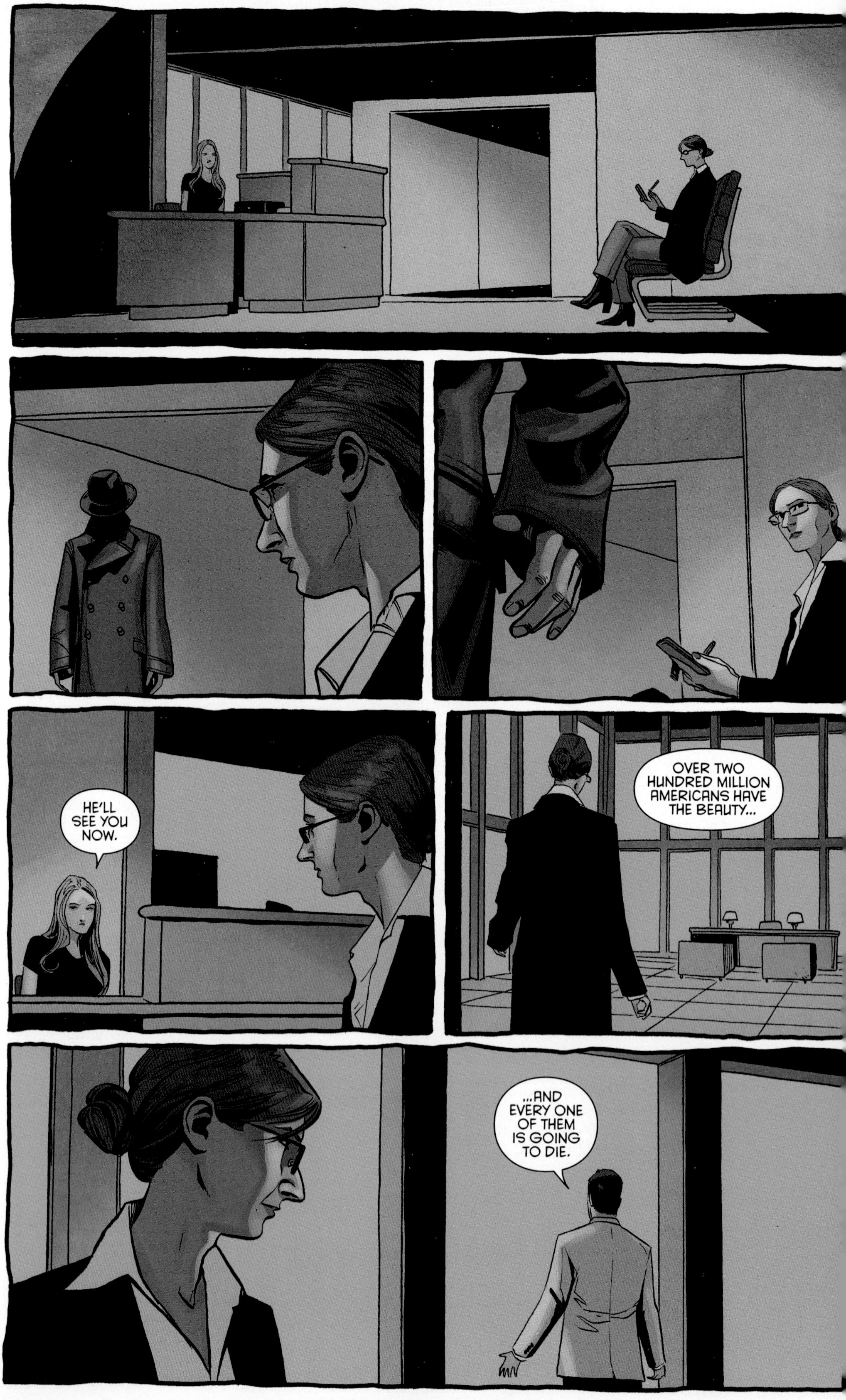
HE'LL SEE YOU NOW.
OVER TWO HUNDRED MILLION AMERICANS HAVE THE BEAUTY...
...AND EVERY ONE OF THEM IS GOING TO DIE.

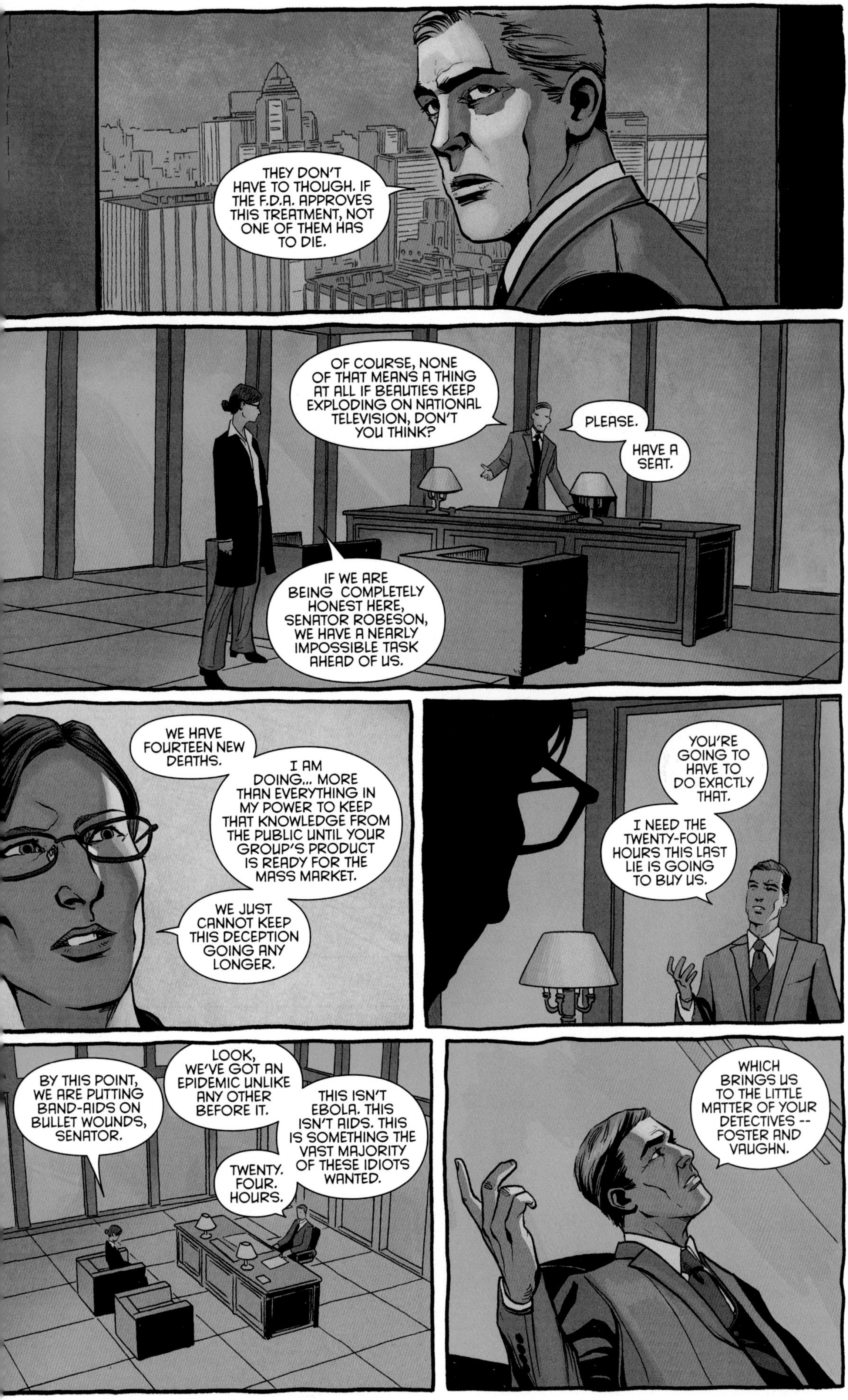
THEY DON'T HAVE TO THOUGH. IF THE F.D.A. APPROVES THIS TREATMENT, NOT ONE OF THEM HAS TO DIE.
OF COURSE, NONE OF THAT MEANS A THING AT ALL IF BEAUTIES KEEP EXPLODING ON NATIONAL TELEVISION, DON'T YOU THINK?
PLEASE.
HAVE A SEAT.
IF WE ARE BEING COMPLETELY HONEST HERE, SENATOR ROBESON, WE HAVE A NEARLY IMPOSSIBLE TASK AHEAD OF US.
WE HAVE FOURTEEN NEW DEATHS.
I AM DOING... MORE THAN EVERYTHING IN MY POWER TO KEEP THAT KNOWLEDGE FROM THE PUBLIC UNTIL YOUR GROUP'S PRODUCT IS READY FOR THE MASS MARKET.
WE JUST CANNOT KEEP THIS DECEPTION GOING ANY LONGER.
YOU'RE GOING TO HAVE TO DO EXACTLY THAT.
I NEED THE TWENTY-FOUR HOURS THIS LAST LIE IS GOING TO BUY US.
BY THIS POINT, WE ARE PUTTING BAND-AIDS ON BULLET WOUNDS, SENATOR.
LOOK, WE'VE GOT AN EPIDEMIC UNLIKE ANY OTHER BEFORE IT.
THIS ISN'T EBOLA. THIS ISN'T AIDS. THIS IS SOMETHING THE VAST MAJORITY OF THESE IDIOTS WANTED.
TWENTY. FOUR. HOURS.
WHICH BRINGS US TO THE LITTLE MATTER OF YOUR DETECTIVES -- FOSTER AND VAUGHN.

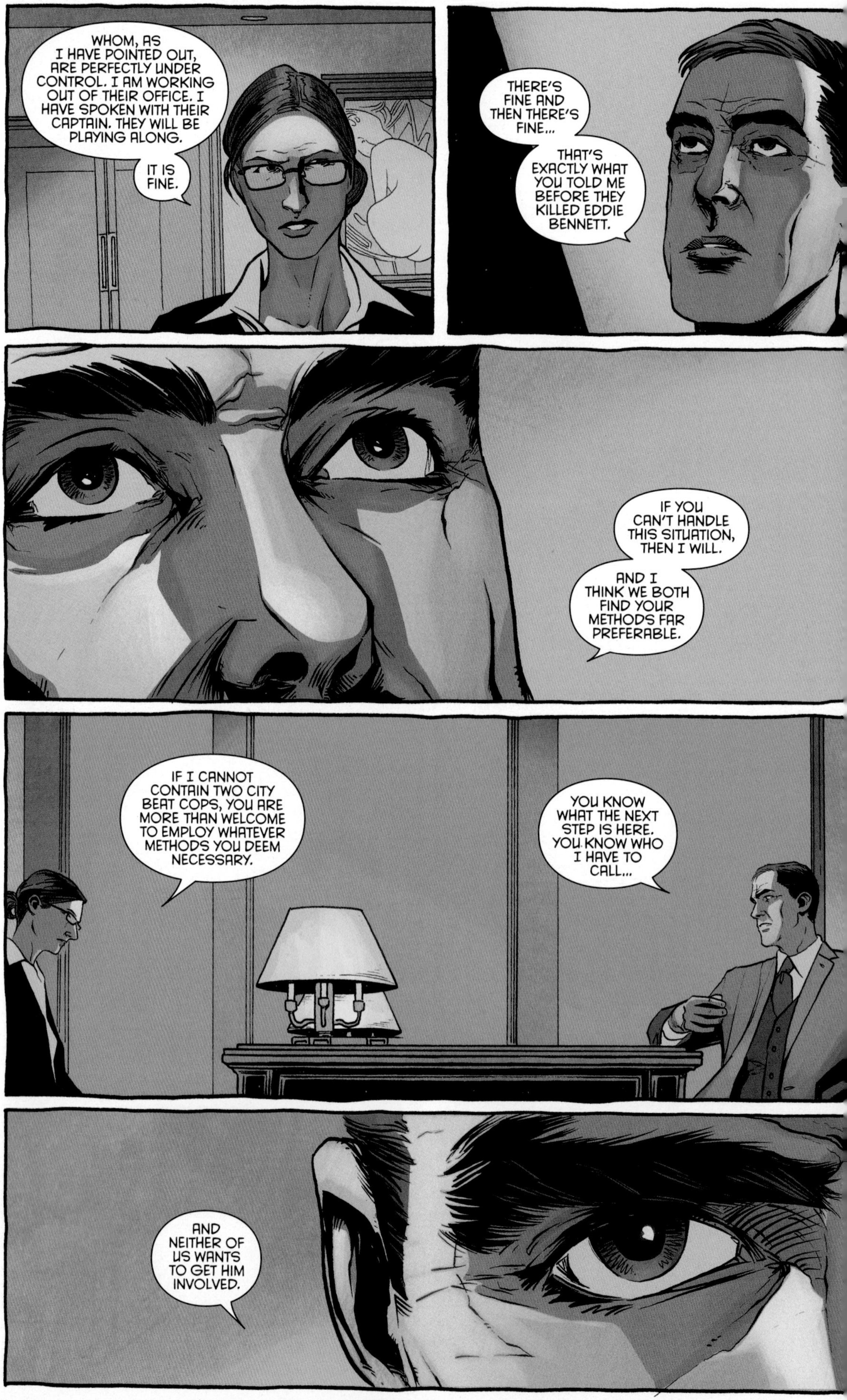
WHOM, AS I HAVE POINTED OUT, ARE PERFECTLY UNDER CONTROL. I AM WORKING OUT OF THEIR OFFICE. I HAVE SPOKEN WITH THEIR CAPTAIN. THEY WILL BE PLAYING ALONG.
IT IS FINE.
THERE'S FINE AND THEN THERE'S FINE...
THAT'S EXACTLY WHAT YOU TOLD ME BEFORE THEY KILLED EDDIE BENNETT.
IF YOU CAN'T HANDLE THIS SITUATION, THEN I WILL.
AND I THINK WE BOTH FIND YOUR METHODS FAR PREFERABLE.
IF I CANNOT CONTAIN TWO CITY BEAT COPS, YOU ARE MORE THAN WELCOME TO EMPLOY WHATEVER METHODS YOU DEEM NECESSARY.
YOU KNOW WHAT THE NEXT STEP IS HERE. YOU KNOW WHO I HAVE TO CALL...
AND NEITHER OF US WANTS TO GET HIM INVOLVED.

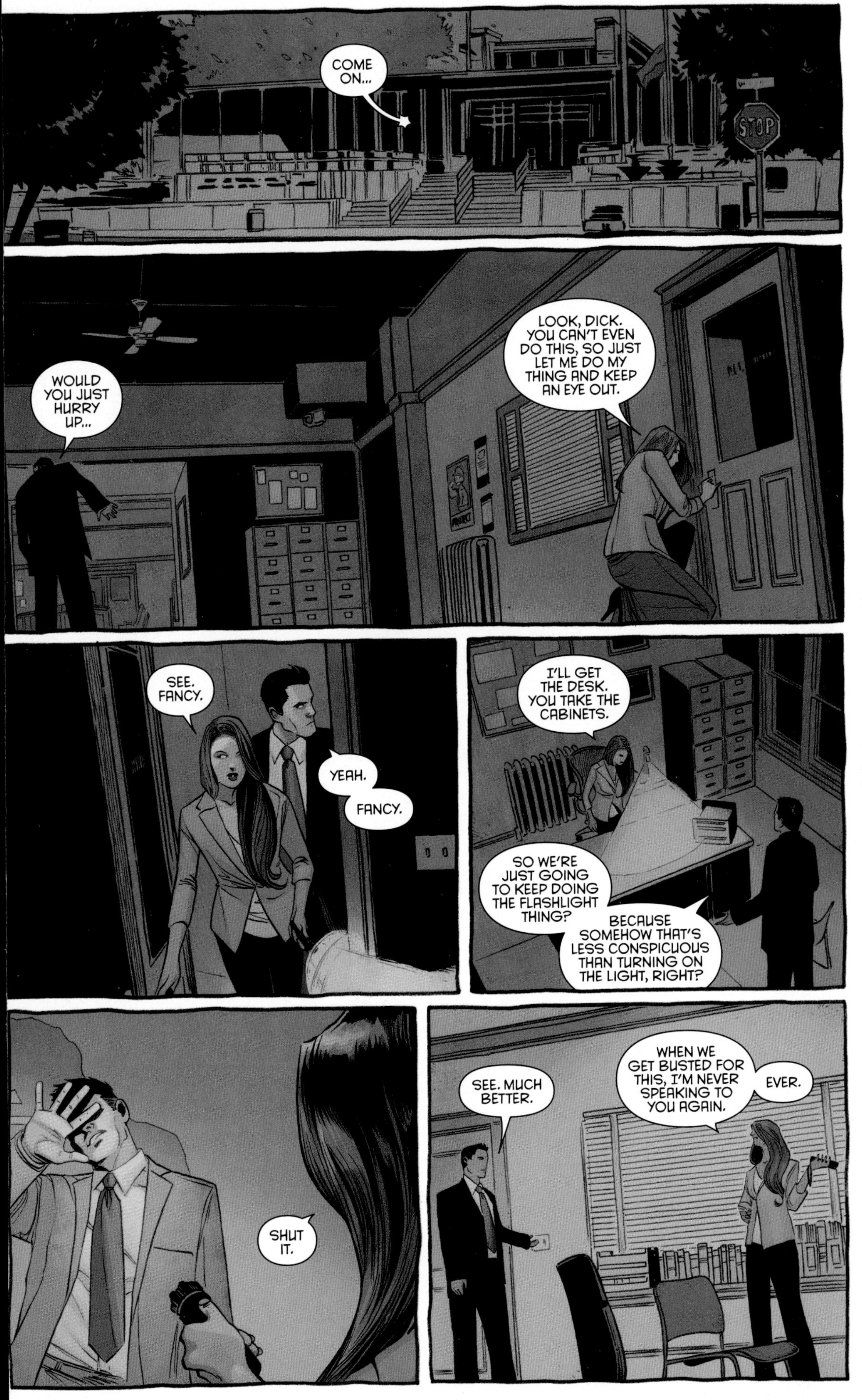
COME ON...
WOULD YOU JUST HURRY UP...
LOOK, DICK. YOU CAN'T EVEN DO THIS, SO JUST LET ME DO MY THING AND KEEP AN EYE OUT.
SEE. FANCY.
YEAH.
FANCY.
I'LL GET THE DESK. YOU TAKE THE CABINETS.
SO WE'RE JUST GOING TO KEEP DOING THE FLASHLIGHT THING?
BECAUSE SOMEHOW THAT'S LESS CONSPICUOUS THAN TURNING ON THE LIGHT, RIGHT?
SHUT IT.
SEE. MUCH BETTER.
WHEN WE GET BUSTED FOR THIS, I'M NEVER SPEAKING TO YOU AGAIN.
EVER.

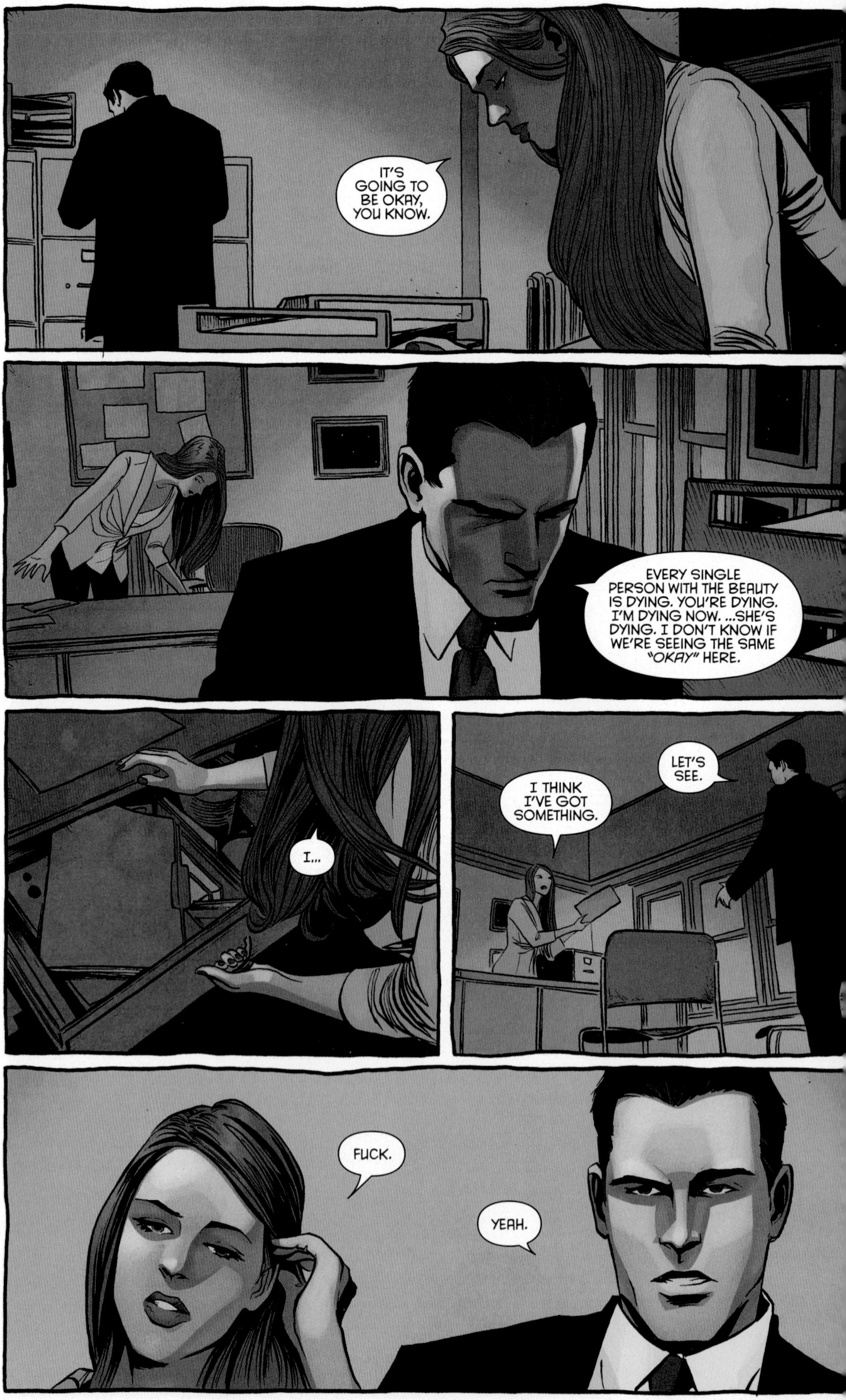
IT'S GOING TO BE OKAY, YOU KNOW.
EVERY SINGLE PERSON WITH THE BEAUTY IS DYING. YOU'RE DYING. I'M DYING NOW. ...SHE'S DYING. I DON'T KNOW IF WE'RE SEEING THE SAME *"OKAY"* HERE.
I...
I THINK I'VE GOT SOMETHING.
LET'S SEE.
FUCK.
YEAH.

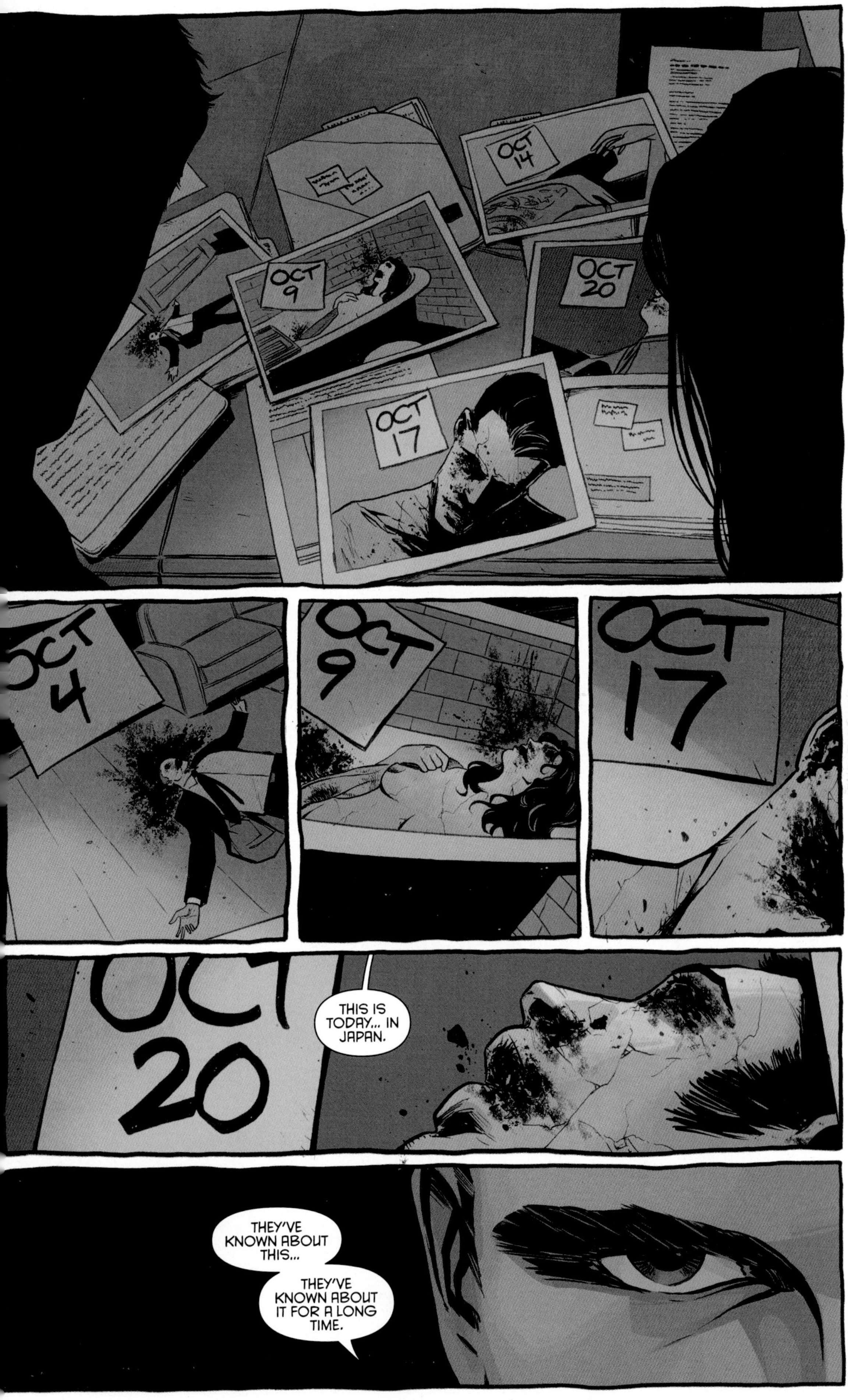
OCT 14
OCT 9
OCT 20
OCT 17
OCT 4
OCT 9
OCT 17
OCT 20
THIS IS TODAY... IN JAPAN.
THEY'VE KNOWN ABOUT THIS...
THEY'VE KNOWN ABOUT IT FOR A LONG TIME.

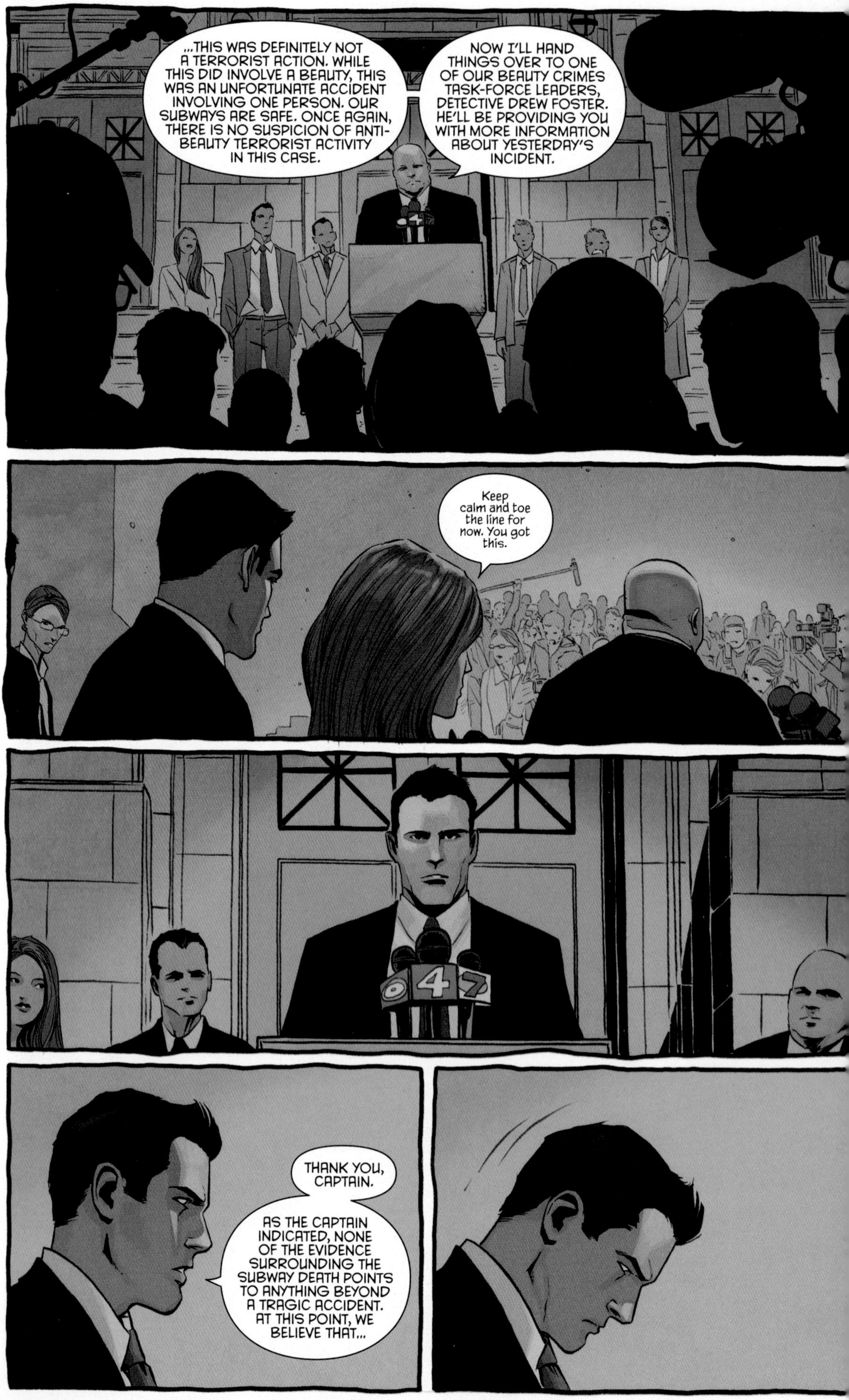
...THIS WAS DEFINITELY NOT A TERRORIST ACTION. WHILE THIS DID INVOLVE A BEAUTY, THIS WAS AN UNFORTUNATE ACCIDENT INVOLVING ONE PERSON. OUR SUBWAYS ARE SAFE. ONCE AGAIN, THERE IS NO SUSPICION OF ANTI-BEAUTY TERRORIST ACTIVITY IN THIS CASE.
NOW I'LL HAND THINGS OVER TO ONE OF OUR BEAUTY CRIMES TASK-FORCE LEADERS, DETECTIVE DREW FOSTER. HE'LL BE PROVIDING YOU WITH MORE INFORMATION ABOUT YESTERDAY'S INCIDENT.
Keep calm and toe the line for now. You got this.
47
THANK YOU, CAPTAIN.
AS THE CAPTAIN INDICATED, NONE OF THE EVIDENCE SURROUNDING THE SUBWAY DEATH POINTS TO ANYTHING BEYOND A TRAGIC ACCIDENT. AT THIS POINT, WE BELIEVE THAT...

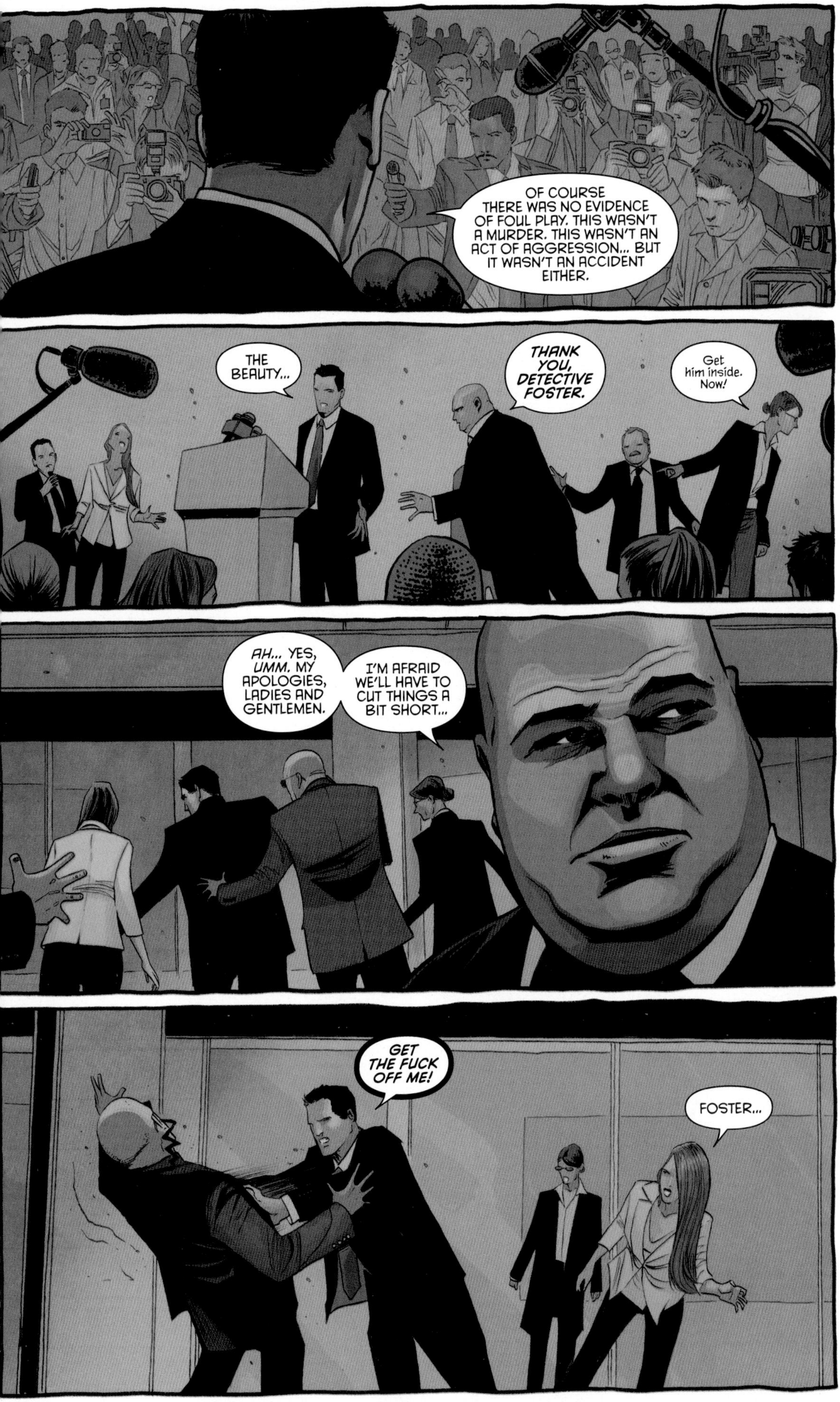

OF COURSE THERE WAS NO EVIDENCE OF FOUL PLAY. THIS WASN'T A MURDER. THIS WASN'T AN ACT OF AGGRESSION... BUT IT WASN'T AN ACCIDENT EITHER.
THE BEAUTY...
THANK YOU, DETECTIVE FOSTER.
Get him inside. Now!
AH... YES, UMM. MY APOLOGIES, LADIES AND GENTLEMEN.
I'M AFRAID WE'LL HAVE TO CUT THINGS A BIT SHORT...
GET THE FUCK OFF ME!
FOSTER...

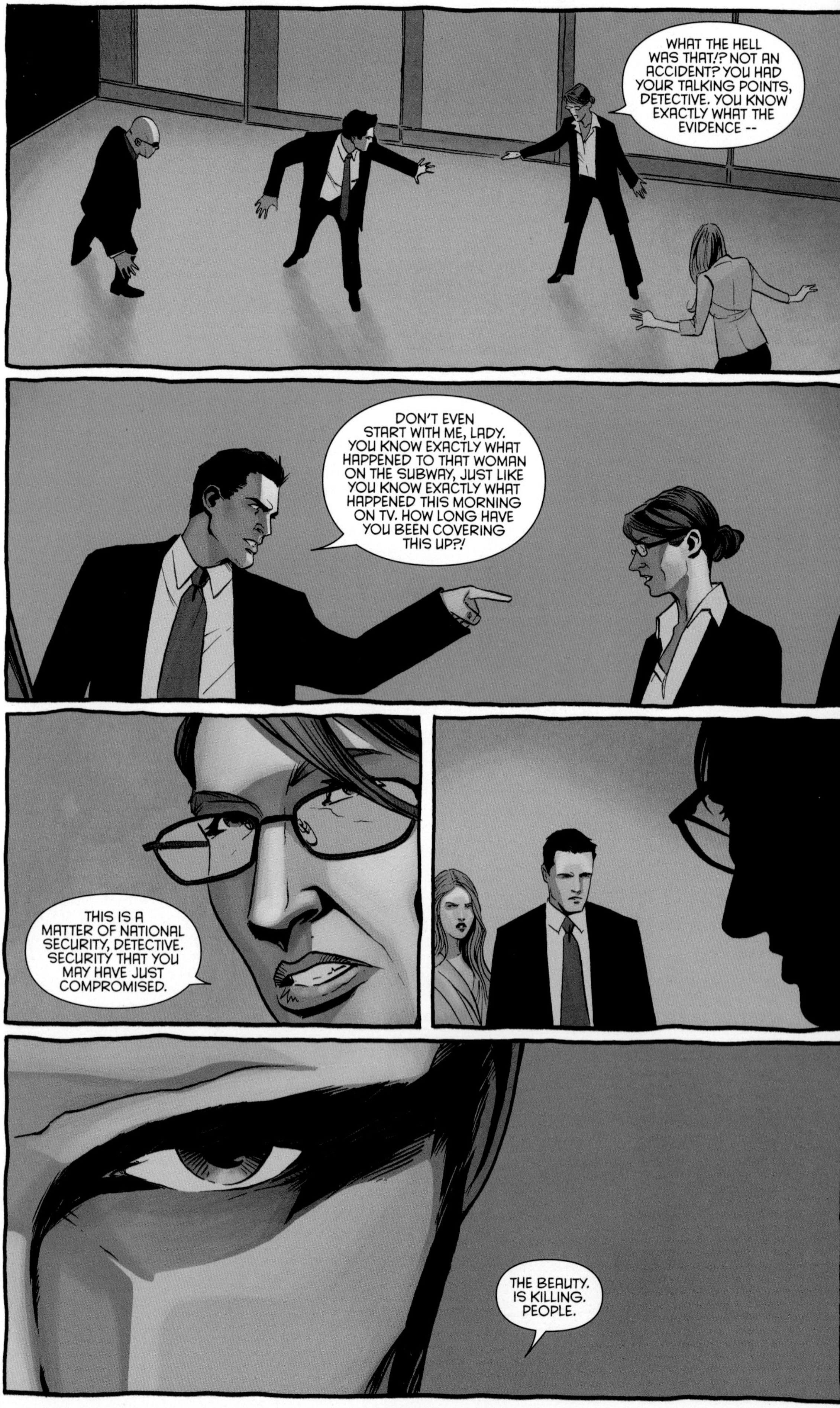
WHAT THE HELL WAS THAT!? NOT AN ACCIDENT? YOU HAD YOUR TALKING POINTS, DETECTIVE. YOU KNOW EXACTLY WHAT THE EVIDENCE --
DON'T EVEN START WITH ME, LADY. YOU KNOW EXACTLY WHAT HAPPENED TO THAT WOMAN ON THE SUBWAY, JUST LIKE YOU KNOW EXACTLY WHAT HAPPENED THIS MORNING ON TV. HOW LONG HAVE YOU BEEN COVERING THIS UP?!
THIS IS A MATTER OF NATIONAL SECURITY, DETECTIVE. SECURITY THAT YOU MAY HAVE JUST COMPROMISED.
THE BEAUTY. IS KILLING. PEOPLE.

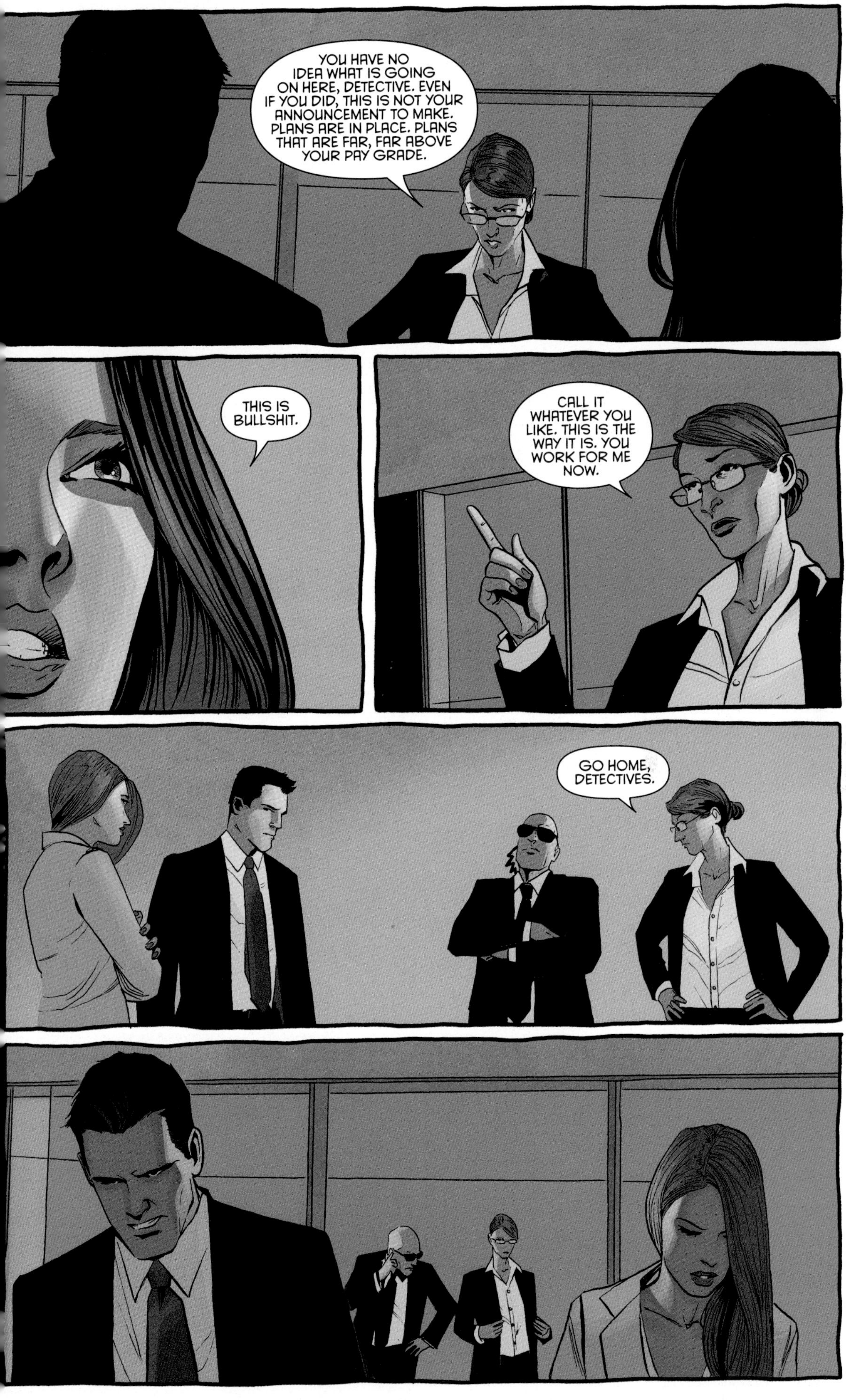
YOU HAVE NO IDEA WHAT IS GOING ON HERE, DETECTIVE. EVEN IF YOU DID, THIS IS NOT YOUR ANNOUNCEMENT TO MAKE. PLANS ARE IN PLACE. PLANS THAT ARE FAR, FAR ABOVE YOUR PAY GRADE.
THIS IS BULLSHIT.
CALL IT WHATEVER YOU LIKE. THIS IS THE WAY IT IS. YOU WORK FOR ME NOW.
GO HOME, DETECTIVES.

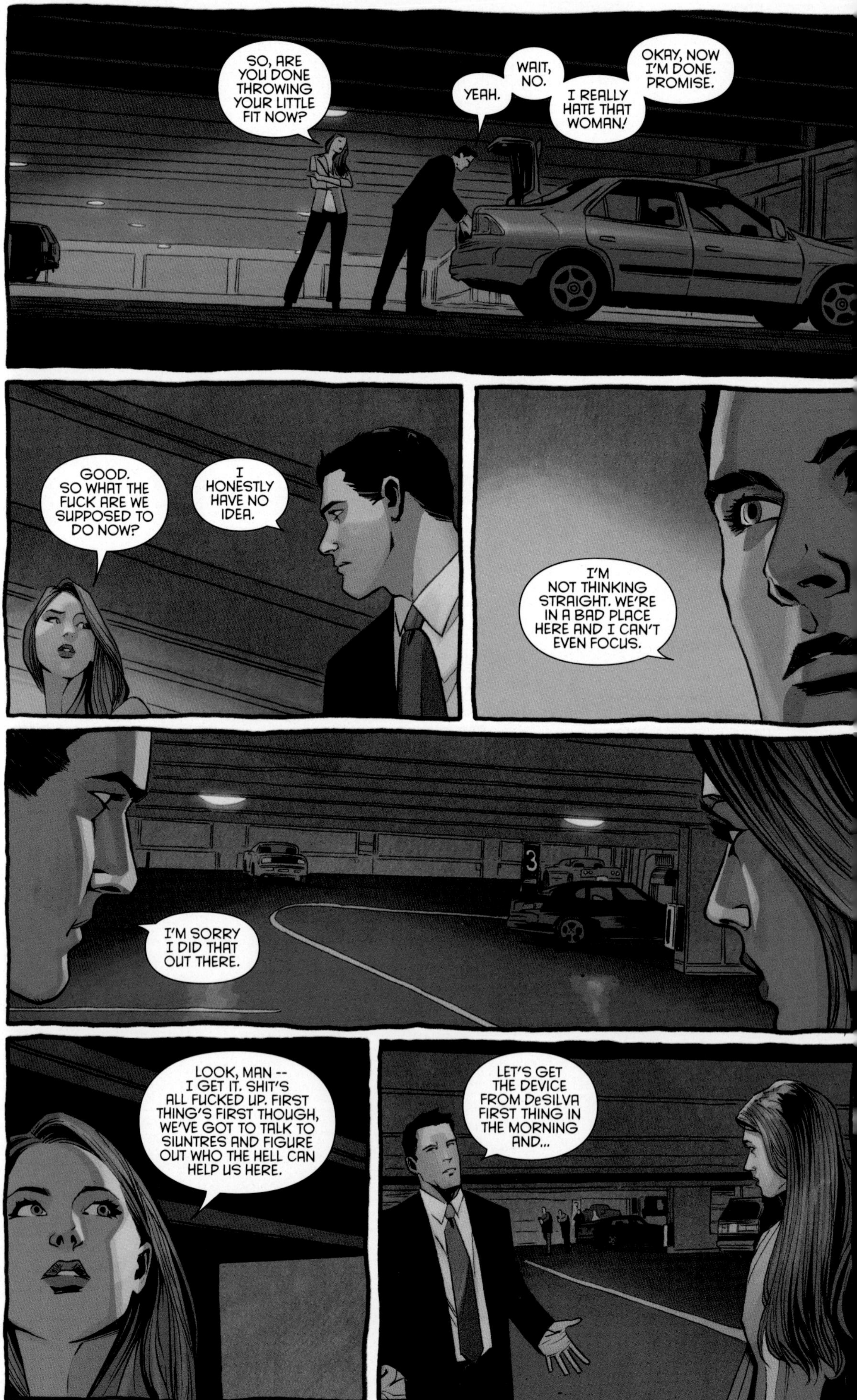
SO, ARE YOU DONE THROWING YOUR LITTLE FIT NOW?
YEAH.
WAIT, NO.
I REALLY HATE THAT WOMAN!
OKAY, NOW I'M DONE. PROMISE.
GOOD. SO WHAT THE FUCK ARE WE SUPPOSED TO DO NOW?
I HONESTLY HAVE NO IDEA.
I'M NOT THINKING STRAIGHT. WE'RE IN A BAD PLACE HERE AND I CAN'T EVEN FOCUS.
I'M SORRY I DID THAT OUT THERE.
LOOK, MAN -- I GET IT. SHIT'S ALL FUCKED UP. FIRST THING'S FIRST THOUGH, WE'VE GOT TO TALK TO SIUNTRES AND FIGURE OUT WHO THE HELL CAN HELP US HERE.
LET'S GET THE DEVICE FROM DeSILVA FIRST THING IN THE MORNING AND...

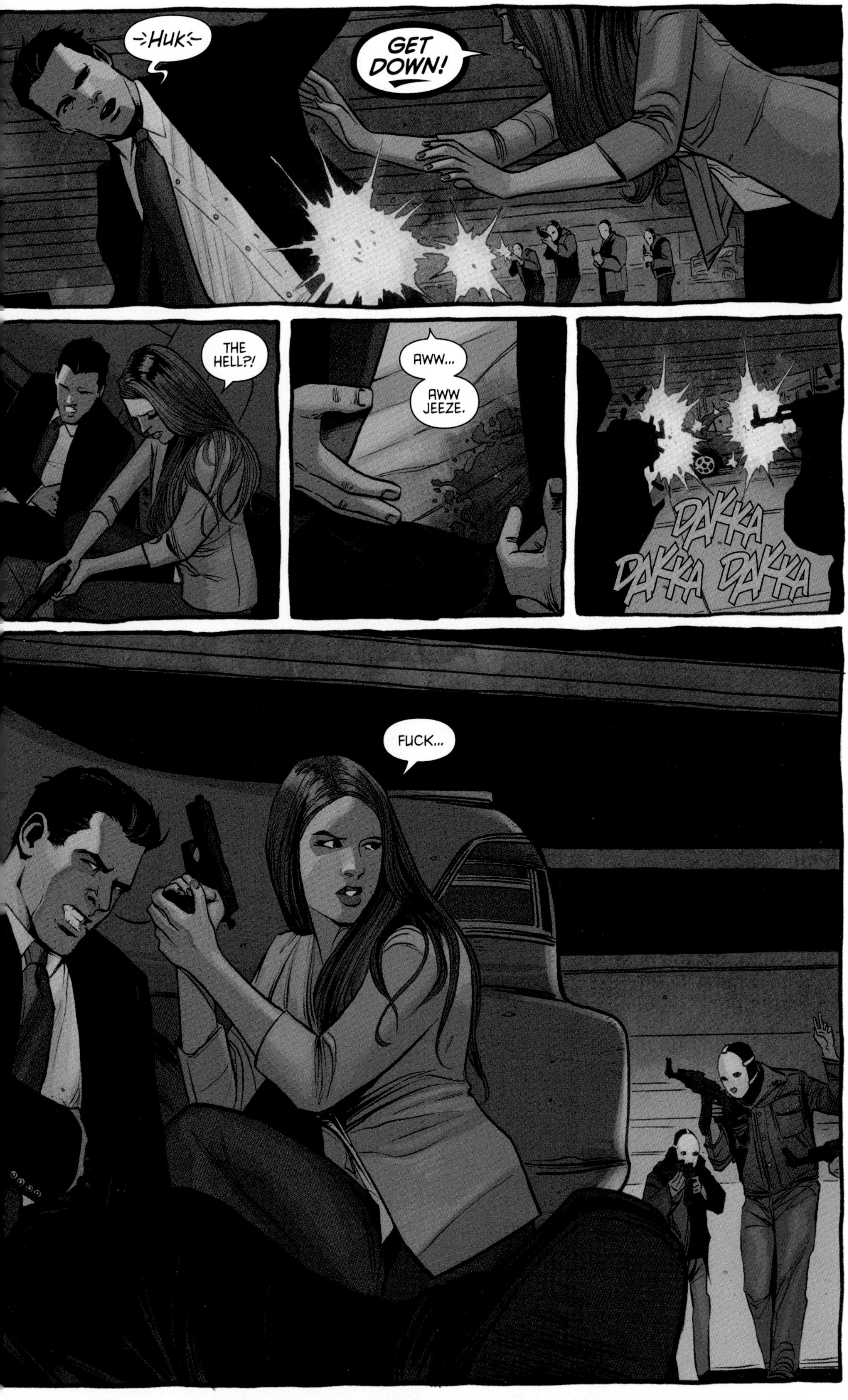

HUK
GET DOWN!
THE HELL?!
AWW...
AWW JEEZE.
DAKKA
DAKKA DAKKA
FUCK...

CHAPTER 5

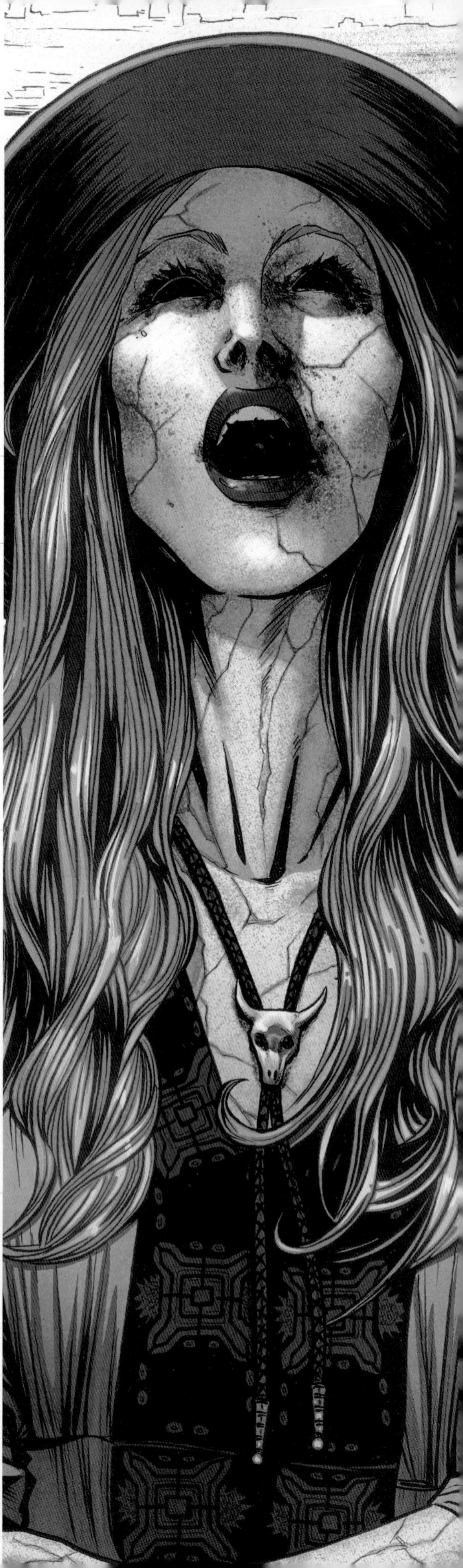

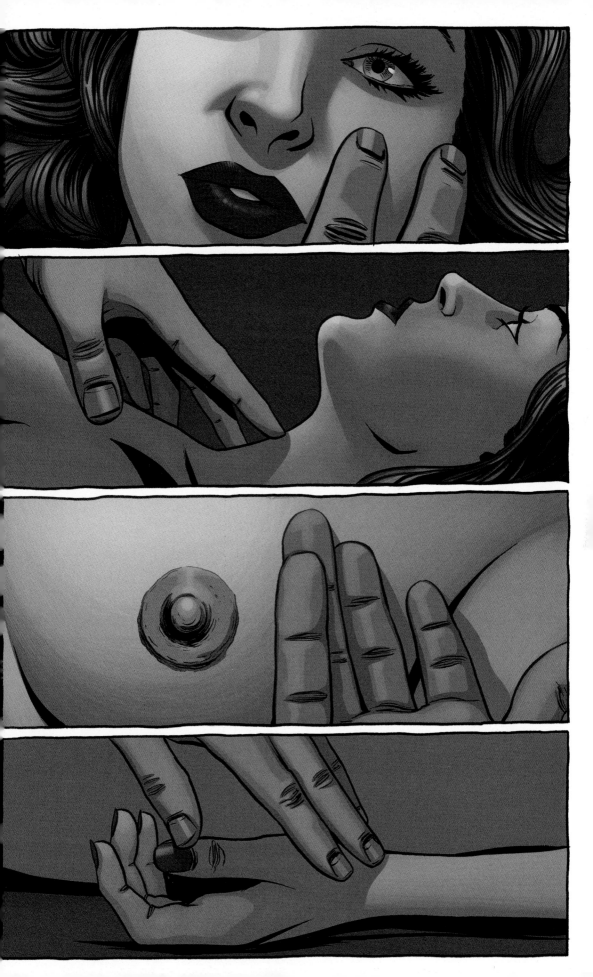

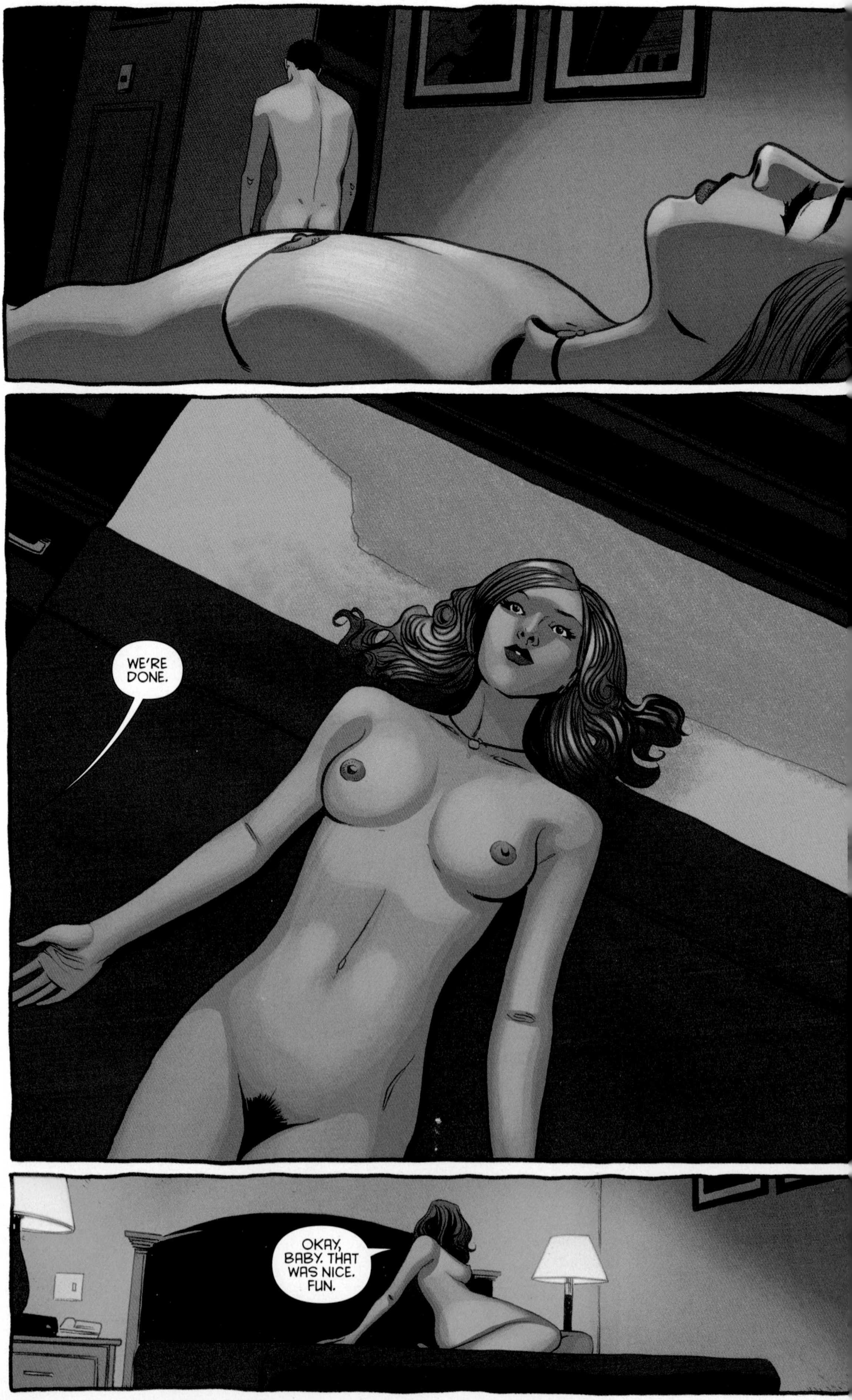
WE'RE DONE.
OKAY, BABY. THAT WAS NICE. FUN.

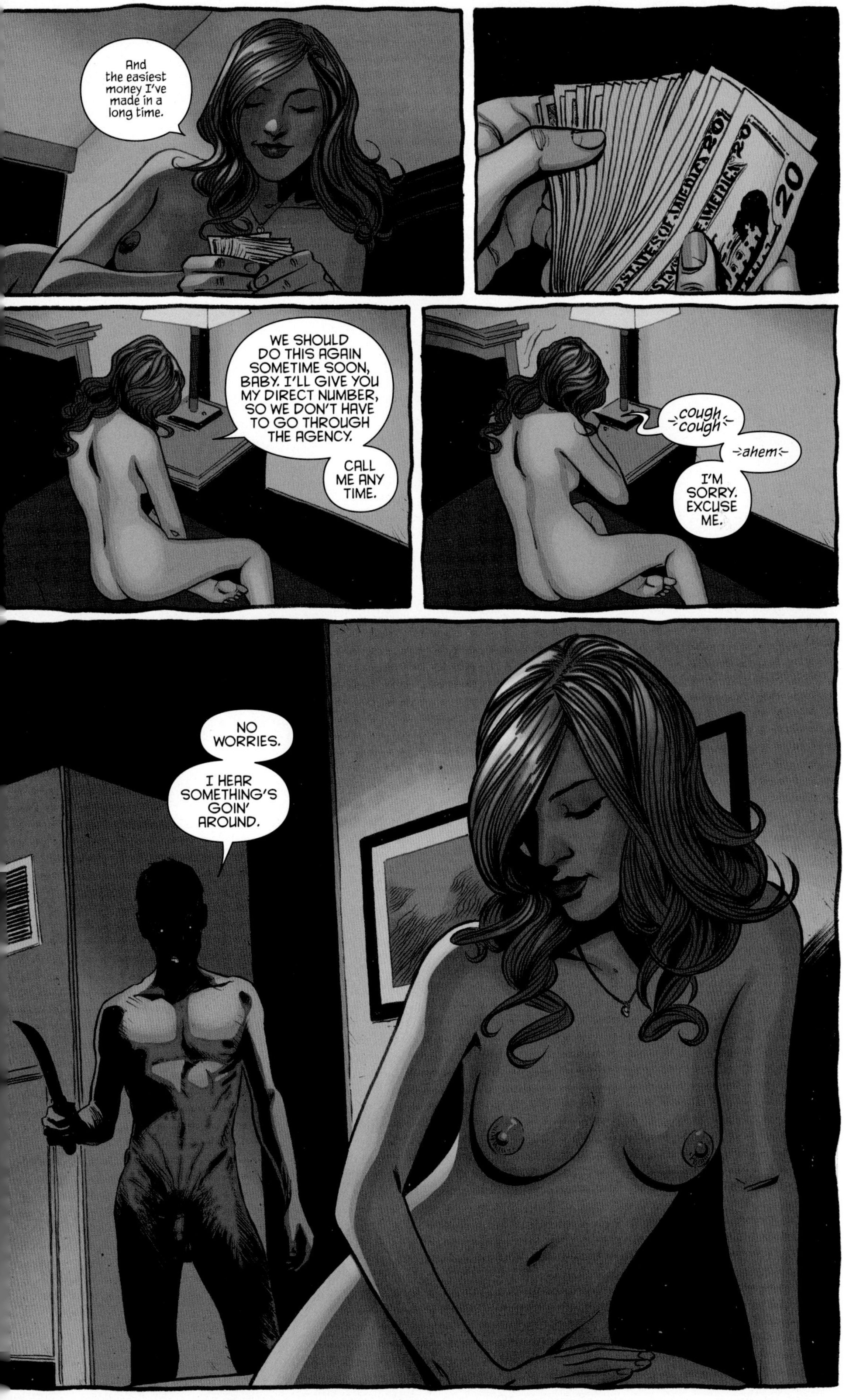
And the easiest money I've made in a long time.
WE SHOULD DO THIS AGAIN SOMETIME SOON, BABY. I'LL GIVE YOU MY DIRECT NUMBER, SO WE DON'T HAVE TO GO THROUGH THE AGENCY.
CALL ME ANY TIME.
cough cough
ahem
I'M SORRY. EXCUSE ME.
NO WORRIES.
I HEAR SOMETHING'S GOIN' AROUND.

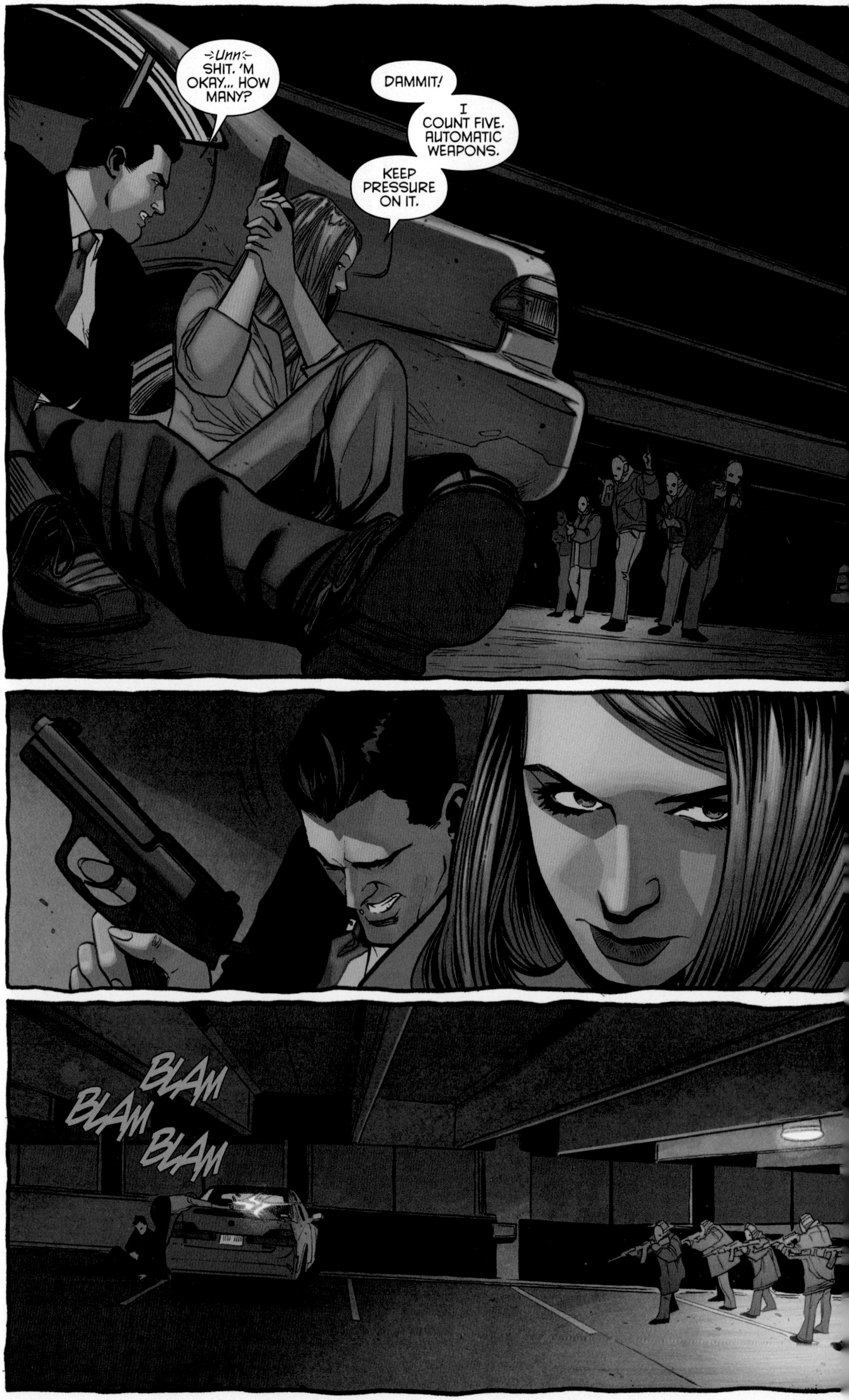
-Unn-
SHIT. 'M OKAY... HOW MANY?
DAMMIT!
I COUNT FIVE. AUTOMATIC WEAPONS.
KEEP PRESSURE ON IT.
BLAM
BLAM
BLAM

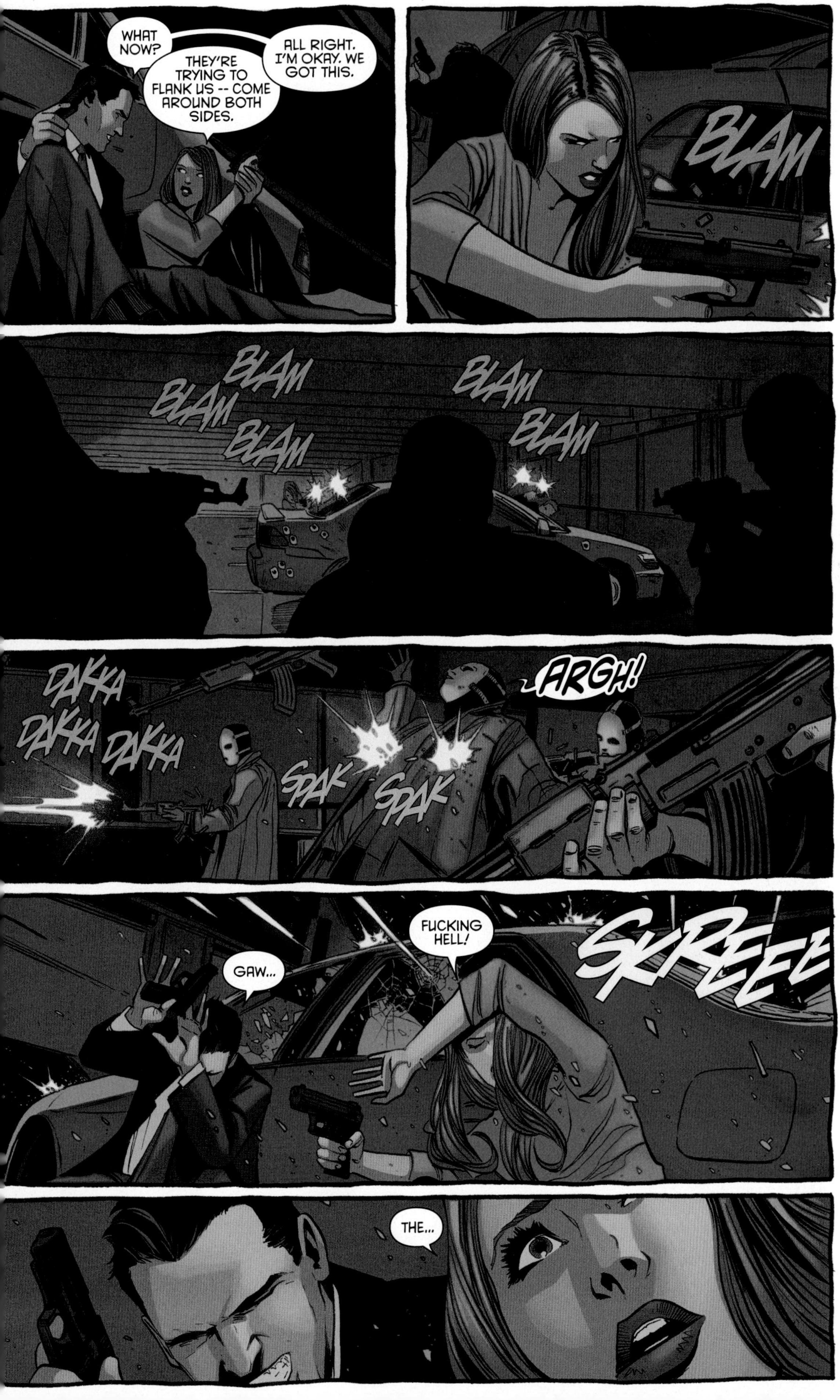
WHAT NOW?
THEY'RE TRYING TO FLANK US -- COME AROUND BOTH SIDES.
ALL RIGHT. I'M OKAY. WE GOT THIS.
BLAM
BLAM
BLAM
BLAM
BLAM
BLAM
DAKKA
DAKKA
DAKKA
SPAK
SPAK
ARGH!
GAW...
FUCKING HELL!
SKREEE
THE...

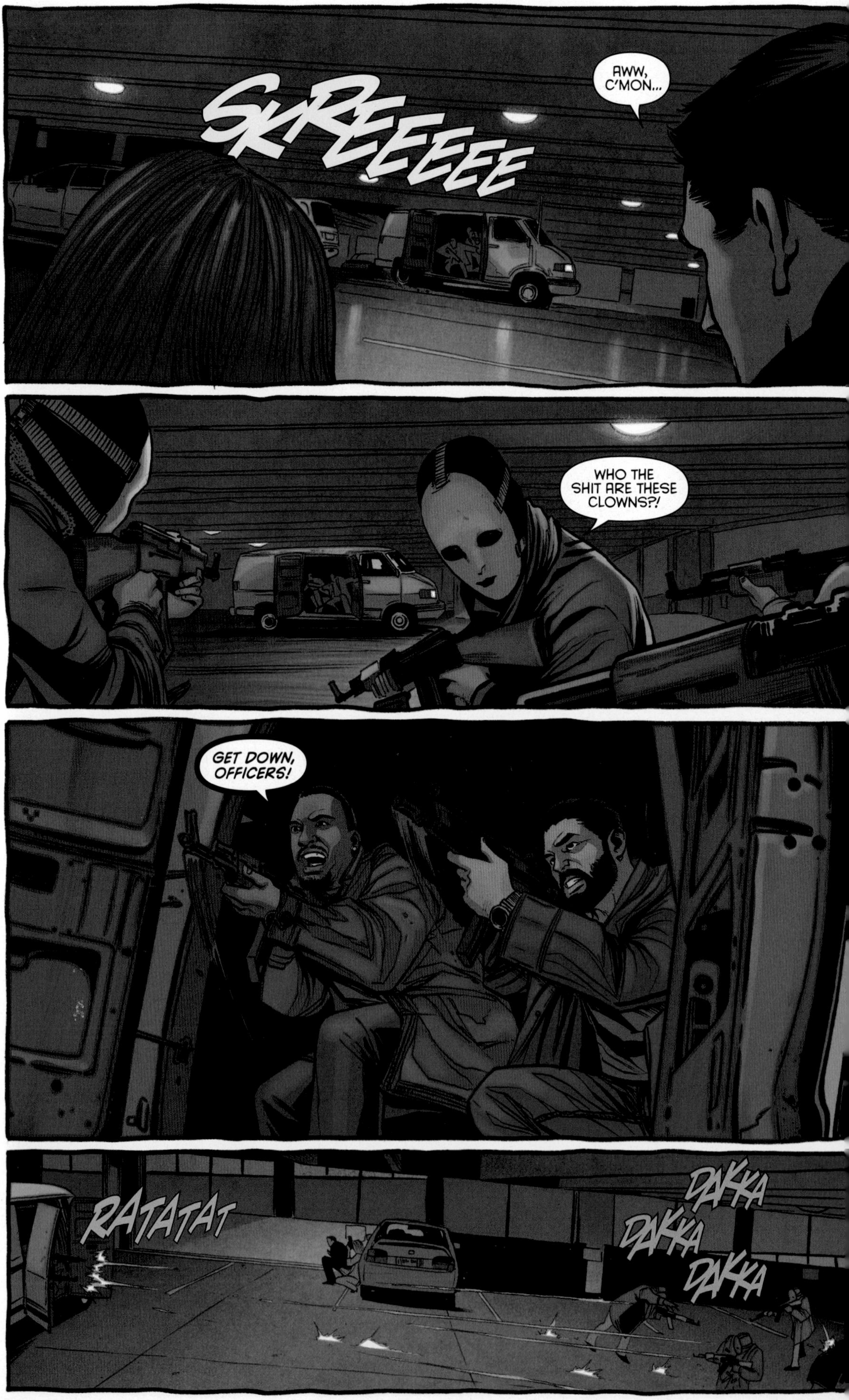
SKREEEEEE
AWW, C'MON...
WHO THE SHIT ARE THESE CLOWNS?!
GET DOWN, OFFICERS!
RATATAT
DAKKA DAKKA DAKKA

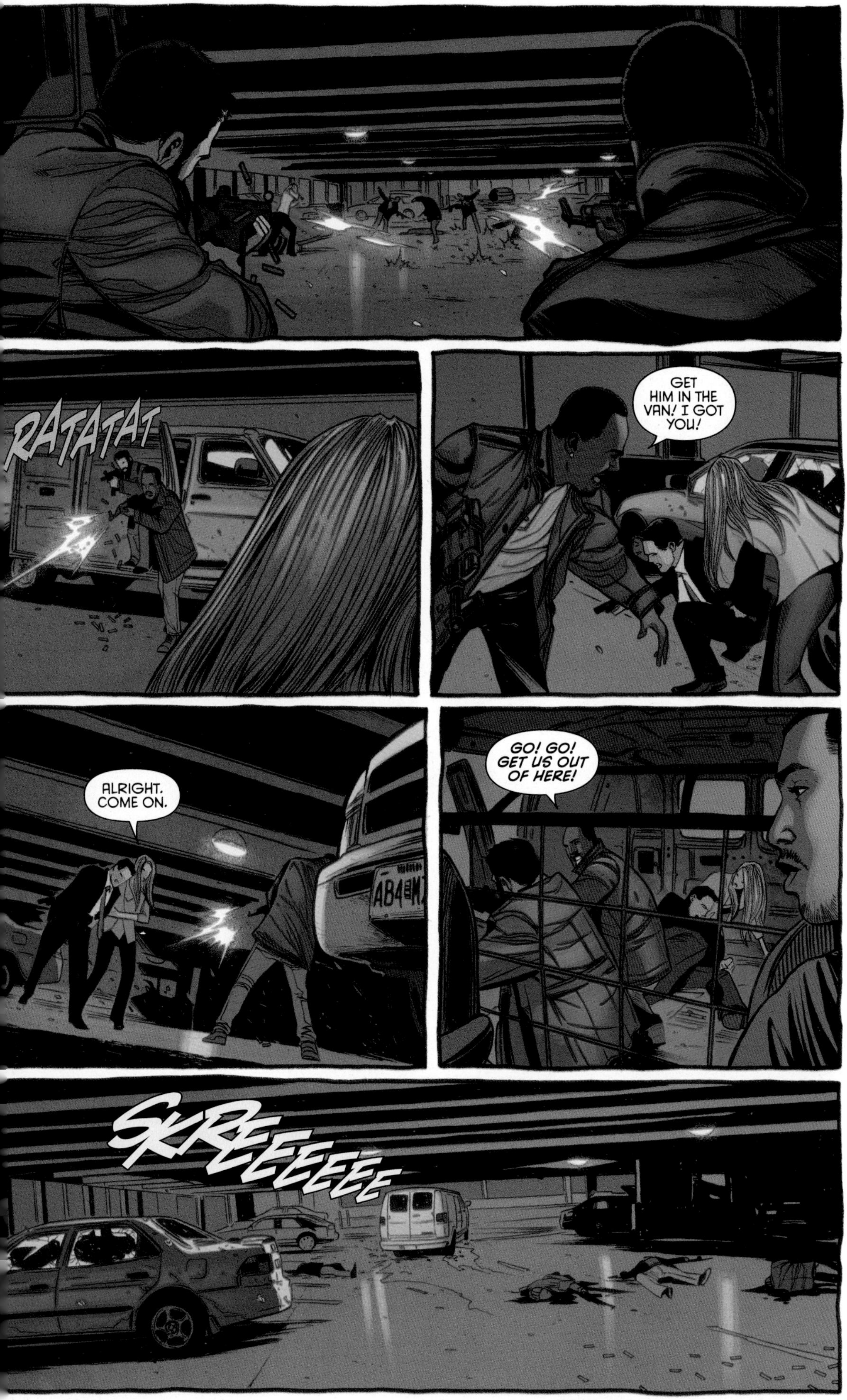
RATATAT
GET HIM IN THE VAN! I GOT YOU!
ALRIGHT. COME ON.
AB4
GO! GO! GET US OUT OF HERE!
SKREEEEEEEE

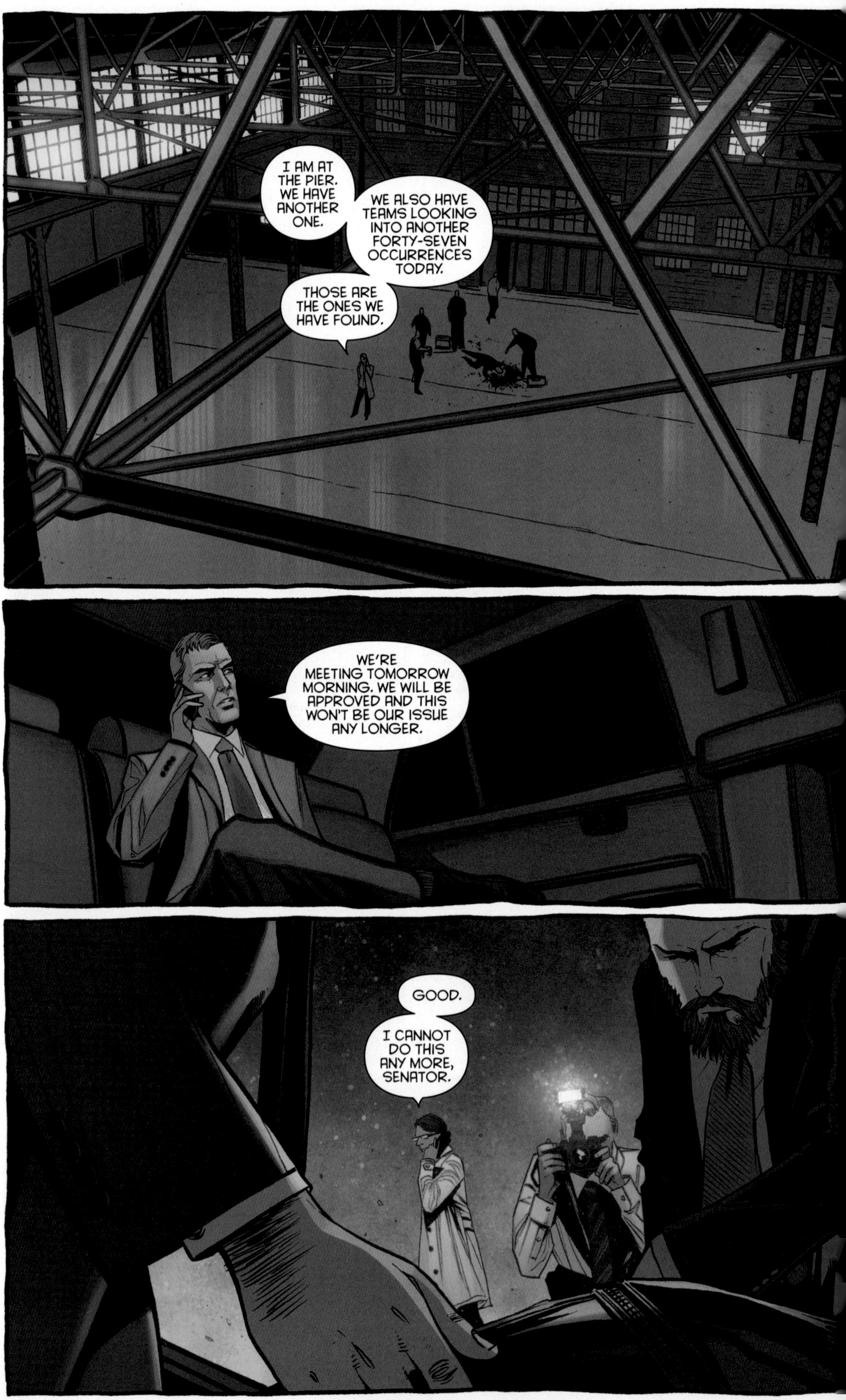
I AM AT THE PIER. WE HAVE ANOTHER ONE.
WE ALSO HAVE TEAMS LOOKING INTO ANOTHER FORTY-SEVEN OCCURRENCES TODAY.
THOSE ARE THE ONES WE HAVE FOUND.
WE'RE MEETING TOMORROW MORNING. WE WILL BE APPROVED AND THIS WON'T BE OUR ISSUE ANY LONGER.
GOOD.
I CANNOT DO THIS ANY MORE, SENATOR.

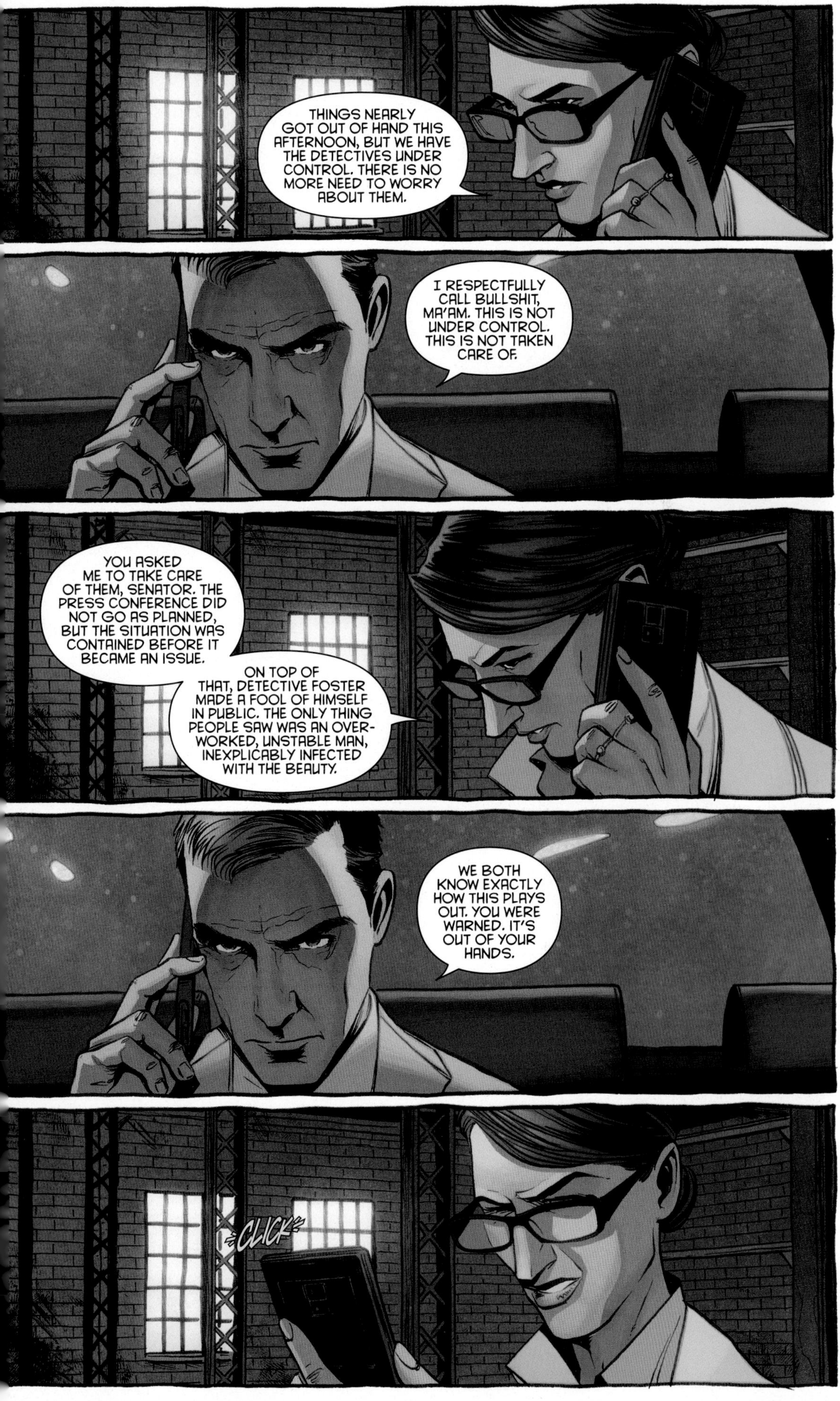
THINGS NEARLY GOT OUT OF HAND THIS AFTERNOON, BUT WE HAVE THE DETECTIVES UNDER CONTROL. THERE IS NO MORE NEED TO WORRY ABOUT THEM.
I RESPECTFULLY CALL BULLSHIT, MA'AM. THIS IS NOT UNDER CONTROL. THIS IS NOT TAKEN CARE OF.
YOU ASKED ME TO TAKE CARE OF THEM, SENATOR. THE PRESS CONFERENCE DID NOT GO AS PLANNED, BUT THE SITUATION WAS CONTAINED BEFORE IT BECAME AN ISSUE.
ON TOP OF THAT, DETECTIVE FOSTER MADE A FOOL OF HIMSELF IN PUBLIC. THE ONLY THING PEOPLE SAW WAS AN OVER-WORKED, UNSTABLE MAN, INEXPLICABLY INFECTED WITH THE BEAUTY.
WE BOTH KNOW EXACTLY HOW THIS PLAYS OUT. YOU WERE WARNED. IT'S OUT OF YOUR HANDS.
CLICK

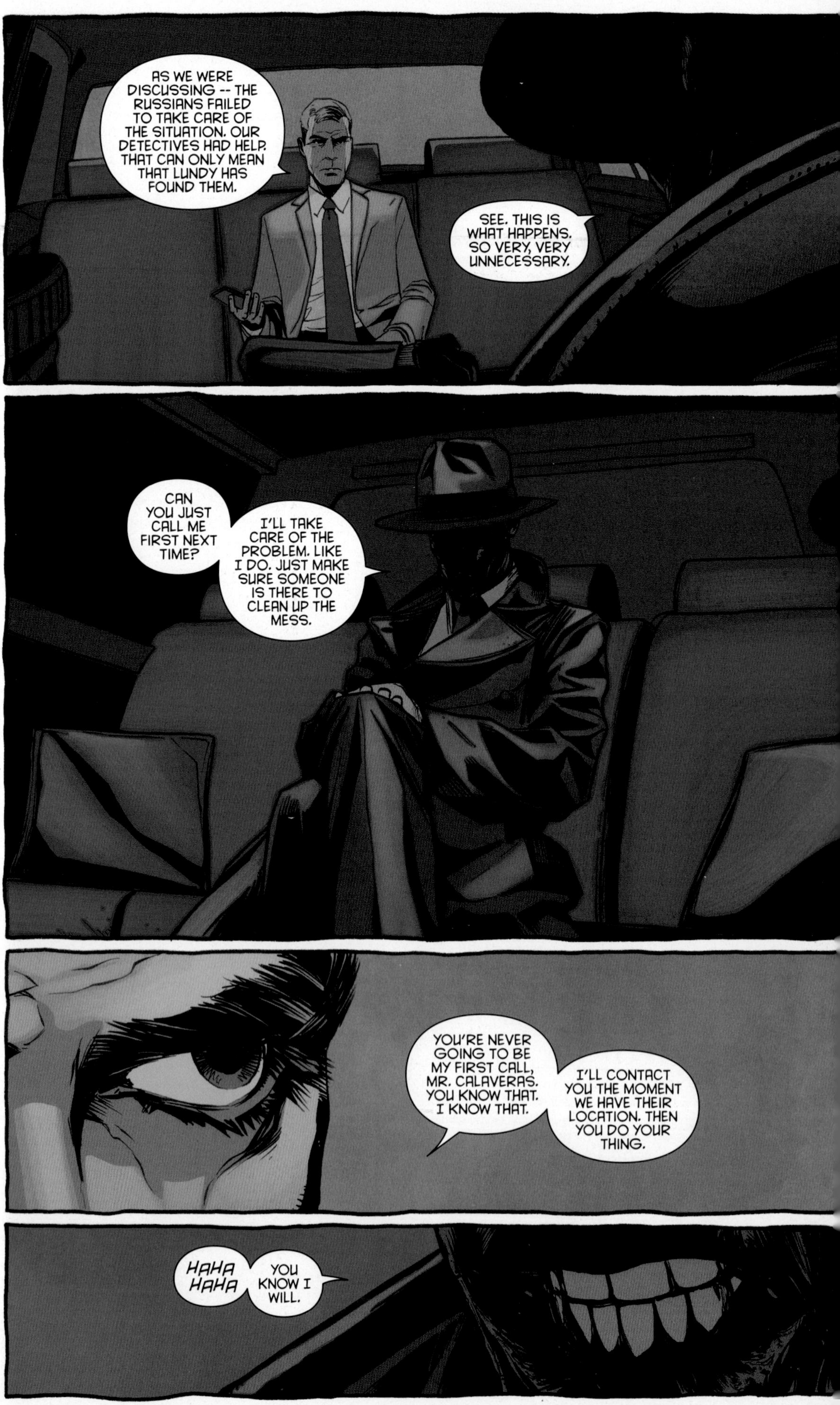
AS WE WERE DISCUSSING -- THE RUSSIANS FAILED TO TAKE CARE OF THE SITUATION. OUR DETECTIVES HAD HELP. THAT CAN ONLY MEAN THAT LUNDY HAS FOUND THEM.
SEE. THIS IS WHAT HAPPENS. SO VERY, VERY UNNECESSARY.
CAN YOU JUST CALL ME FIRST NEXT TIME?
I'LL TAKE CARE OF THE PROBLEM. LIKE I DO. JUST MAKE SURE SOMEONE IS THERE TO CLEAN UP THE MESS.
YOU'RE NEVER GOING TO BE MY FIRST CALL, MR. CALAVERAS. YOU KNOW THAT. I KNOW THAT.
I'LL CONTACT YOU THE MOMENT WE HAVE THEIR LOCATION. THEN YOU DO YOUR THING.
HAHA HAHA
YOU KNOW I WILL.

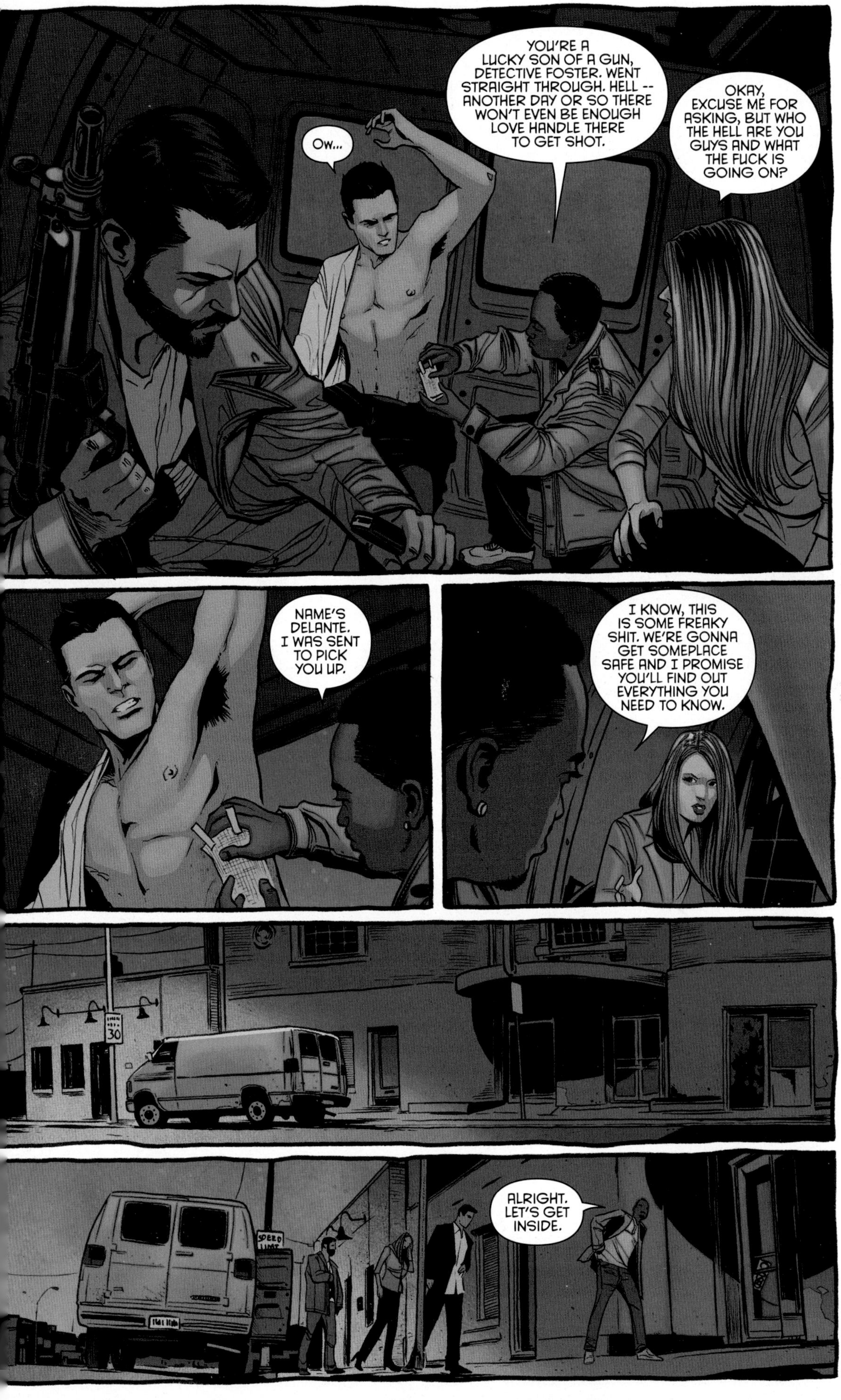
OW...
YOU'RE A LUCKY SON OF A GUN, DETECTIVE FOSTER. WENT STRAIGHT THROUGH. HELL -- ANOTHER DAY OR SO THERE WON'T EVEN BE ENOUGH LOVE HANDLE THERE TO GET SHOT.
OKAY, EXCUSE ME FOR ASKING, BUT WHO THE HELL ARE YOU GUYS AND WHAT THE FUCK IS GOING ON?
NAME'S DELANTE. I WAS SENT TO PICK YOU UP.
I KNOW, THIS IS SOME FREAKY SHIT. WE'RE GONNA GET SOMEPLACE SAFE AND I PROMISE YOU'LL FIND OUT EVERYTHING YOU NEED TO KNOW.
30
ALRIGHT. LET'S GET INSIDE.

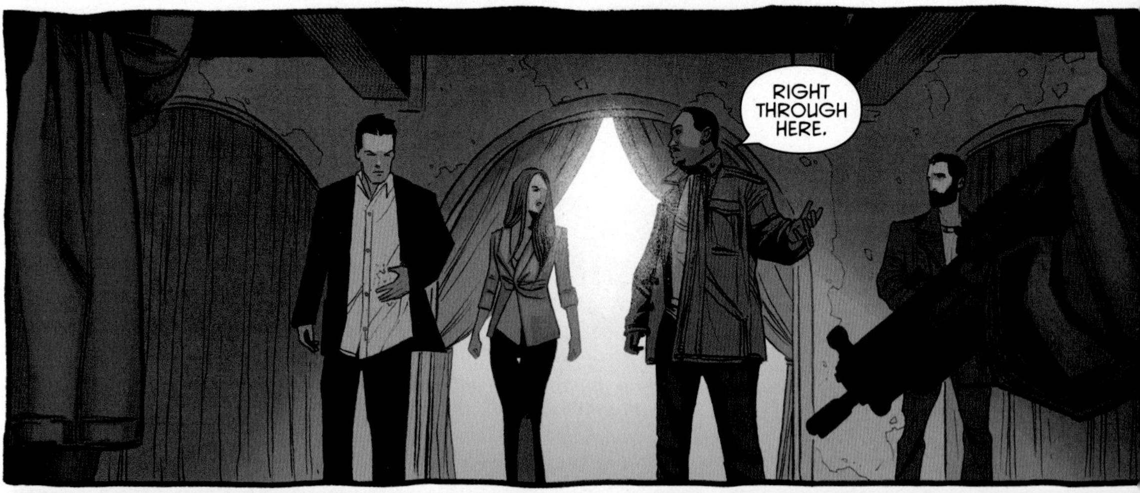
RIGHT THROUGH HERE.

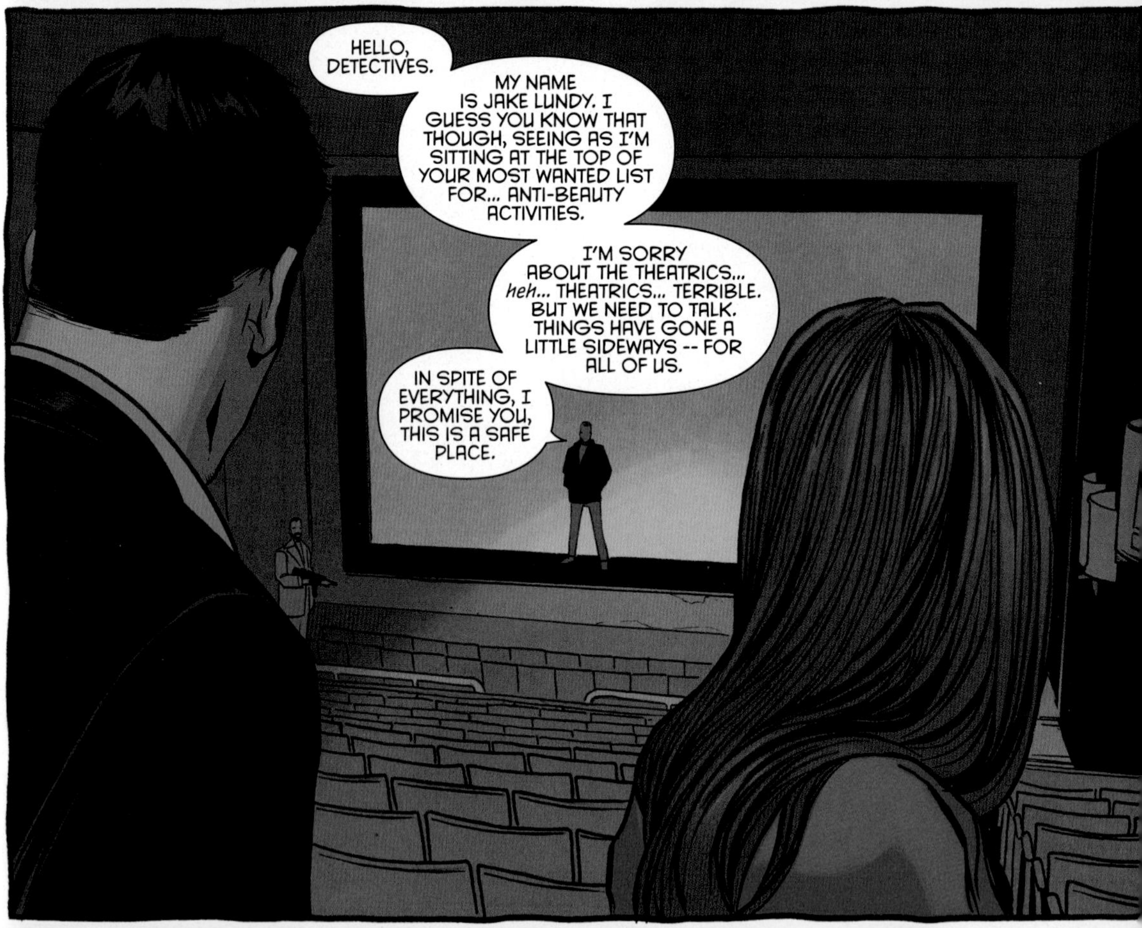
HELLO, DETECTIVES.
MY NAME IS JAKE LUNDY. I GUESS YOU KNOW THAT THOUGH, SEEING AS I'M SITTING AT THE TOP OF YOUR MOST WANTED LIST FOR... ANTI-BEAUTY ACTIVITIES.
I'M SORRY ABOUT THE THEATRICS... *heh*... THEATRICS... TERRIBLE. BUT WE NEED TO TALK. THINGS HAVE GONE A LITTLE SIDEWAYS -- FOR ALL OF US.
IN SPITE OF EVERYTHING, I PROMISE YOU, THIS IS A SAFE PLACE.

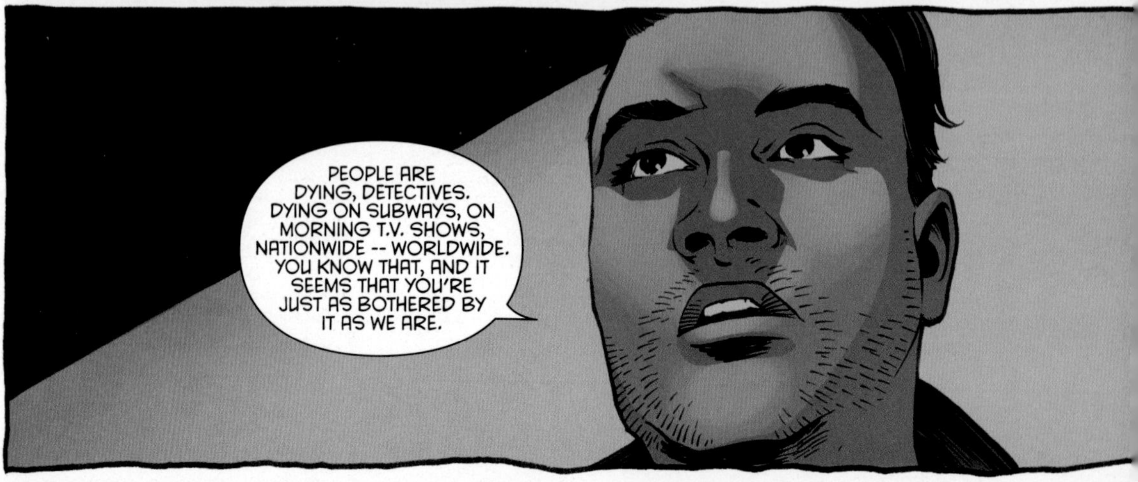
PEOPLE ARE DYING, DETECTIVES. DYING ON SUBWAYS, ON MORNING T.V. SHOWS, NATIONWIDE -- WORLDWIDE. YOU KNOW THAT, AND IT SEEMS THAT YOU'RE JUST AS BOTHERED BY IT AS WE ARE.

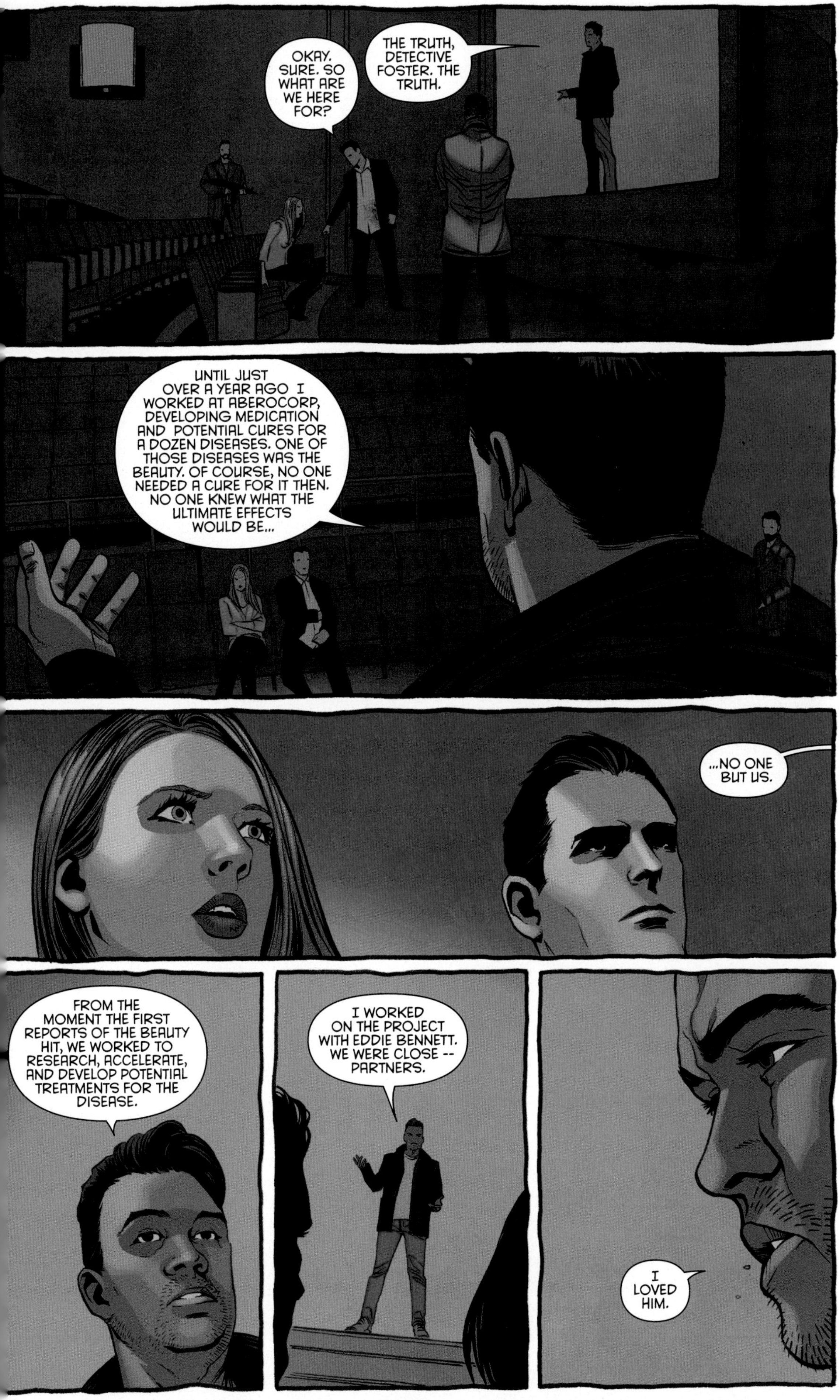
OKAY. SURE. SO WHAT ARE WE HERE FOR?
THE TRUTH, DETECTIVE FOSTER. THE TRUTH.
UNTIL JUST OVER A YEAR AGO I WORKED AT ABEROCORP, DEVELOPING MEDICATION AND POTENTIAL CURES FOR A DOZEN DISEASES. ONE OF THOSE DISEASES WAS THE BEAUTY. OF COURSE, NO ONE NEEDED A CURE FOR IT THEN. NO ONE KNEW WHAT THE ULTIMATE EFFECTS WOULD BE...
...NO ONE BUT US.
FROM THE MOMENT THE FIRST REPORTS OF THE BEAUTY HIT, WE WORKED TO RESEARCH, ACCELERATE, AND DEVELOP POTENTIAL TREATMENTS FOR THE DISEASE.
I WORKED ON THE PROJECT WITH EDDIE BENNETT. WE WERE CLOSE -- PARTNERS.
I LOVED HIM.

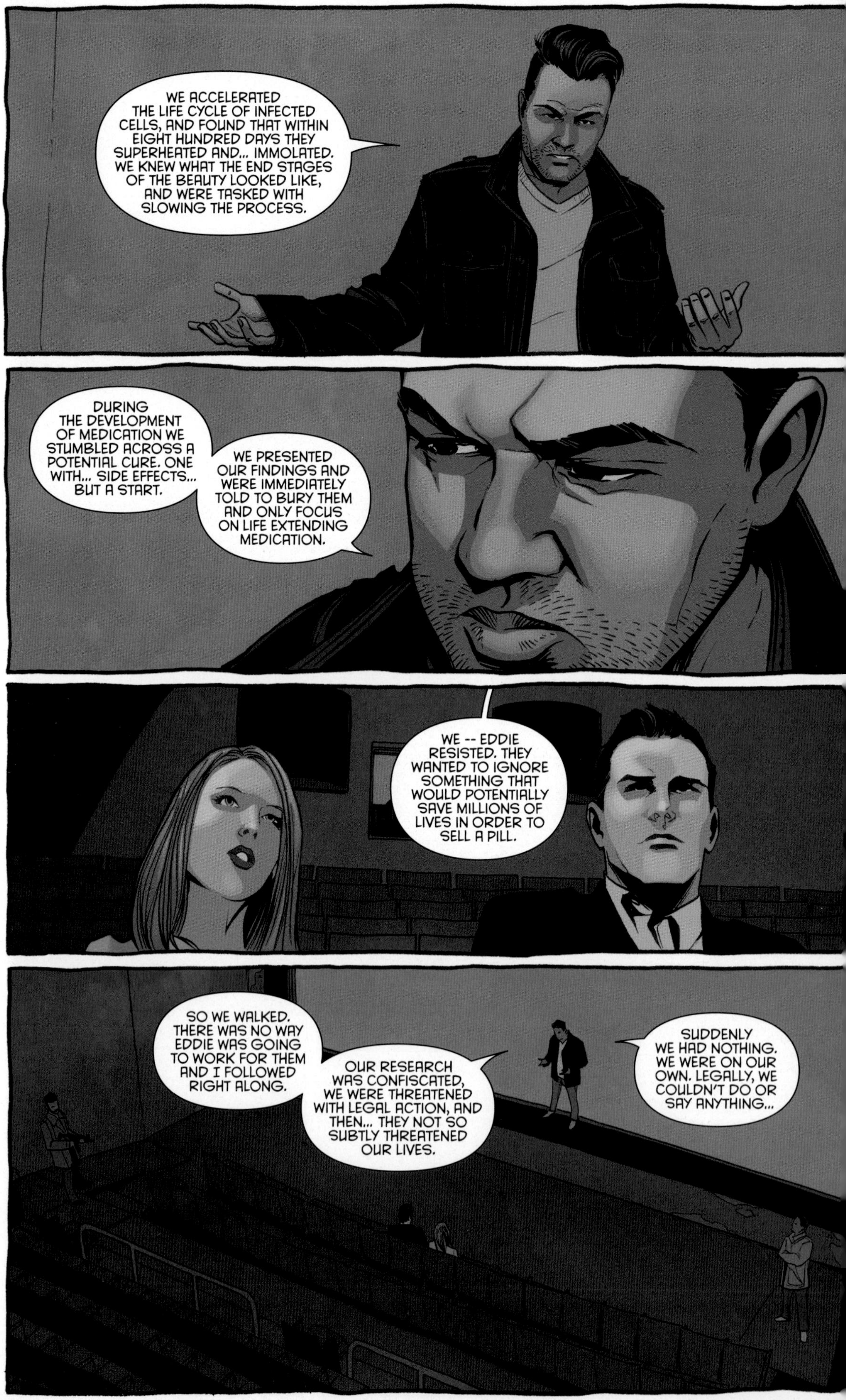
WE ACCELERATED THE LIFE CYCLE OF INFECTED CELLS, AND FOUND THAT WITHIN EIGHT HUNDRED DAYS THEY SUPERHEATED AND... IMMOLATED. WE KNEW WHAT THE END STAGES OF THE BEAUTY LOOKED LIKE, AND WERE TASKED WITH SLOWING THE PROCESS.
DURING THE DEVELOPMENT OF MEDICATION WE STUMBLED ACROSS A POTENTIAL CURE. ONE WITH... SIDE EFFECTS... BUT A START.
WE PRESENTED OUR FINDINGS AND WERE IMMEDIATELY TOLD TO BURY THEM AND ONLY FOCUS ON LIFE EXTENDING MEDICATION.
WE -- EDDIE RESISTED. THEY WANTED TO IGNORE SOMETHING THAT WOULD POTENTIALLY SAVE MILLIONS OF LIVES IN ORDER TO SELL A PILL.
SO WE WALKED. THERE WAS NO WAY EDDIE WAS GOING TO WORK FOR THEM AND I FOLLOWED RIGHT ALONG.
OUR RESEARCH WAS CONFISCATED, WE WERE THREATENED WITH LEGAL ACTION, AND THEN... THEY NOT SO SUBTLY THREATENED OUR LIVES.
SUDDENLY WE HAD NOTHING. WE WERE ON OUR OWN. LEGALLY, WE COULDN'T DO OR SAY ANYTHING...

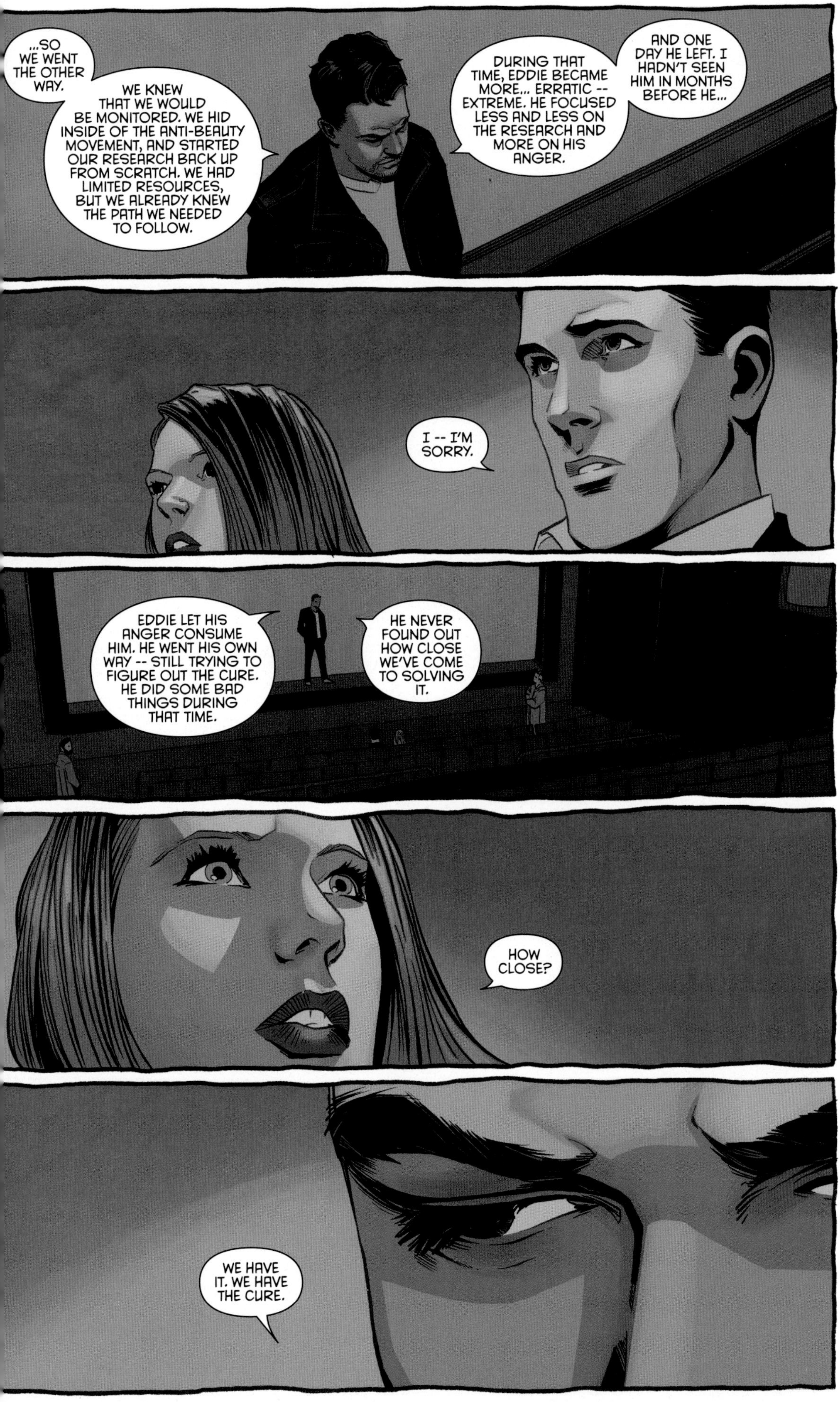
...SO WE WENT THE OTHER WAY.
WE KNEW THAT WE WOULD BE MONITORED. WE HID INSIDE OF THE ANTI-BEAUTY MOVEMENT, AND STARTED OUR RESEARCH BACK UP FROM SCRATCH. WE HAD LIMITED RESOURCES, BUT WE ALREADY KNEW THE PATH WE NEEDED TO FOLLOW.
DURING THAT TIME, EDDIE BECAME MORE... ERRATIC -- EXTREME. HE FOCUSED LESS AND LESS ON THE RESEARCH AND MORE ON HIS ANGER.
AND ONE DAY HE LEFT. I HADN'T SEEN HIM IN MONTHS BEFORE HE...
I -- I'M SORRY.
EDDIE LET HIS ANGER CONSUME HIM. HE WENT HIS OWN WAY -- STILL TRYING TO FIGURE OUT THE CURE. HE DID SOME BAD THINGS DURING THAT TIME.
HE NEVER FOUND OUT HOW CLOSE WE'VE COME TO SOLVING IT.
HOW CLOSE?
WE HAVE IT. WE HAVE THE CURE.

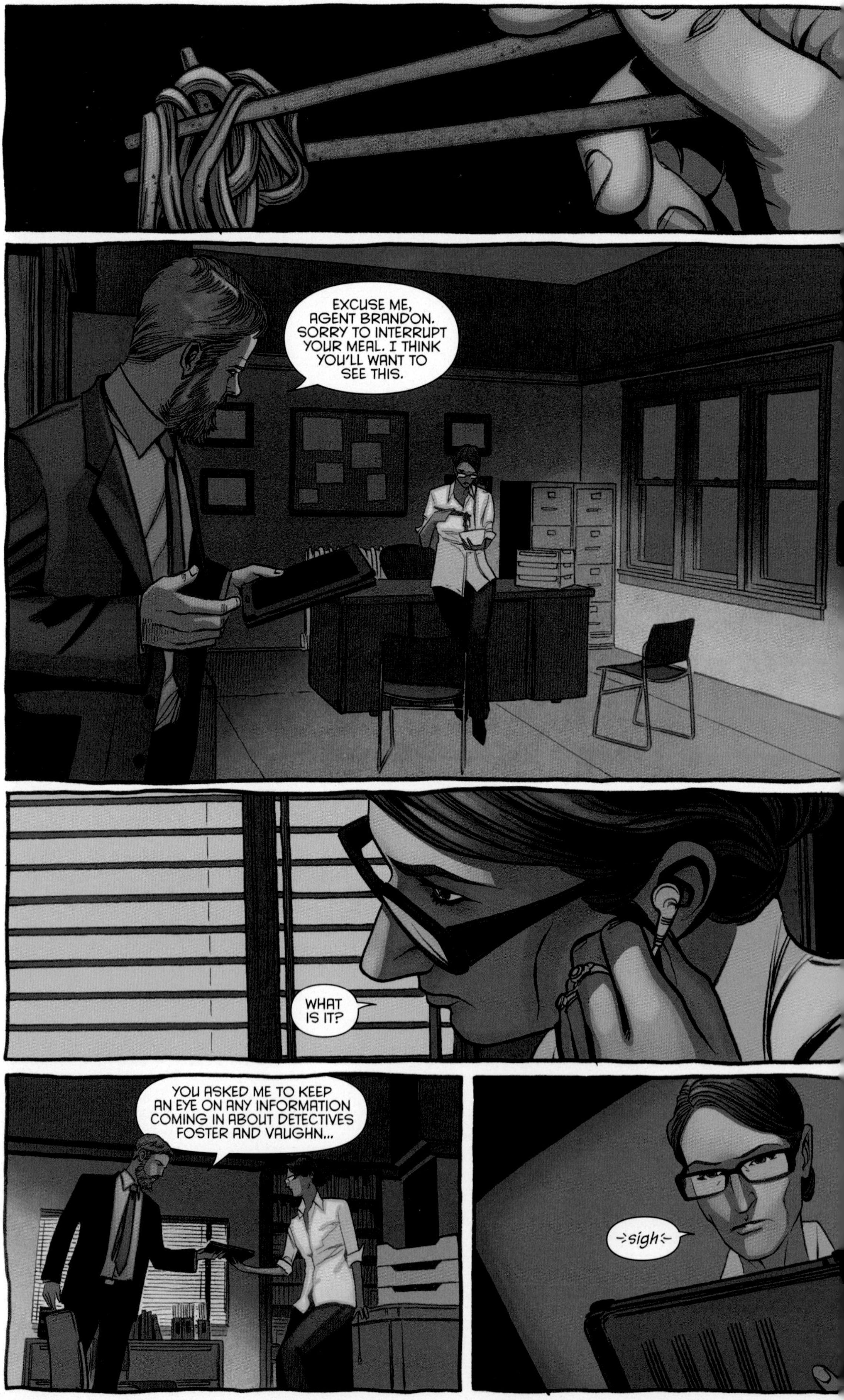
EXCUSE ME, AGENT BRANDON. SORRY TO INTERRUPT YOUR MEAL. I THINK YOU'LL WANT TO SEE THIS.
WHAT IS IT?
YOU ASKED ME TO KEEP AN EYE ON ANY INFORMATION COMING IN ABOUT DETECTIVES FOSTER AND VAUGHN...
sigh

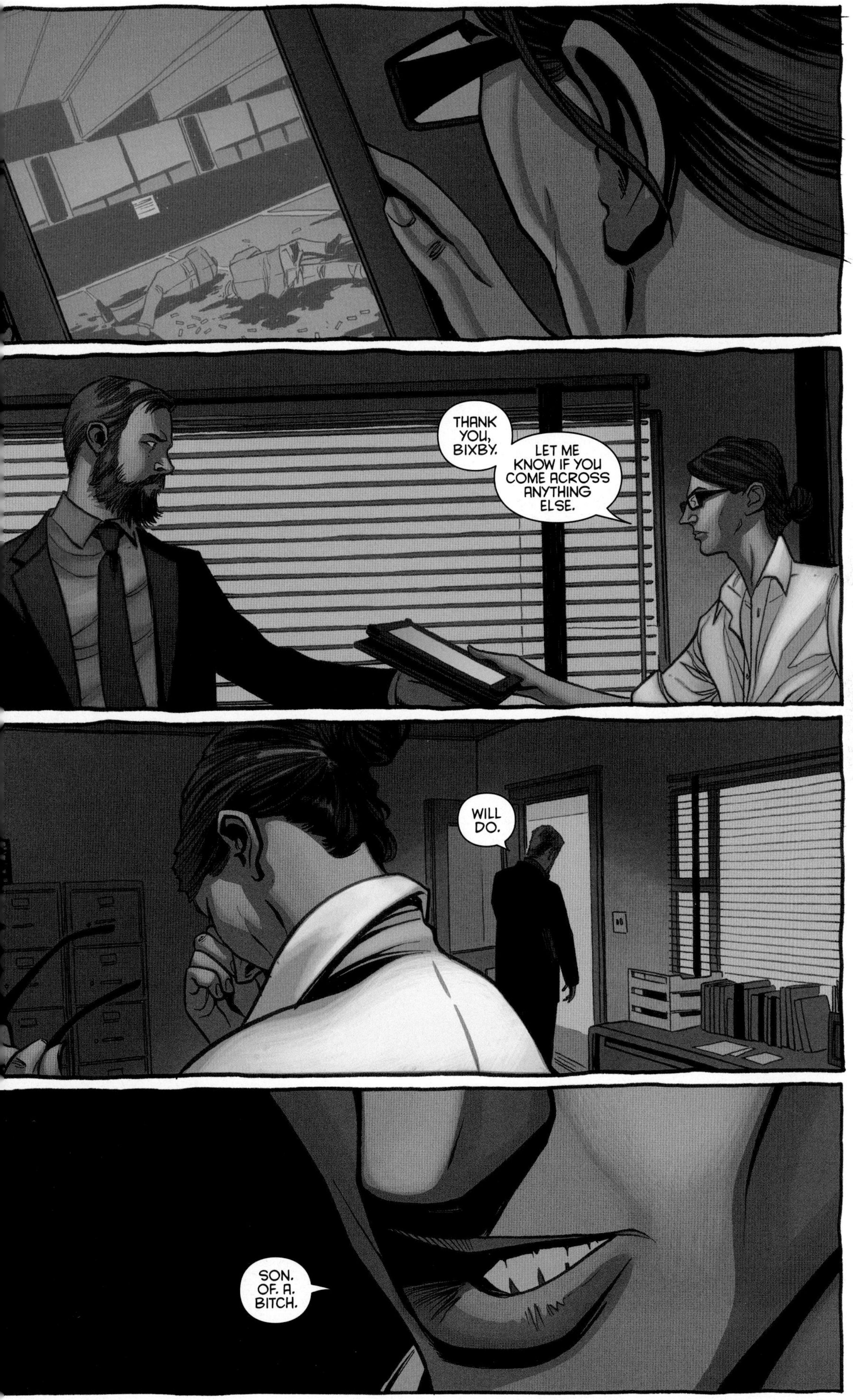
THANK YOU, BIXBY.
LET ME KNOW IF YOU COME ACROSS ANYTHING ELSE.
WILL DO.
SON. OF. A. BITCH.

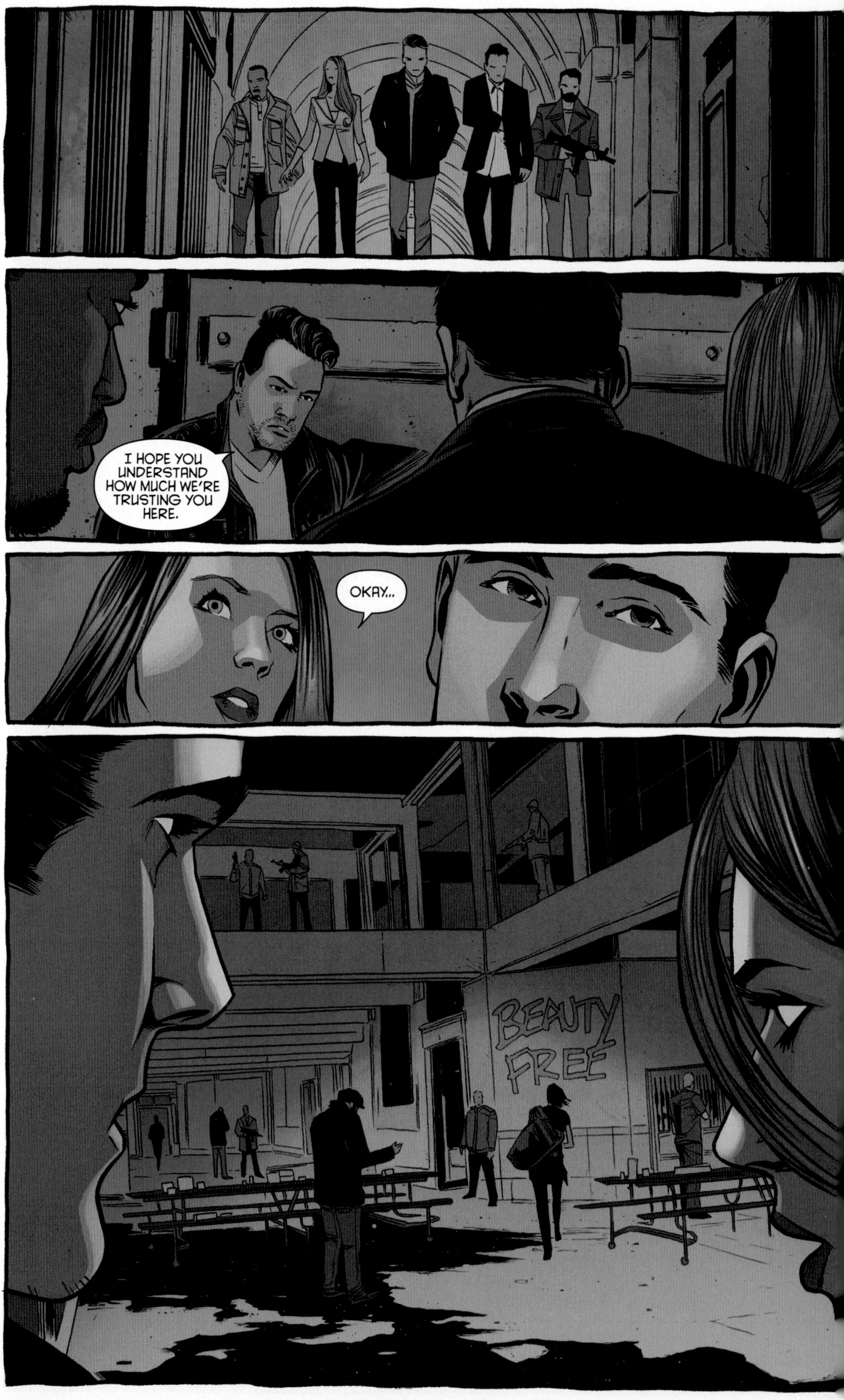
I HOPE YOU UNDERSTAND HOW MUCH WE'RE TRUSTING YOU HERE.
OKAY...
BEAUTY FREE

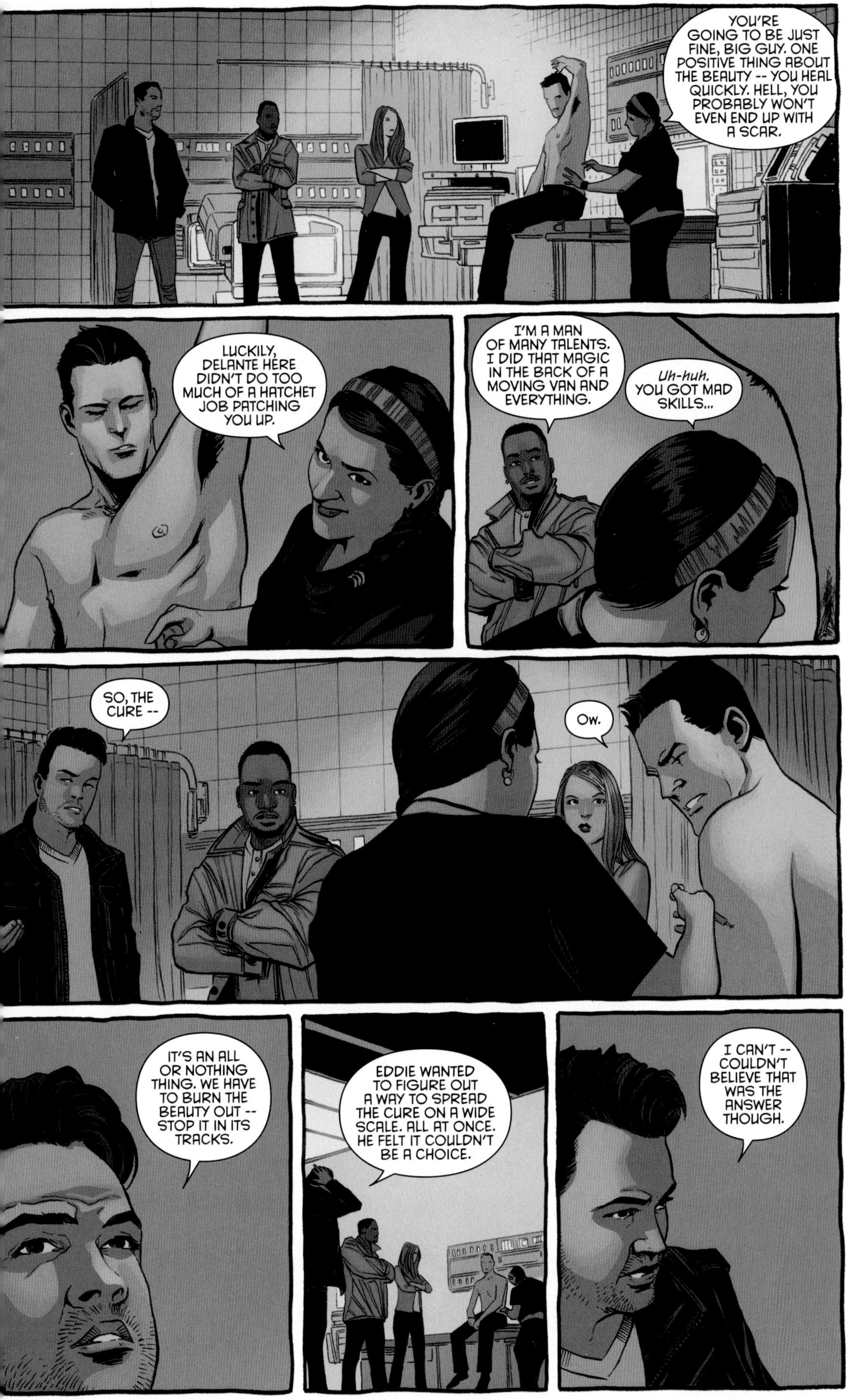

YOU'RE GOING TO BE JUST FINE, BIG GUY. ONE POSITIVE THING ABOUT THE BEAUTY -- YOU HEAL QUICKLY. HELL, YOU PROBABLY WON'T EVEN END UP WITH A SCAR.
LUCKILY, DELANTE HERE DIDN'T DO TOO MUCH OF A HATCHET JOB PATCHING YOU UP.
I'M A MAN OF MANY TALENTS. I DID THAT MAGIC IN THE BACK OF A MOVING VAN AND EVERYTHING.
Uh-huh. YOU GOT MAD SKILLS...
SO, THE CURE --
Ow.
IT'S AN ALL OR NOTHING THING. WE HAVE TO BURN THE BEAUTY OUT -- STOP IT IN ITS TRACKS.
EDDIE WANTED TO FIGURE OUT A WAY TO SPREAD THE CURE ON A WIDE SCALE. ALL AT ONCE. HE FELT IT COULDN'T BE A CHOICE.
I CAN'T -- COULDN'T BELIEVE THAT WAS THE ANSWER THOUGH.

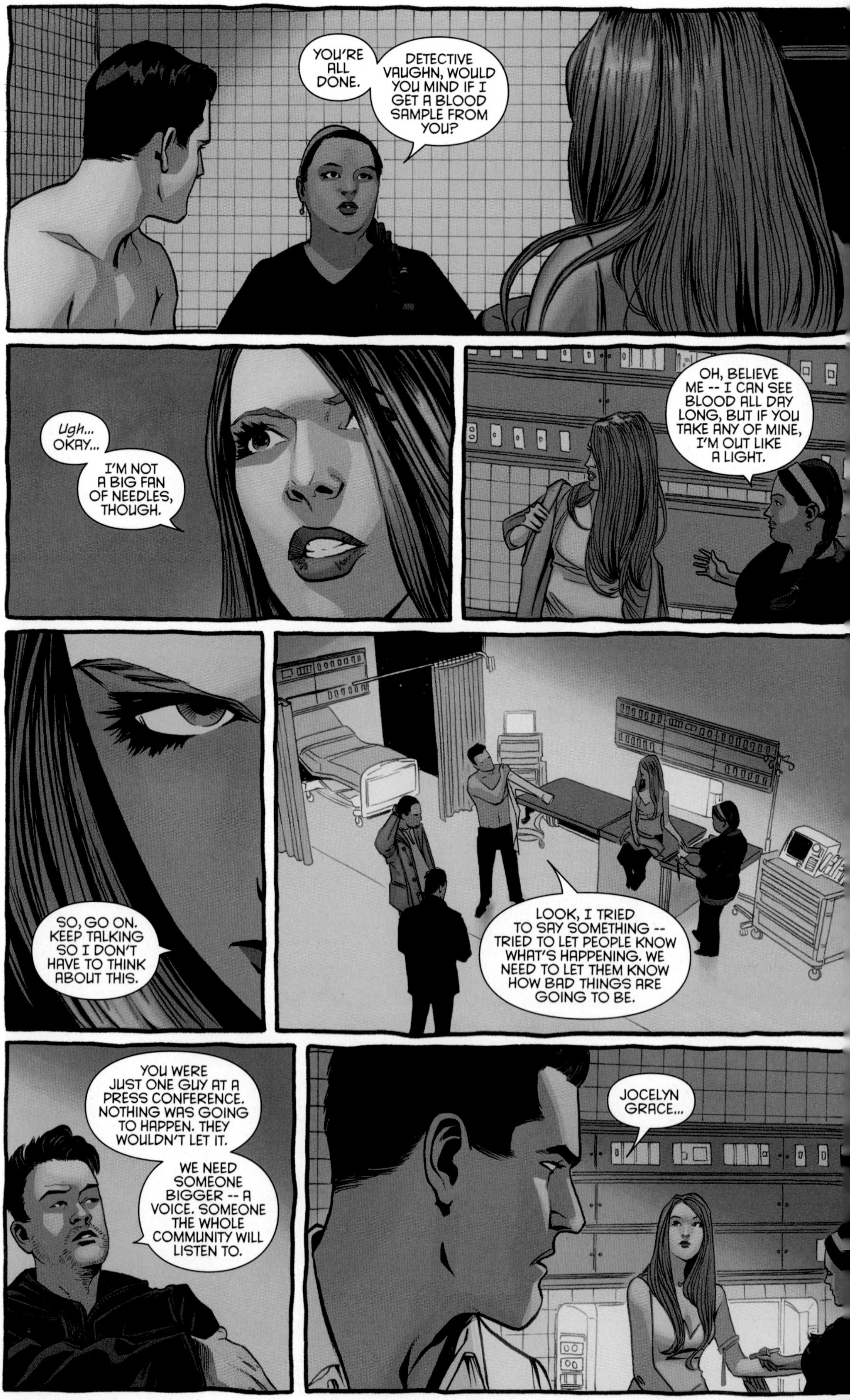

YOU'RE ALL DONE.
DETECTIVE VAUGHN, WOULD YOU MIND IF I GET A BLOOD SAMPLE FROM YOU?
Ugh... OKAY...
I'M NOT A BIG FAN OF NEEDLES, THOUGH.
OH, BELIEVE ME -- I CAN SEE BLOOD ALL DAY LONG, BUT IF YOU TAKE ANY OF MINE, I'M OUT LIKE A LIGHT.
SO, GO ON. KEEP TALKING SO I DON'T HAVE TO THINK ABOUT THIS.
LOOK, I TRIED TO SAY SOMETHING -- TRIED TO LET PEOPLE KNOW WHAT'S HAPPENING. WE NEED TO LET THEM KNOW HOW BAD THINGS ARE GOING TO BE.
YOU WERE JUST ONE GUY AT A PRESS CONFERENCE. NOTHING WAS GOING TO HAPPEN. THEY WOULDN'T LET IT.
WE NEED SOMEONE BIGGER -- A VOICE. SOMEONE THE WHOLE COMMUNITY WILL LISTEN TO.
JOCELYN GRACE...

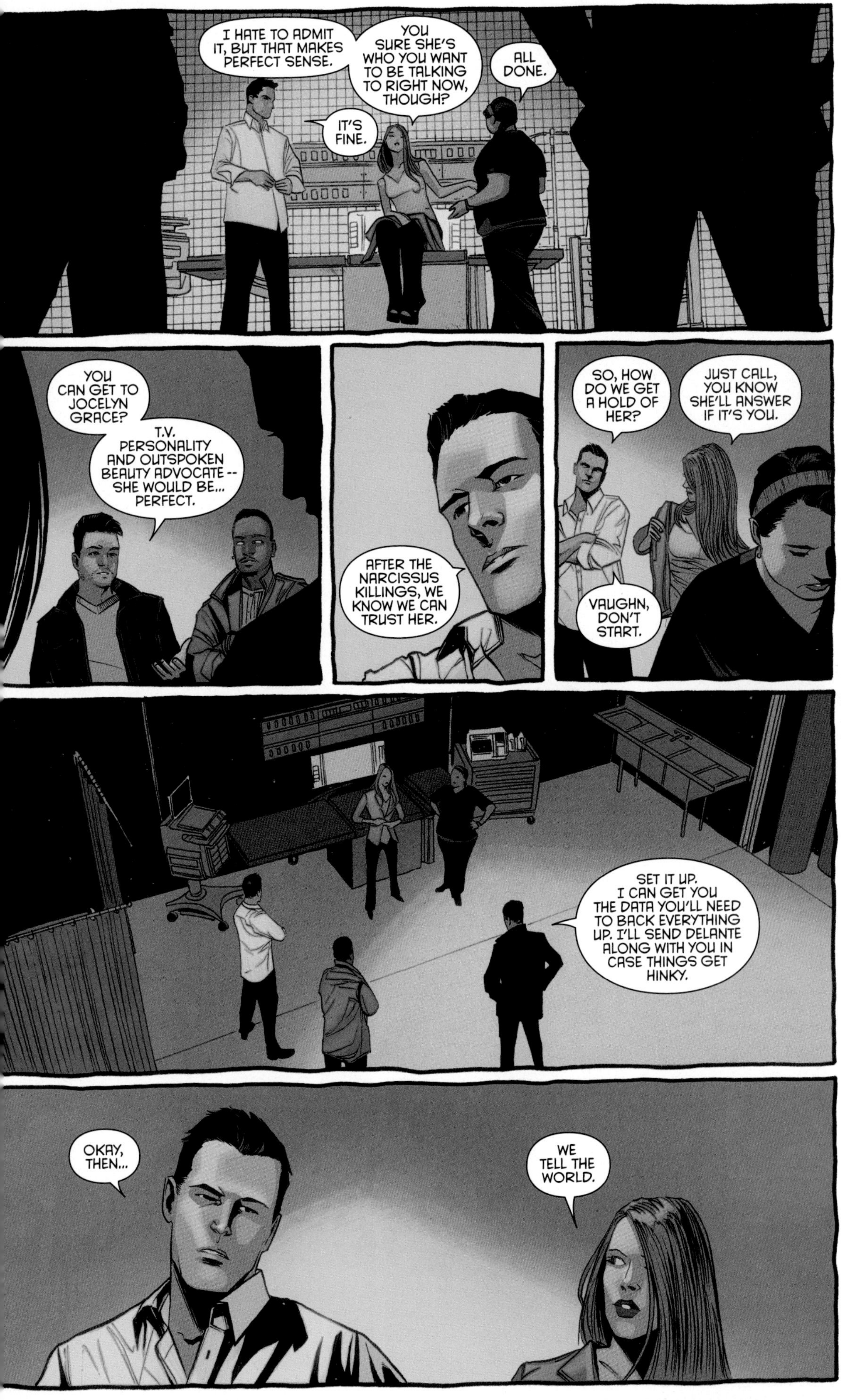

I HATE TO ADMIT IT, BUT THAT MAKES PERFECT SENSE.
YOU SURE SHE'S WHO YOU WANT TO BE TALKING TO RIGHT NOW, THOUGH?
ALL DONE.
IT'S FINE.
YOU CAN GET TO JOCELYN GRACE?
T.V. PERSONALITY AND OUTSPOKEN BEAUTY ADVOCATE -- SHE WOULD BE... PERFECT.
AFTER THE NARCISSUS KILLINGS, WE KNOW WE CAN TRUST HER.
SO, HOW DO WE GET A HOLD OF HER?
JUST CALL, YOU KNOW SHE'LL ANSWER IF IT'S YOU.
VAUGHN, DON'T START.
SET IT UP. I CAN GET YOU THE DATA YOU'LL NEED TO BACK EVERYTHING UP. I'LL SEND DELANTE ALONG WITH YOU IN CASE THINGS GET HINKY.
OKAY, THEN...
WE TELL THE WORLD.

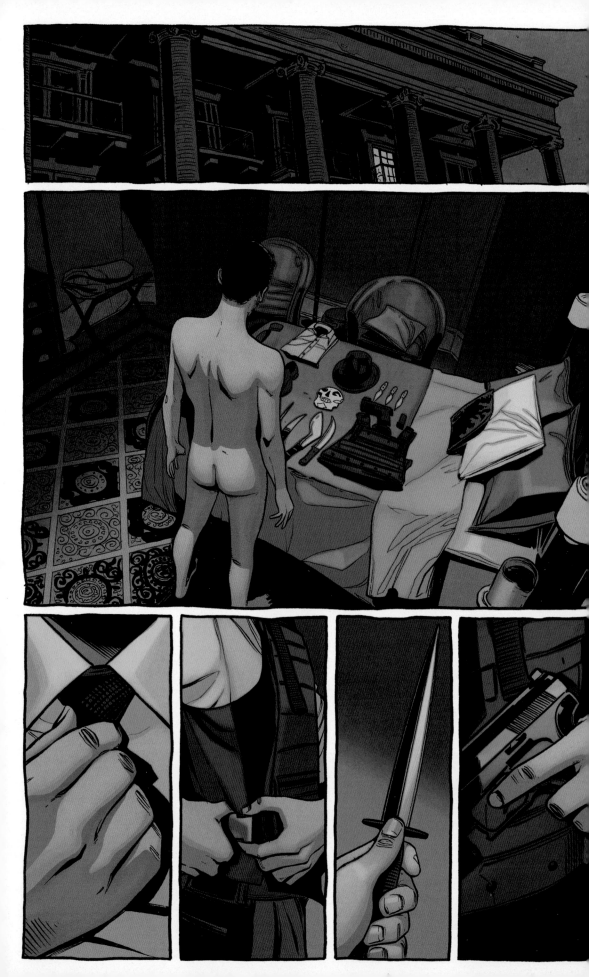

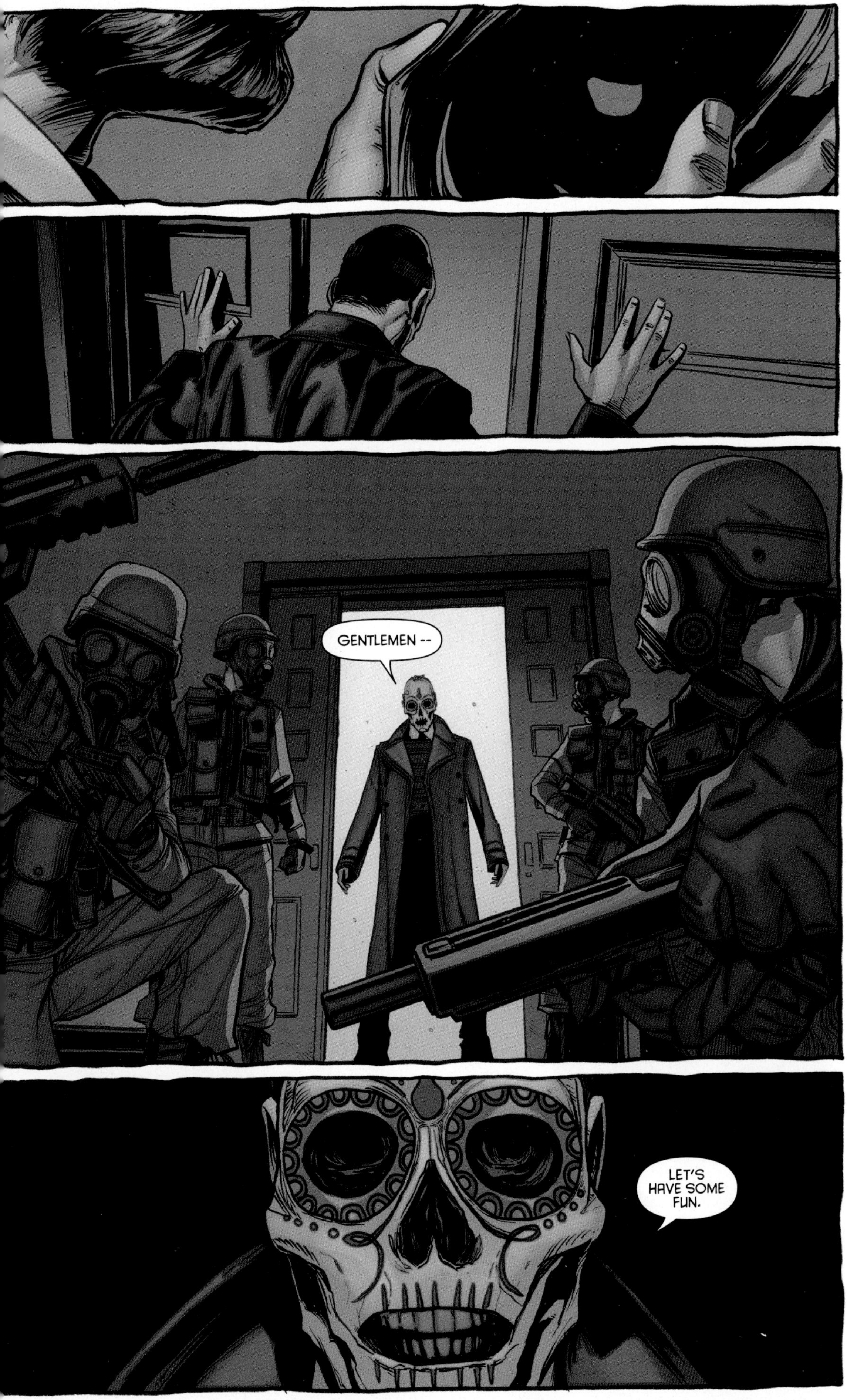
GENTLEMEN --
LET'S HAVE SOME FUN.

CHAPTER

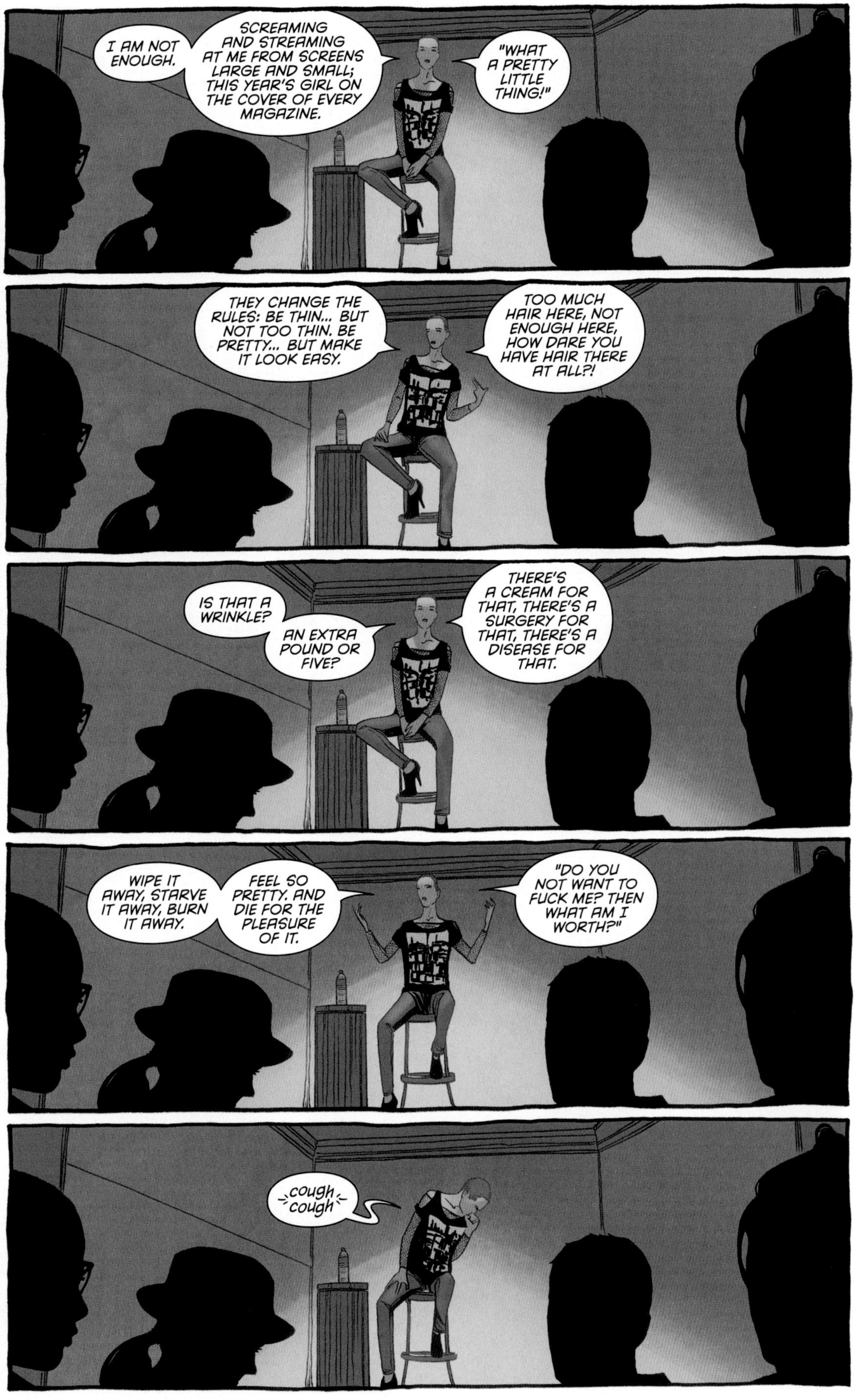
I AM NOT ENOUGH.
SCREAMING AND STREAMING AT ME FROM SCREENS LARGE AND SMALL; THIS YEAR'S GIRL ON THE COVER OF EVERY MAGAZINE.
"WHAT A PRETTY LITTLE THING!"
THEY CHANGE THE RULES: BE THIN... BUT NOT TOO THIN. BE PRETTY... BUT MAKE IT LOOK EASY.
TOO MUCH HAIR HERE, NOT ENOUGH HERE, HOW DARE YOU HAVE HAIR THERE AT ALL?!
IS THAT A WRINKLE?
AN EXTRA POUND OR FIVE?
THERE'S A CREAM FOR THAT, THERE'S A SURGERY FOR THAT, THERE'S A DISEASE FOR THAT.
WIPE IT AWAY, STARVE IT AWAY, BURN IT AWAY.
FEEL SO PRETTY. AND DIE FOR THE PLEASURE OF IT.
"DO YOU NOT WANT TO FUCK ME? THEN WHAT AM I WORTH?"
cough cough

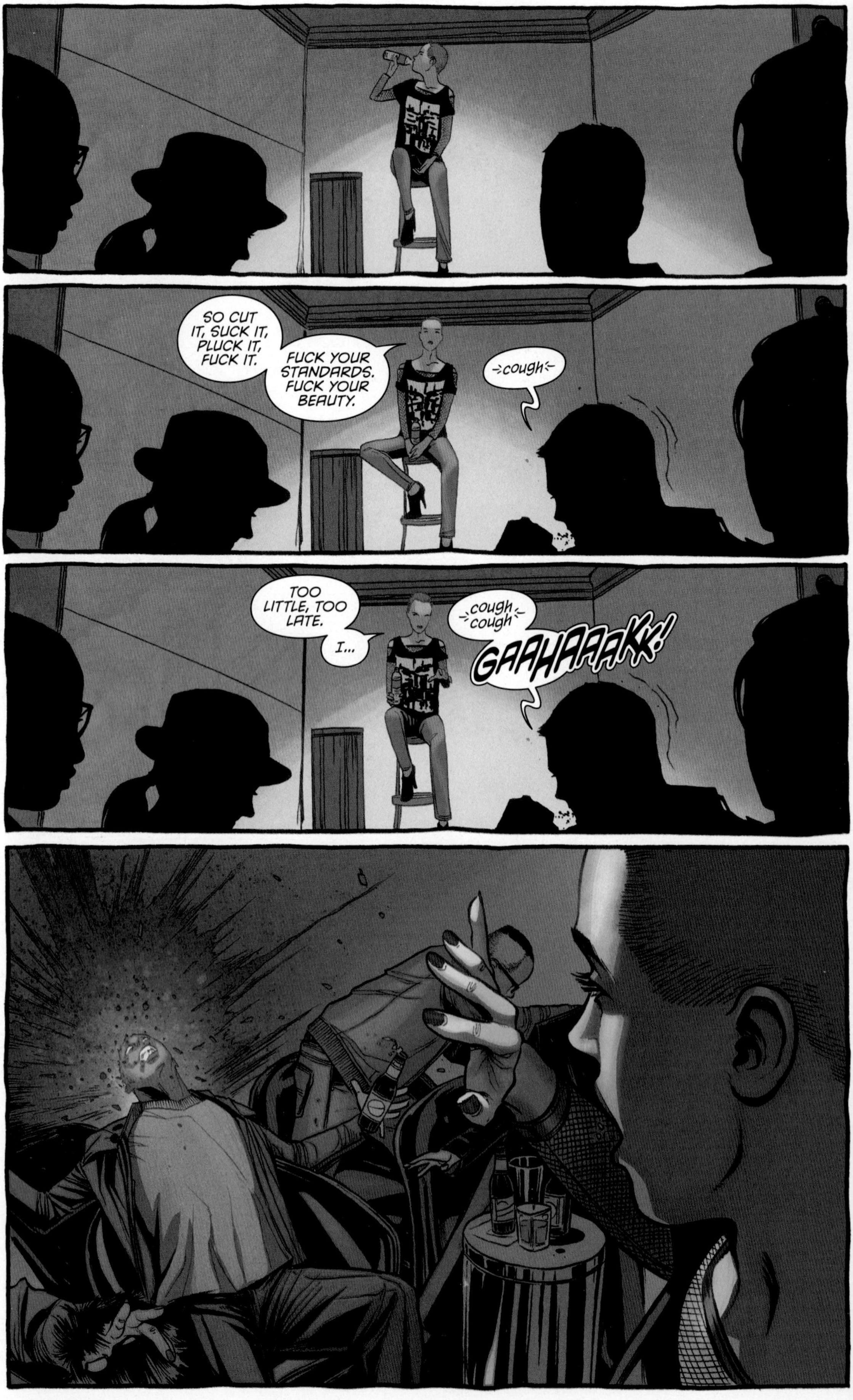
SO CUT IT, SUCK IT, PLUCK IT, FUCK IT.
FUCK YOUR STANDARDS. FUCK YOUR BEAUTY.
cough
TOO LITTLE, TOO LATE.
I...
cough cough
GAAHAAAKK!

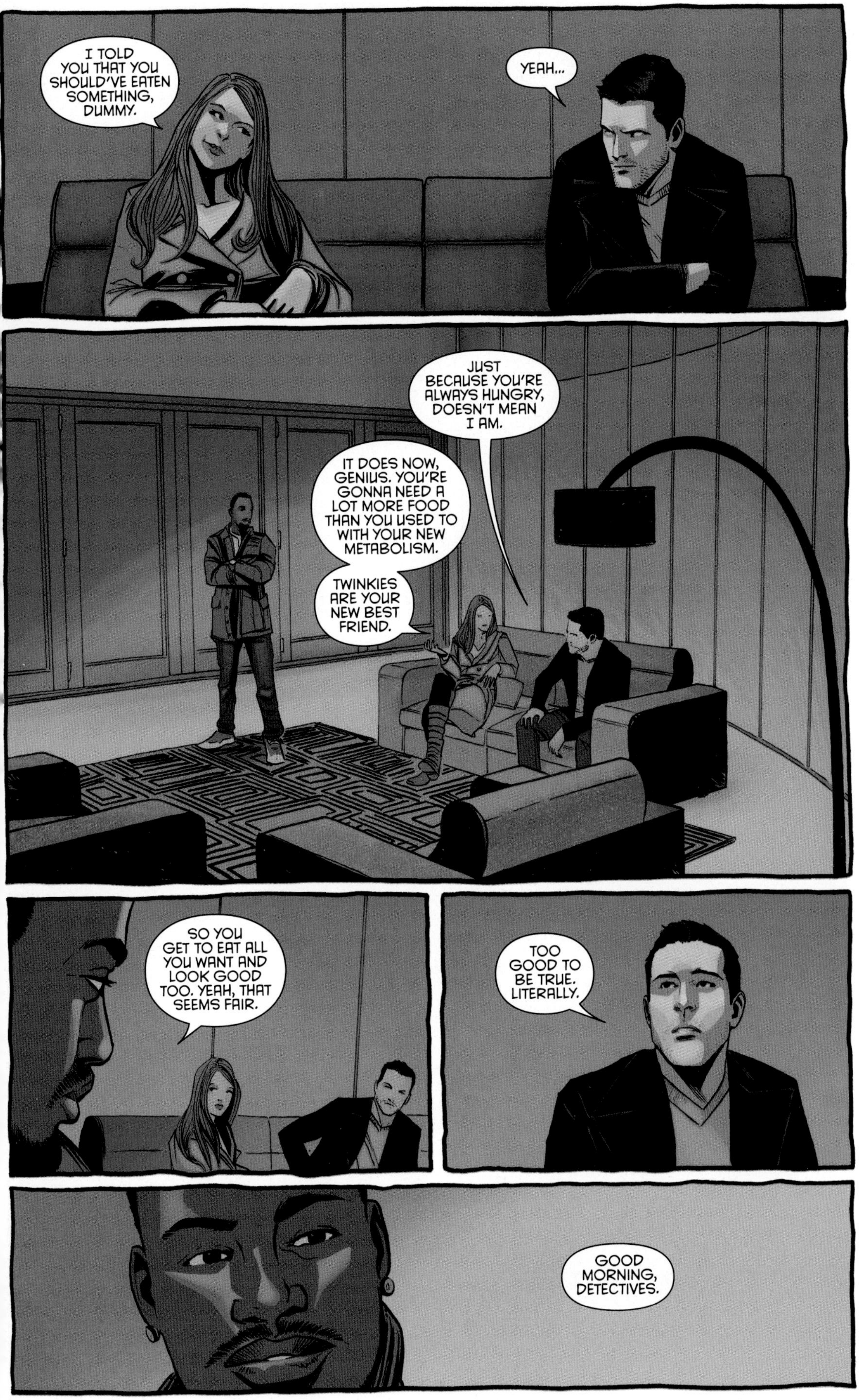
I TOLD YOU THAT YOU SHOULD'VE EATEN SOMETHING, DUMMY.
YEAH...
JUST BECAUSE YOU'RE ALWAYS HUNGRY, DOESN'T MEAN I AM.
IT DOES NOW, GENIUS. YOU'RE GONNA NEED A LOT MORE FOOD THAN YOU USED TO WITH YOUR NEW METABOLISM.
TWINKIES ARE YOUR NEW BEST FRIEND.
SO YOU GET TO EAT ALL YOU WANT AND LOOK GOOD TOO. YEAH, THAT SEEMS FAIR.
TOO GOOD TO BE TRUE. LITERALLY.
GOOD MORNING, DETECTIVES.

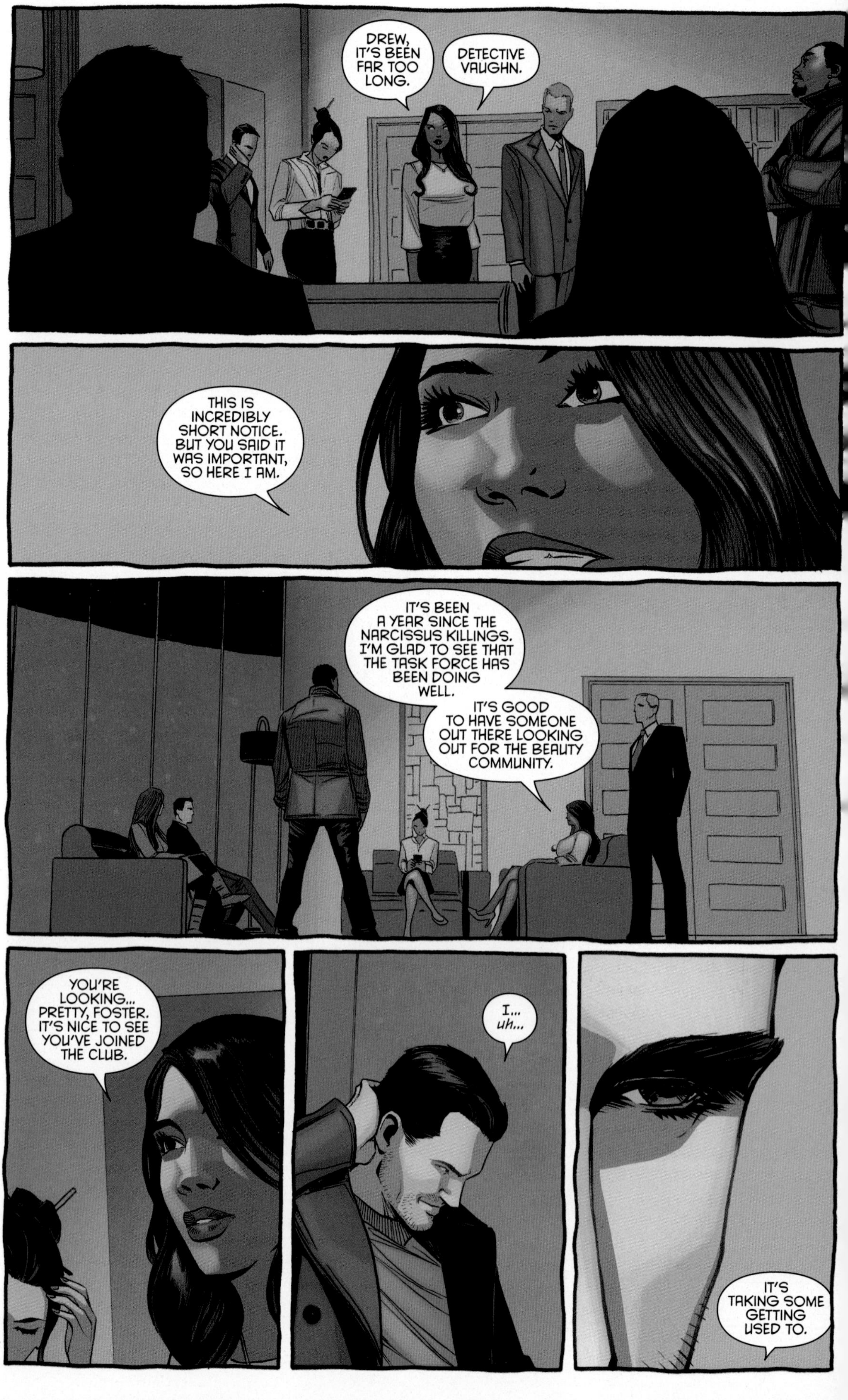
DREW, IT'S BEEN FAR TOO LONG.
DETECTIVE VAUGHN.
THIS IS INCREDIBLY SHORT NOTICE. BUT YOU SAID IT WAS IMPORTANT, SO HERE I AM.
IT'S BEEN A YEAR SINCE THE NARCISSUS KILLINGS. I'M GLAD TO SEE THAT THE TASK FORCE HAS BEEN DOING WELL.
IT'S GOOD TO HAVE SOMEONE OUT THERE LOOKING OUT FOR THE BEAUTY COMMUNITY.
YOU'RE LOOKING... PRETTY, FOSTER. IT'S NICE TO SEE YOU'VE JOINED THE CLUB.
I... uh...
IT'S TAKING SOME GETTING USED TO.

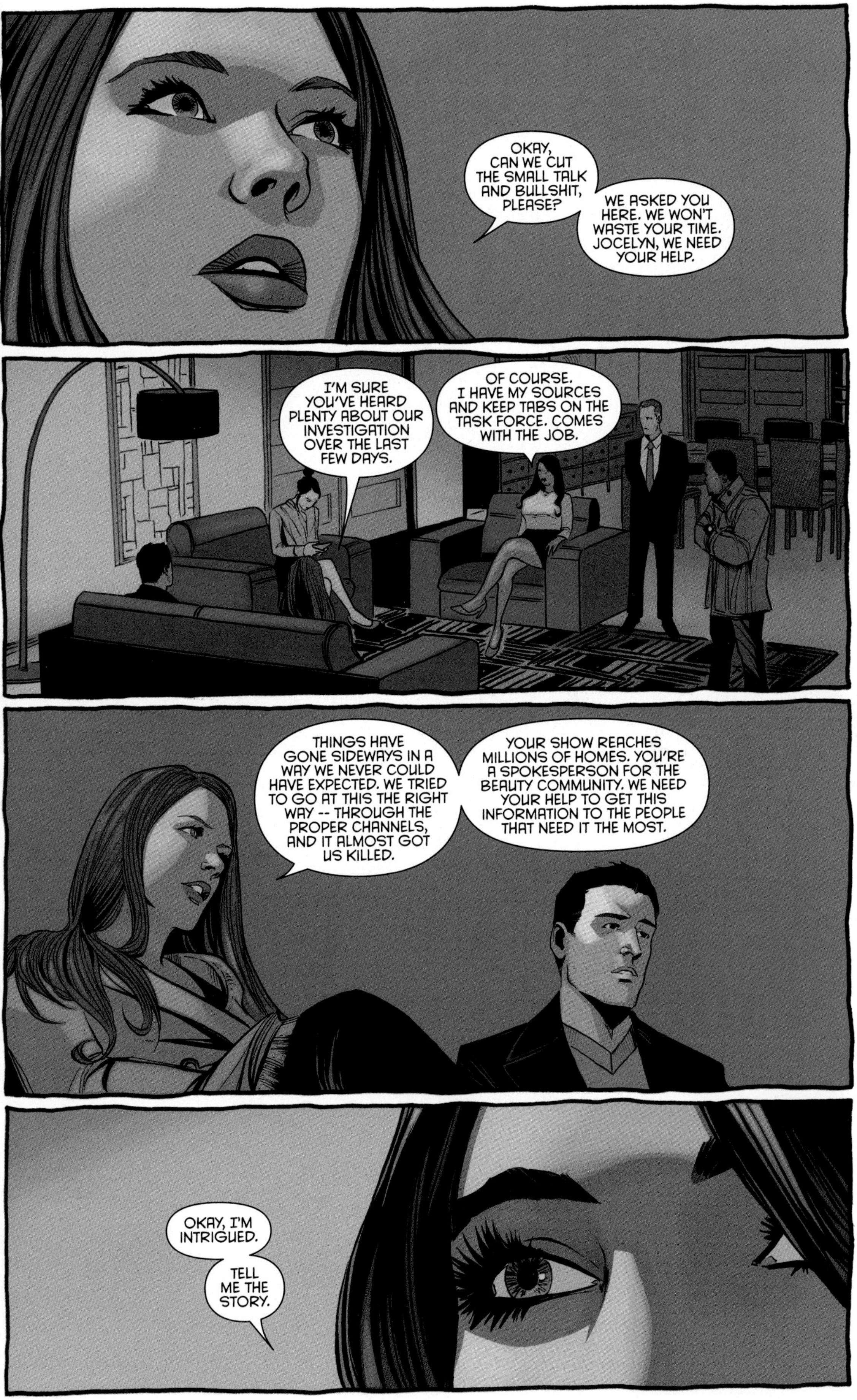
OKAY, CAN WE CUT THE SMALL TALK AND BULLSHIT, PLEASE?
WE ASKED YOU HERE. WE WON'T WASTE YOUR TIME. JOCELYN, WE NEED YOUR HELP.
I'M SURE YOU'VE HEARD PLENTY ABOUT OUR INVESTIGATION OVER THE LAST FEW DAYS.
OF COURSE. I HAVE MY SOURCES AND KEEP TABS ON THE TASK FORCE. COMES WITH THE JOB.
THINGS HAVE GONE SIDEWAYS IN A WAY WE NEVER COULD HAVE EXPECTED. WE TRIED TO GO AT THIS THE RIGHT WAY -- THROUGH THE PROPER CHANNELS, AND IT ALMOST GOT US KILLED.
YOUR SHOW REACHES MILLIONS OF HOMES. YOU'RE A SPOKESPERSON FOR THE BEAUTY COMMUNITY. WE NEED YOUR HELP TO GET THIS INFORMATION TO THE PEOPLE THAT NEED IT THE MOST.
OKAY, I'M INTRIGUED.
TELL ME THE STORY.

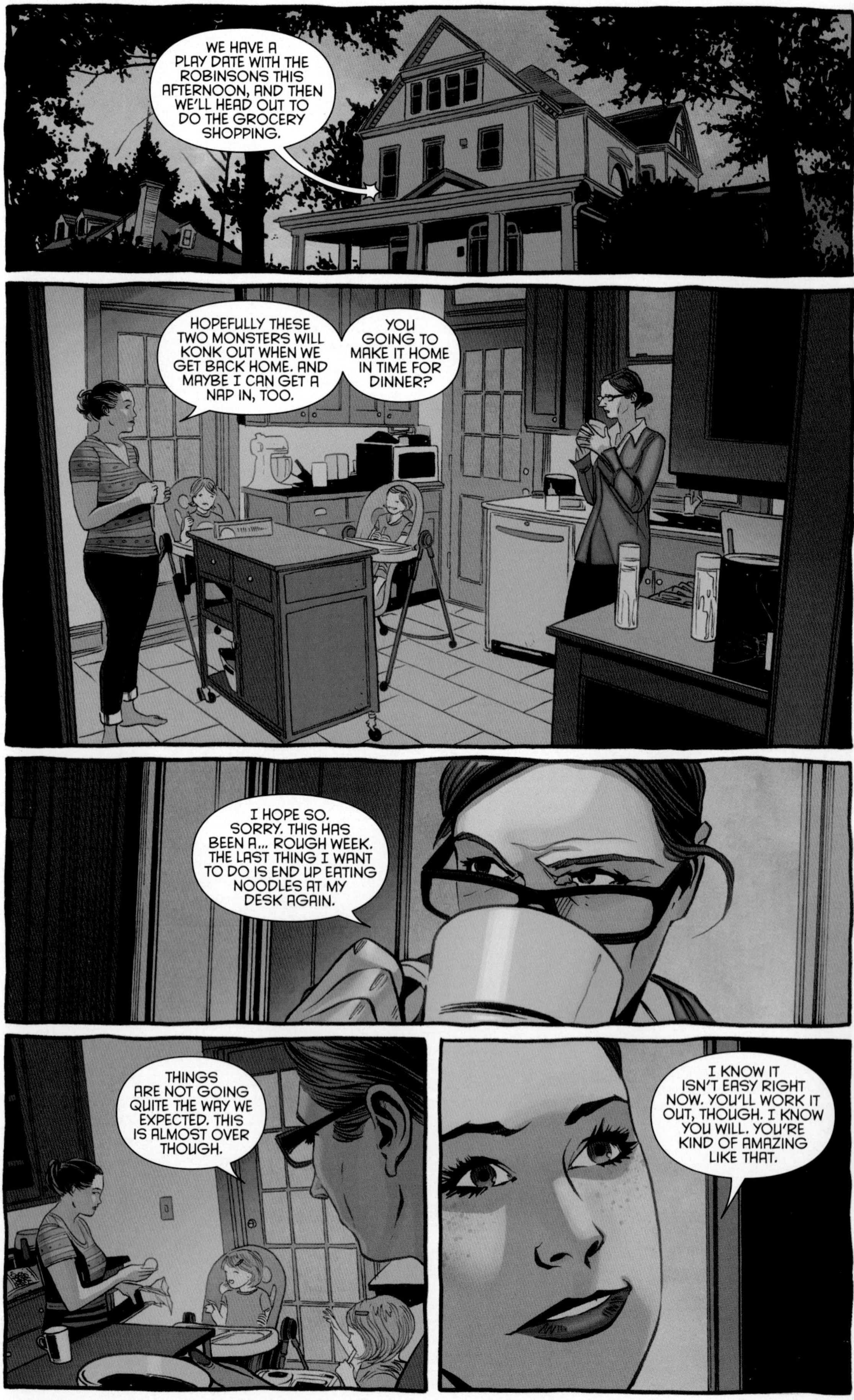
WE HAVE A PLAY DATE WITH THE ROBINSONS THIS AFTERNOON, AND THEN WE'LL HEAD OUT TO DO THE GROCERY SHOPPING.
HOPEFULLY THESE TWO MONSTERS WILL KONK OUT WHEN WE GET BACK HOME. AND MAYBE I CAN GET A NAP IN, TOO.
YOU GOING TO MAKE IT HOME IN TIME FOR DINNER?
I HOPE SO. SORRY. THIS HAS BEEN A... ROUGH WEEK. THE LAST THING I WANT TO DO IS END UP EATING NOODLES AT MY DESK AGAIN.
THINGS ARE NOT GOING QUITE THE WAY WE EXPECTED. THIS IS ALMOST OVER THOUGH.
I KNOW IT ISN'T EASY RIGHT NOW. YOU'LL WORK IT OUT, THOUGH. I KNOW YOU WILL. YOU'RE KIND OF AMAZING LIKE THAT.

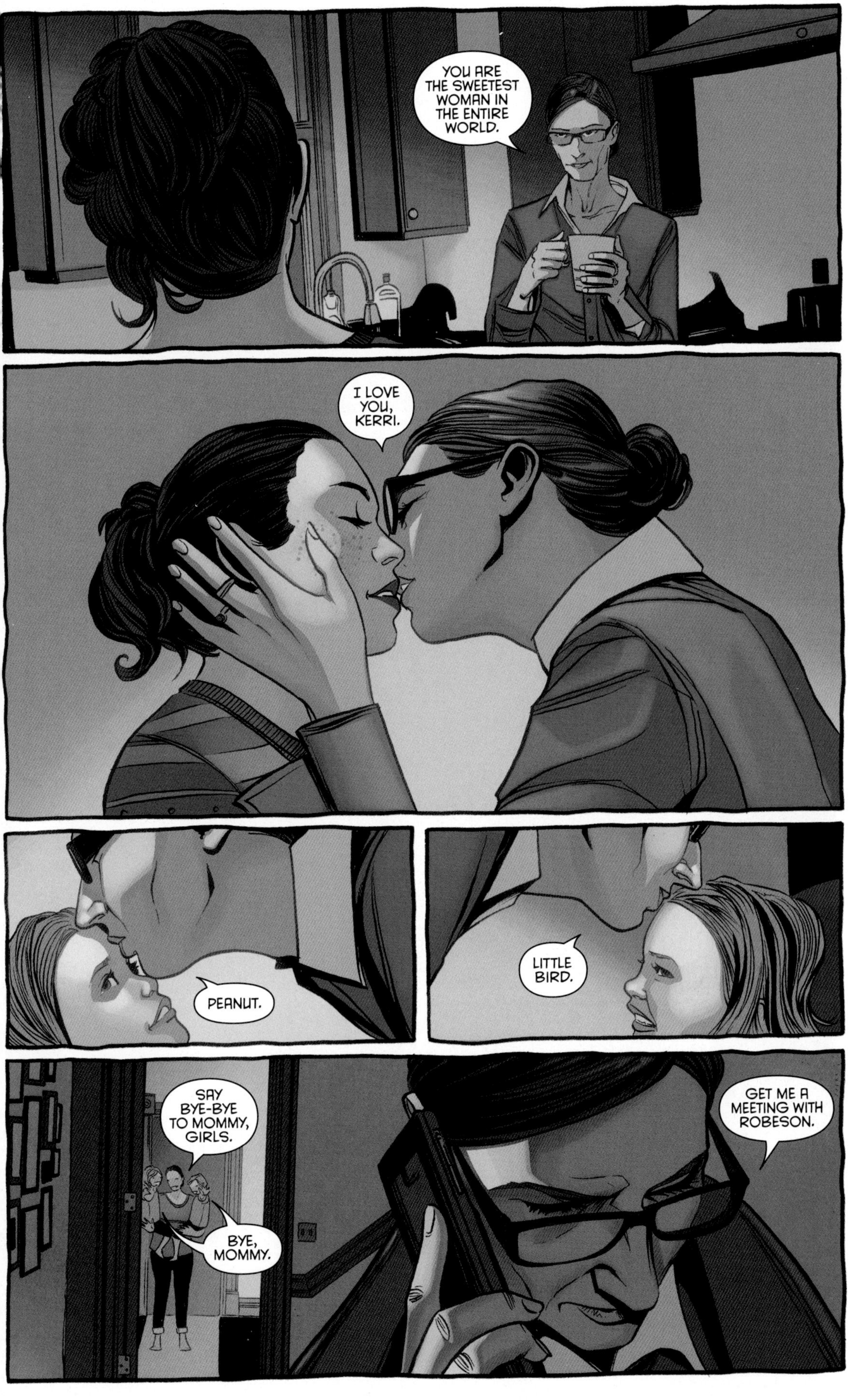

YOU ARE THE SWEETEST WOMAN IN THE ENTIRE WORLD.
I LOVE YOU, KERRI.
PEANUT.
LITTLE BIRD.
SAY BYE-BYE TO MOMMY, GIRLS.
BYE, MOMMY.
GET ME A MEETING WITH ROBESON.

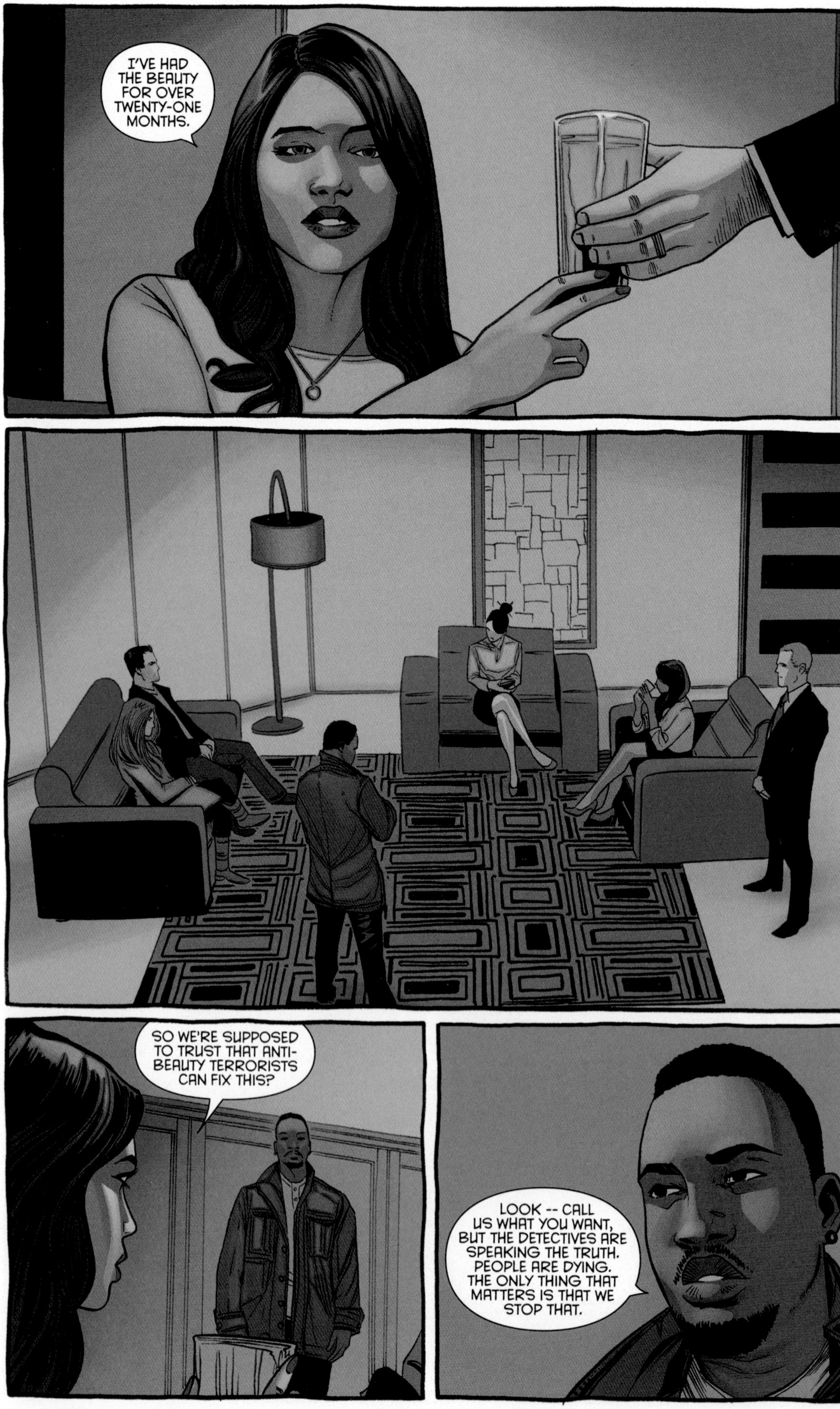
I'VE HAD THE BEAUTY FOR OVER TWENTY-ONE MONTHS.
SO WE'RE SUPPOSED TO TRUST THAT ANTI-BEAUTY TERRORISTS CAN FIX THIS?
LOOK -- CALL US WHAT YOU WANT, BUT THE DETECTIVES ARE SPEAKING THE TRUTH. PEOPLE ARE DYING. THE ONLY THING THAT MATTERS IS THAT WE STOP THAT.

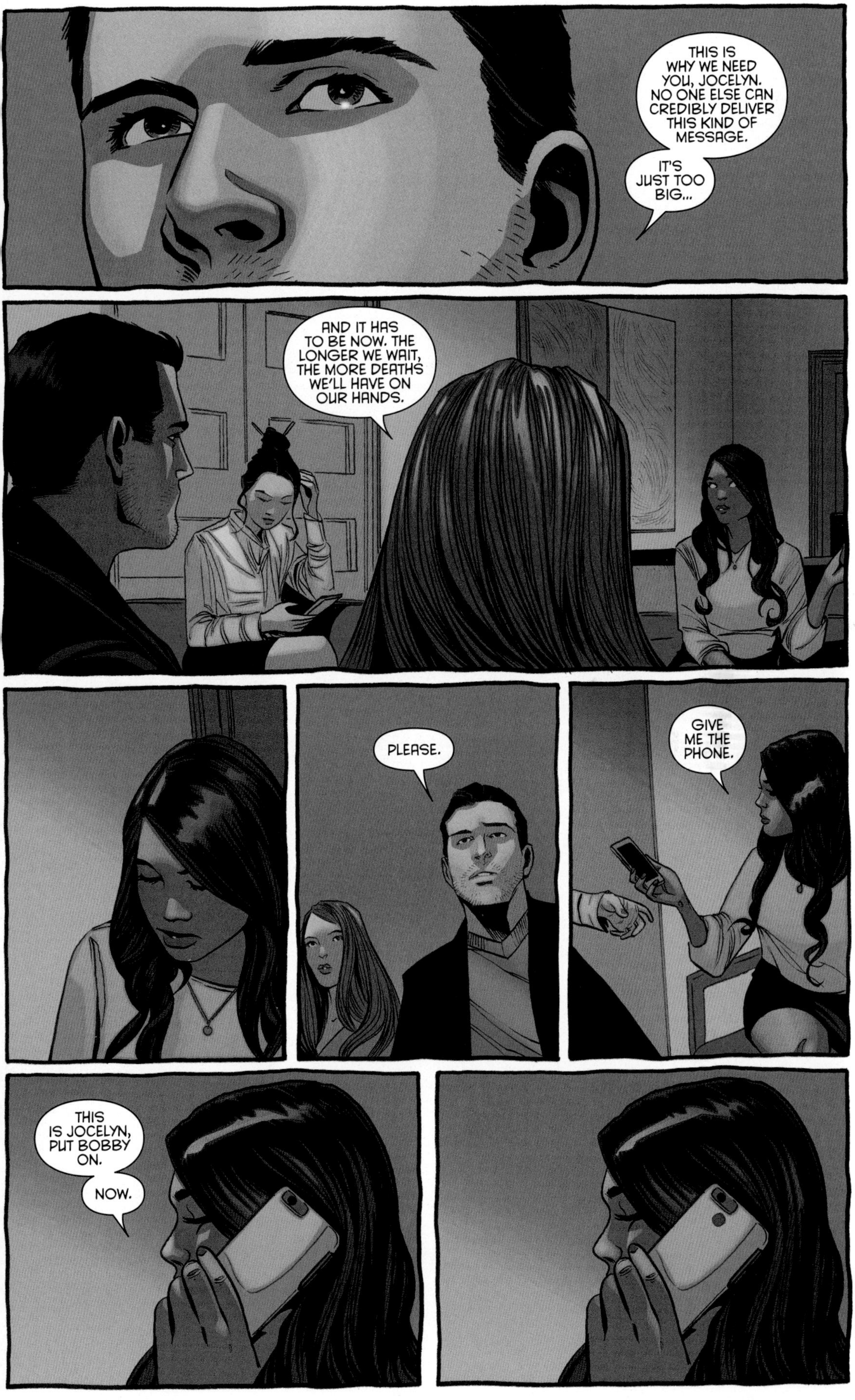
THIS IS WHY WE NEED YOU, JOCELYN. NO ONE ELSE CAN CREDIBLY DELIVER THIS KIND OF MESSAGE.
IT'S JUST TOO BIG...
AND IT HAS TO BE NOW. THE LONGER WE WAIT, THE MORE DEATHS WE'LL HAVE ON OUR HANDS.
PLEASE.
GIVE ME THE PHONE.
THIS IS JOCELYN, PUT BOBBY ON.
NOW.

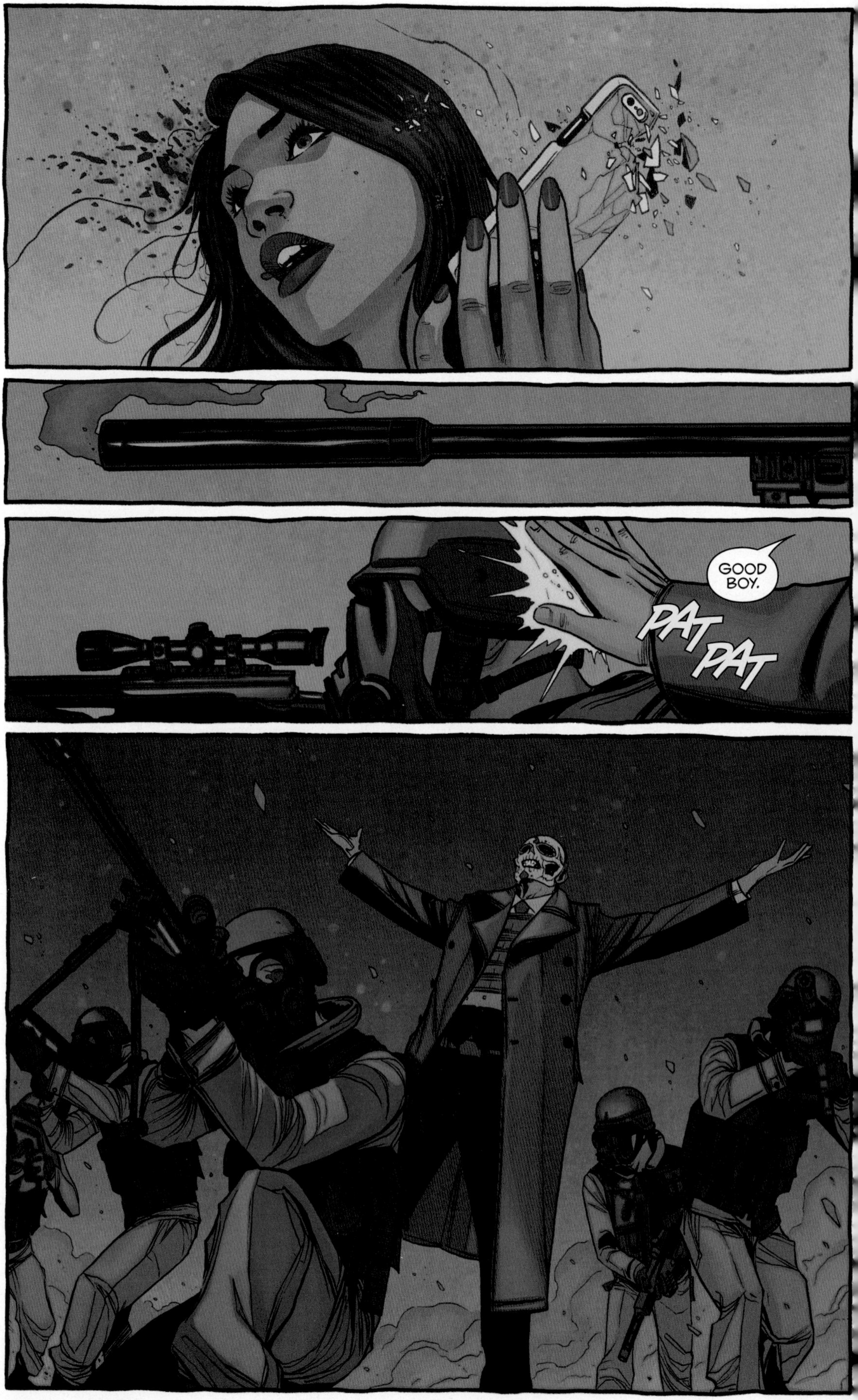
GOOD BOY.
PAT PAT

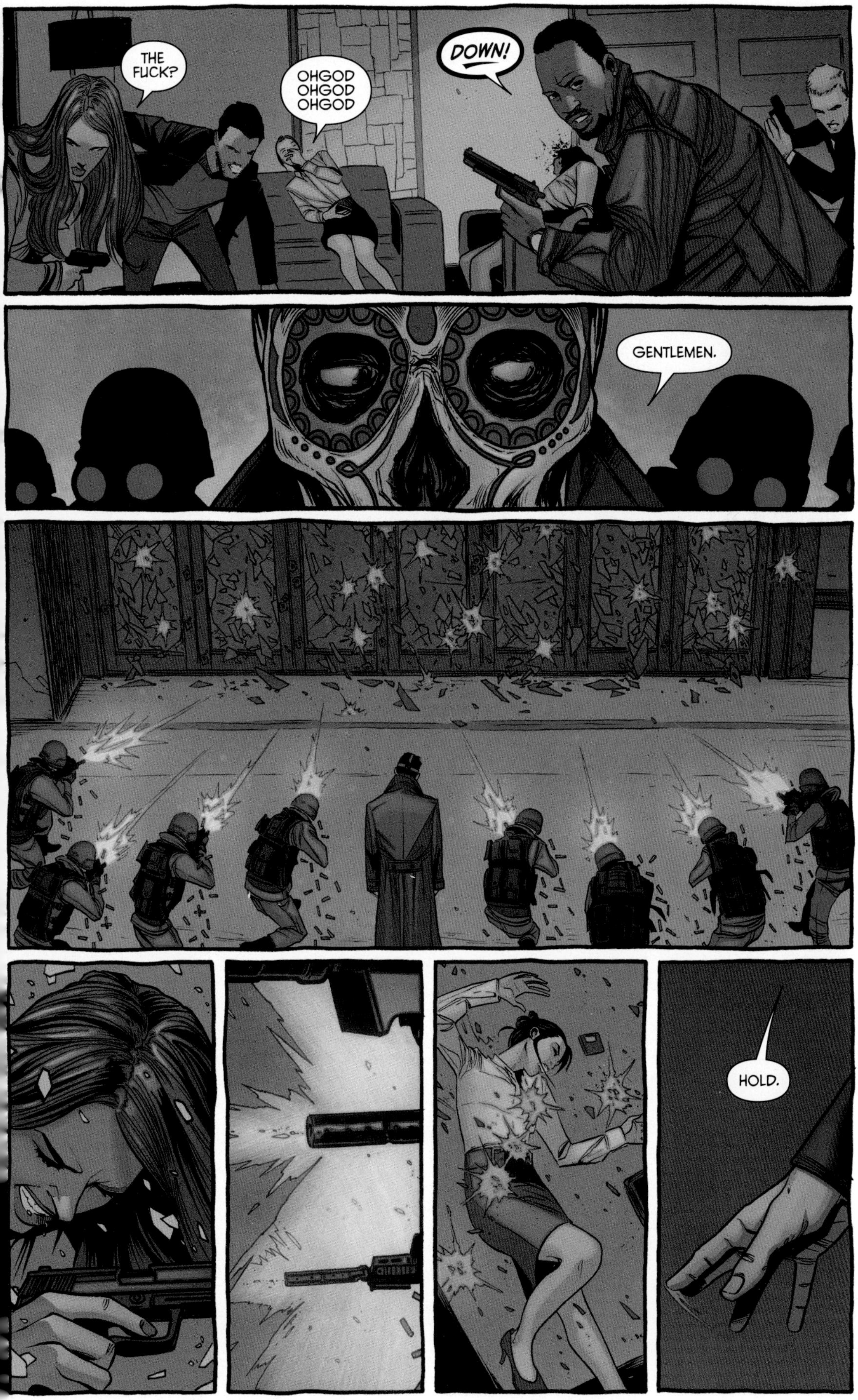
THE FUCK?
OHGOD OHGOD OHGOD
DOWN!
GENTLEMEN.
HOLD.

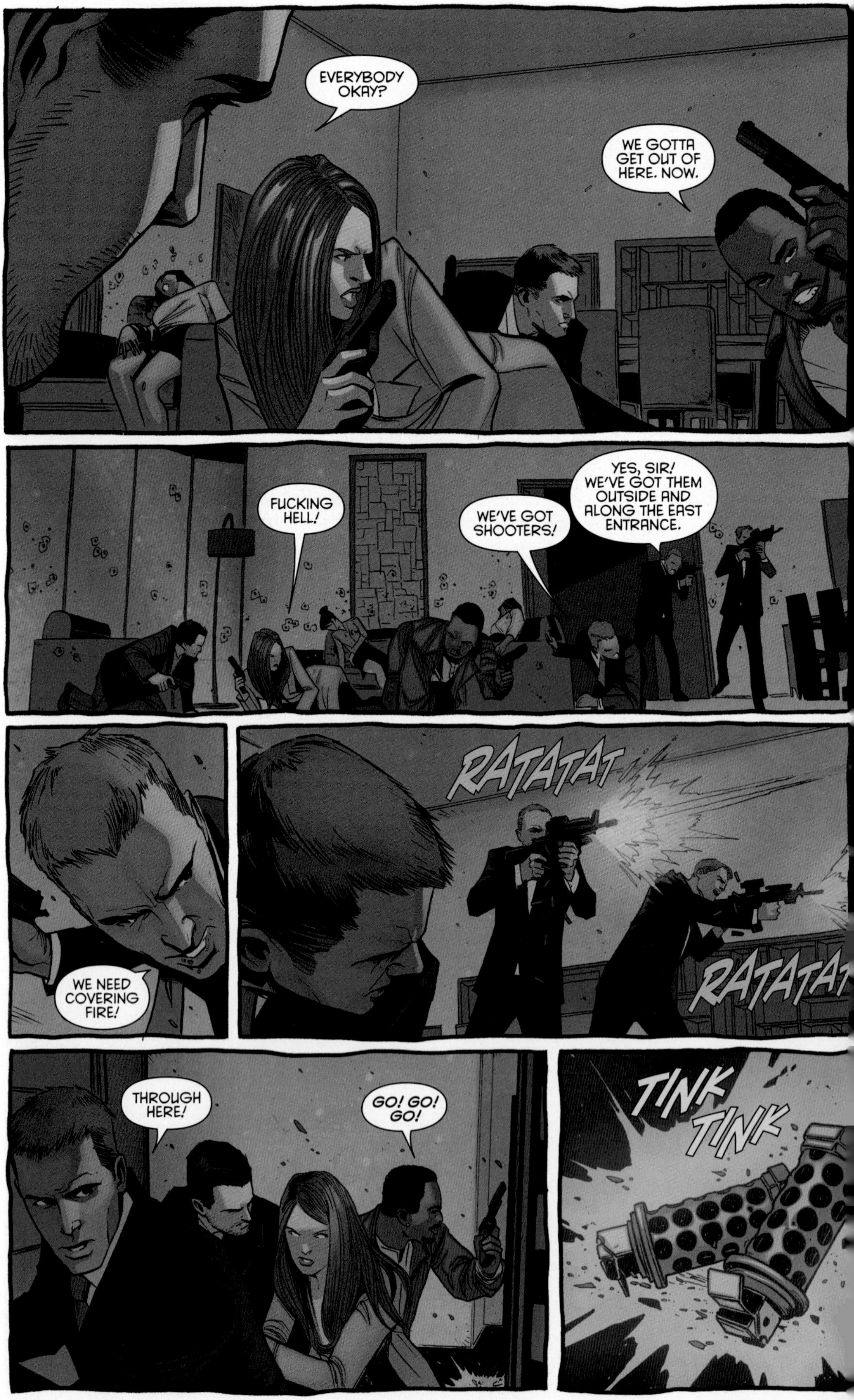
EVERYBODY OKAY?
WE GOTTA GET OUT OF HERE. NOW.
FUCKING HELL!
WE'VE GOT SHOOTERS!
YES, SIR! WE'VE GOT THEM OUTSIDE AND ALONG THE EAST ENTRANCE.
WE NEED COVERING FIRE!
RATATAT
RATATAT
THROUGH HERE!
GO! GO! GO!
TINK
TINK

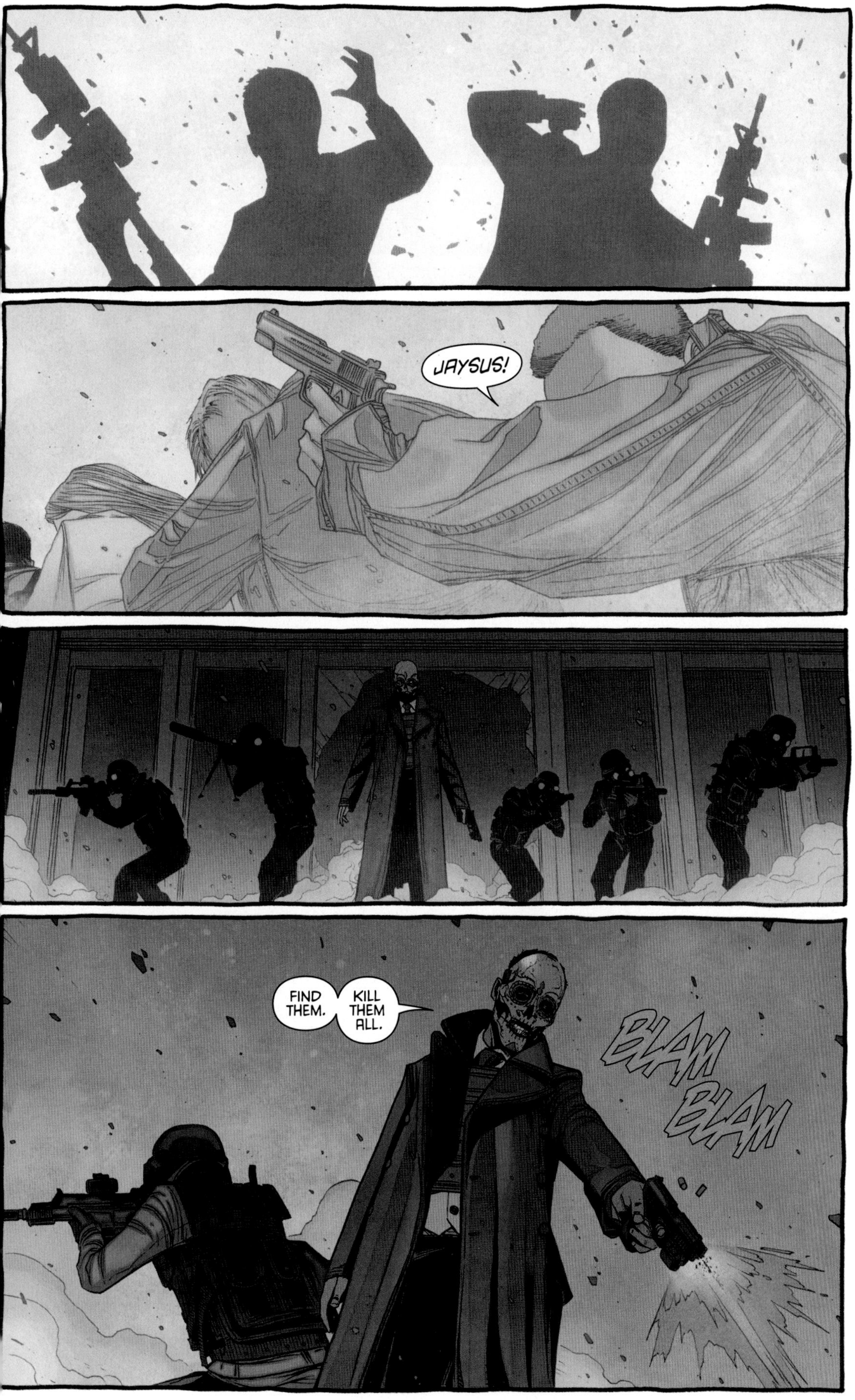
JAYSUS!
FIND THEM.
KILL THEM ALL.
BLAM
BLAM

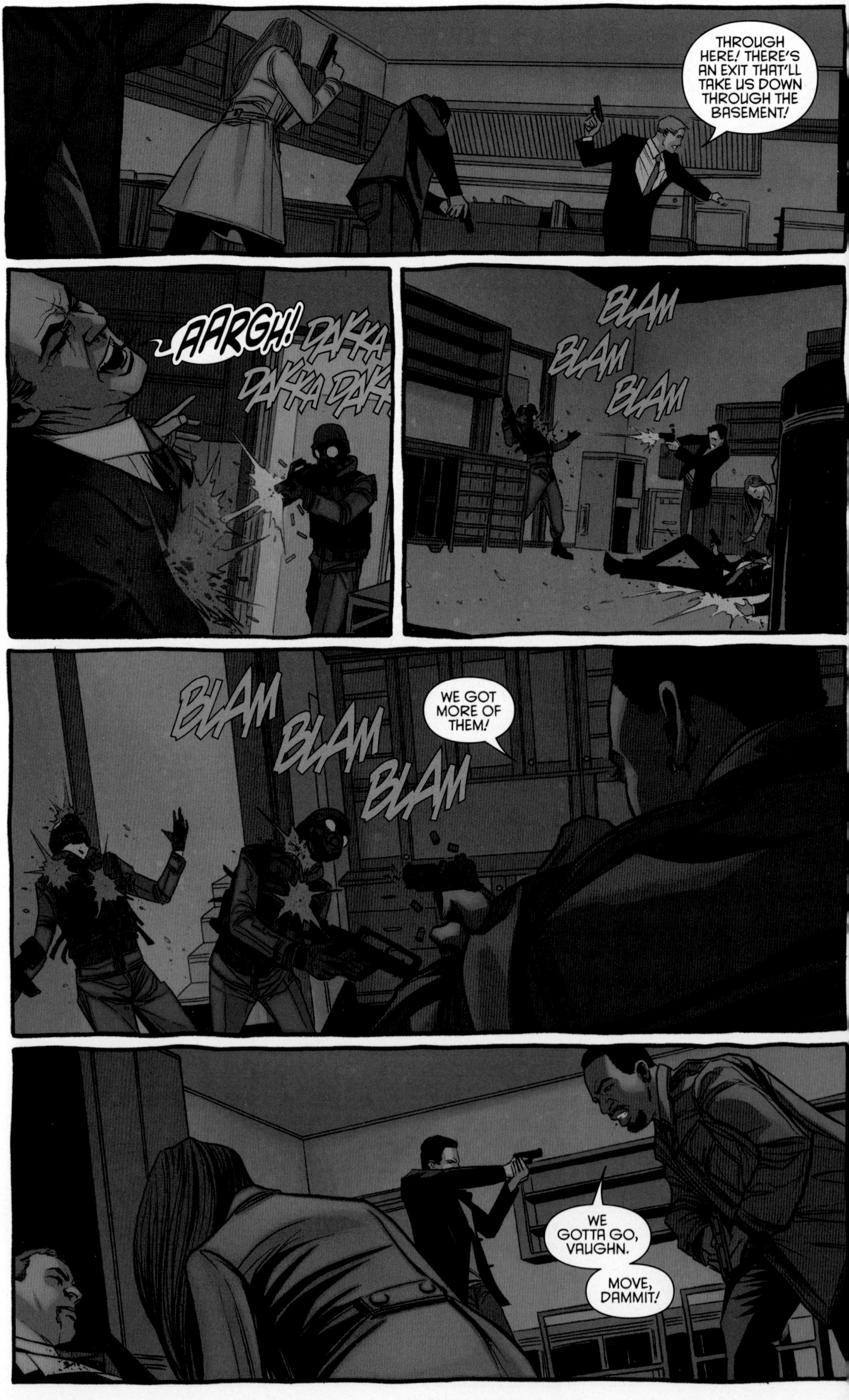
THROUGH HERE! THERE'S AN EXIT THAT'LL TAKE US DOWN THROUGH THE BASEMENT!
AARGH!
DAKKA DAKKA DAKKA
BLAM BLAM BLAM
BLAM BLAM BLAM
WE GOT MORE OF THEM!
WE GOTTA GO, VAUGHN.
MOVE, DAMMIT!

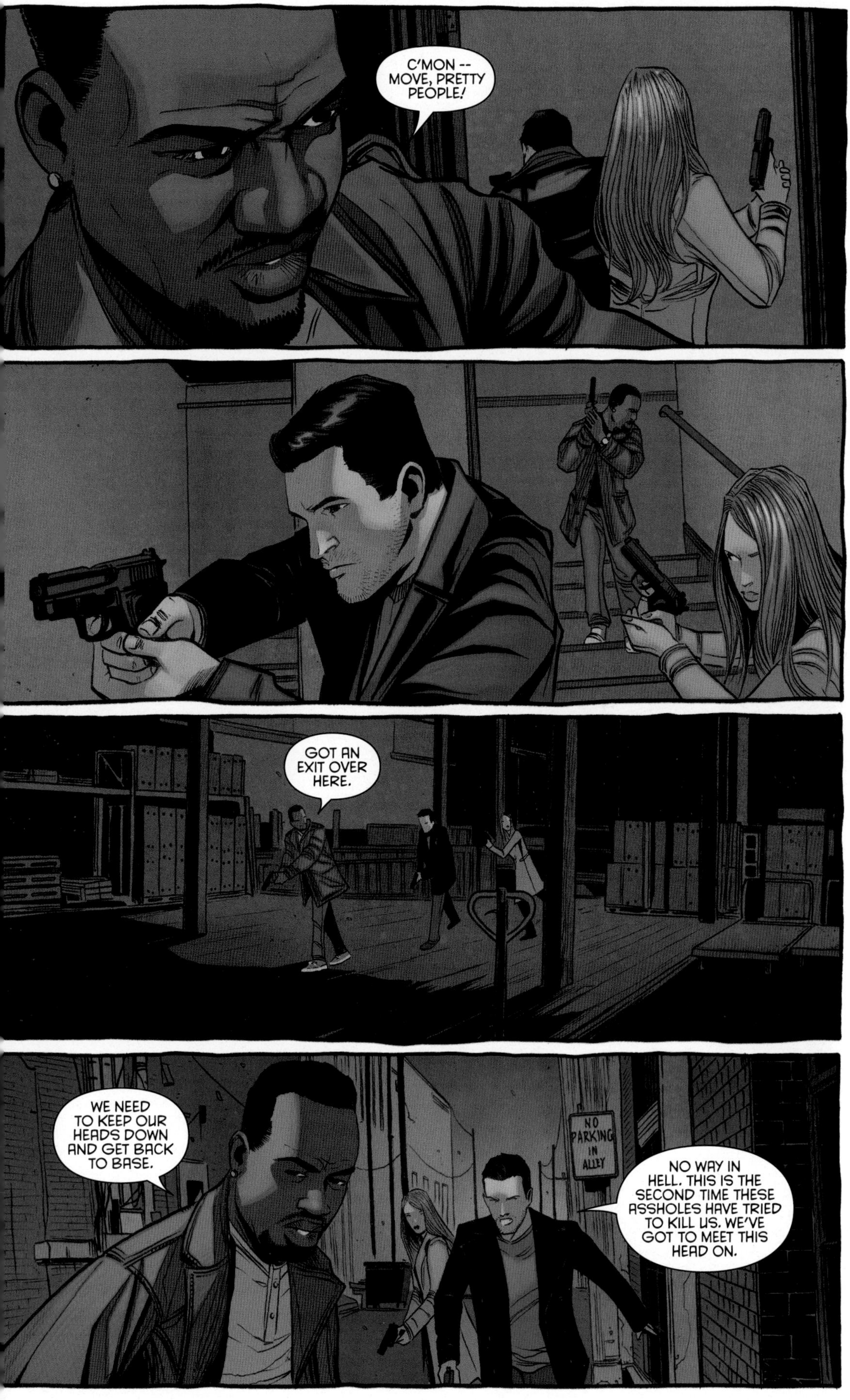

C'MON -- MOVE, PRETTY PEOPLE!
GOT AN EXIT OVER HERE.
WE NEED TO KEEP OUR HEADS DOWN AND GET BACK TO BASE.
NO PARKING IN ALLEY
NO WAY IN HELL. THIS IS THE SECOND TIME THESE ASSHOLES HAVE TRIED TO KILL US. WE'VE GOT TO MEET THIS HEAD ON.

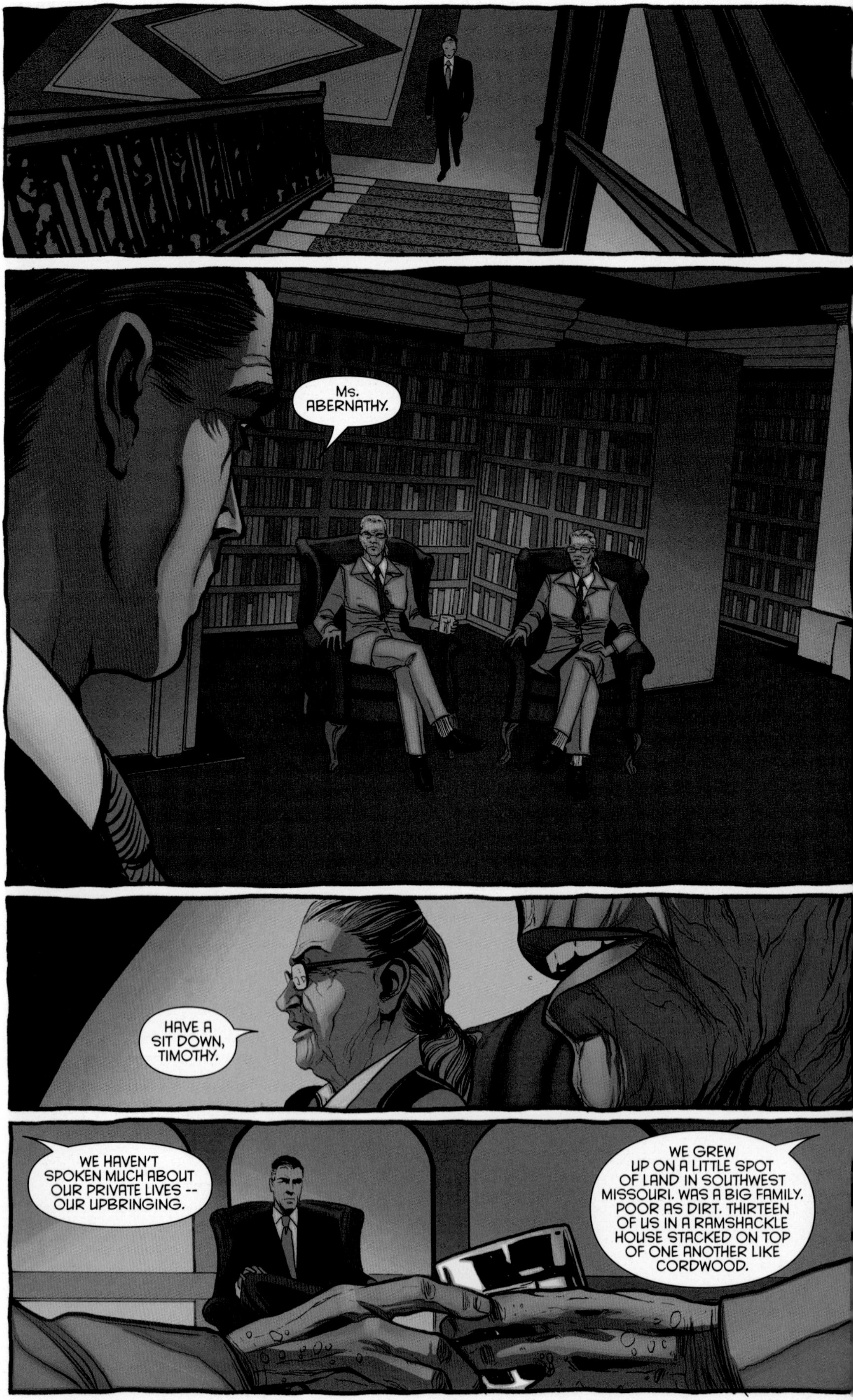
Ms. ABERNATHY.
HAVE A SIT DOWN, TIMOTHY.
WE HAVEN'T SPOKEN MUCH ABOUT OUR PRIVATE LIVES -- OUR UPBRINGING.
WE GREW UP ON A LITTLE SPOT OF LAND IN SOUTHWEST MISSOURI. WAS A BIG FAMILY. POOR AS DIRT. THIRTEEN OF US IN A RAMSHACKLE HOUSE STACKED ON TOP OF ONE ANOTHER LIKE CORDWOOD.

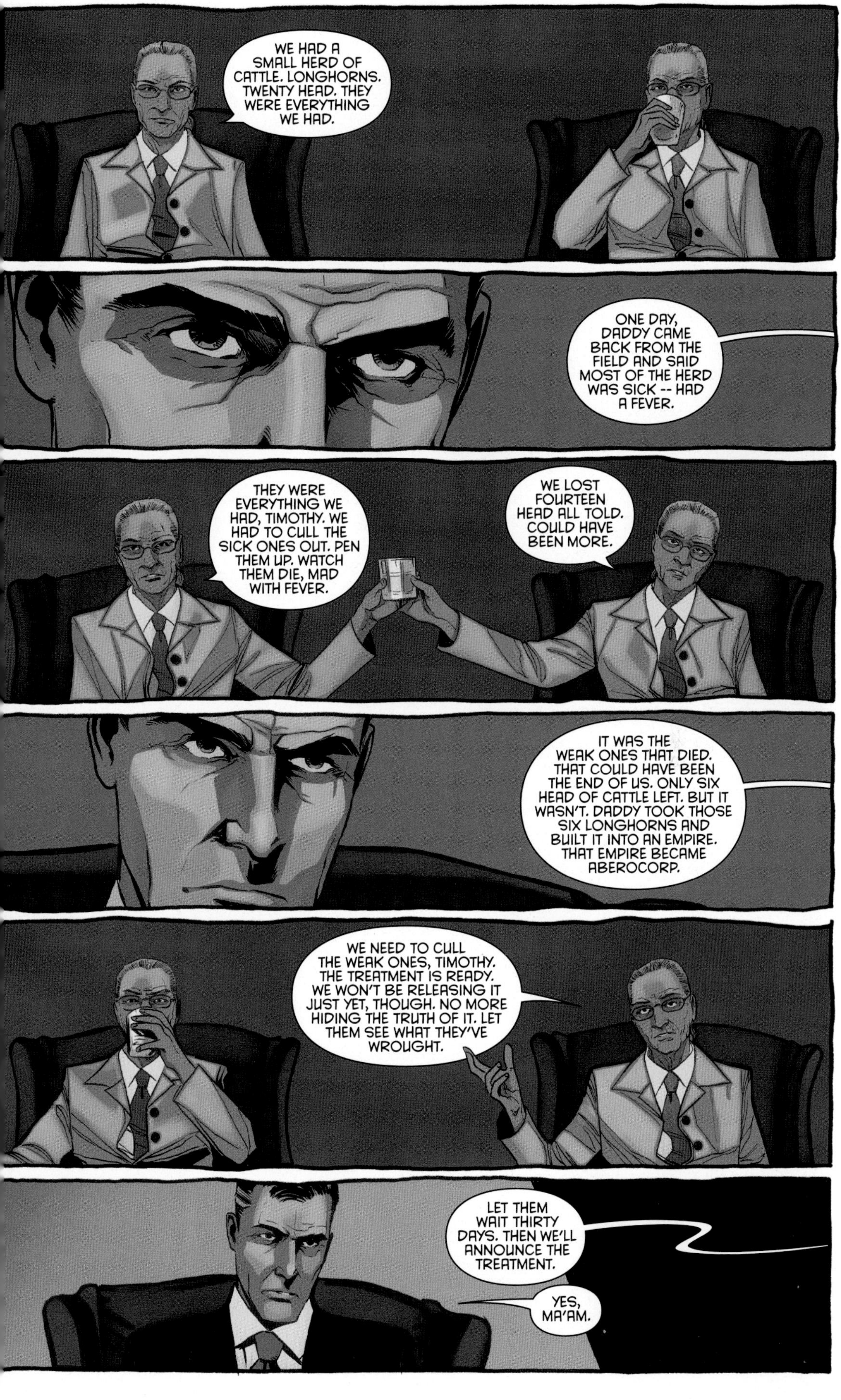
WE HAD A SMALL HERD OF CATTLE. LONGHORNS. TWENTY HEAD. THEY WERE EVERYTHING WE HAD.
ONE DAY, DADDY CAME BACK FROM THE FIELD AND SAID MOST OF THE HERD WAS SICK -- HAD A FEVER.
THEY WERE EVERYTHING WE HAD, TIMOTHY. WE HAD TO CULL THE SICK ONES OUT. PEN THEM UP. WATCH THEM DIE, MAD WITH FEVER.
WE LOST FOURTEEN HEAD ALL TOLD. COULD HAVE BEEN MORE.
IT WAS THE WEAK ONES THAT DIED. THAT COULD HAVE BEEN THE END OF US. ONLY SIX HEAD OF CATTLE LEFT. BUT IT WASN'T. DADDY TOOK THOSE SIX LONGHORNS AND BUILT IT INTO AN EMPIRE. THAT EMPIRE BECAME ABEROCORP.
WE NEED TO CULL THE WEAK ONES, TIMOTHY. THE TREATMENT IS READY. WE WON'T BE RELEASING IT JUST YET, THOUGH. NO MORE HIDING THE TRUTH OF IT. LET THEM SEE WHAT THEY'VE WROUGHT.
LET THEM WAIT THIRTY DAYS. THEN WE'LL ANNOUNCE THE TREATMENT.
YES, MA'AM.

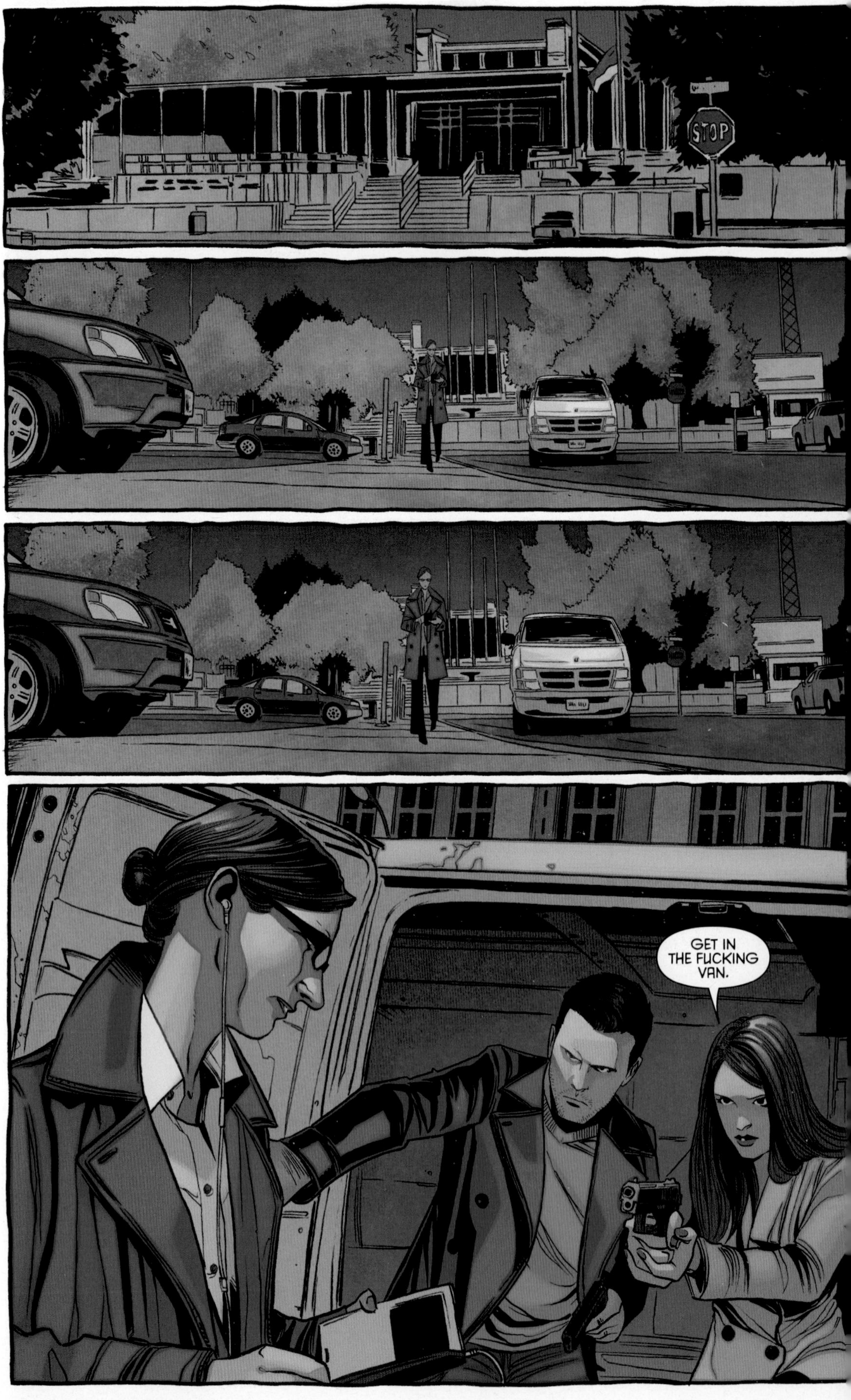
GET IN THE FUCKING VAN.

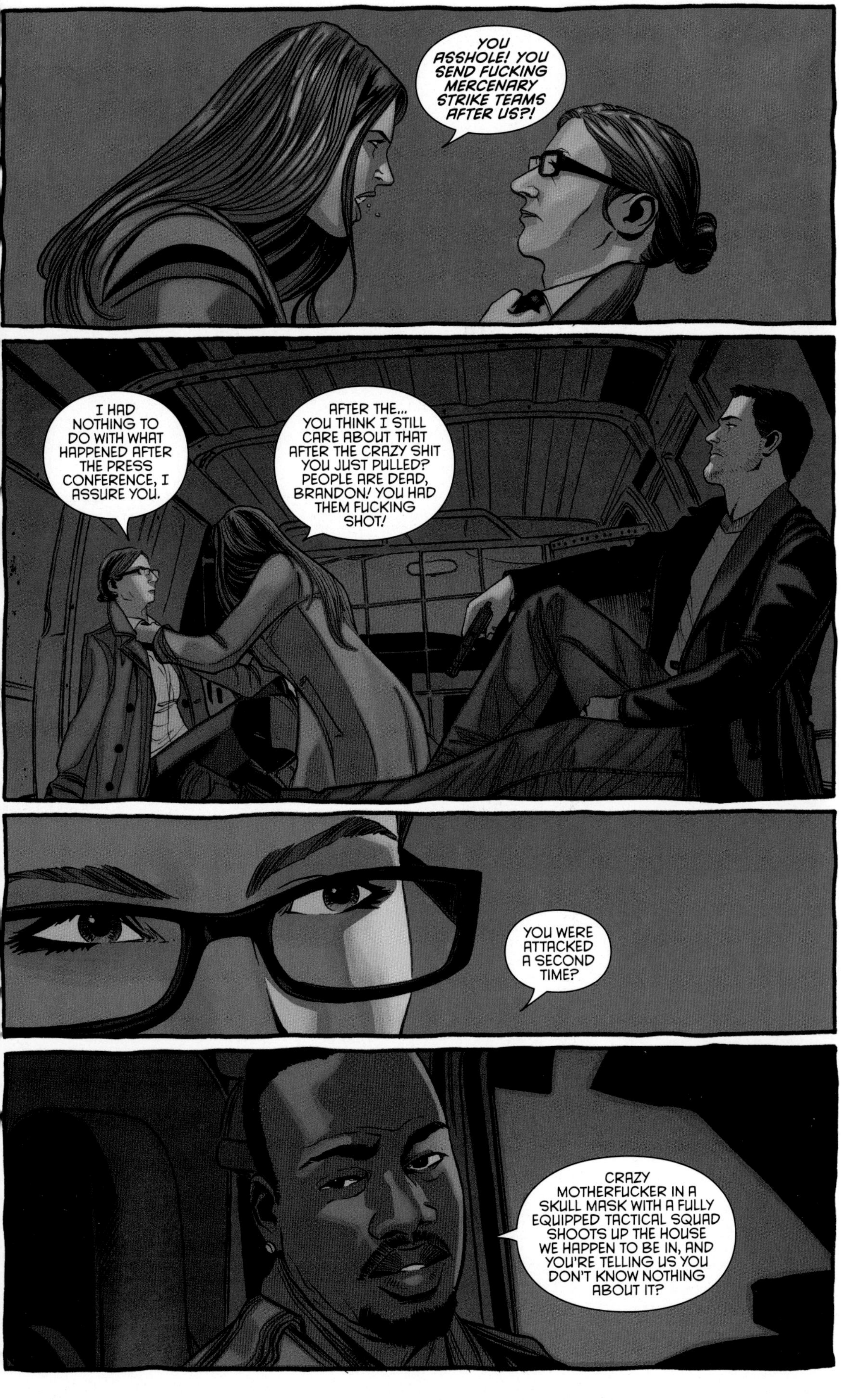
YOU ASSHOLE! YOU SEND FUCKING MERCENARY STRIKE TEAMS AFTER US?!
I HAD NOTHING TO DO WITH WHAT HAPPENED AFTER THE PRESS CONFERENCE, I ASSURE YOU.
AFTER THE... YOU THINK I STILL CARE ABOUT THAT AFTER THE CRAZY SHIT YOU JUST PULLED? PEOPLE ARE DEAD, BRANDON! YOU HAD THEM FUCKING SHOT!
YOU WERE ATTACKED A SECOND TIME?
CRAZY MOTHERFUCKER IN A SKULL MASK WITH A FULLY EQUIPPED TACTICAL SQUAD SHOOTS UP THE HOUSE WE HAPPEN TO BE IN, AND YOU'RE TELLING US YOU DON'T KNOW NOTHING ABOUT IT?

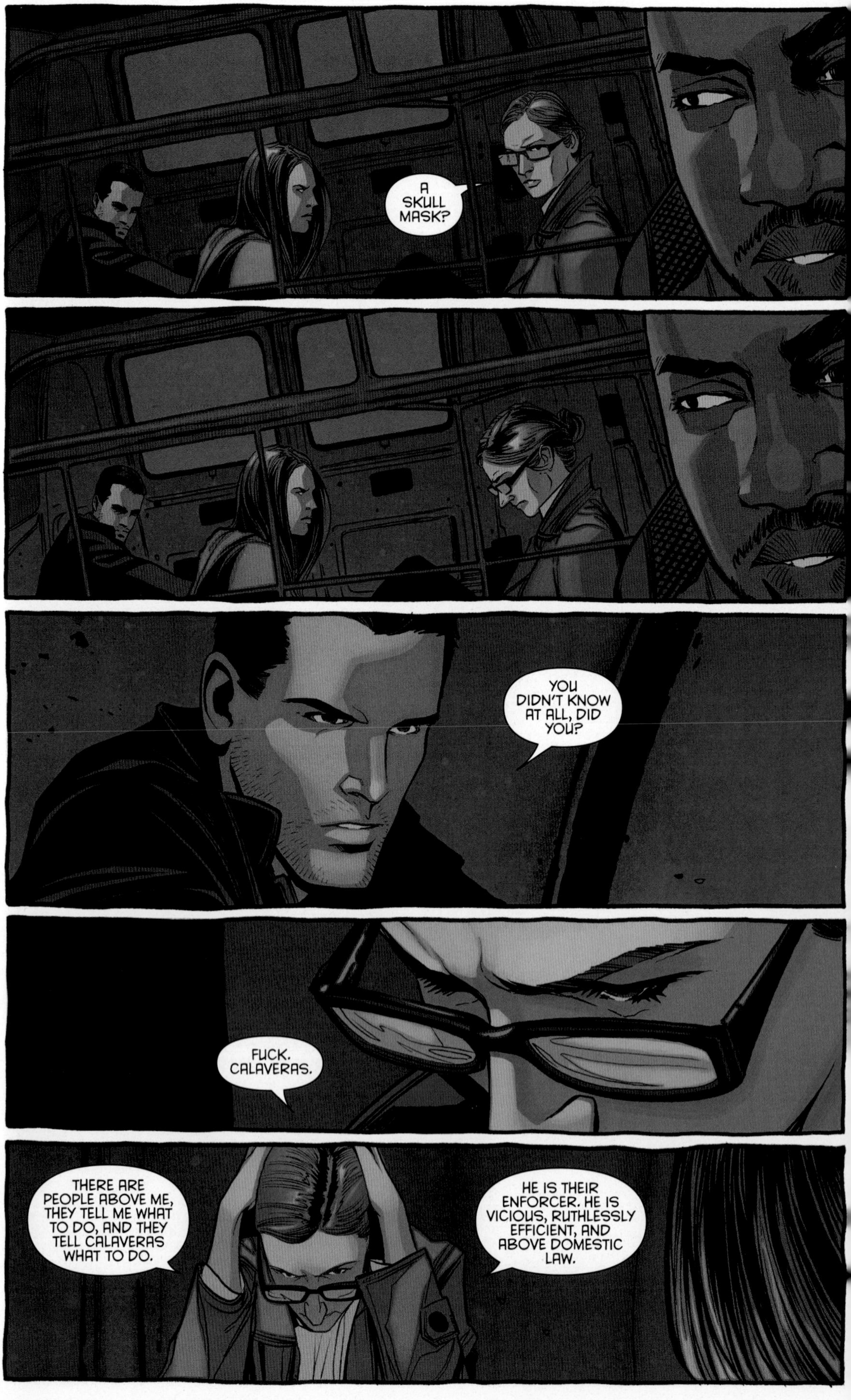
A SKULL MASK?
YOU DIDN'T KNOW AT ALL, DID YOU?
FUCK. CALAVERAS.
THERE ARE PEOPLE ABOVE ME, THEY TELL ME WHAT TO DO, AND THEY TELL CALAVERAS WHAT TO DO.
HE IS THEIR ENFORCER. HE IS VICIOUS, RUTHLESSLY EFFICIENT, AND ABOVE DOMESTIC LAW.

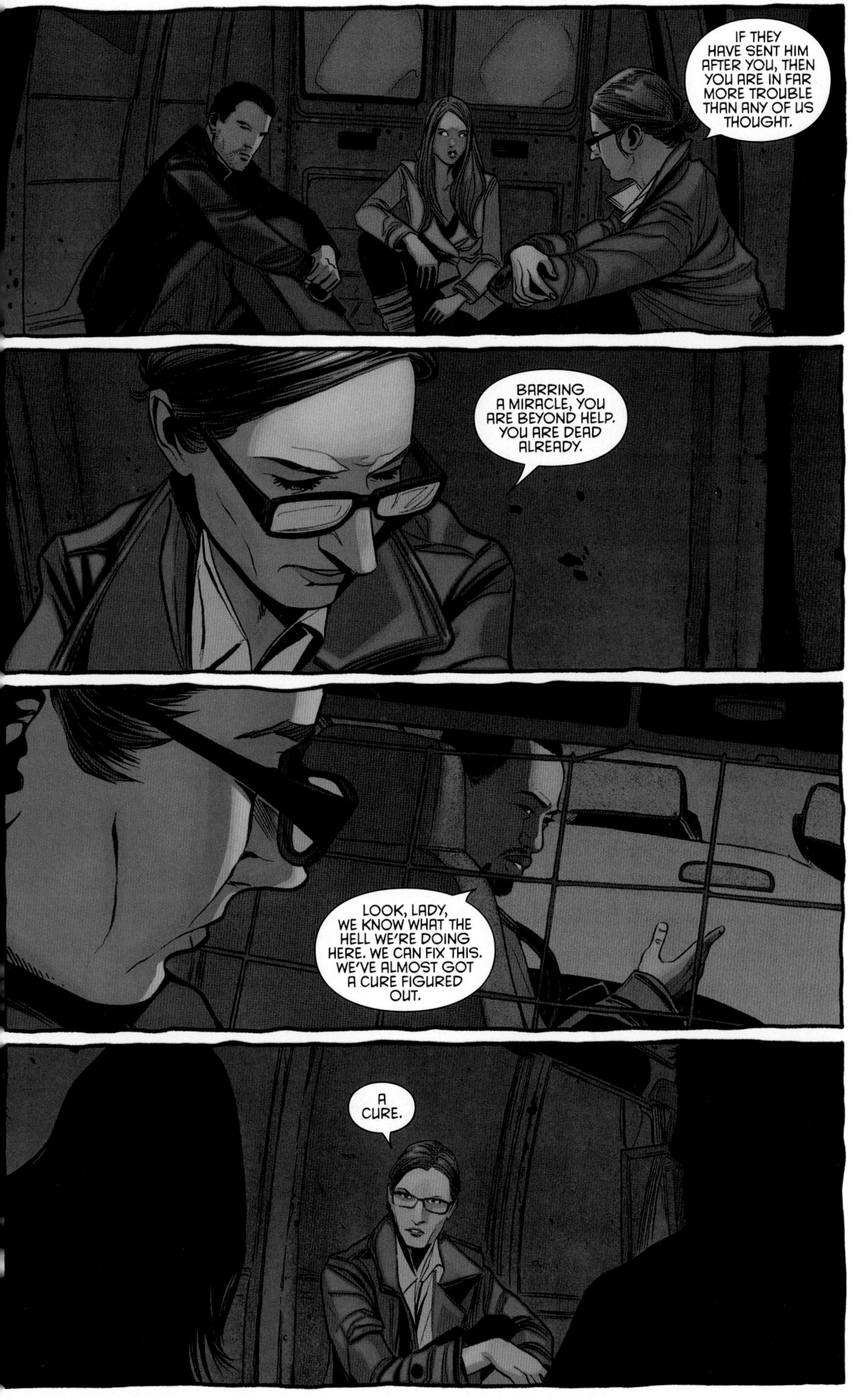
IF THEY HAVE SENT HIM AFTER YOU, THEN YOU ARE IN FAR MORE TROUBLE THAN ANY OF US THOUGHT.
BARRING A MIRACLE, YOU ARE BEYOND HELP. YOU ARE DEAD ALREADY.
LOOK, LADY, WE KNOW WHAT THE HELL WE'RE DOING HERE. WE CAN FIX THIS. WE'VE ALMOST GOT A CURE FIGURED OUT.
A CURE.

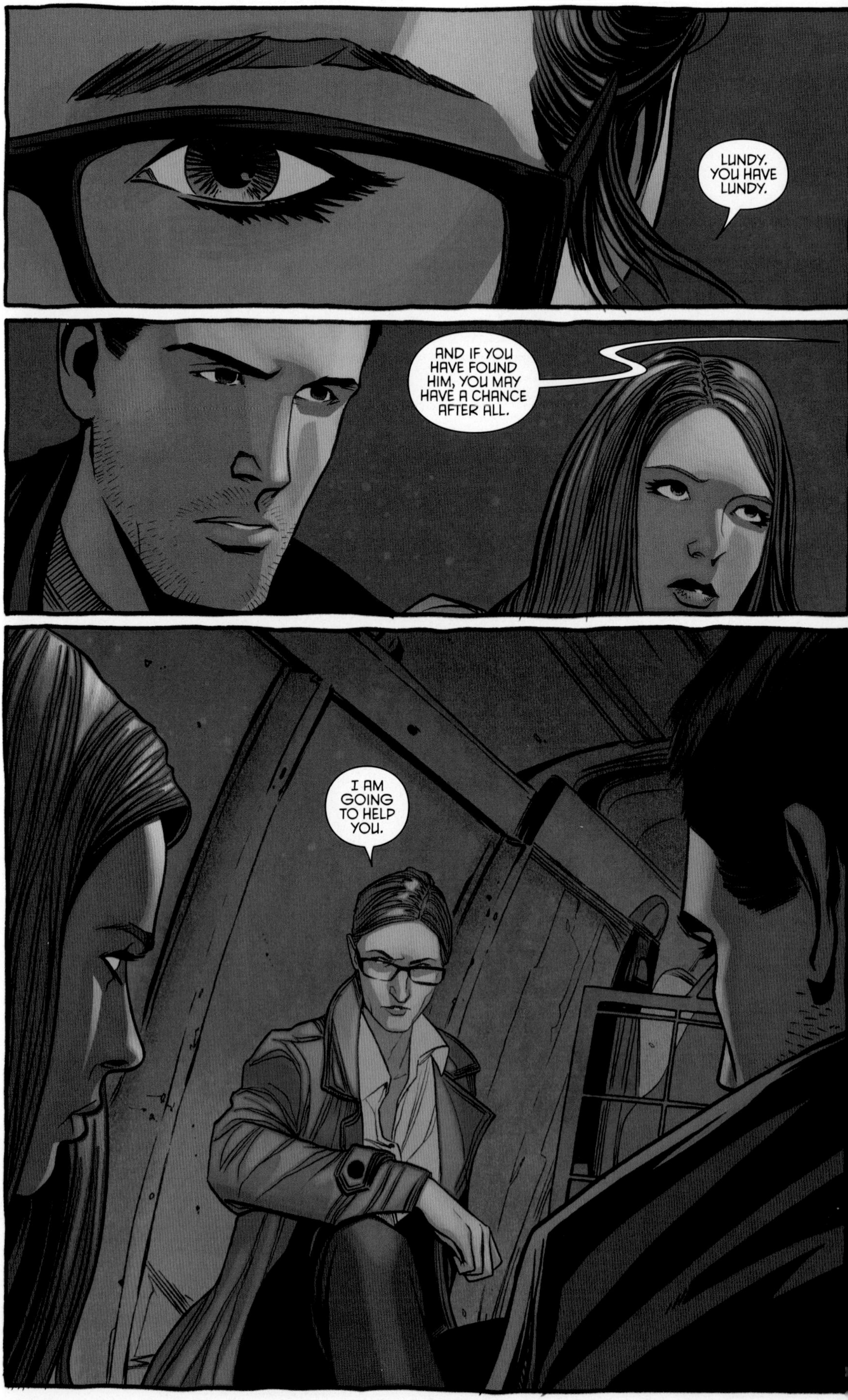
LUNDY. YOU HAVE LUNDY.
AND IF YOU HAVE FOUND HIM, YOU MAY HAVE A CHANCE AFTER ALL.
I AM GOING TO HELP YOU.

CHAPTER

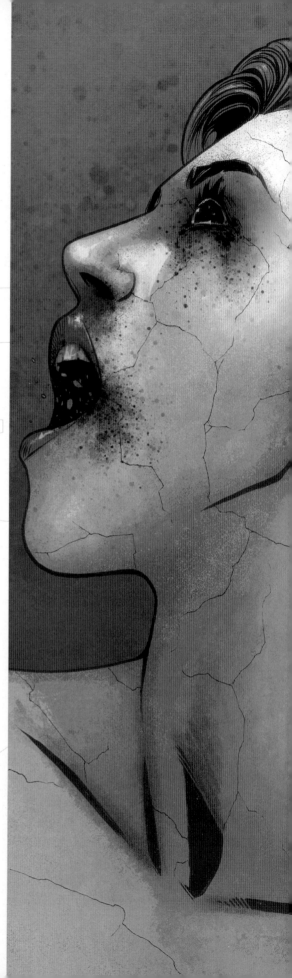

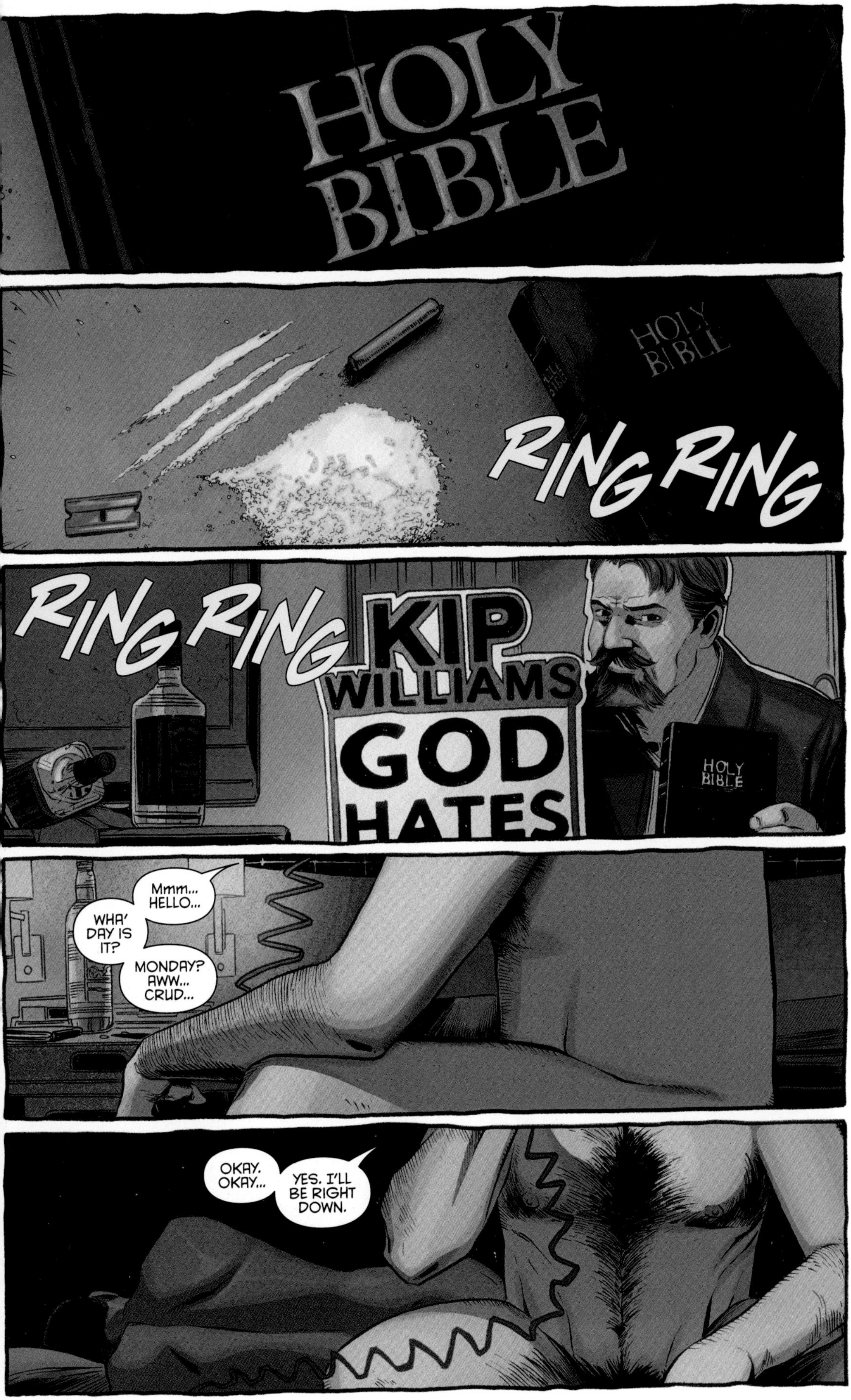
HOLY BIBLE
HOLY BIBLE
RING RING
RING RING
KIP WILLIAMS
GOD HATES
HOLY BIBLE
Mmm... HELLO...
WHA' DAY IS IT?
MONDAY? AWW... CRUD...
OKAY. OKAY...
YES. I'LL BE RIGHT DOWN.

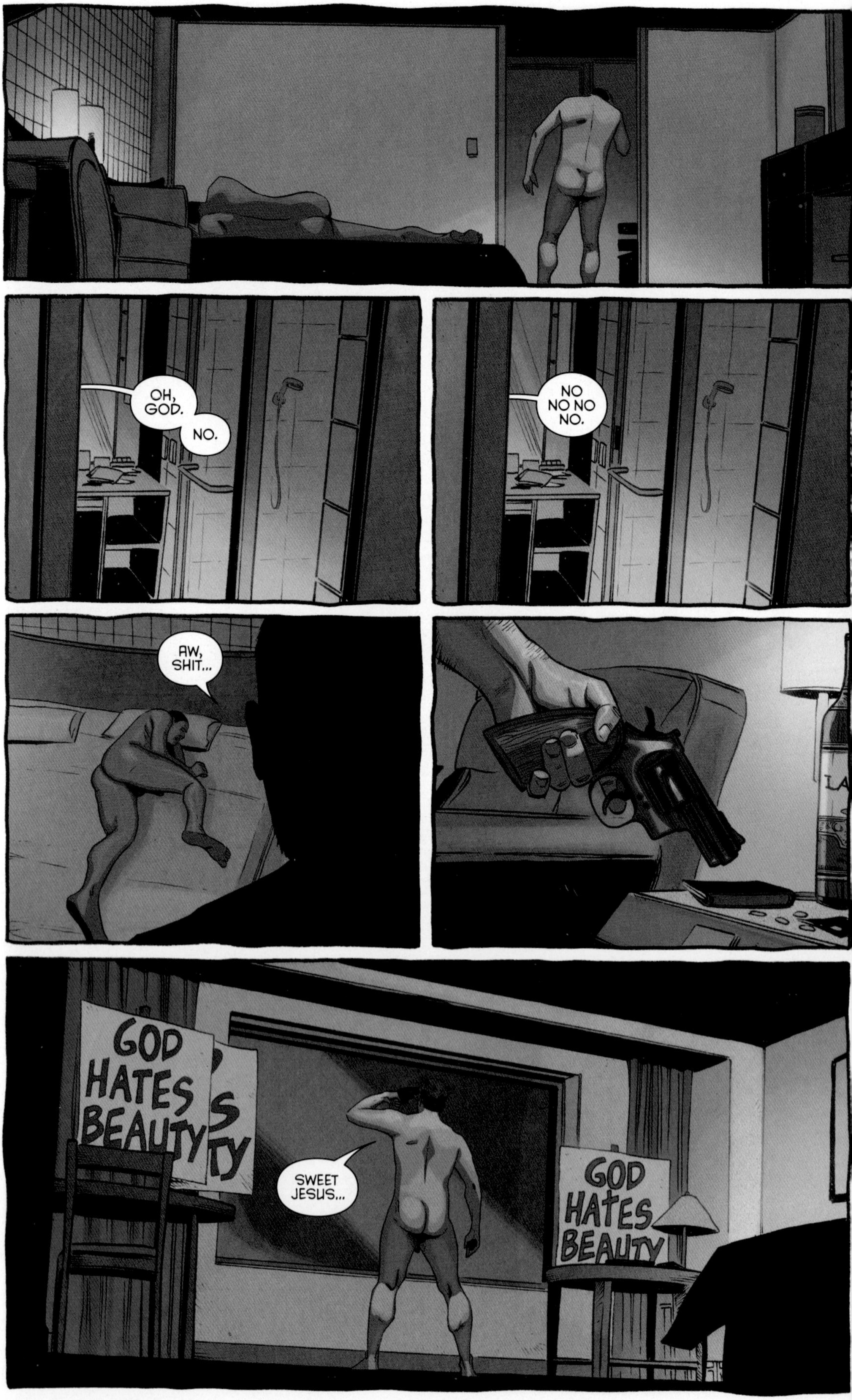
OH, GOD.
NO.
NO NO NO NO.
AW, SHIT...
GOD HATES BEAUTY
SWEET JESUS...
GOD HATES BEAUTY

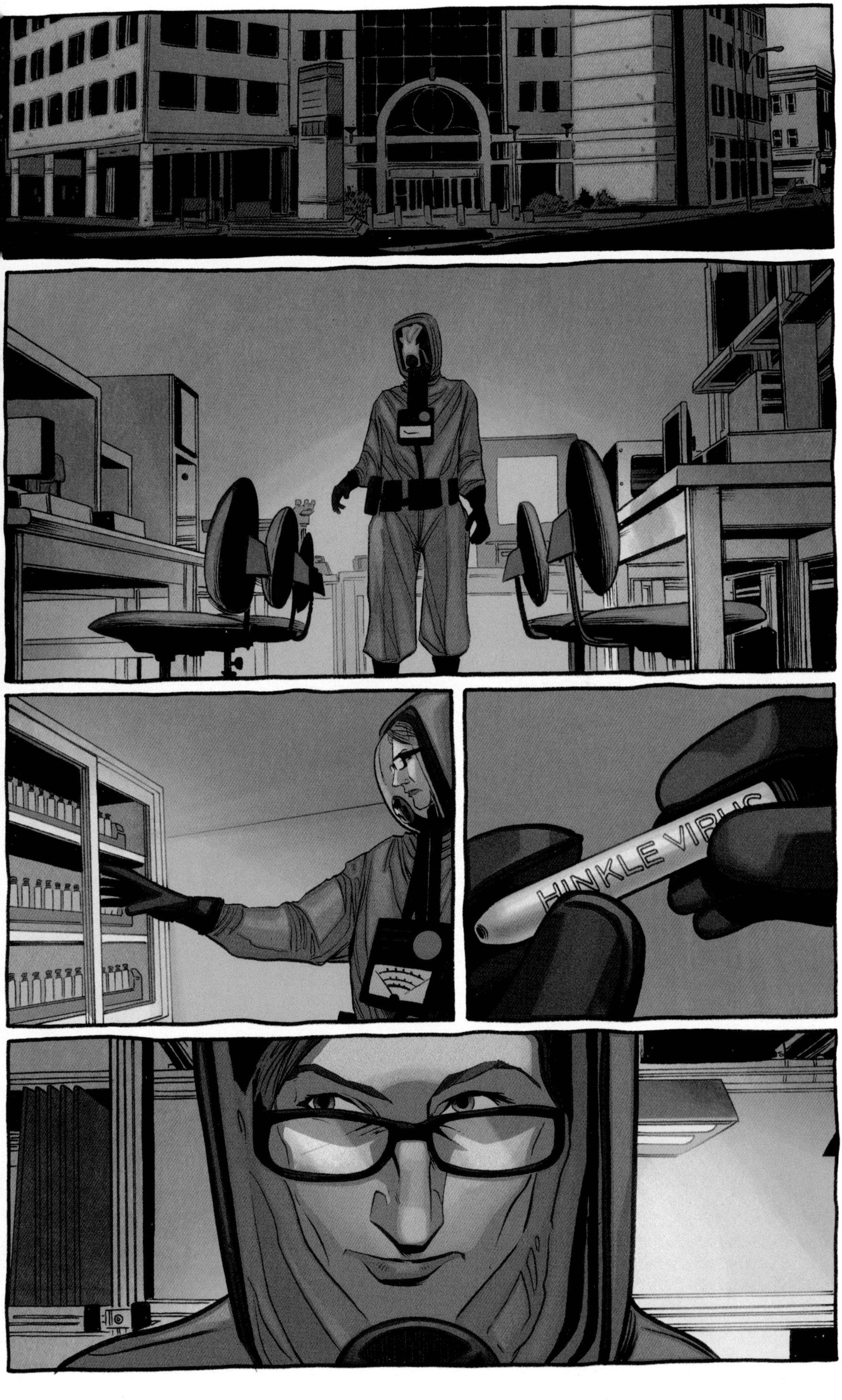
HINKLE VIRUS

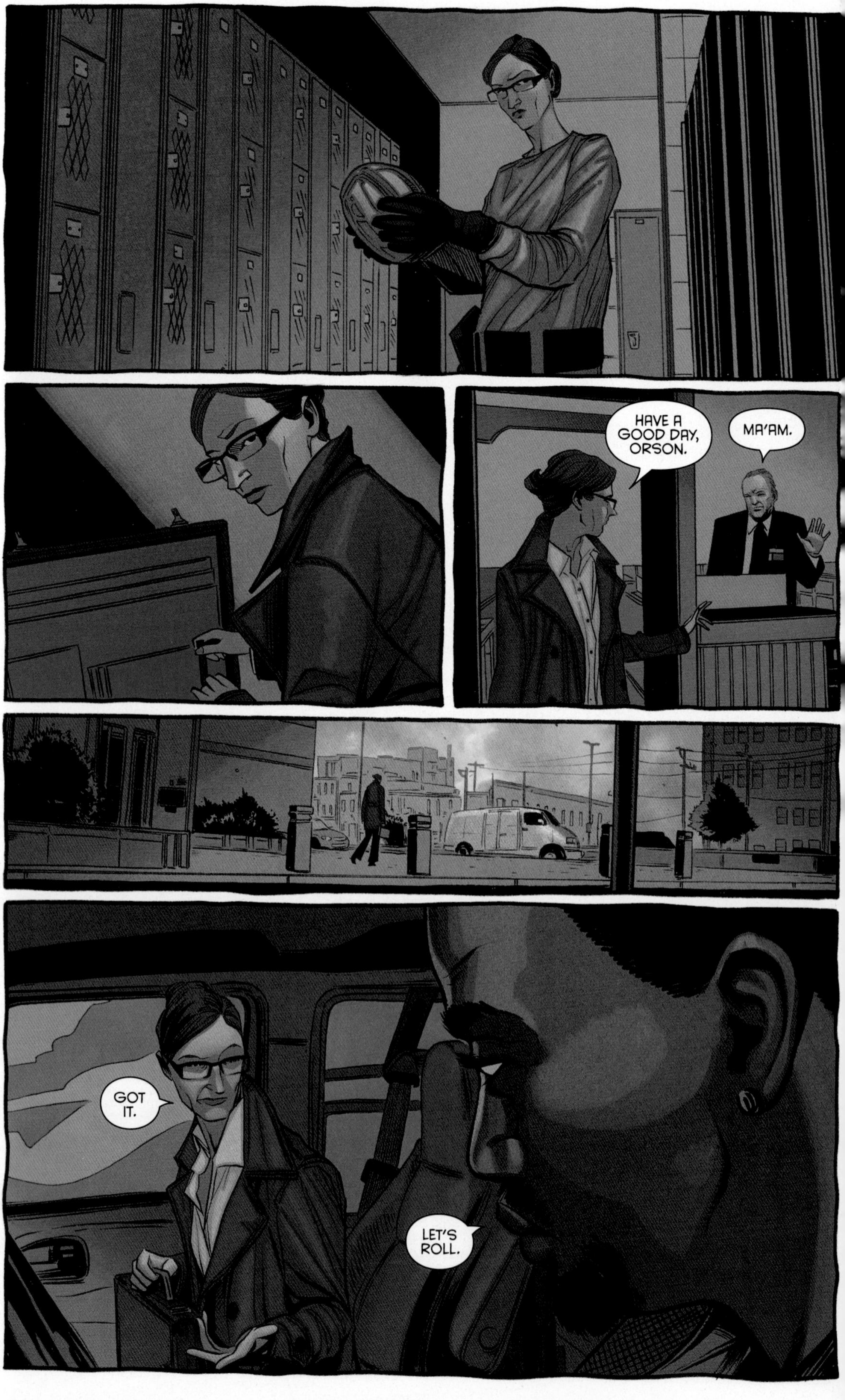
HAVE A GOOD DAY, ORSON.
MA'AM.
GOT IT.
LET'S ROLL.

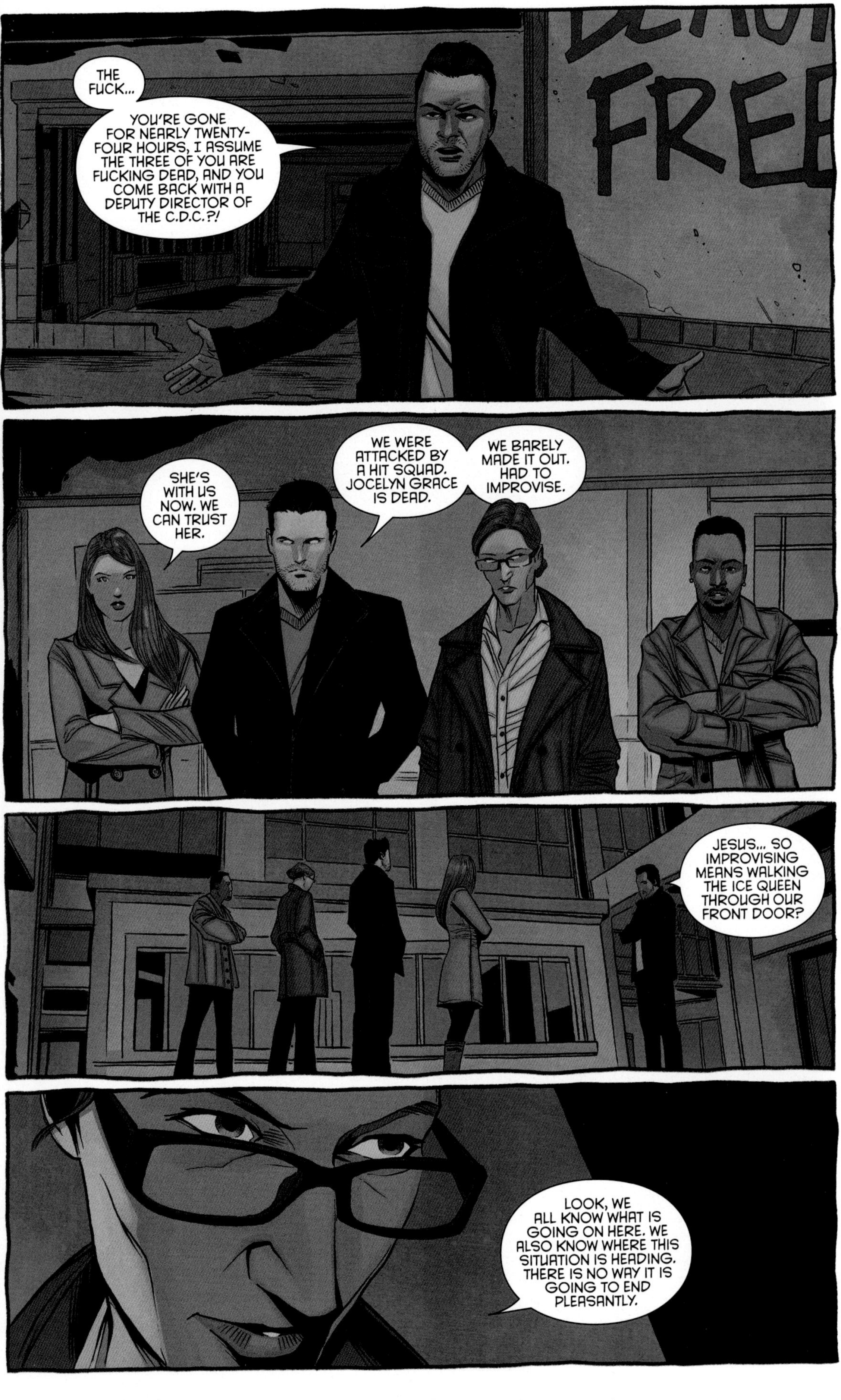
DEATH
FREE
THE FUCK...
YOU'RE GONE FOR NEARLY TWENTY-FOUR HOURS, I ASSUME THE THREE OF YOU ARE FUCKING DEAD, AND YOU COME BACK WITH A DEPUTY DIRECTOR OF THE C.D.C.?!
SHE'S WITH US NOW. WE CAN TRUST HER.
WE WERE ATTACKED BY A HIT SQUAD. JOCELYN GRACE IS DEAD.
WE BARELY MADE IT OUT. HAD TO IMPROVISE.
JESUS... SO IMPROVISING MEANS WALKING THE ICE QUEEN THROUGH OUR FRONT DOOR?
LOOK, WE ALL KNOW WHAT IS GOING ON HERE. WE ALSO KNOW WHERE THIS SITUATION IS HEADING. THERE IS NO WAY IT IS GOING TO END PLEASANTLY.

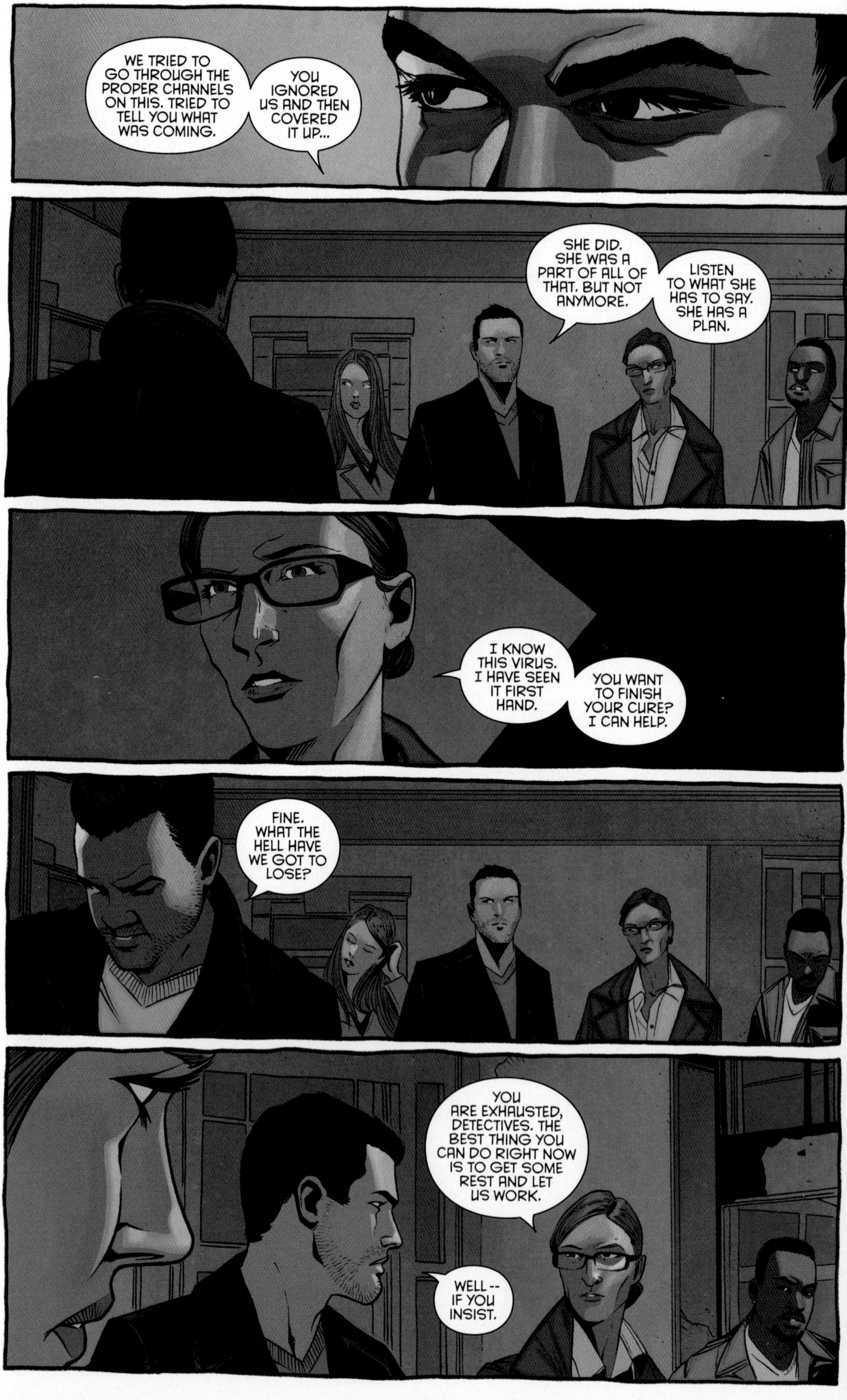
WE TRIED TO GO THROUGH THE PROPER CHANNELS ON THIS. TRIED TO TELL YOU WHAT WAS COMING.
YOU IGNORED US AND THEN COVERED IT UP...
SHE DID. SHE WAS A PART OF ALL OF THAT. BUT NOT ANYMORE.
LISTEN TO WHAT SHE HAS TO SAY. SHE HAS A PLAN.
I KNOW THIS VIRUS. I HAVE SEEN IT FIRST HAND.
YOU WANT TO FINISH YOUR CURE? I CAN HELP.
FINE. WHAT THE HELL HAVE WE GOT TO LOSE?
YOU ARE EXHAUSTED, DETECTIVES. THE BEST THING YOU CAN DO RIGHT NOW IS TO GET SOME REST AND LET US WORK.
WELL -- IF YOU INSIST.

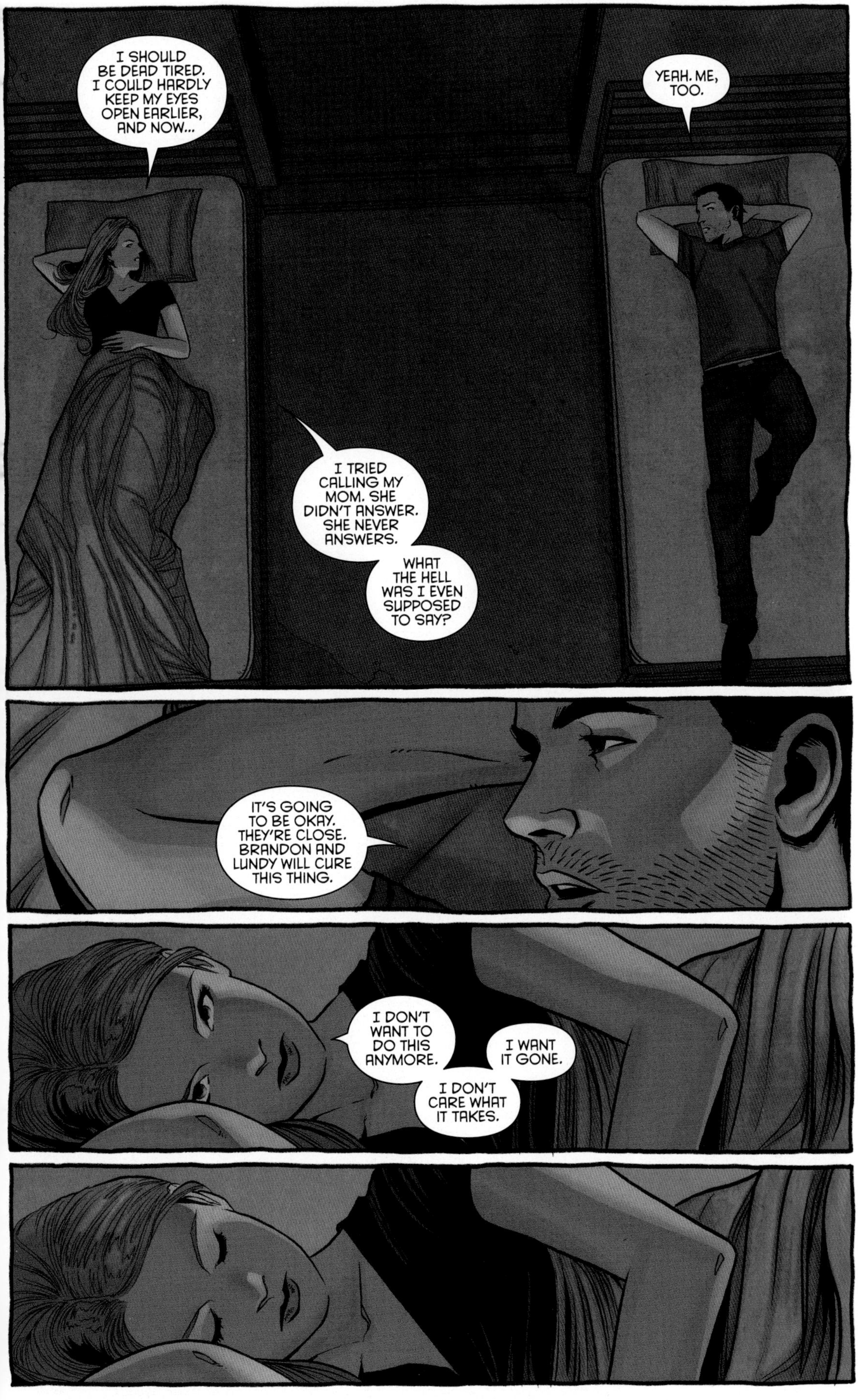
I SHOULD BE DEAD TIRED. I COULD HARDLY KEEP MY EYES OPEN EARLIER, AND NOW...
YEAH. ME, TOO.
I TRIED CALLING MY MOM. SHE DIDN'T ANSWER. SHE NEVER ANSWERS.
WHAT THE HELL WAS I EVEN SUPPOSED TO SAY?
IT'S GOING TO BE OKAY. THEY'RE CLOSE. BRANDON AND LUNDY WILL CURE THIS THING.
I DON'T WANT TO DO THIS ANYMORE.
I WANT IT GONE.
I DON'T CARE WHAT IT TAKES.

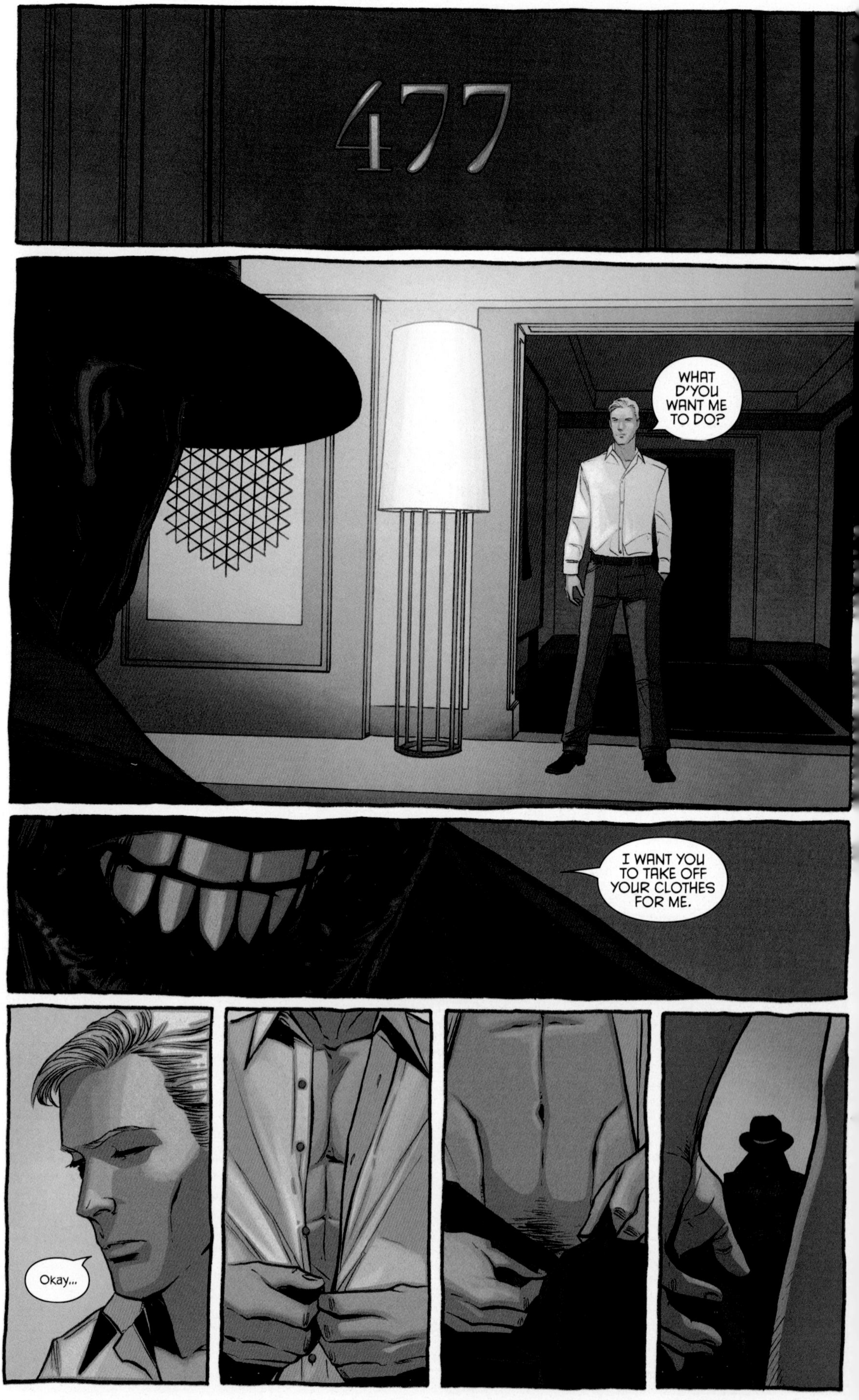
477
WHAT D'YOU WANT ME TO DO?
I WANT YOU TO TAKE OFF YOUR CLOTHES FOR ME.
Okay...

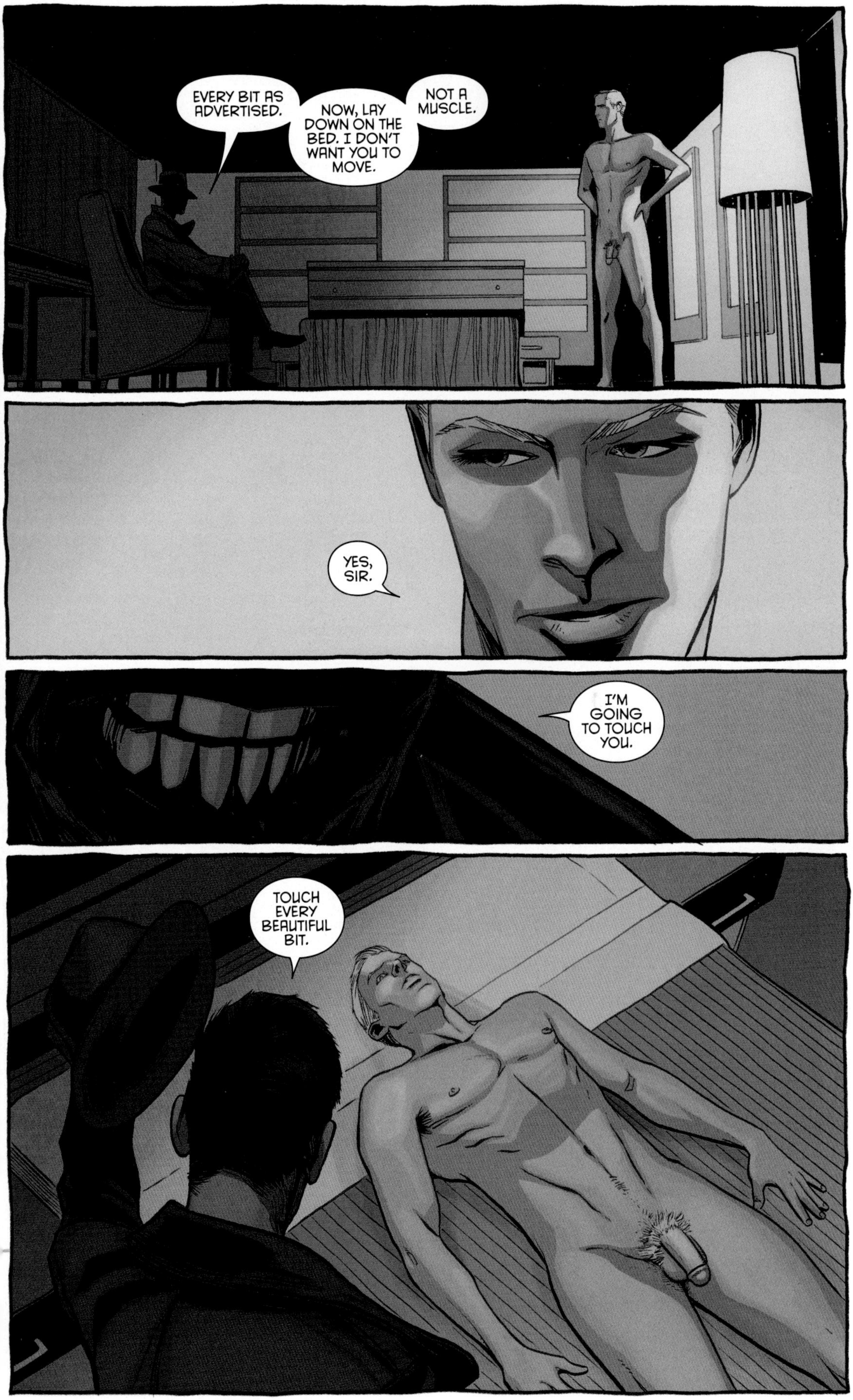
EVERY BIT AS ADVERTISED.
NOW, LAY DOWN ON THE BED. I DON'T WANT YOU TO MOVE.
NOT A MUSCLE.
YES, SIR.
I'M GOING TO TOUCH YOU.
TOUCH EVERY BEAUTIFUL BIT.

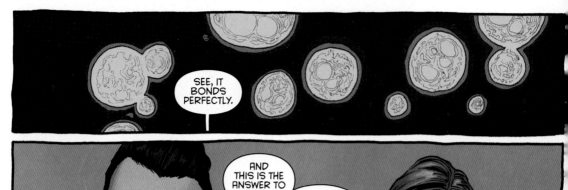

SEE, IT BONDS PERFECTLY.

AND THIS IS THE ANSWER TO IT ALL... WE PIGGY-BACK THE CURE ONTO YOUR SUPERFLU AND SPREAD IT LIKE WILDFIRE.

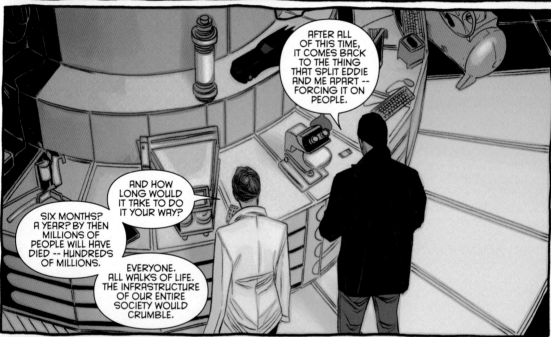

AFTER ALL OF THIS TIME, IT COMES BACK TO THE THING THAT SPLIT EDDIE AND ME APART -- FORCING IT ON PEOPLE.

AND HOW LONG WOULD IT TAKE TO DO IT YOUR WAY?

SIX MONTHS? A YEAR? BY THEN MILLIONS OF PEOPLE WILL HAVE DIED -- HUNDREDS OF MILLIONS.

EVERYONE. ALL WALKS OF LIFE. THE INFRASTRUCTURE OF OUR ENTIRE SOCIETY WOULD CRUMBLE.

I... YEAH...

WE HAVE TO STOP THIS THING DEAD. BURN IT OUT. IF WE DON'T ERADICATE IT, IT WILL COME BACK STRONGER, COMPLETELY RESISTANT.

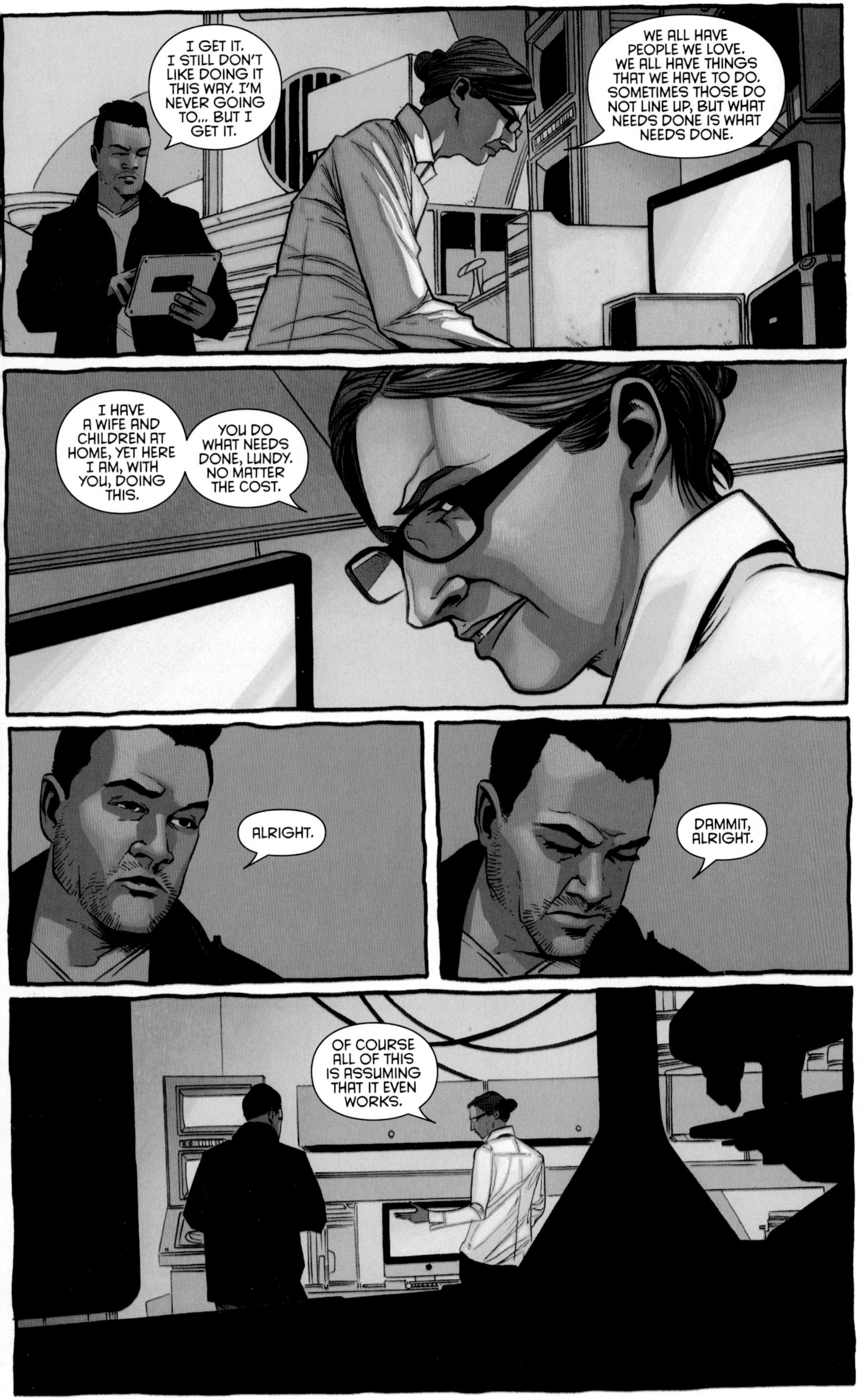
I GET IT. I STILL DON'T LIKE DOING IT THIS WAY. I'M NEVER GOING TO... BUT I GET IT.
WE ALL HAVE PEOPLE WE LOVE. WE ALL HAVE THINGS THAT WE HAVE TO DO. SOMETIMES THOSE DO NOT LINE UP, BUT WHAT NEEDS DONE IS WHAT NEEDS DONE.
I HAVE A WIFE AND CHILDREN AT HOME, YET HERE I AM, WITH YOU, DOING THIS.
YOU DO WHAT NEEDS DONE, LUNDY. NO MATTER THE COST.
ALRIGHT.
DAMMIT, ALRIGHT.
OF COURSE ALL OF THIS IS ASSUMING THAT IT EVEN WORKS.

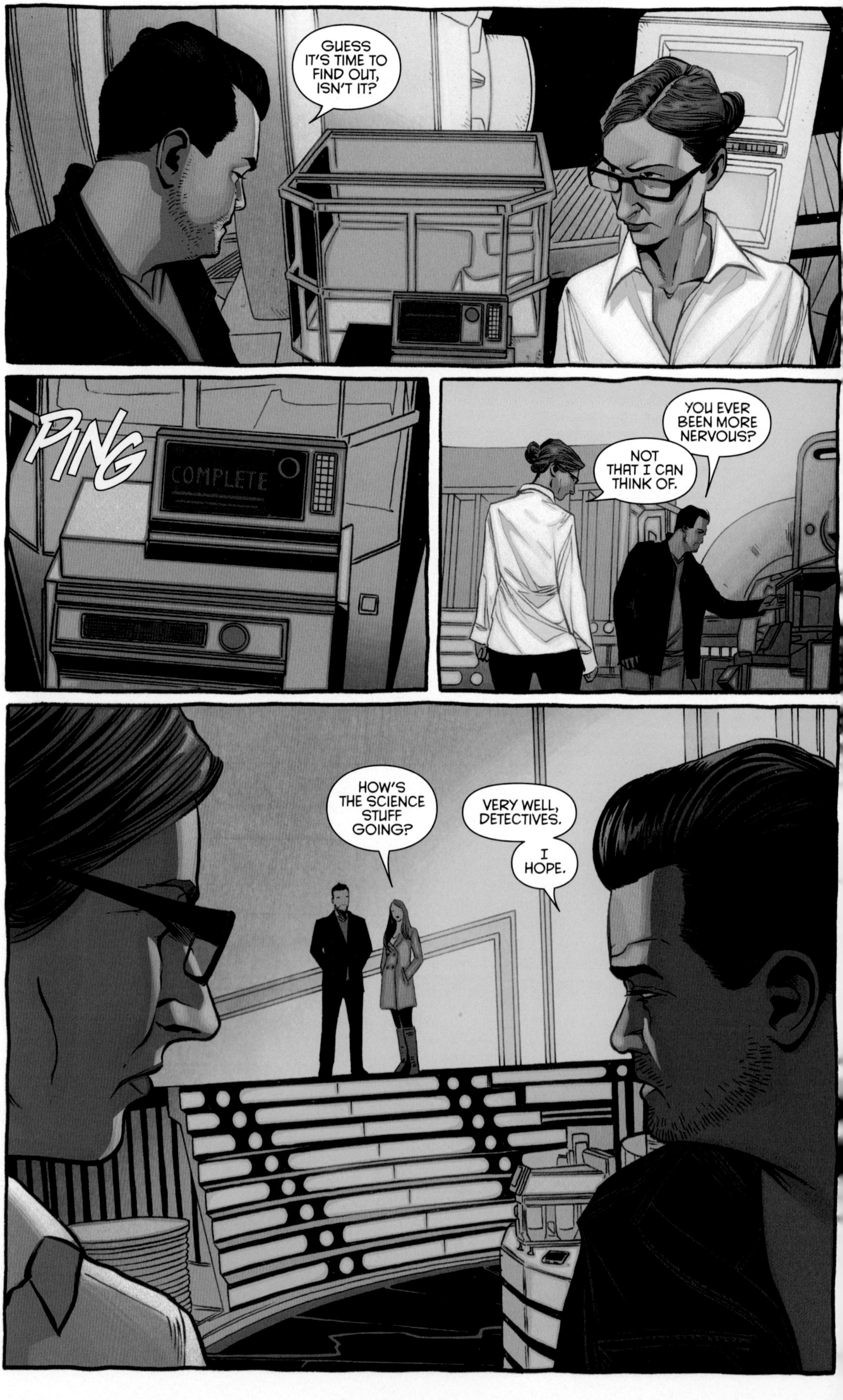
GUESS IT'S TIME TO FIND OUT, ISN'T IT?
PING
COMPLETE
YOU EVER BEEN MORE NERVOUS?
NOT THAT I CAN THINK OF.
HOW'S THE SCIENCE STUFF GOING?
VERY WELL, DETECTIVES.
I HOPE.

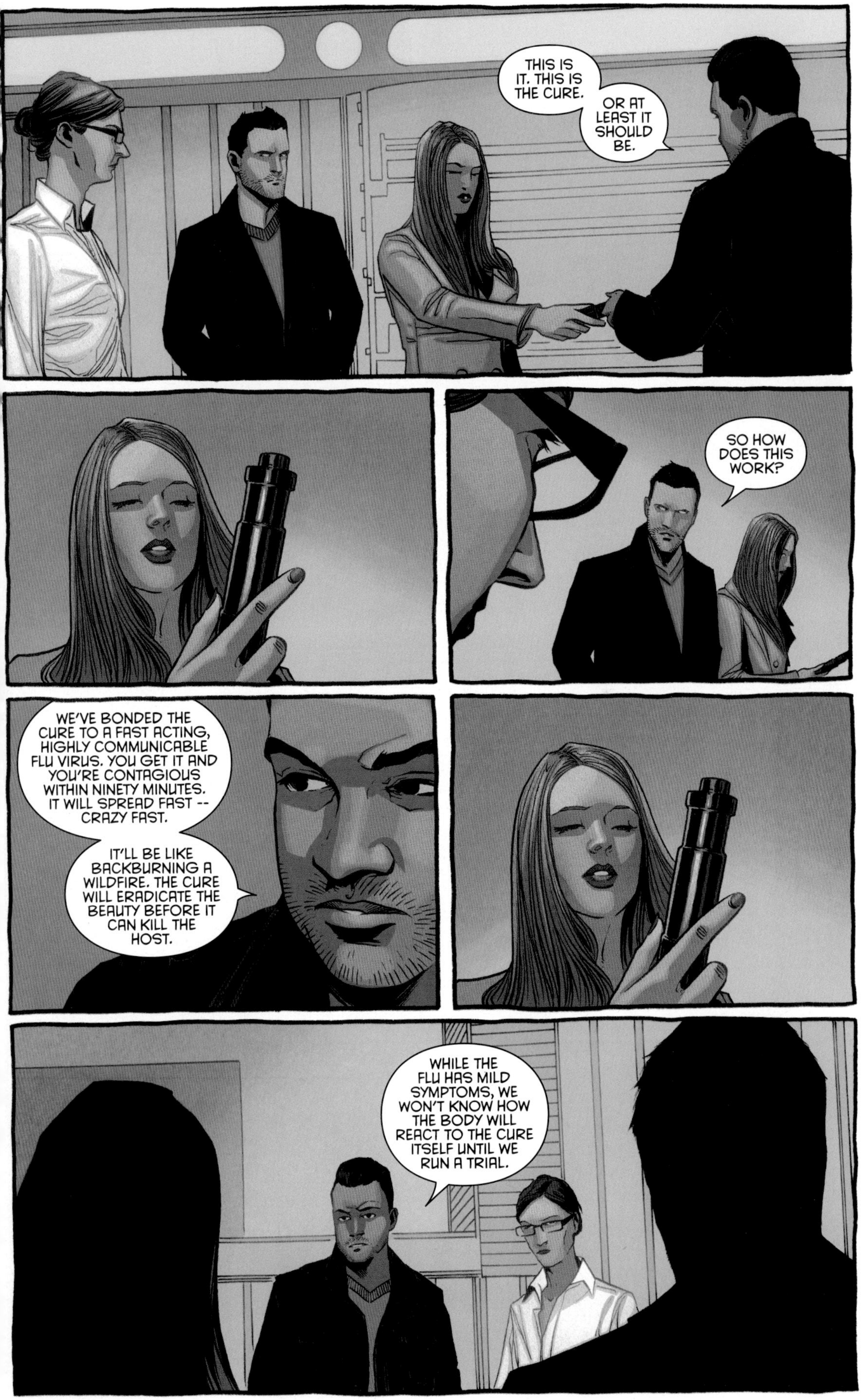
THIS IS IT. THIS IS THE CURE.
OR AT LEAST IT SHOULD BE.
SO HOW DOES THIS WORK?
WE'VE BONDED THE CURE TO A FAST ACTING, HIGHLY COMMUNICABLE FLU VIRUS. YOU GET IT AND YOU'RE CONTAGIOUS WITHIN NINETY MINUTES. IT WILL SPREAD FAST -- CRAZY FAST.
IT'LL BE LIKE BACKBURNING A WILDFIRE. THE CURE WILL ERADICATE THE BEAUTY BEFORE IT CAN KILL THE HOST.
WHILE THE FLU HAS MILD SYMPTOMS, WE WON'T KNOW HOW THE BODY WILL REACT TO THE CURE ITSELF UNTIL WE RUN A TRIAL.

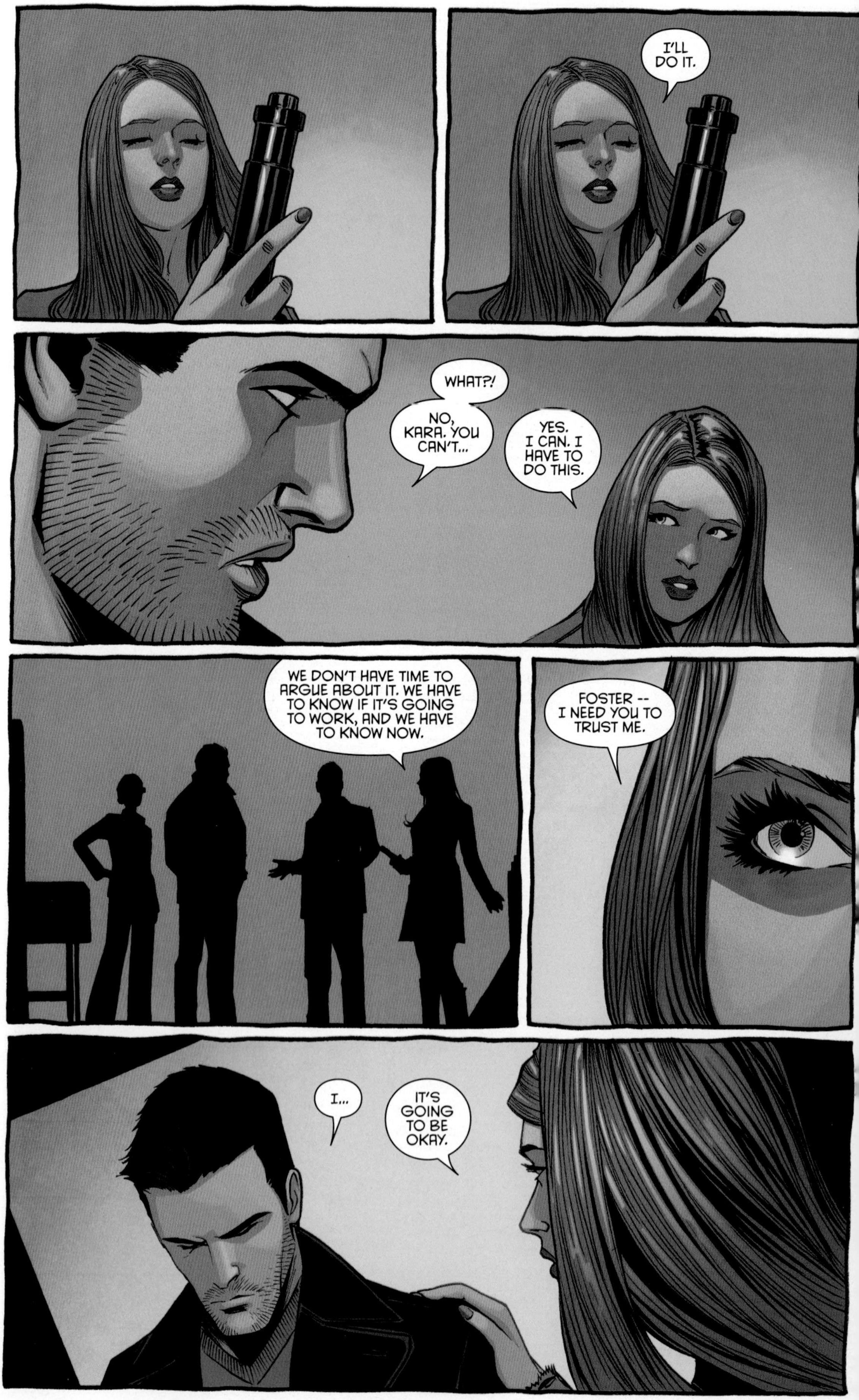
I'LL DO IT.
WHAT?!
NO, KARA. YOU CAN'T...
YES. I CAN. I HAVE TO DO THIS.
WE DON'T HAVE TIME TO ARGUE ABOUT IT. WE HAVE TO KNOW IF IT'S GOING TO WORK, AND WE HAVE TO KNOW NOW.
FOSTER -- I NEED YOU TO TRUST ME.
I...
IT'S GOING TO BE OKAY.

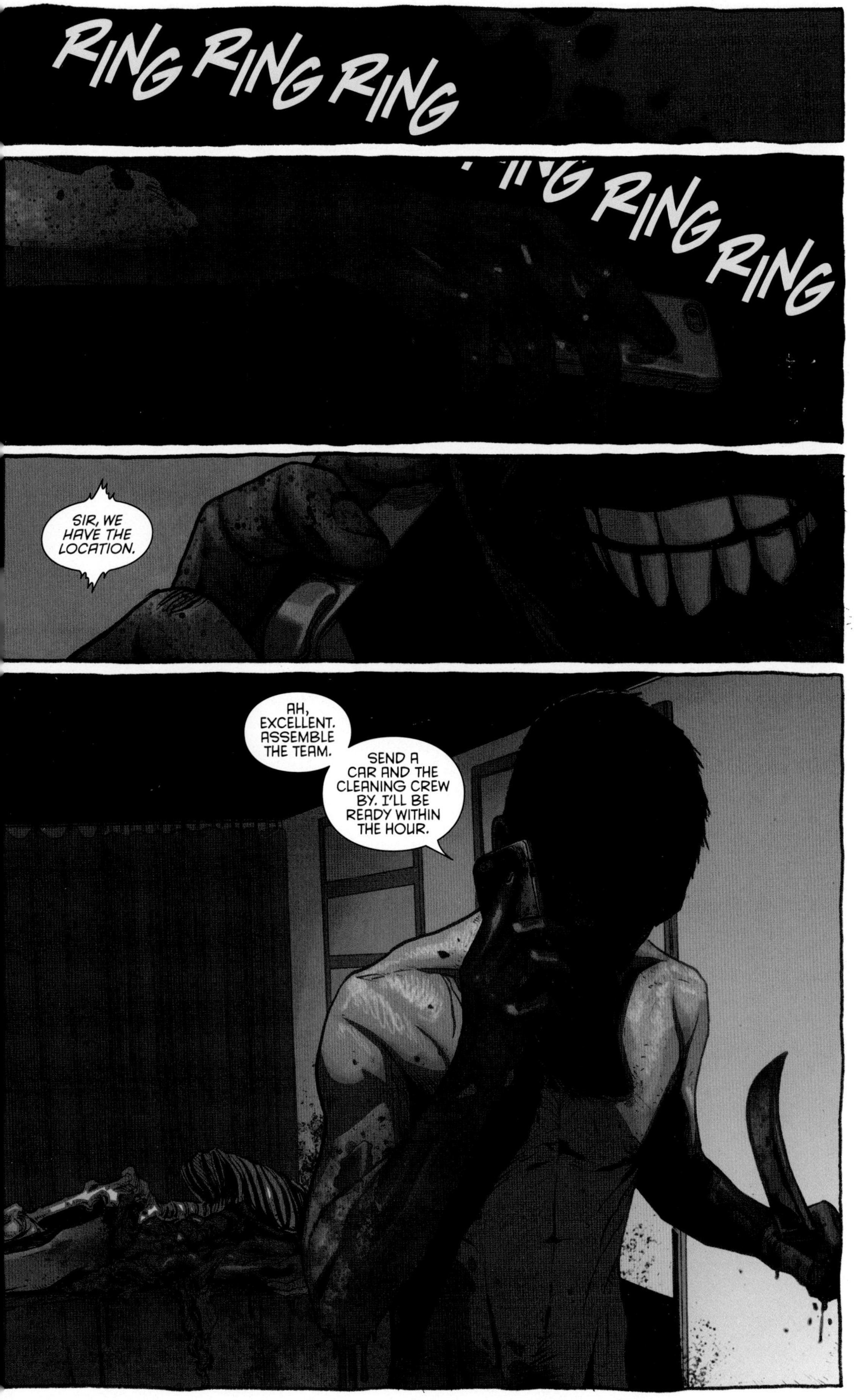
RING RING RING
RING RING RING
SIR, WE HAVE THE LOCATION.
AH, EXCELLENT. ASSEMBLE THE TEAM.
SEND A CAR AND THE CLEANING CREW BY. I'LL BE READY WITHIN THE HOUR.

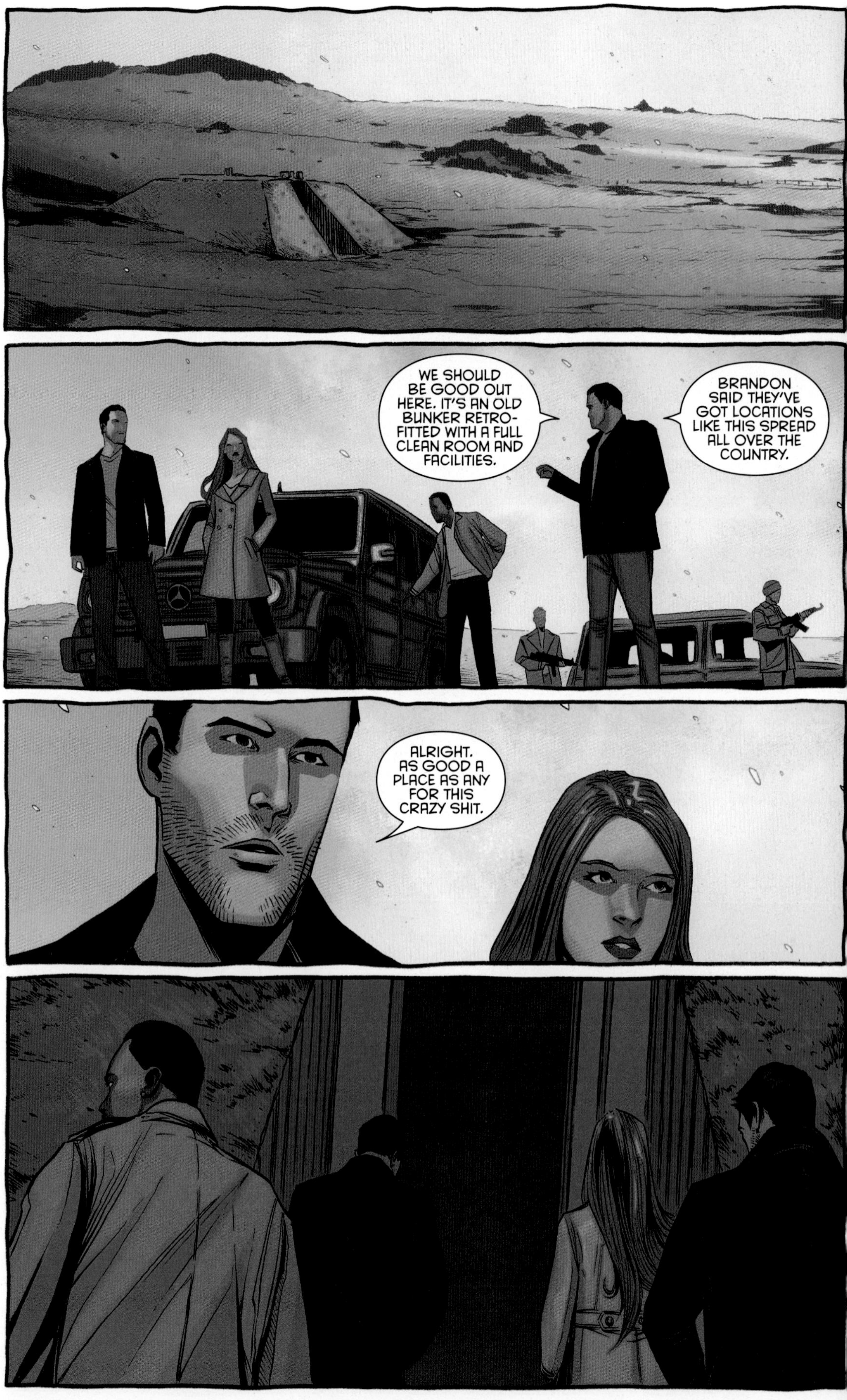

WE SHOULD BE GOOD OUT HERE. IT'S AN OLD BUNKER RETRO-FITTED WITH A FULL CLEAN ROOM AND FACILITIES.
BRANDON SAID THEY'VE GOT LOCATIONS LIKE THIS SPREAD ALL OVER THE COUNTRY.
ALRIGHT. AS GOOD A PLACE AS ANY FOR THIS CRAZY SHIT.

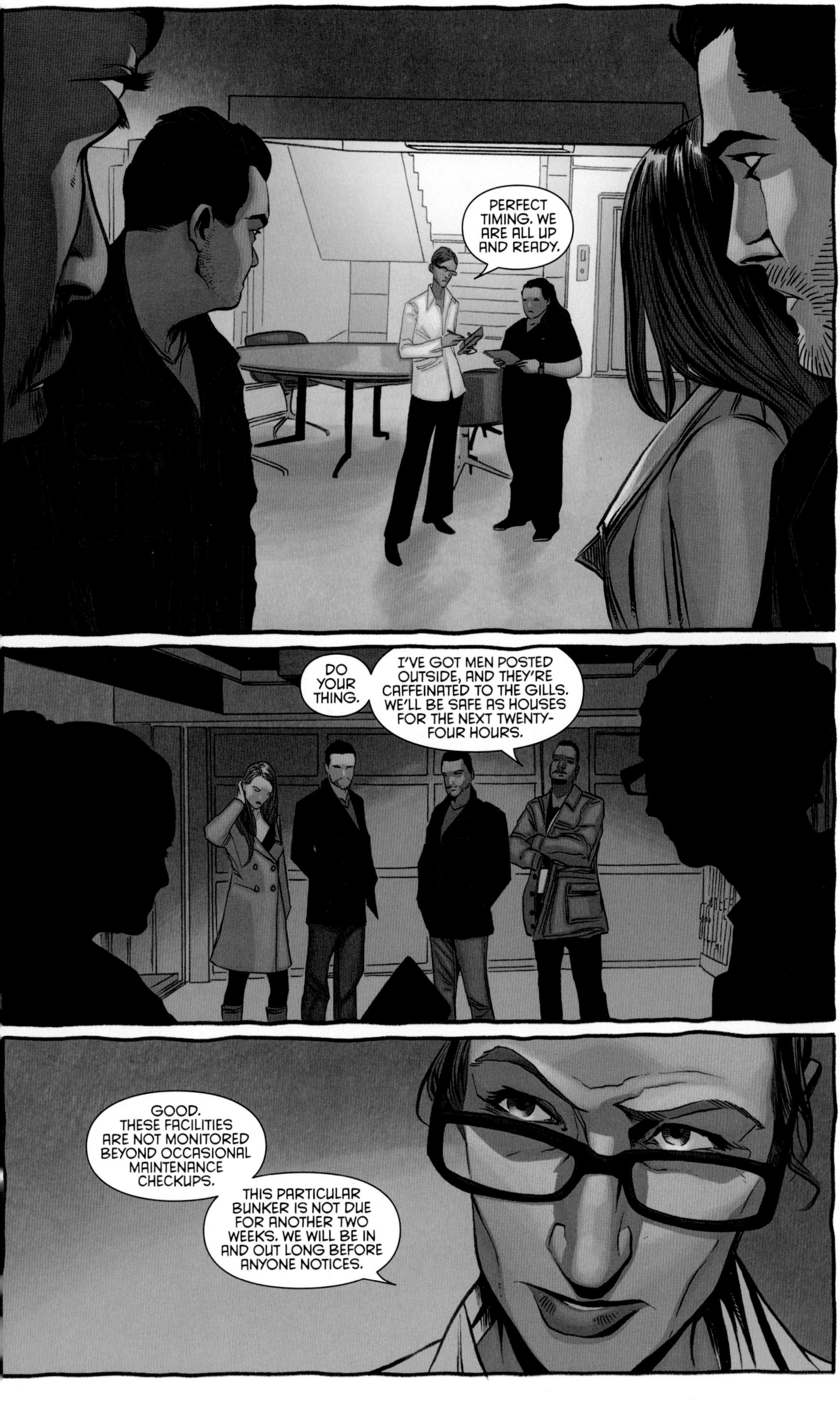

PERFECT TIMING. WE ARE ALL UP AND READY.
DO YOUR THING.
I'VE GOT MEN POSTED OUTSIDE, AND THEY'RE CAFFEINATED TO THE GILLS. WE'LL BE SAFE AS HOUSES FOR THE NEXT TWENTY-FOUR HOURS.
GOOD. THESE FACILITIES ARE NOT MONITORED BEYOND OCCASIONAL MAINTENANCE CHECKUPS.
THIS PARTICULAR BUNKER IS NOT DUE FOR ANOTHER TWO WEEKS. WE WILL BE IN AND OUT LONG BEFORE ANYONE NOTICES.

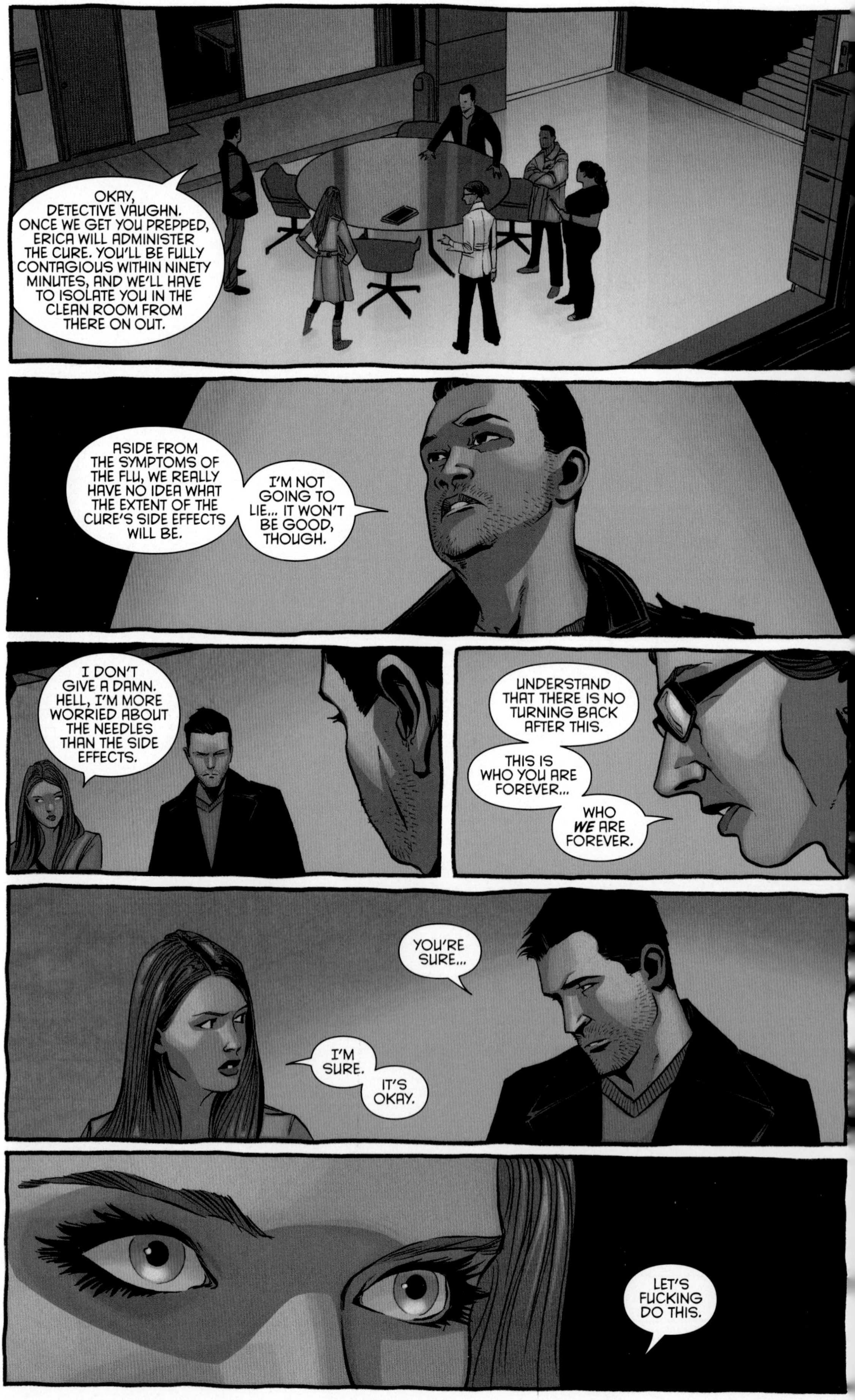
OKAY, DETECTIVE VAUGHN. ONCE WE GET YOU PREPPED, ERICA WILL ADMINISTER THE CURE. YOU'LL BE FULLY CONTAGIOUS WITHIN NINETY MINUTES, AND WE'LL HAVE TO ISOLATE YOU IN THE CLEAN ROOM FROM THERE ON OUT.
ASIDE FROM THE SYMPTOMS OF THE FLU, WE REALLY HAVE NO IDEA WHAT THE EXTENT OF THE CURE'S SIDE EFFECTS WILL BE.
I'M NOT GOING TO LIE... IT WON'T BE GOOD, THOUGH.
I DON'T GIVE A DAMN. HELL, I'M MORE WORRIED ABOUT THE NEEDLES THAN THE SIDE EFFECTS.
UNDERSTAND THAT THERE IS NO TURNING BACK AFTER THIS.
THIS IS WHO YOU ARE FOREVER...
WHO *WE* ARE FOREVER.
YOU'RE SURE...
I'M SURE.
IT'S OKAY.
LET'S FUCKING DO THIS.

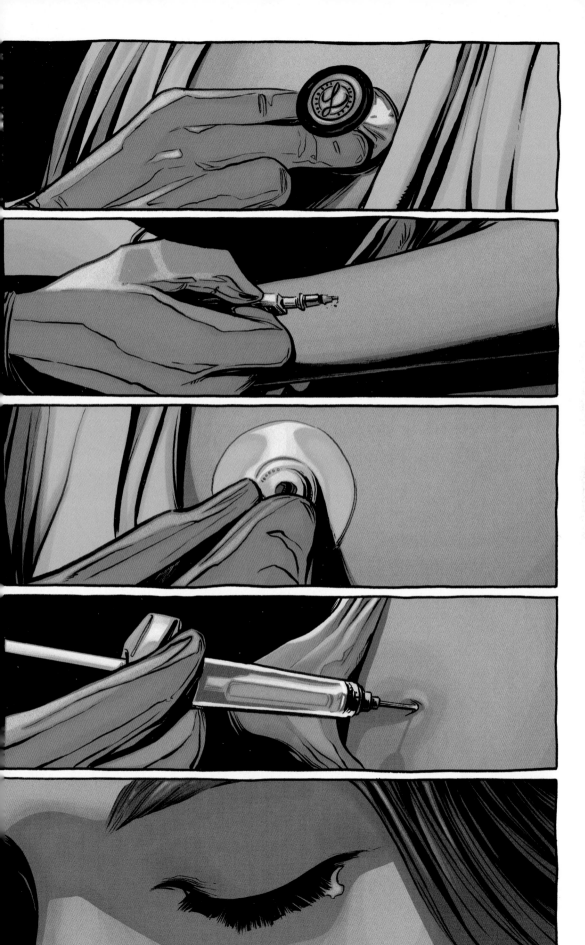

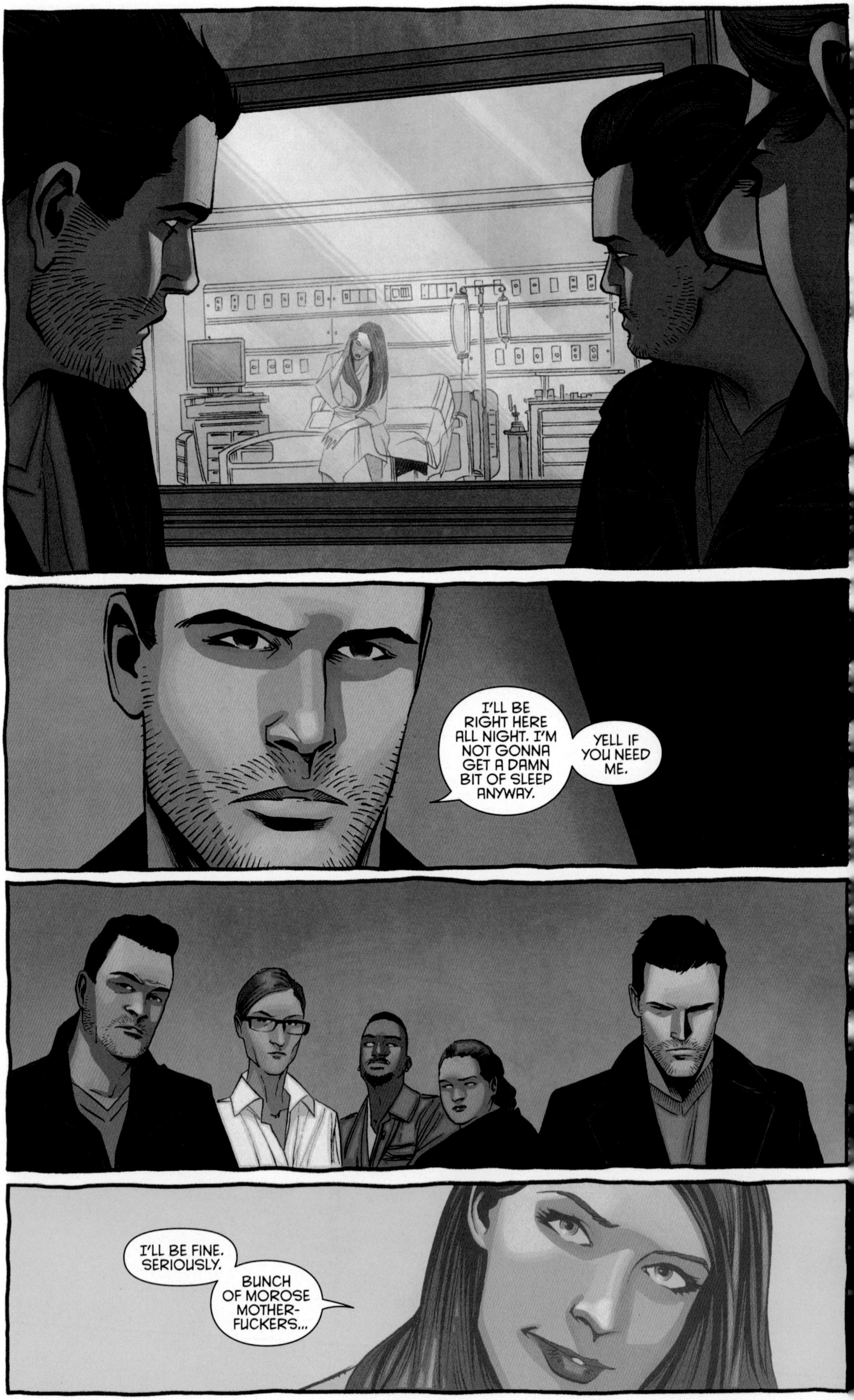
I'LL BE RIGHT HERE ALL NIGHT. I'M NOT GONNA GET A DAMN BIT OF SLEEP ANYWAY.
YELL IF YOU NEED ME.
I'LL BE FINE. SERIOUSLY.
BUNCH OF MOROSE MOTHER-FUCKERS...

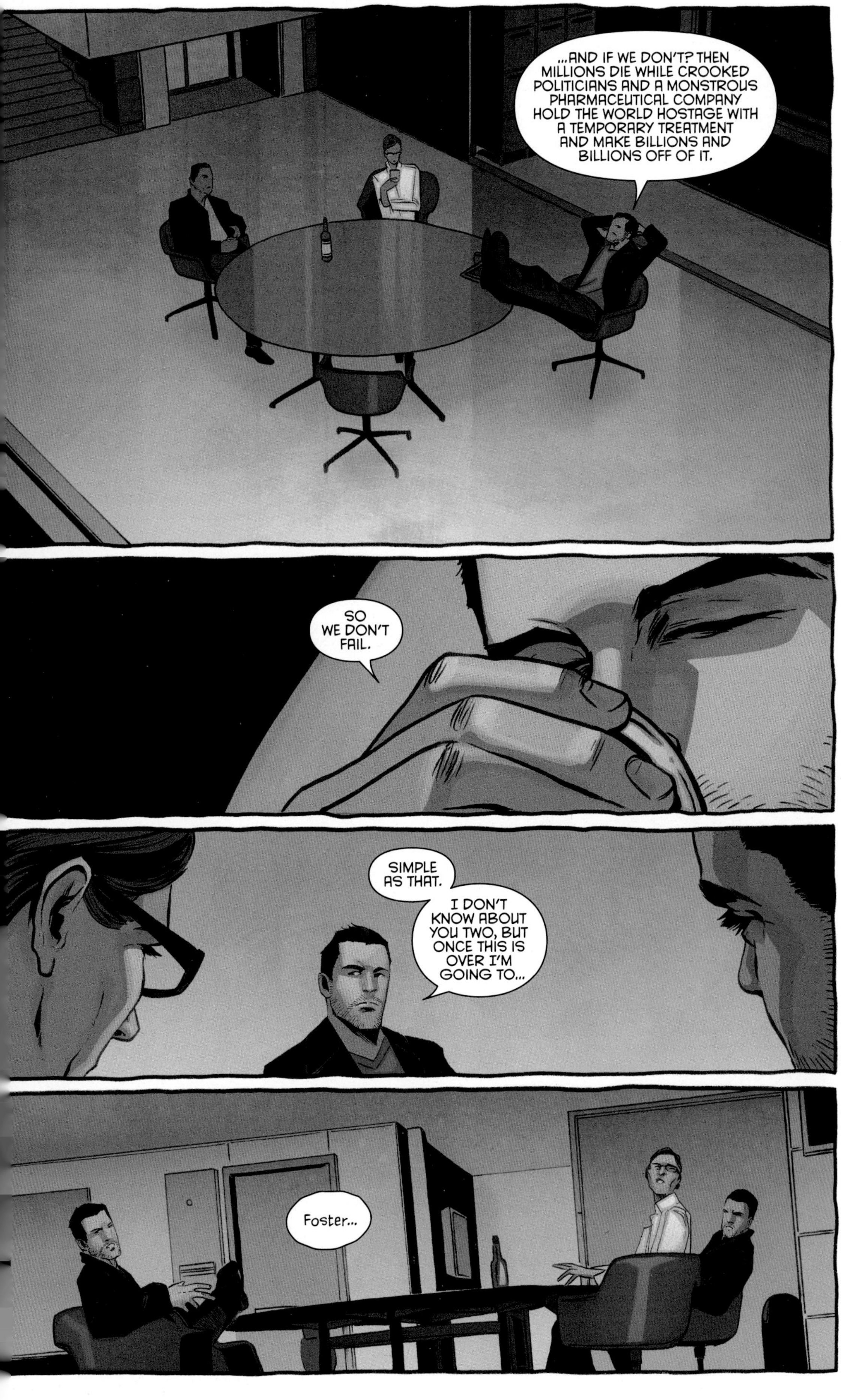
...AND IF WE DON'T? THEN MILLIONS DIE WHILE CROOKED POLITICIANS AND A MONSTROUS PHARMACEUTICAL COMPANY HOLD THE WORLD HOSTAGE WITH A TEMPORARY TREATMENT AND MAKE BILLIONS AND BILLIONS OFF OF IT.
SO WE DON'T FAIL.
SIMPLE AS THAT.
I DON'T KNOW ABOUT YOU TWO, BUT ONCE THIS IS OVER I'M GOING TO...
Foster...

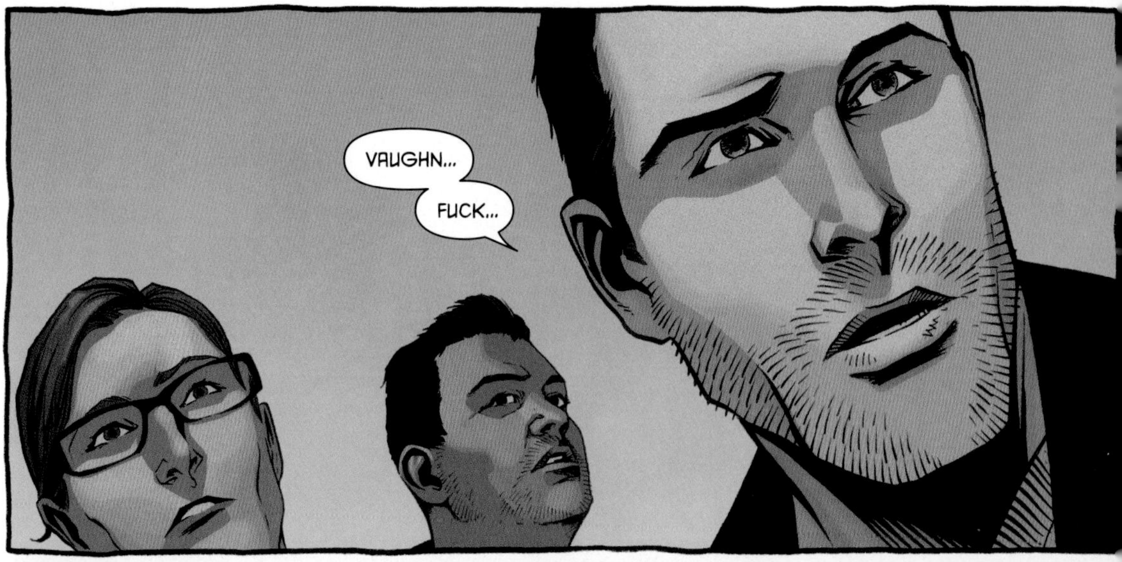
VAUGHN...
FUCK...
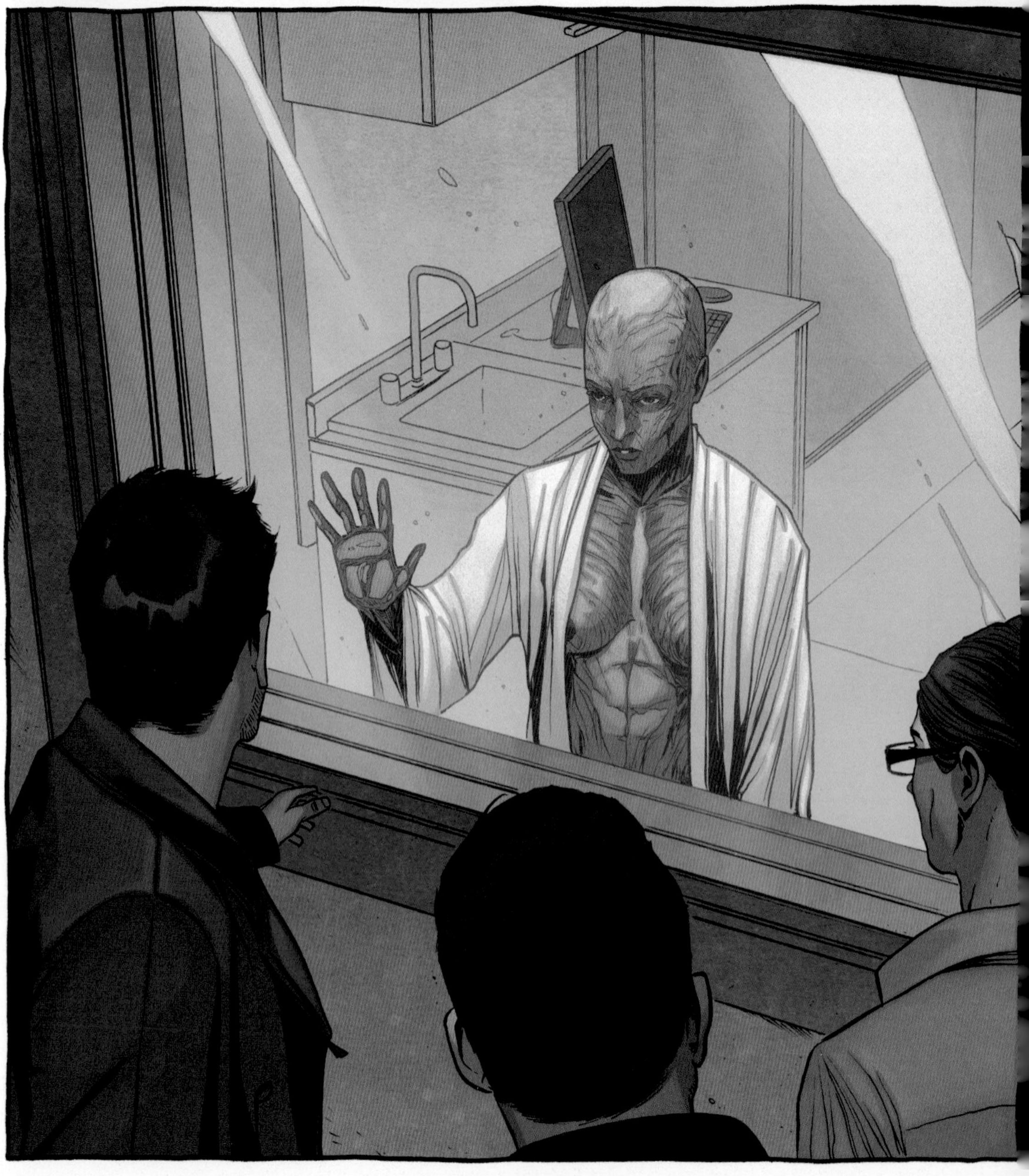

CHAPTER

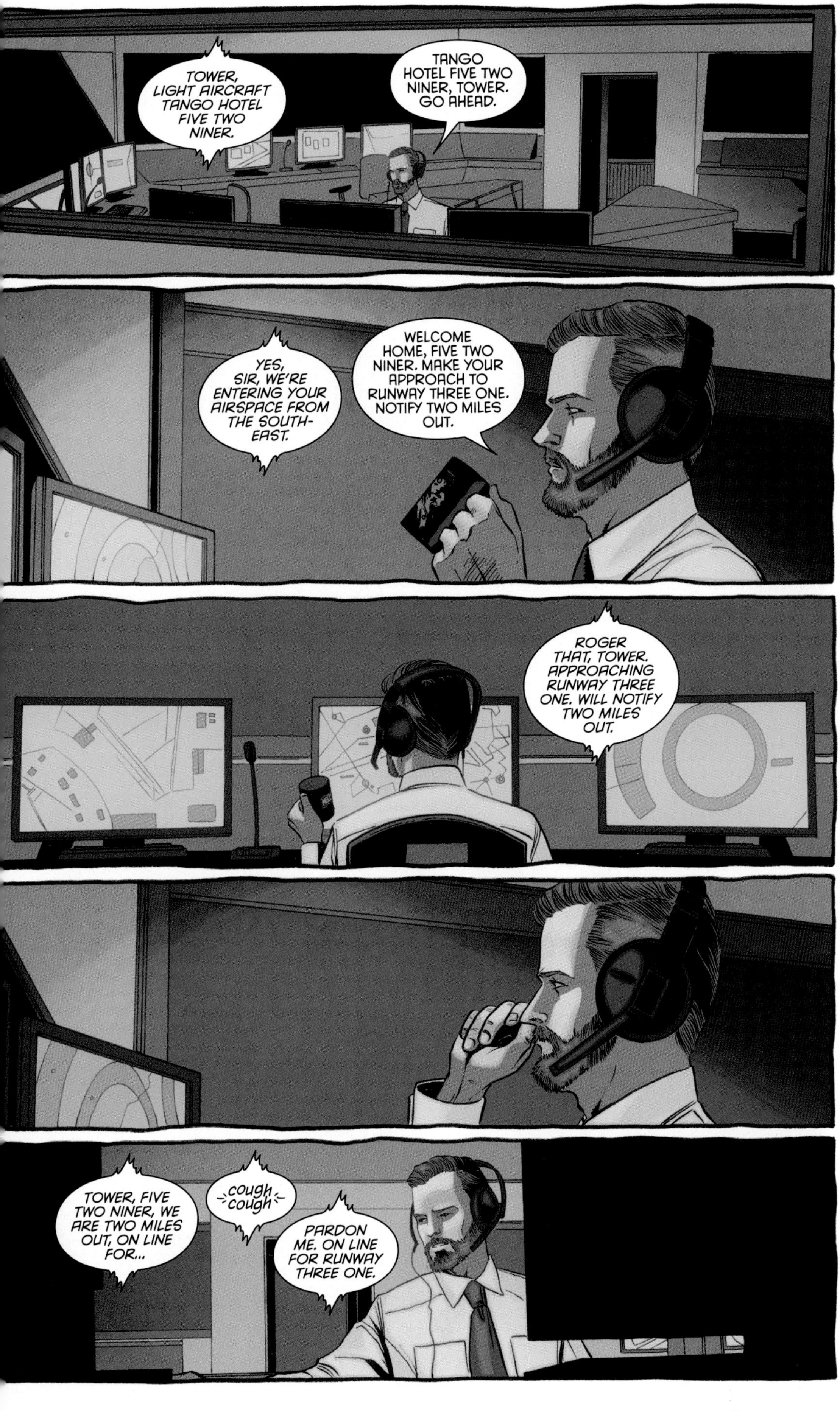
TOWER, LIGHT AIRCRAFT TANGO HOTEL FIVE TWO NINER.
TANGO HOTEL FIVE TWO NINER, TOWER. GO AHEAD.
YES, SIR, WE'RE ENTERING YOUR AIRSPACE FROM THE SOUTH-EAST.
WELCOME HOME, FIVE TWO NINER. MAKE YOUR APPROACH TO RUNWAY THREE ONE. NOTIFY TWO MILES OUT.
ROGER THAT, TOWER. APPROACHING RUNWAY THREE ONE. WILL NOTIFY TWO MILES OUT.
TOWER, FIVE TWO NINER, WE ARE TWO MILES OUT, ON LINE FOR...
cough cough
PARDON ME. ON LINE FOR RUNWAY THREE ONE.

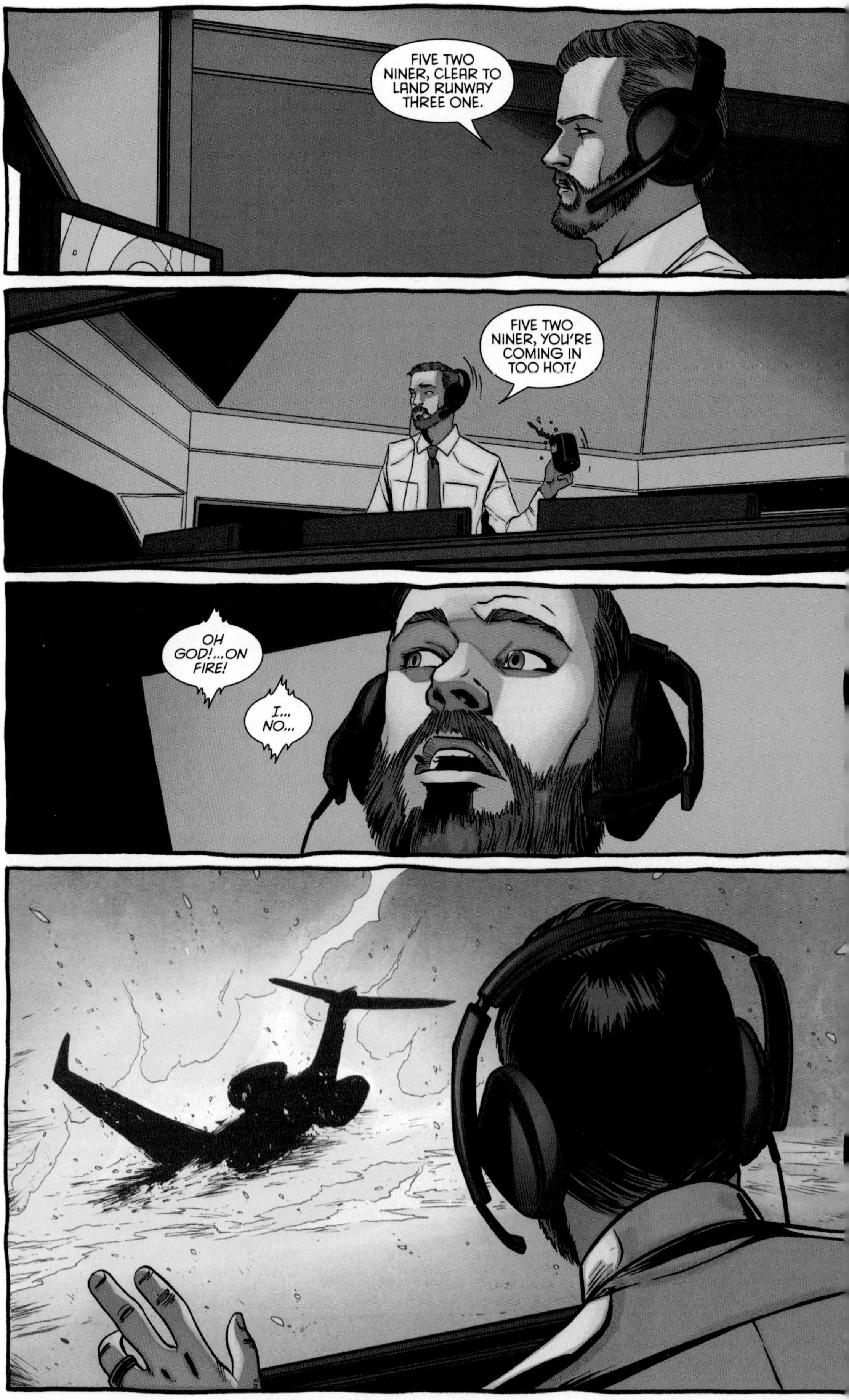
FIVE TWO NINER, CLEAR TO LAND RUNWAY THREE ONE.
FIVE TWO NINER, YOU'RE COMING IN TOO HOT!
OH GOD!...ON FIRE!
I... NO...

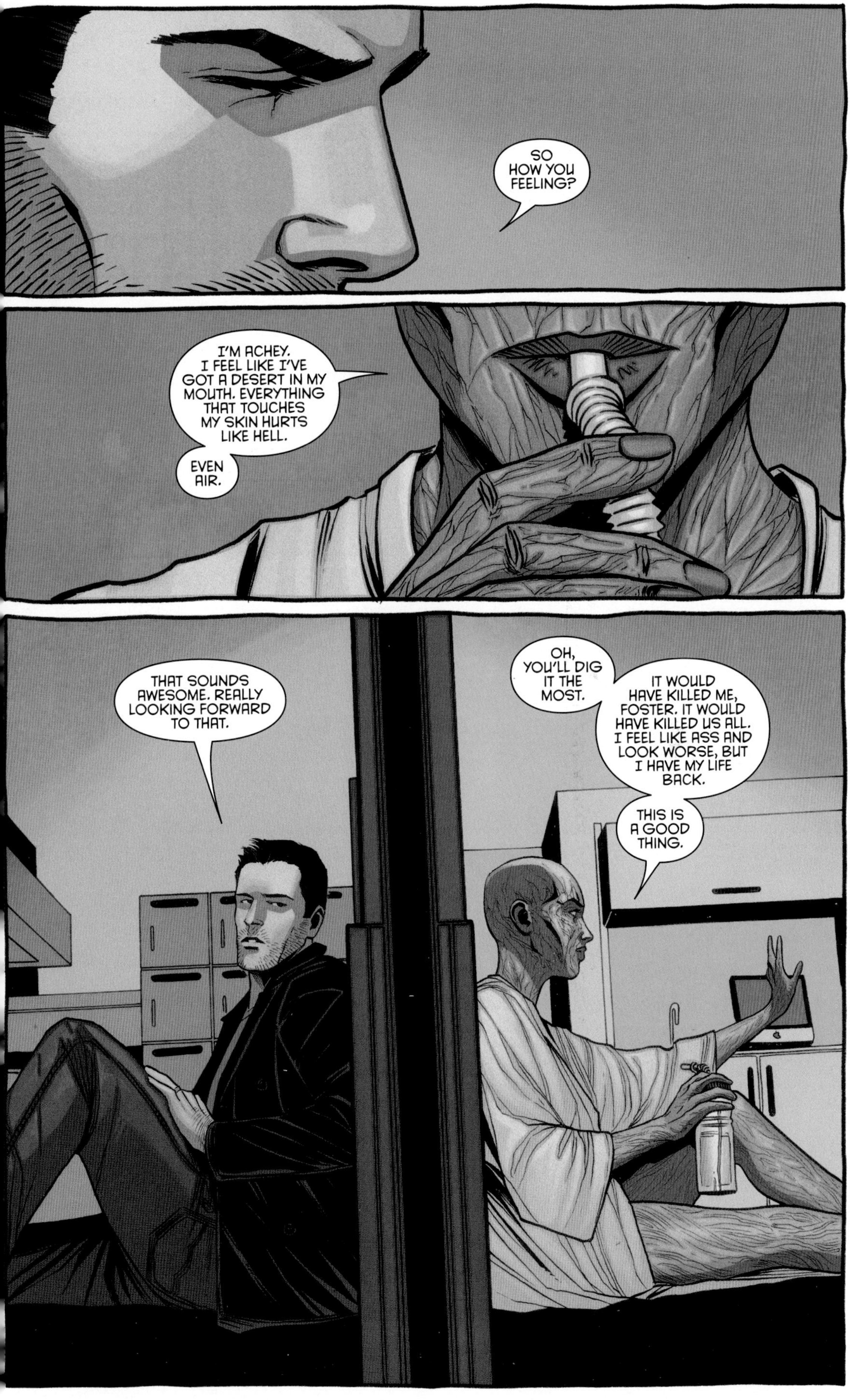
SO HOW YOU FEELING?
I'M ACHEY. I FEEL LIKE I'VE GOT A DESERT IN MY MOUTH. EVERYTHING THAT TOUCHES MY SKIN HURTS LIKE HELL.
EVEN AIR.
THAT SOUNDS AWESOME. REALLY LOOKING FORWARD TO THAT.
OH, YOU'LL DIG IT THE MOST.
IT WOULD HAVE KILLED ME, FOSTER. IT WOULD HAVE KILLED US ALL. I FEEL LIKE ASS AND LOOK WORSE, BUT I HAVE MY LIFE BACK.
THIS IS A GOOD THING.

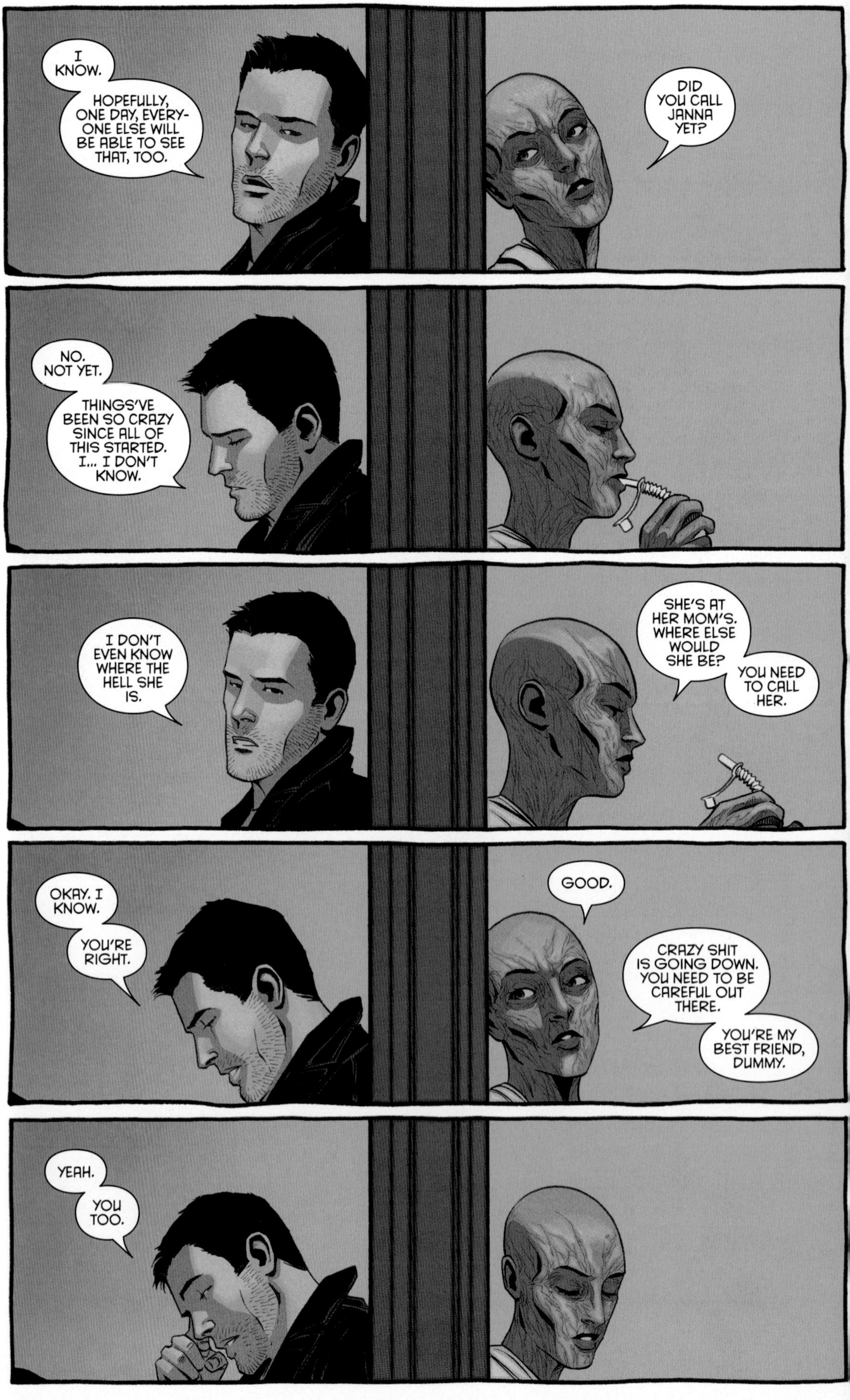
I KNOW.
HOPEFULLY, ONE DAY, EVERY-ONE ELSE WILL BE ABLE TO SEE THAT, TOO.
DID YOU CALL JANNA YET?
NO. NOT YET.
THINGS'VE BEEN SO CRAZY SINCE ALL OF THIS STARTED. I... I DON'T KNOW.
I DON'T EVEN KNOW WHERE THE HELL SHE IS.
SHE'S AT HER MOM'S. WHERE ELSE WOULD SHE BE?
YOU NEED TO CALL HER.
OKAY. I KNOW.
YOU'RE RIGHT.
GOOD.
CRAZY SHIT IS GOING DOWN. YOU NEED TO BE CAREFUL OUT THERE.
YOU'RE MY BEST FRIEND, DUMMY.
YEAH.
YOU TOO.

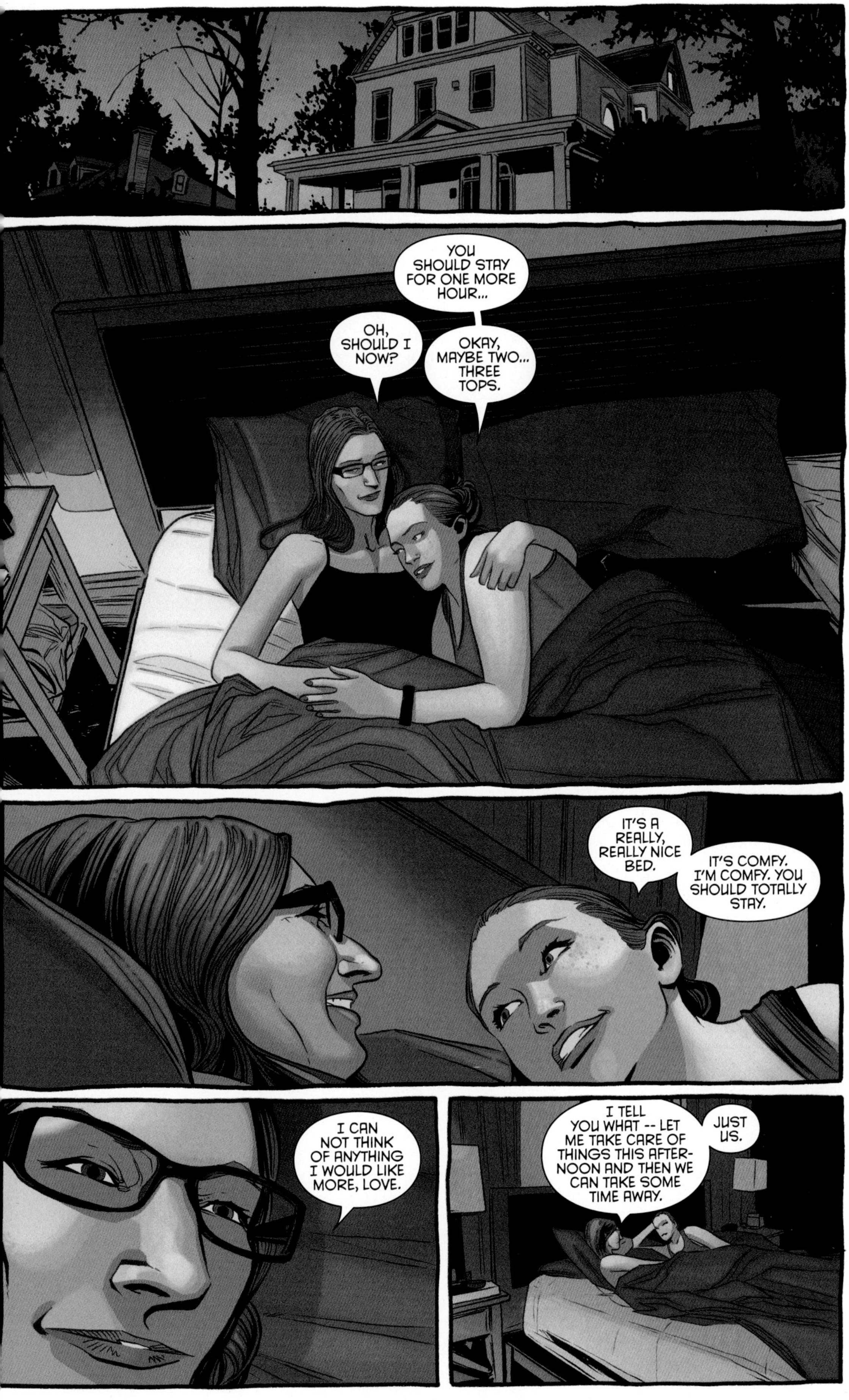
YOU SHOULD STAY FOR ONE MORE HOUR...
OH, SHOULD I NOW?
OKAY, MAYBE TWO... THREE TOPS.
IT'S A REALLY, REALLY NICE BED.
IT'S COMFY. I'M COMFY. YOU SHOULD TOTALLY STAY.
I CAN NOT THINK OF ANYTHING I WOULD LIKE MORE, LOVE.
I TELL YOU WHAT -- LET ME TAKE CARE OF THINGS THIS AFTER-NOON AND THEN WE CAN TAKE SOME TIME AWAY.
JUST US.

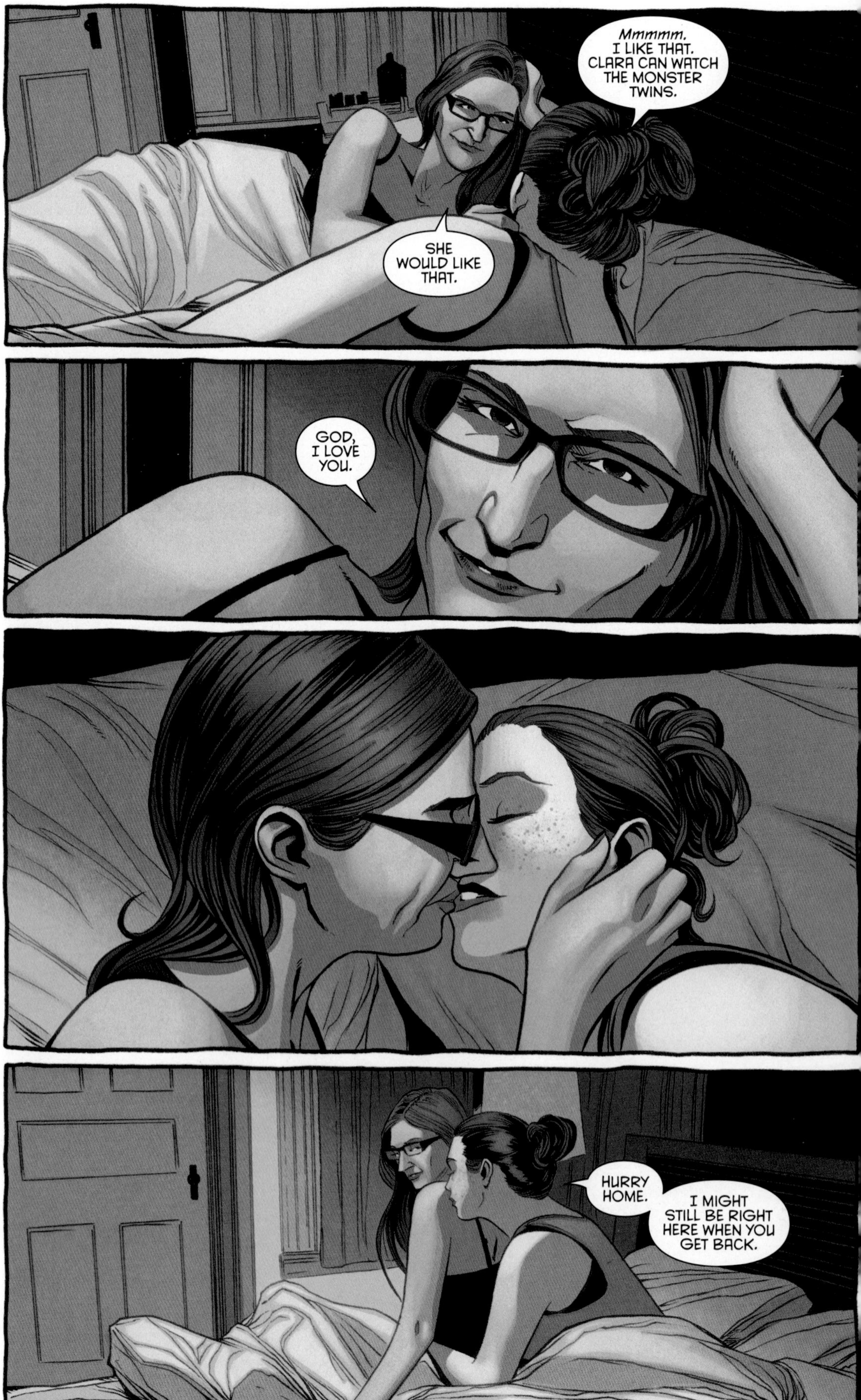
Mmmmm. I LIKE THAT. CLARA CAN WATCH THE MONSTER TWINS.
SHE WOULD LIKE THAT.
GOD, I LOVE YOU.
HURRY HOME.
I MIGHT STILL BE RIGHT HERE WHEN YOU GET BACK.

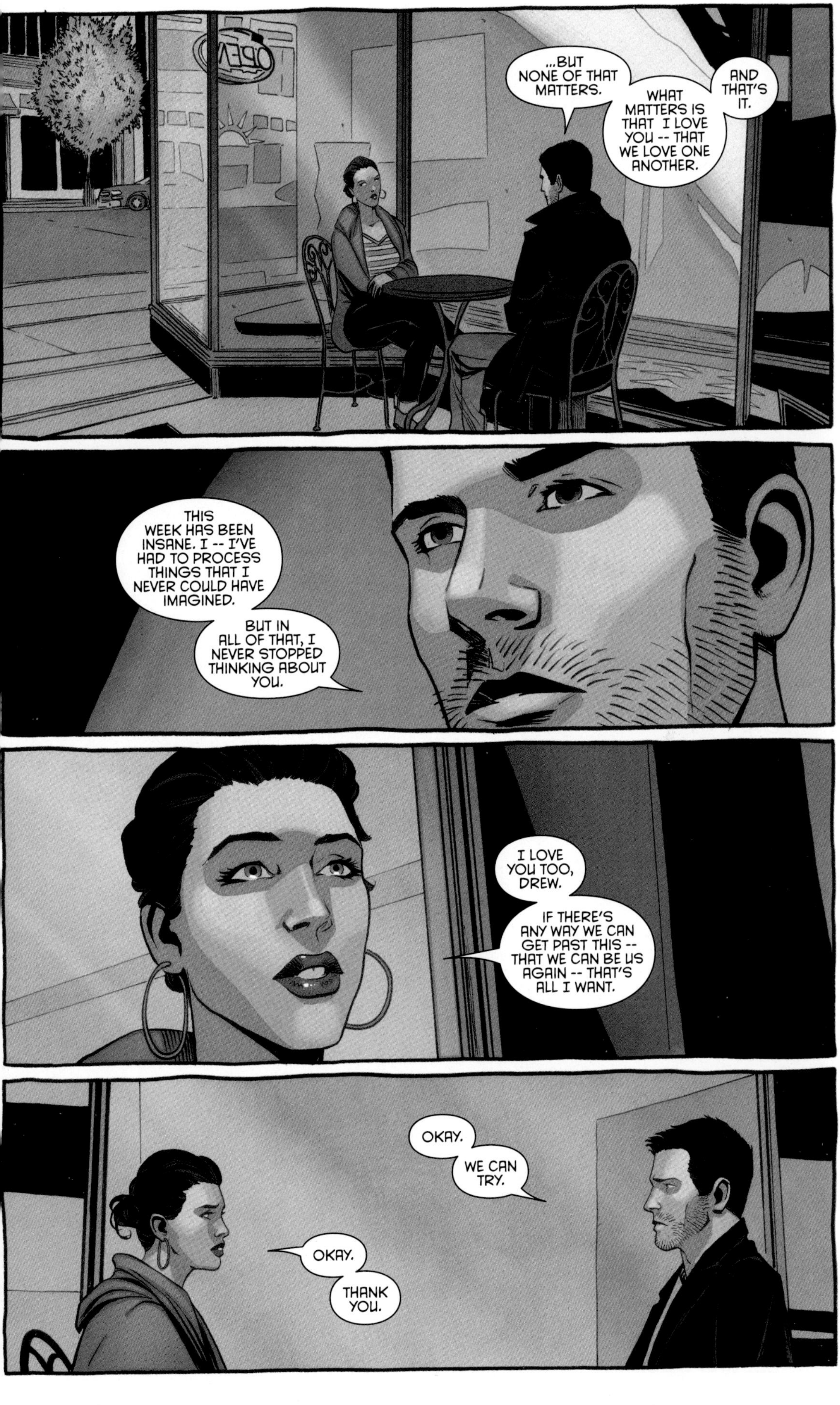
...BUT NONE OF THAT MATTERS.
WHAT MATTERS IS THAT I LOVE YOU -- THAT WE LOVE ONE ANOTHER.
AND THAT'S IT.
THIS WEEK HAS BEEN INSANE. I -- I'VE HAD TO PROCESS THINGS THAT I NEVER COULD HAVE IMAGINED.
BUT IN ALL OF THAT, I NEVER STOPPED THINKING ABOUT YOU.
I LOVE YOU TOO, DREW.
IF THERE'S ANY WAY WE CAN GET PAST THIS -- THAT WE CAN BE US AGAIN -- THAT'S ALL I WANT.
OKAY.
WE CAN TRY.
OKAY.
THANK YOU.

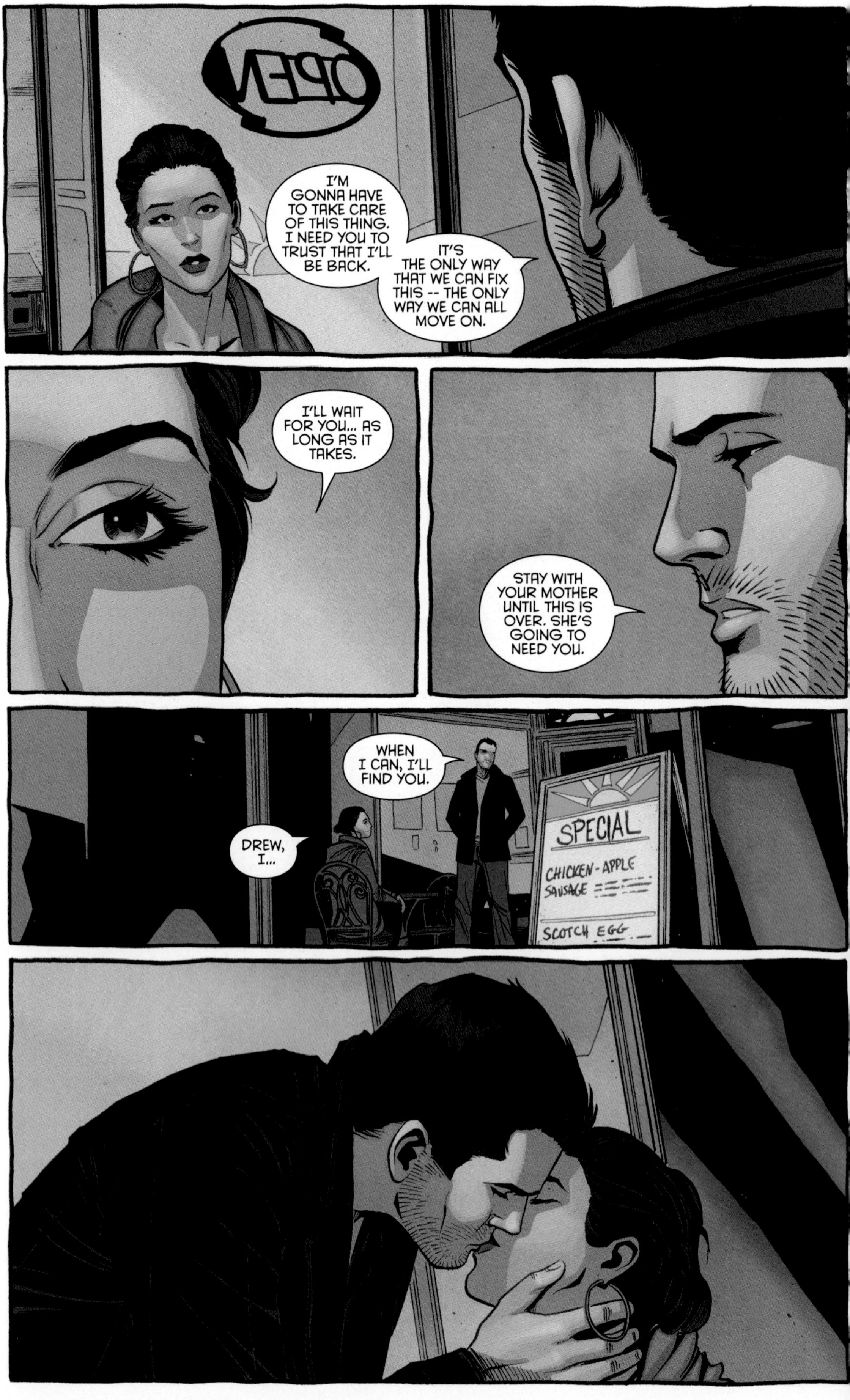
OPEN
I'M GONNA HAVE TO TAKE CARE OF THIS THING. I NEED YOU TO TRUST THAT I'LL BE BACK.
IT'S THE ONLY WAY THAT WE CAN FIX THIS -- THE ONLY WAY WE CAN ALL MOVE ON.
I'LL WAIT FOR YOU... AS LONG AS IT TAKES.
STAY WITH YOUR MOTHER UNTIL THIS IS OVER. SHE'S GOING TO NEED YOU.
WHEN I CAN, I'LL FIND YOU.
DREW, I...
SPECIAL
CHICKEN-APPLE SAUSAGE
SCOTCH EGG

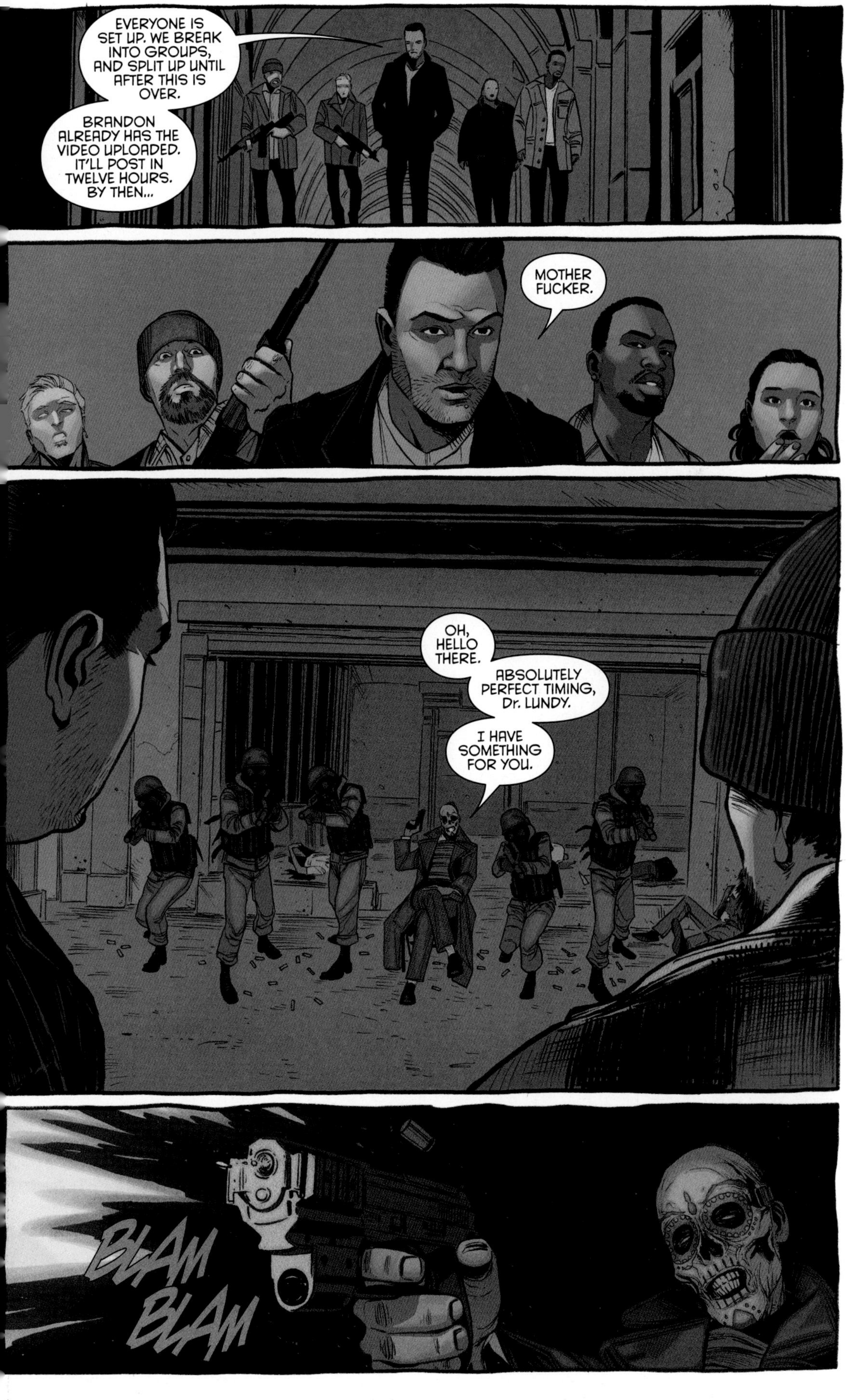
EVERYONE IS SET UP. WE BREAK INTO GROUPS, AND SPLIT UP UNTIL AFTER THIS IS OVER.
BRANDON ALREADY HAS THE VIDEO UPLOADED. IT'LL POST IN TWELVE HOURS. BY THEN...
MOTHER FUCKER.
OH, HELLO THERE.
ABSOLUTELY PERFECT TIMING, Dr. LUNDY.
I HAVE SOMETHING FOR YOU.
BLAM BLAM

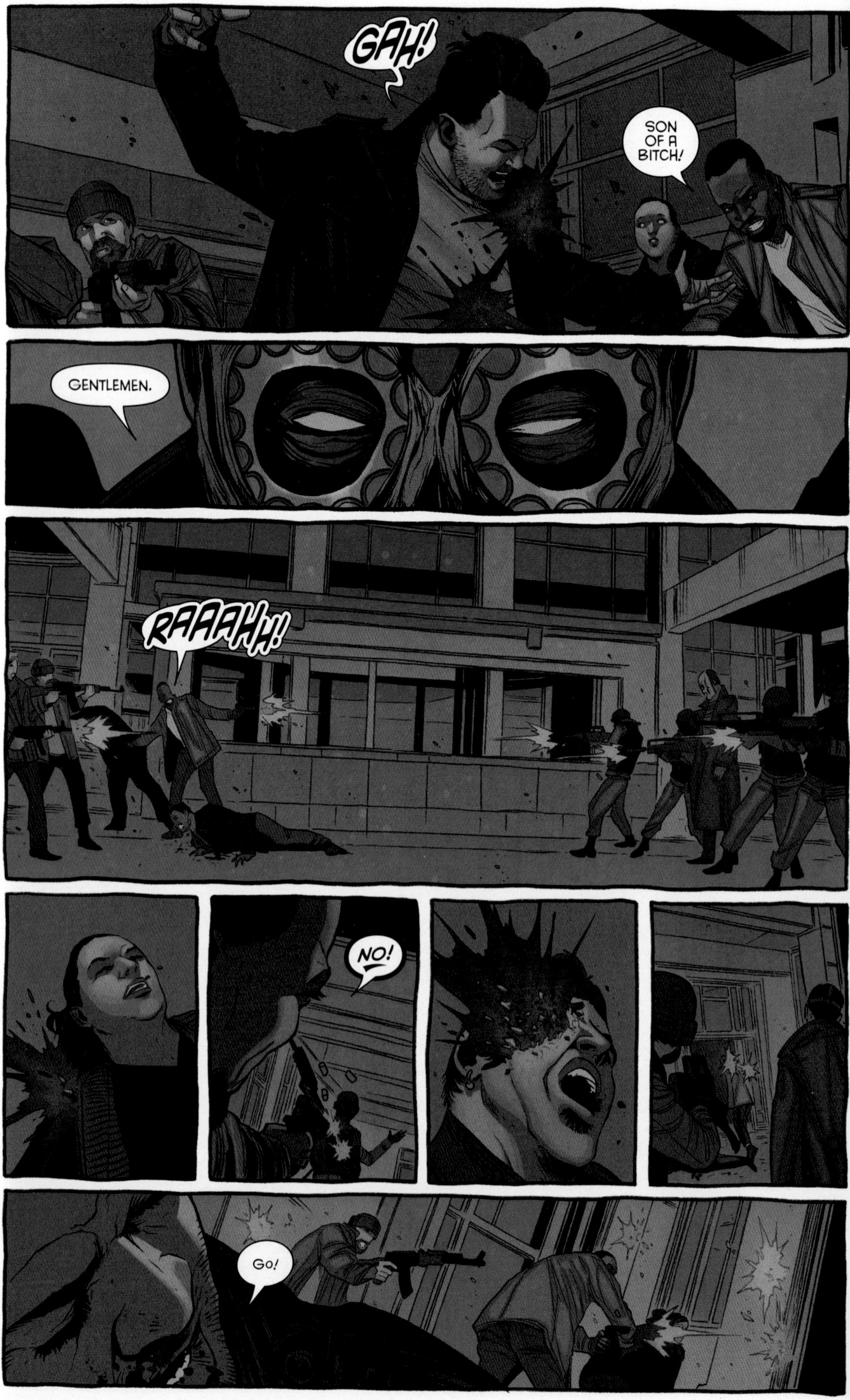
GAH!
SON OF A BITCH!
GENTLEMEN.
RAAAHH!
NO!
Go!

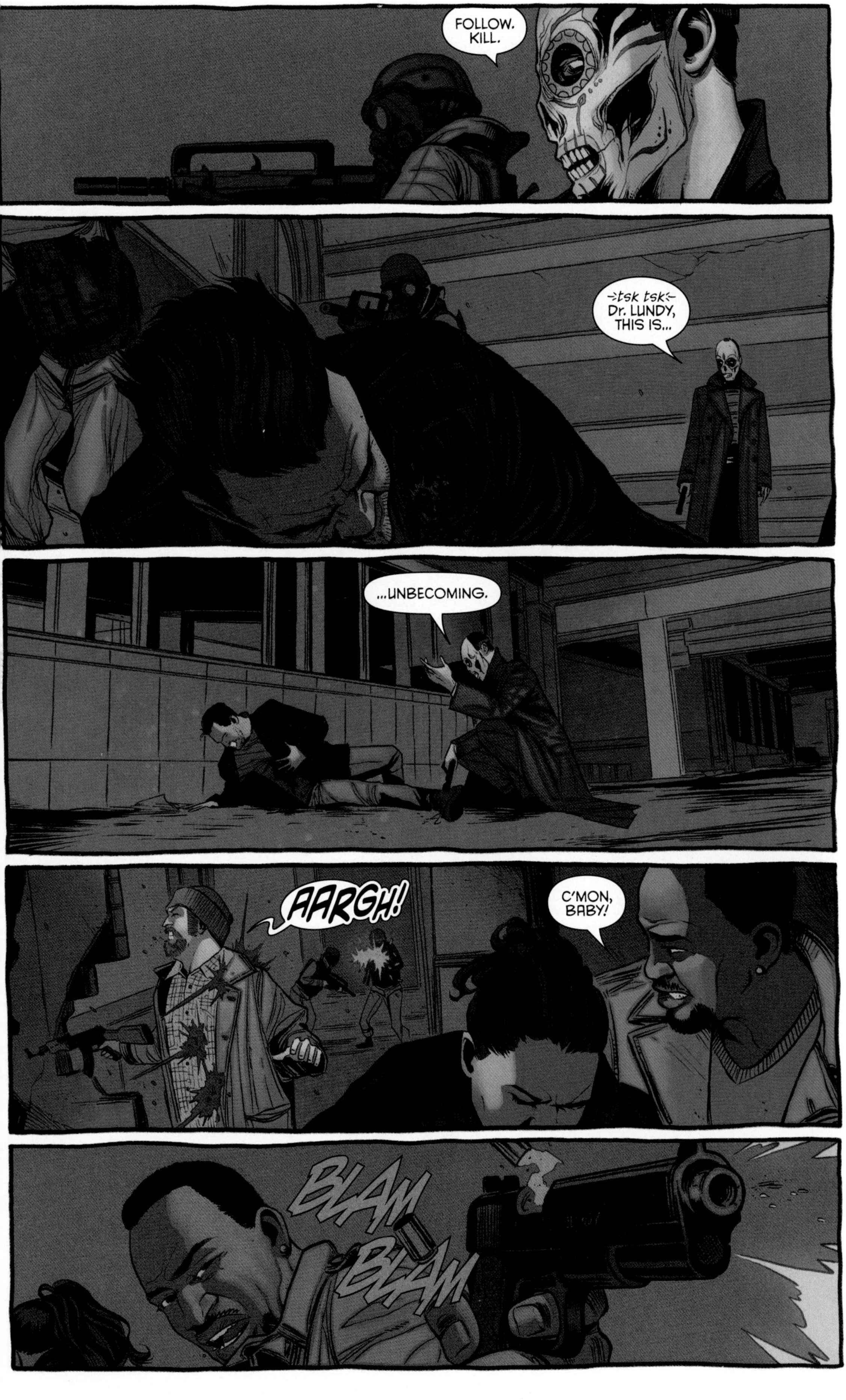

FOLLOW. KILL.
tsk tsk
Dr. LUNDY, THIS IS...
...UNBECOMING.
AARGH!
C'MON, BABY!
BLAM
BLAM

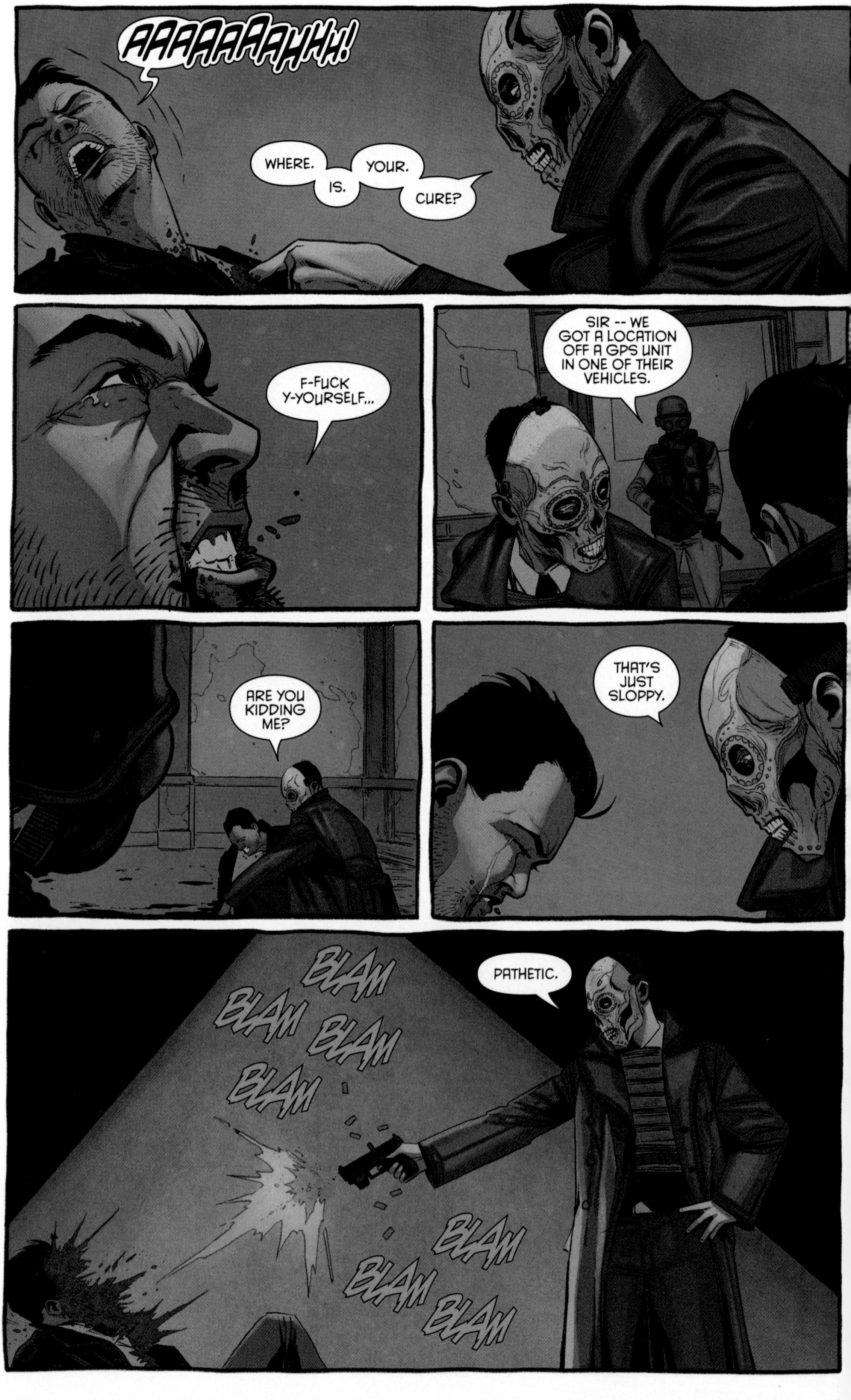
AAAAAAAAHHH!
WHERE. IS. YOUR. CURE?
F-FUCK Y-YOURSELF...
SIR -- WE GOT A LOCATION OFF A GPS UNIT IN ONE OF THEIR VEHICLES.
ARE YOU KIDDING ME?
THAT'S JUST SLOPPY.
PATHETIC.
BLAM BLAM BLAM BLAM
BLAM BLAM BLAM BLAM

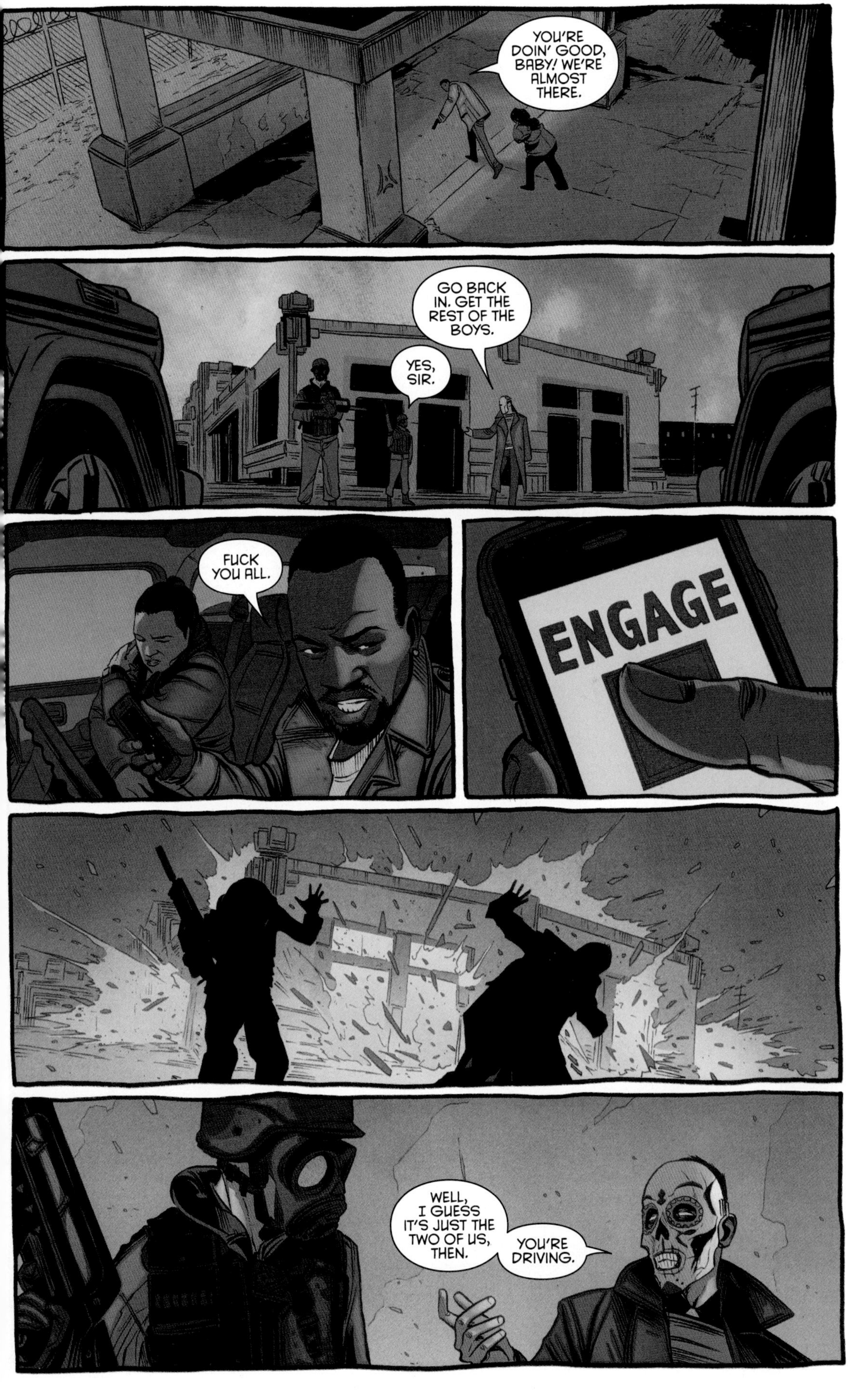
YOU'RE DOIN' GOOD, BABY! WE'RE ALMOST THERE.
GO BACK IN. GET THE REST OF THE BOYS.
YES, SIR.
FUCK YOU ALL.
ENGAGE
WELL, I GUESS IT'S JUST THE TWO OF US, THEN.
YOU'RE DRIVING.

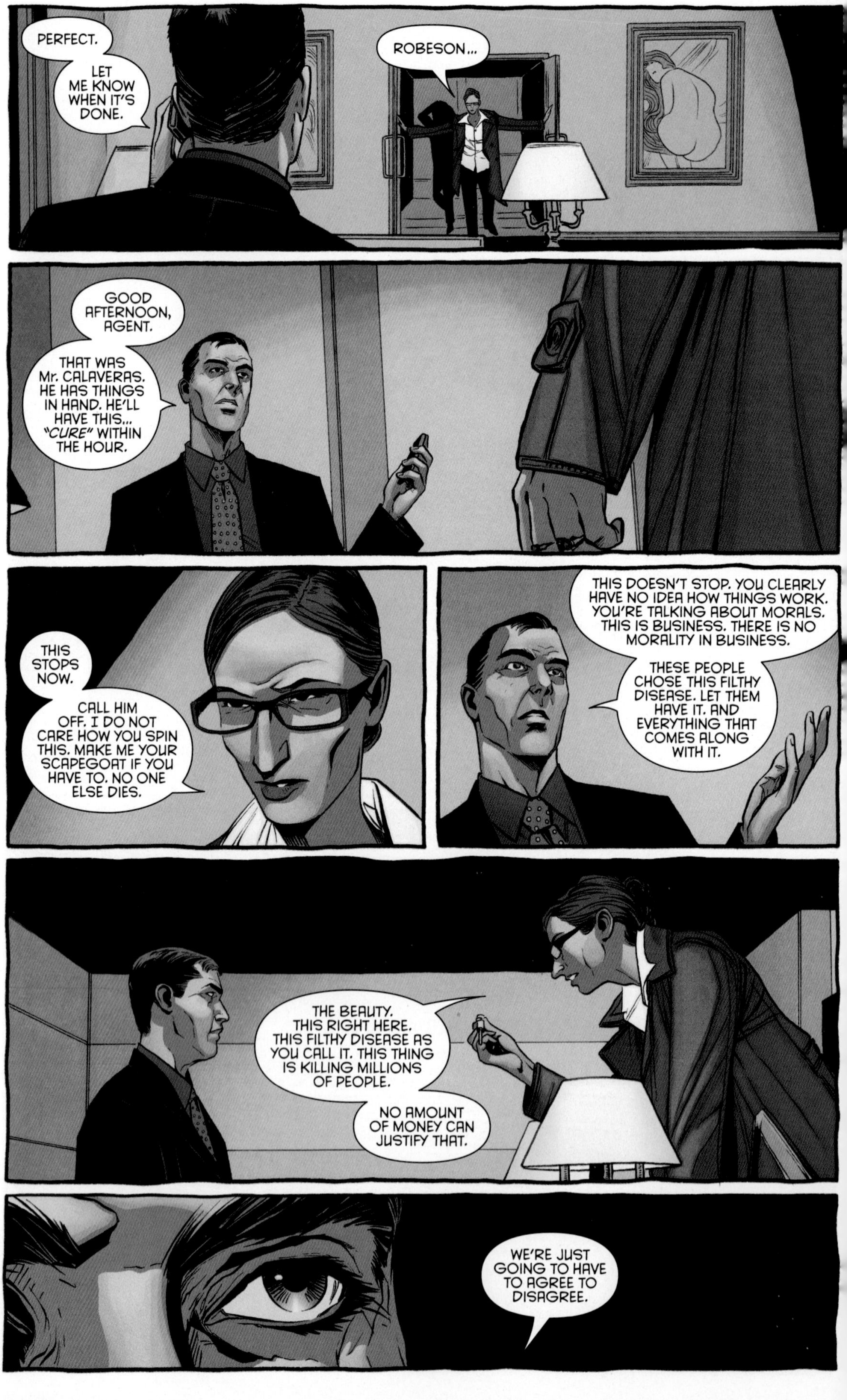
PERFECT.
LET ME KNOW WHEN IT'S DONE.
ROBESON...
GOOD AFTERNOON, AGENT.
THAT WAS Mr. CALAVERAS. HE HAS THINGS IN HAND. HE'LL HAVE THIS... "CURE" WITHIN THE HOUR.
THIS STOPS NOW.
CALL HIM OFF. I DO NOT CARE HOW YOU SPIN THIS. MAKE ME YOUR SCAPEGOAT IF YOU HAVE TO. NO ONE ELSE DIES.
THIS DOESN'T STOP. YOU CLEARLY HAVE NO IDEA HOW THINGS WORK. YOU'RE TALKING ABOUT MORALS. THIS IS BUSINESS. THERE IS NO MORALITY IN BUSINESS.
THESE PEOPLE CHOSE THIS FILTHY DISEASE. LET THEM HAVE IT. AND EVERYTHING THAT COMES ALONG WITH IT.
THE BEAUTY. THIS RIGHT HERE. THIS FILTHY DISEASE AS YOU CALL IT. THIS THING IS KILLING MILLIONS OF PEOPLE.
NO AMOUNT OF MONEY CAN JUSTIFY THAT.
WE'RE JUST GOING TO HAVE TO AGREE TO DISAGREE.

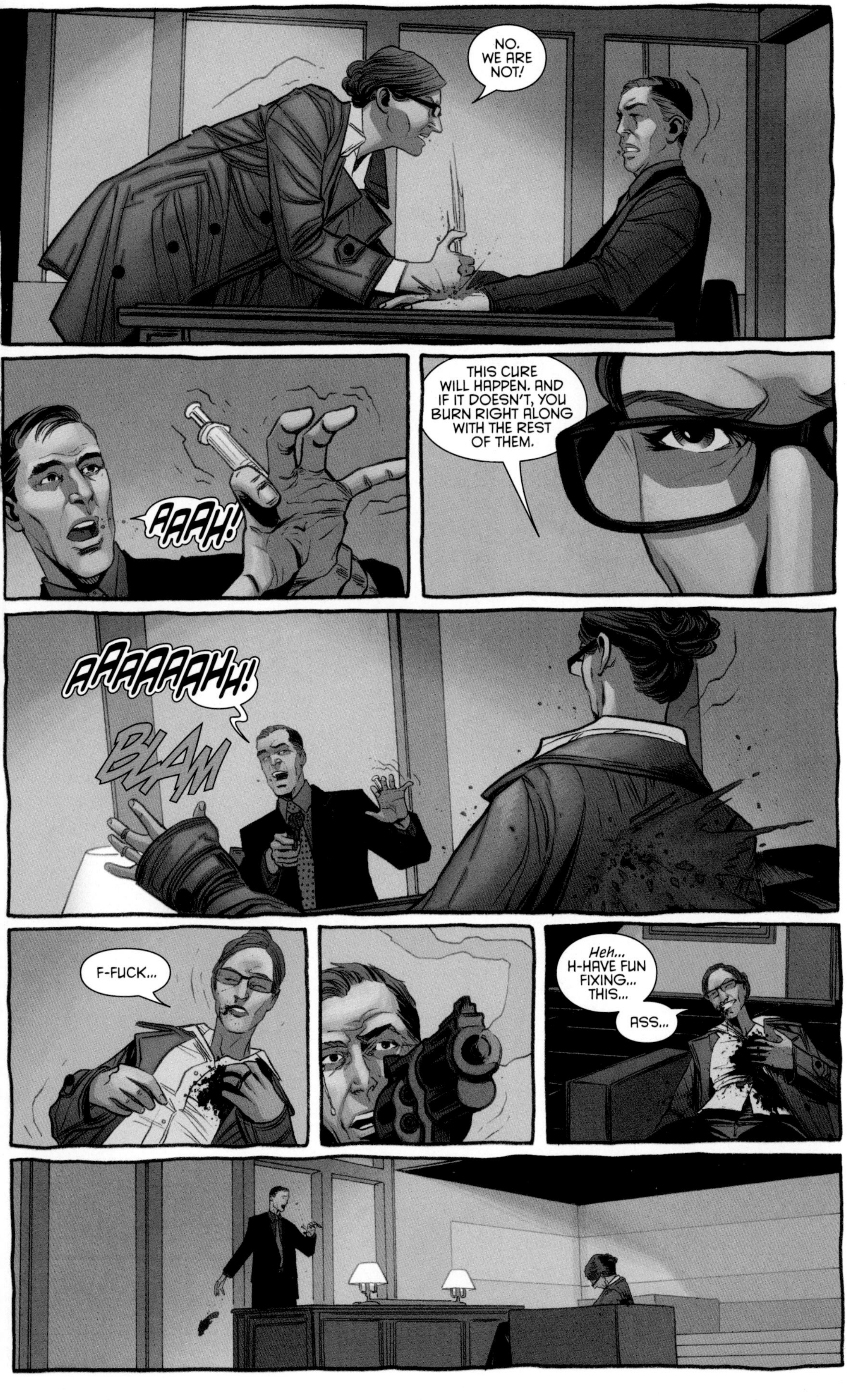
NO. WE ARE NOT!
AAAH!
THIS CURE WILL HAPPEN. AND IF IT DOESN'T, YOU BURN RIGHT ALONG WITH THE REST OF THEM.
AAAAAAHH!
BLAM
F-FUCK...
Heh... H-HAVE FUN FIXING... THIS...
ASS...

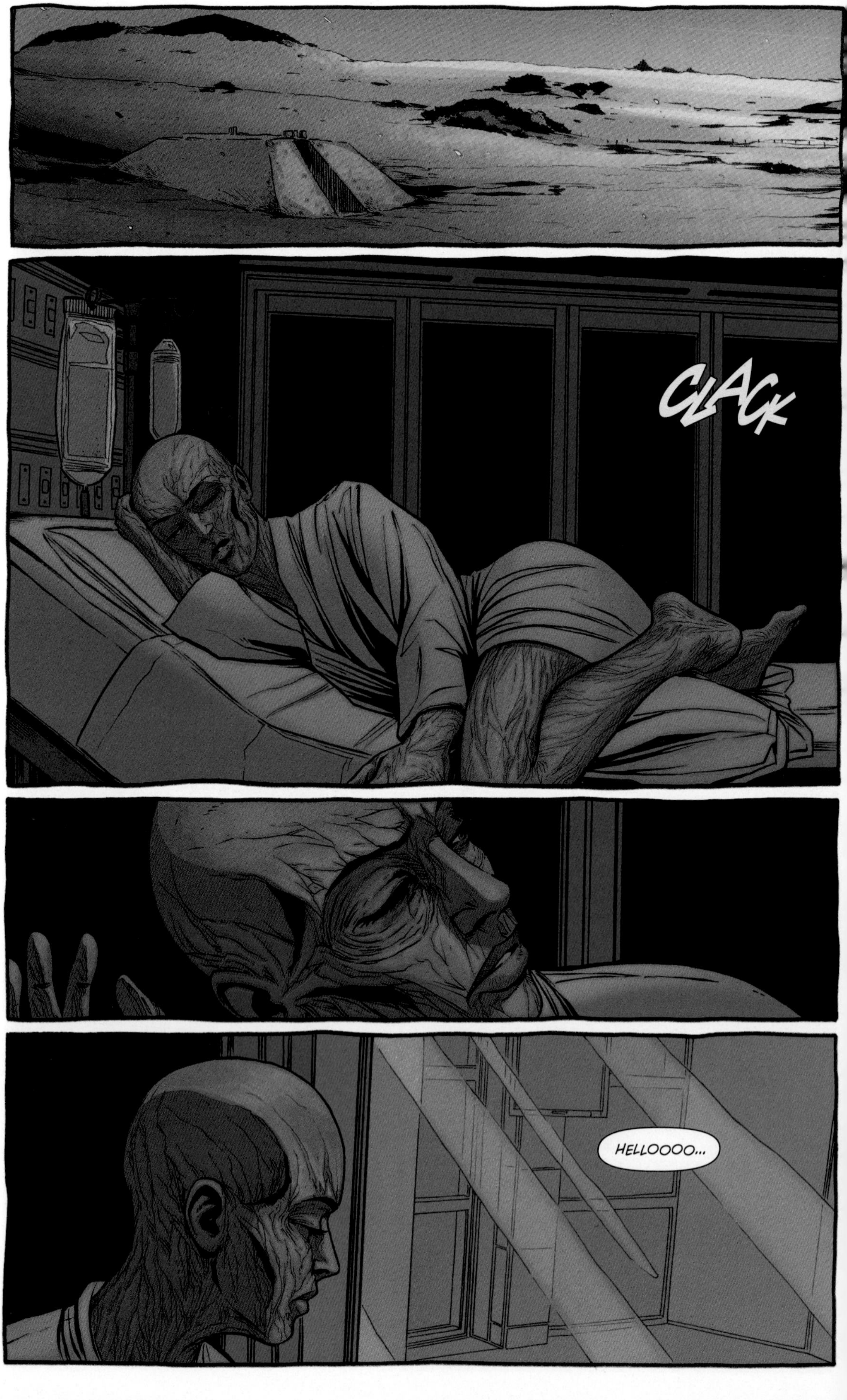
CLACK
HELLOOOO...

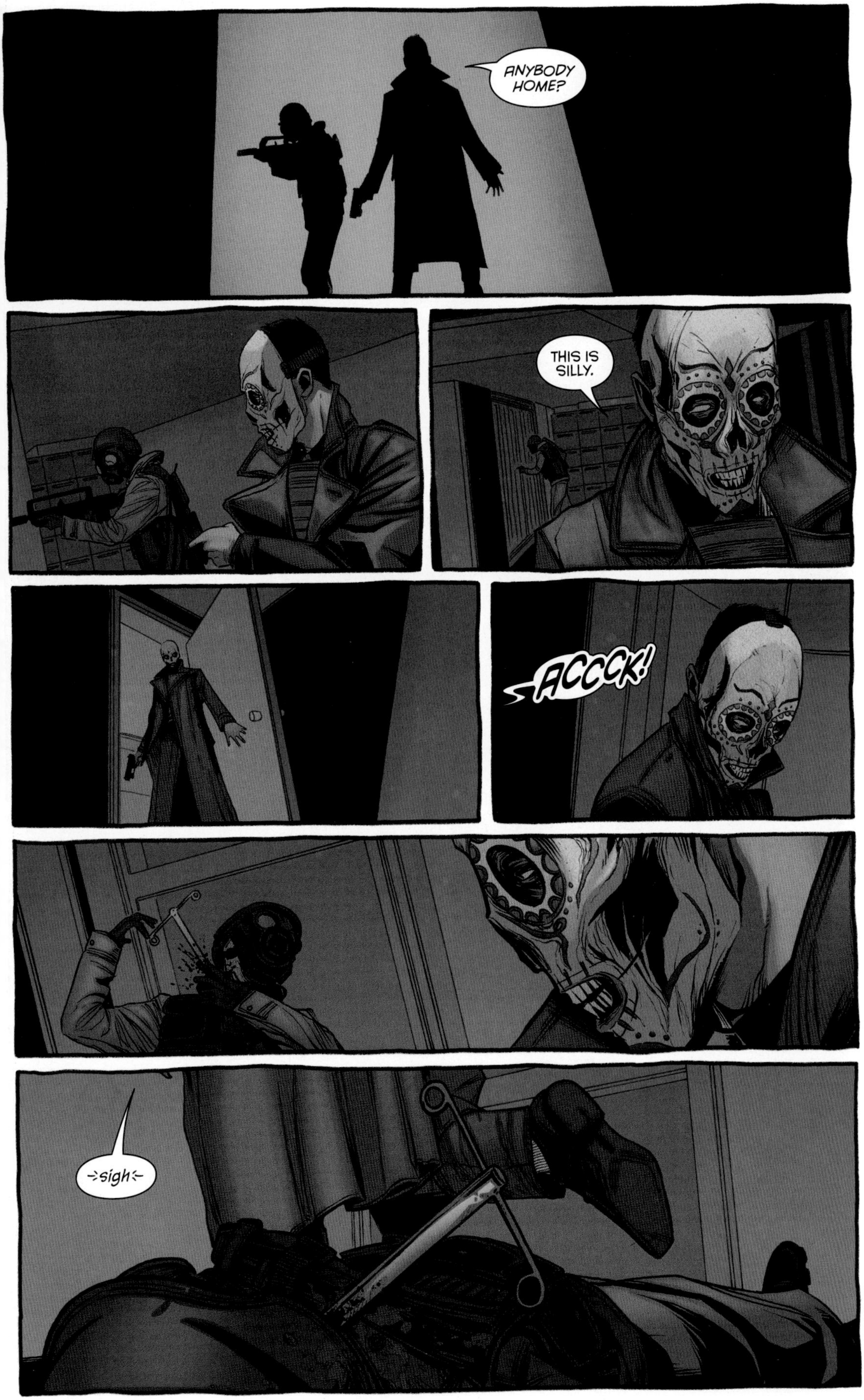
ANYBODY HOME?
THIS IS SILLY.
ACCCK!
-sigh-

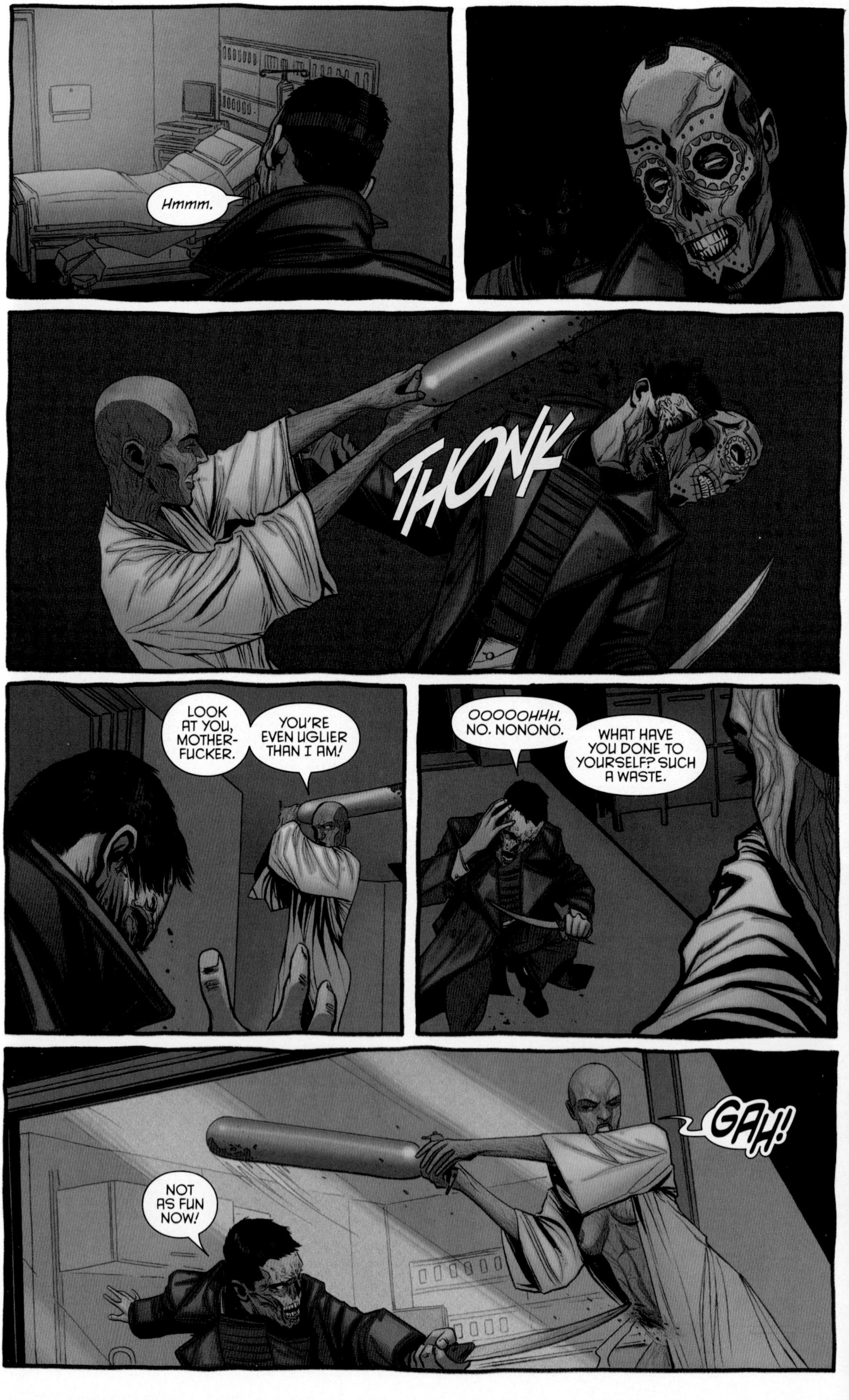
Hmmm.
THONK
LOOK AT YOU, MOTHER-FUCKER.
YOU'RE EVEN UGLIER THAN I AM!
OOOOOHHH. NO. NONONO.
WHAT HAVE YOU DONE TO YOURSELF? SUCH A WASTE.
GAH!
NOT AS FUN NOW!

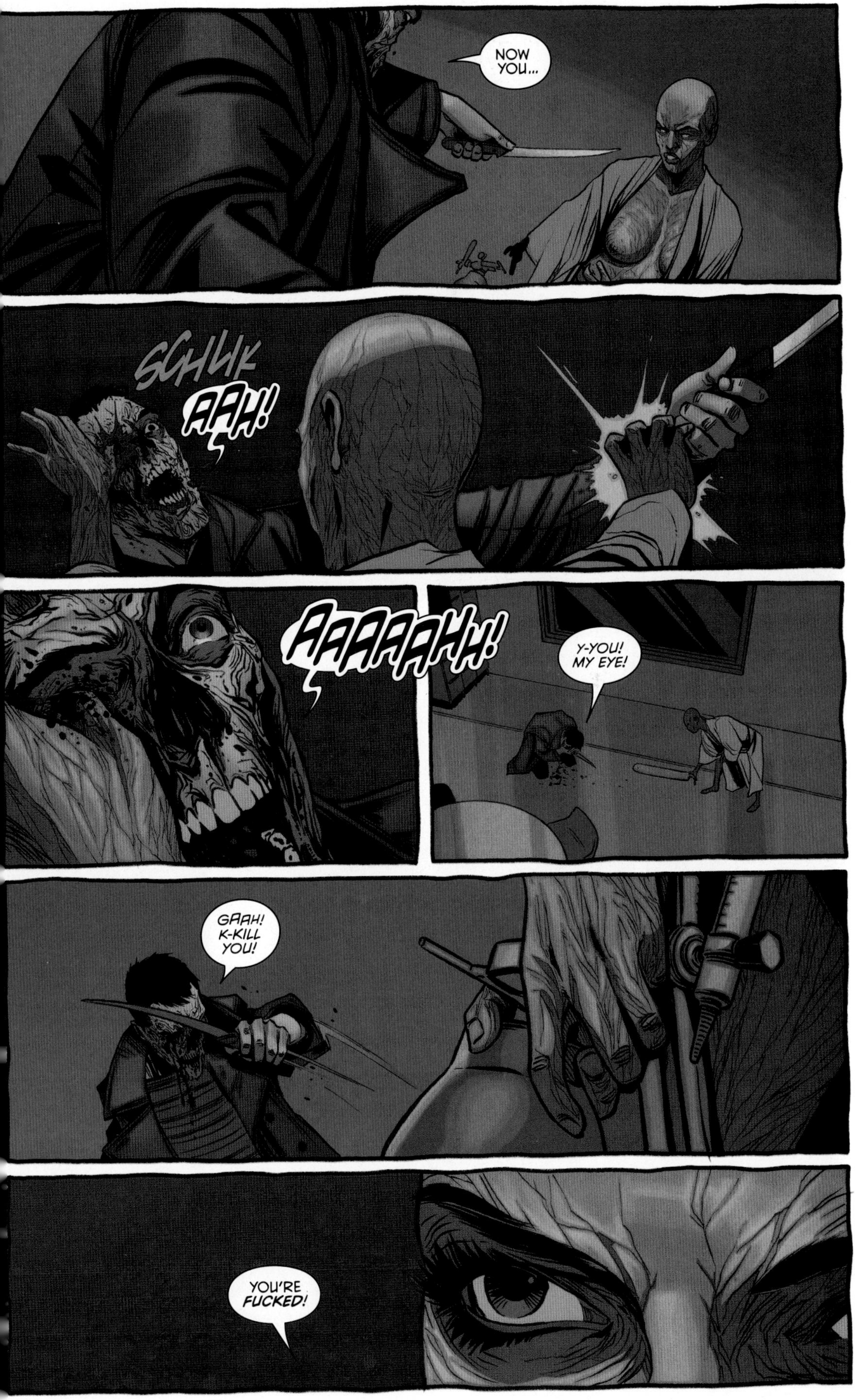
NOW YOU...
SCHLIK
AAH!
AAAAAAHH!
Y-YOU! MY EYE!
GAAH! K-KILL YOU!
YOU'RE FUCKED!

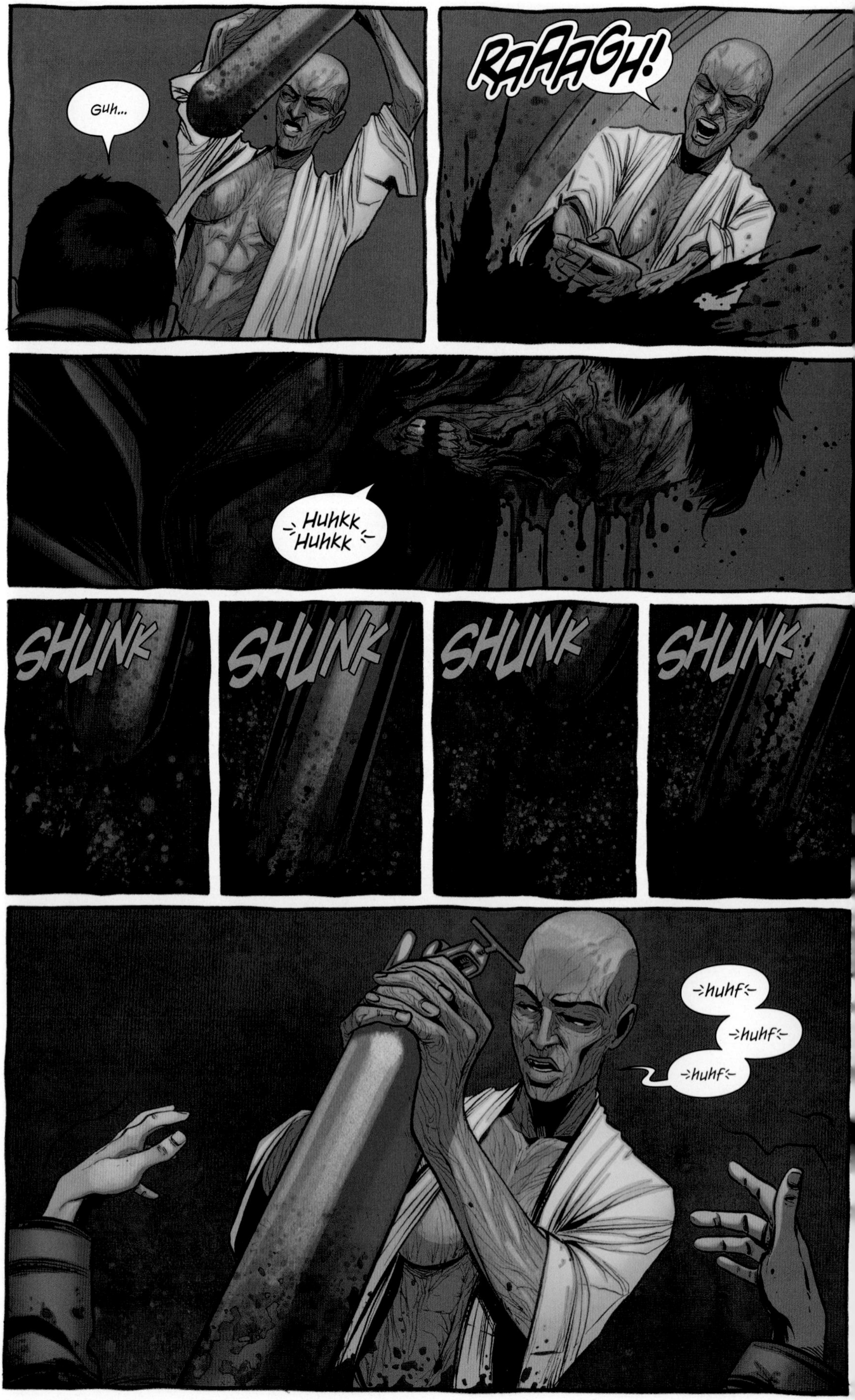
Guh...
RAAAGH!
Hunkk Hunkk
SHUNK
SHUNK
SHUNK
SHUNK
huhf
huhf
huhf

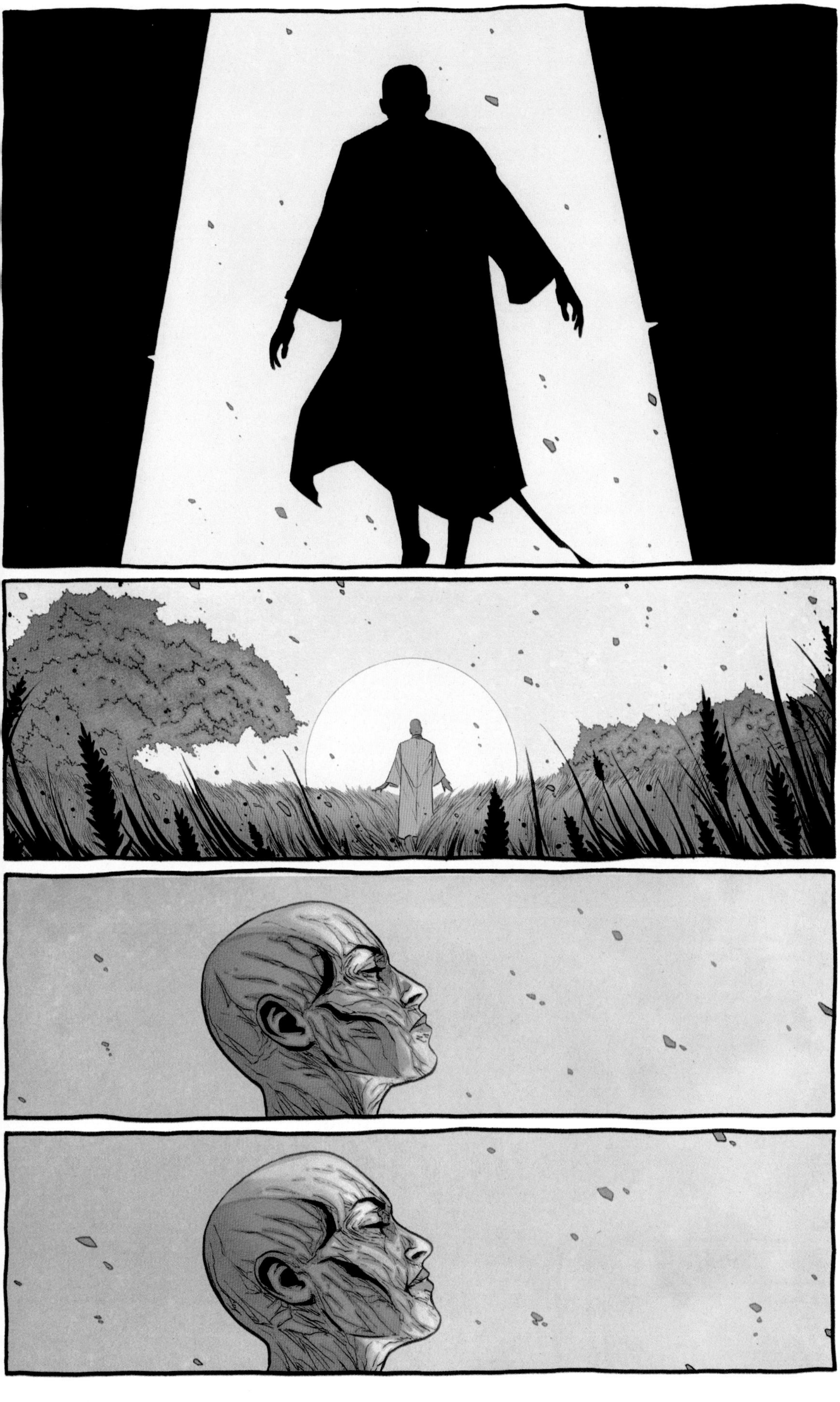

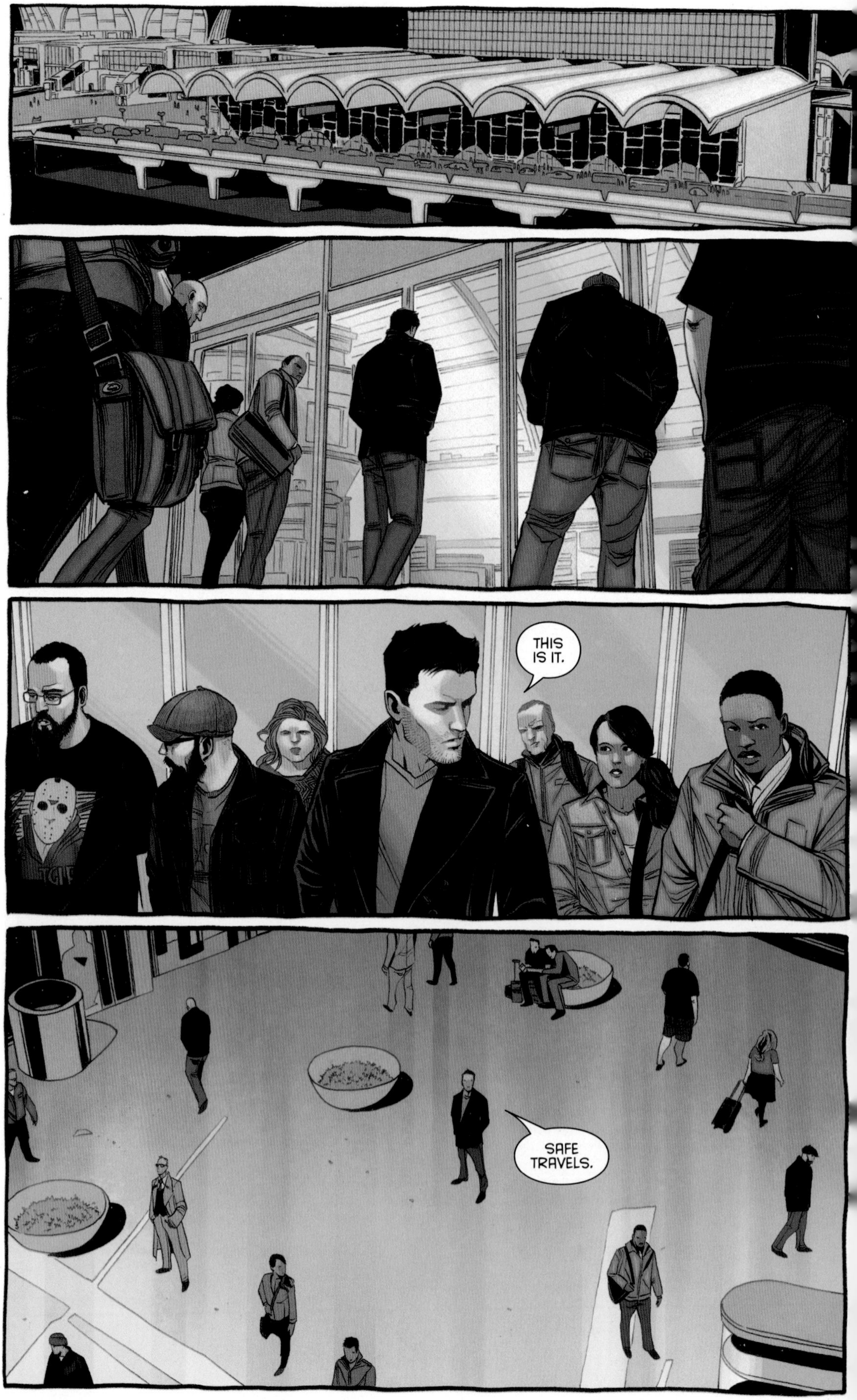
THIS IS IT.
SAFE TRAVELS.

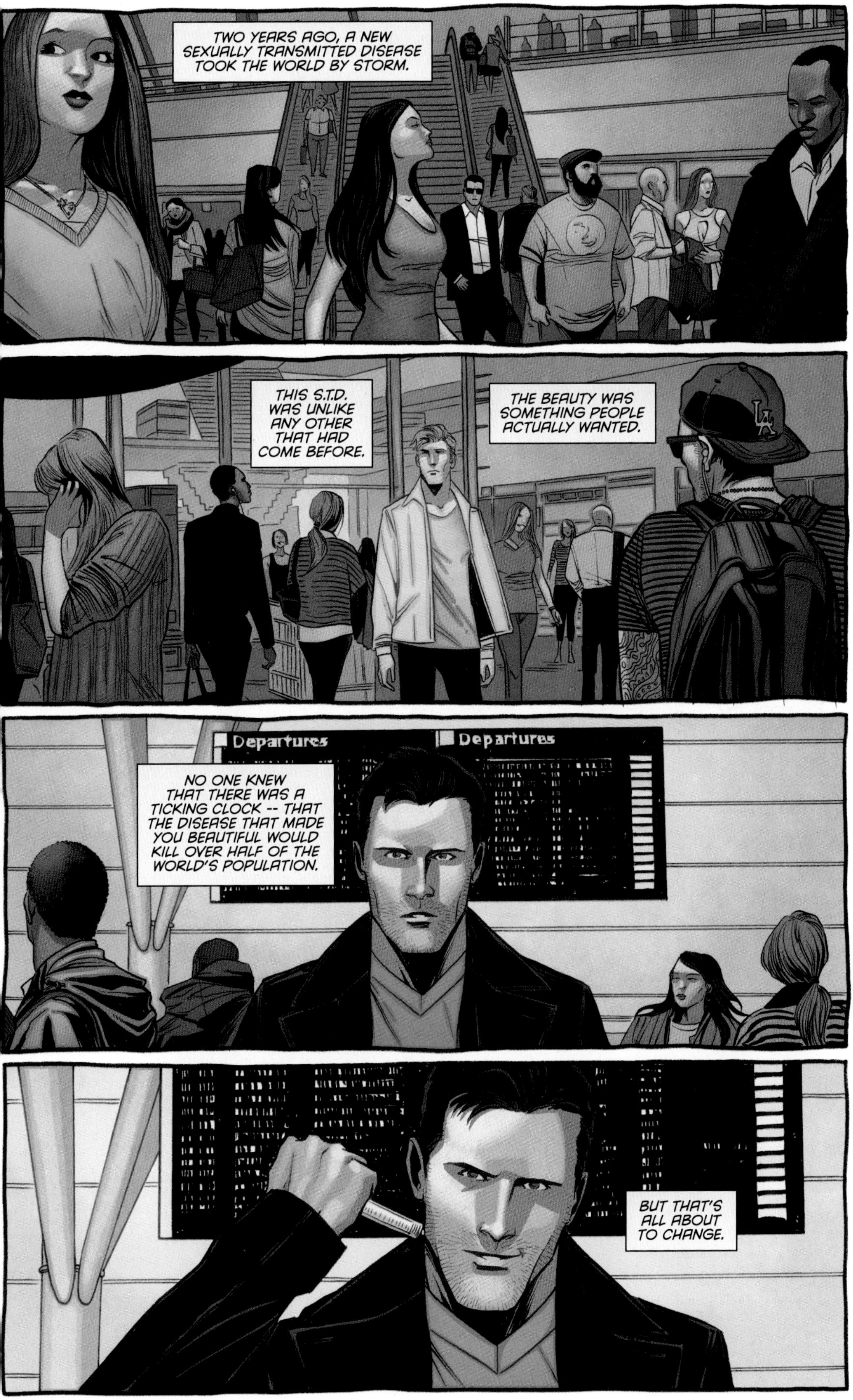
TWO YEARS AGO, A NEW SEXUALLY TRANSMITTED DISEASE TOOK THE WORLD BY STORM.
THIS S.T.D. WAS UNLIKE ANY OTHER THAT HAD COME BEFORE.
THE BEAUTY WAS SOMETHING PEOPLE ACTUALLY WANTED.
Departures
Departures
NO ONE KNEW THAT THERE WAS A TICKING CLOCK -- THAT THE DISEASE THAT MADE YOU BEAUTIFUL WOULD KILL OVER HALF OF THE WORLD'S POPULATION.
BUT THAT'S ALL ABOUT TO CHANGE.

COVERS

JEREMY HAUN
JASON A. HURLEY
JOHN RAUCH
THE BEAUTY
1
$3.50
image

ISSUE #1
Cover A
Jeremy Haun
& John Rauch

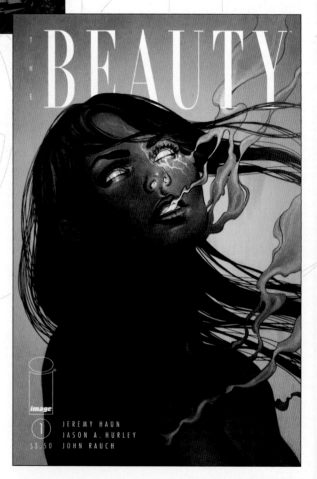

ISSUE #1
Cover B
Jenny Frison

THE BEAUTY
image
1
$3.50
JEREMY HAUN
JASON A. HURLEY
JOHN RAUCH

THE
BEAUTY
1
JEREMY HAUN
JASON A. HURLEY
JOHN RAUCH
$3.50

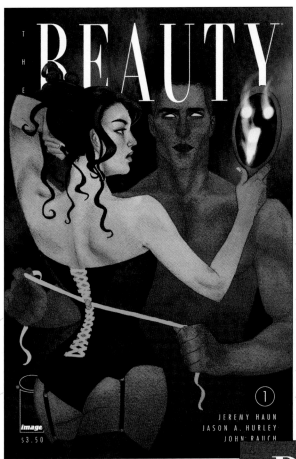

ISSUE #1

Cover C

Kevin Wada

ISSUE #1

Cover D

NYCC EXCLUSIVE

Andrew Robinson

THE
BEAUTY
1
NYCC
JEREMY HAUN
JASON A. HURLEY
JOHN RAUCH

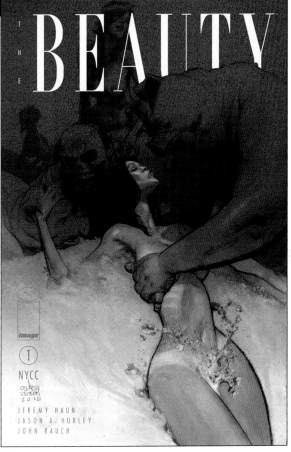

FROM THE ARTIST OF "BATWOMAN" AND "CONSTANTINE"
AND A GUY THAT RUNS A COMIC SHOP IN MIDDLE AMERICA
THE
BEAUTY
HAUN + HURLEY
1
SECRET EDITION

ISSUE #1

Cover E

SECRET EDITION
featuring
Jeremy Haun &
Jason A. Hurley

ISSUE #2

Cover A

Jeremy Haun
& John Rauch

JEREMY HAUN | JASON A. HURLEY | JOHN RAUCH
THE
BEAUTY
2
$3.50

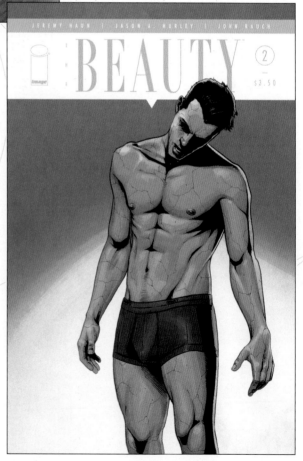

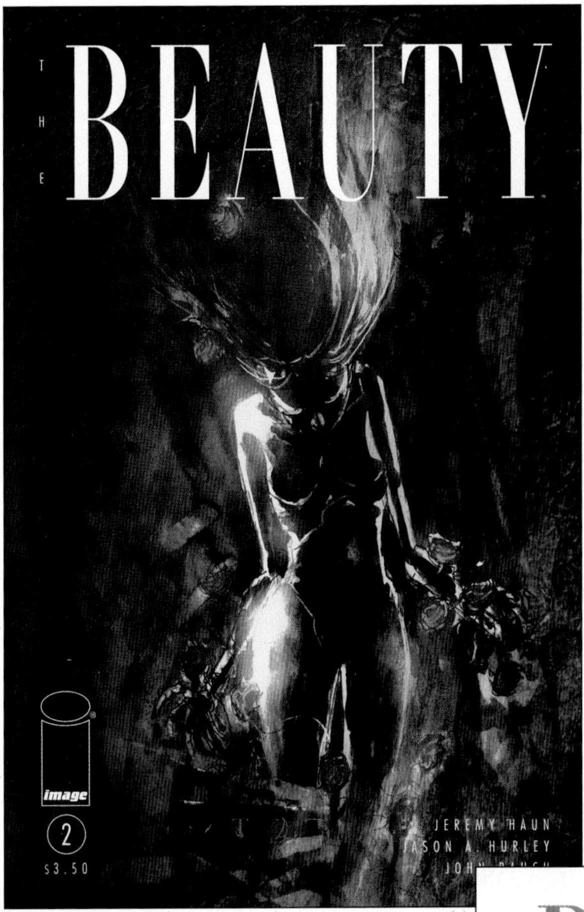
THE
BEAUTY
2
$3.50
JEREMY HAUN
JASON A. HURLEY
JOHN RAUCH

ISSUE #2
Cover B
Ben Templesmith

ISSUE #2
Cover C
Robbi Rodriguez

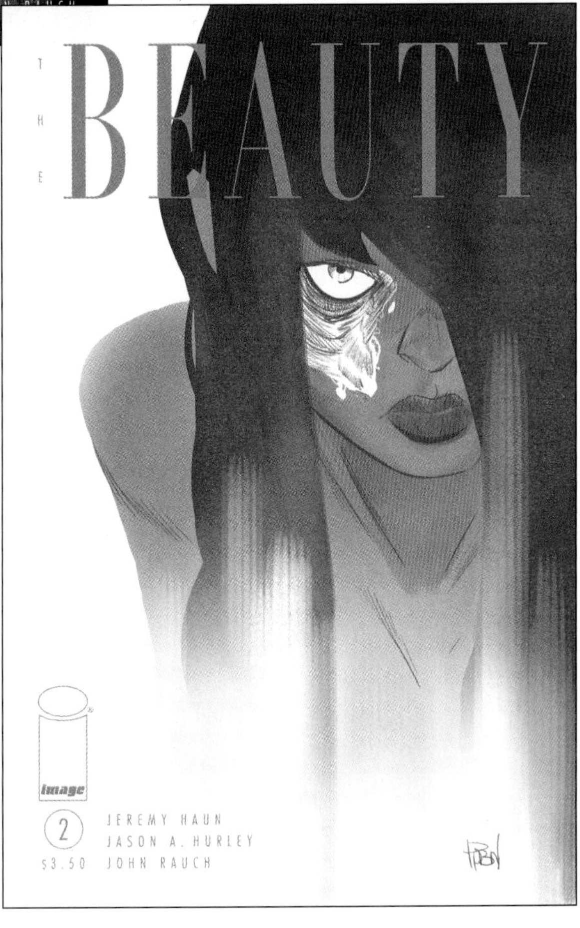
THE
BEAUTY
2
$3.50
JEREMY HAUN
JASON A. HURLEY
JOHN RAUCH

JEREMY HAUN | JASON A. HURLEY | JOHN RAUCH
THE
BEAUTY
3
$3.50
image

ISSUE #3
Cover B
Christopher Mitten

ISSUE #3
Cover A
Jeremy Haun
& John Rauch

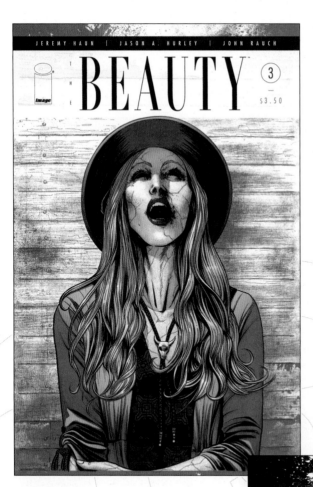

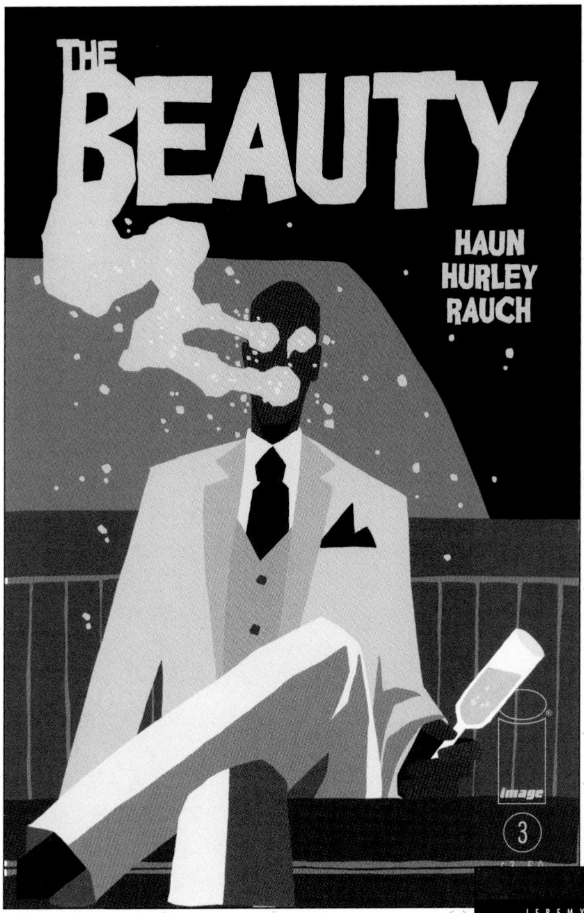
THE BEAUTY
HAUN
HURLEY
RAUCH
image
3

ISSUE #3
Cover C
Jeremy Haun

ISSUE #4
Cover A
Jeremy Haun
& John Rauch

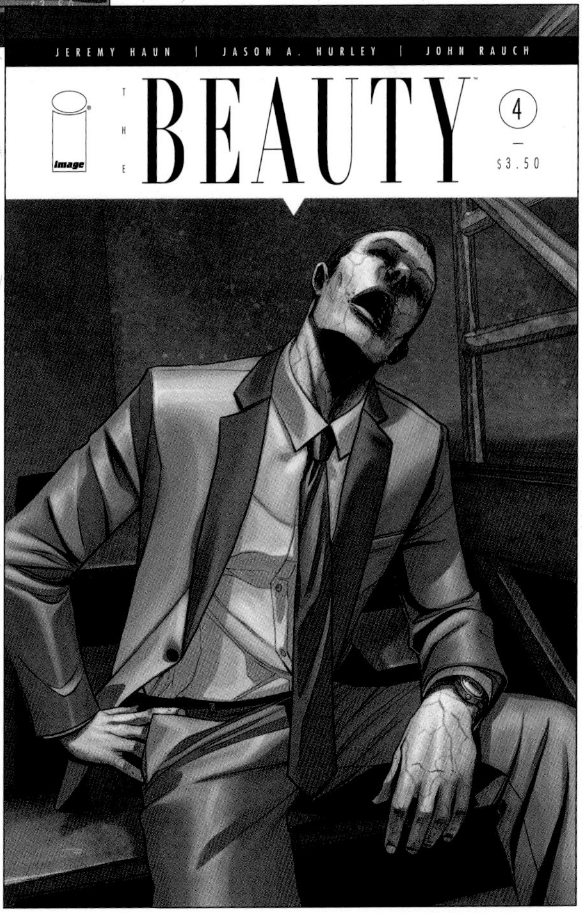
JEREMY HAUN | JASON A. HURLEY | JOHN RAUCH
THE BEAUTY
image
4
$3.50

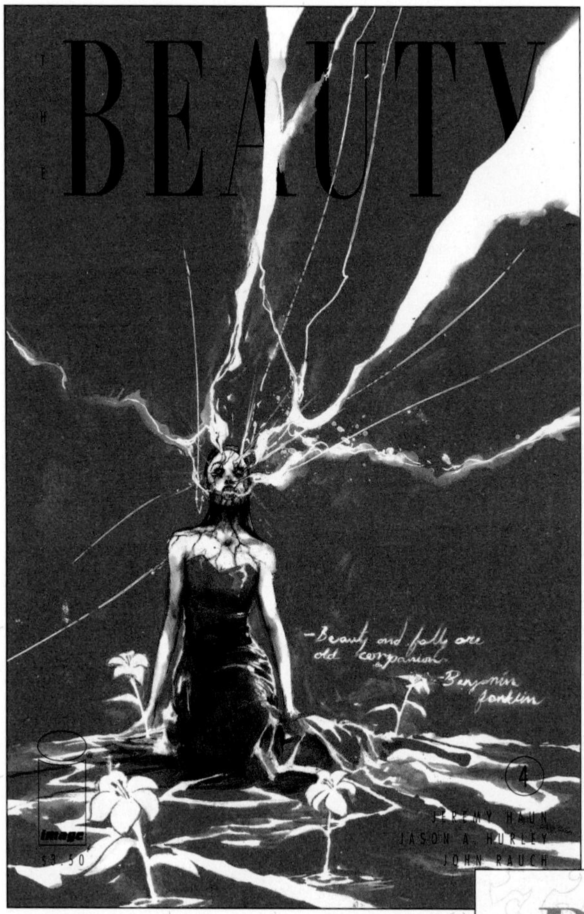
THE
BEAUTY
—Beauty and folly are old companions.
—Benjamin Franklin
4
JEREMY HAUN
JASON A. HURLEY
JOHN RAUCH
image
$3.50

ISSUE #4
Cover B
Riley Rossmo

ISSUE #4
Cover C
Brian Koschak

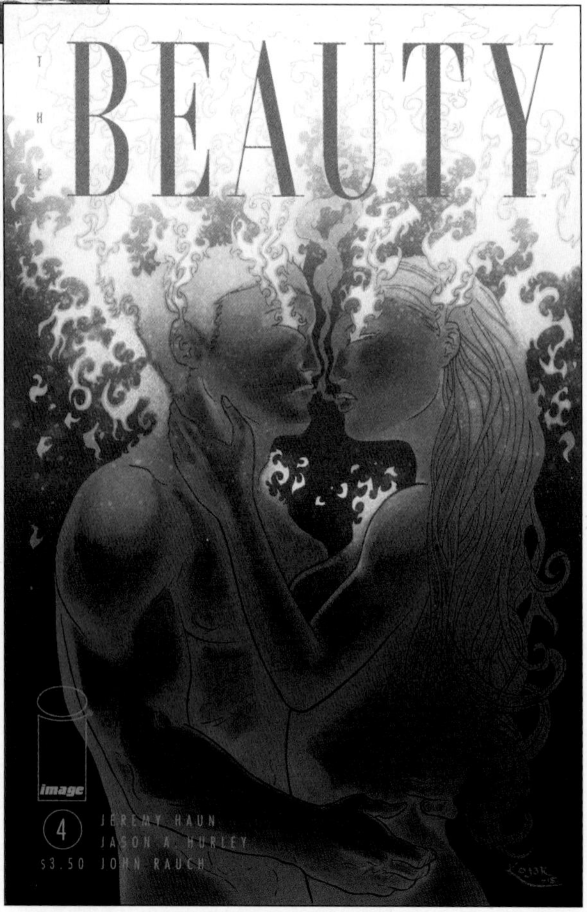
THE
BEAUTY
image
4
JEREMY HAUN
JASON A. HURLEY
$3.50
JOHN RAUCH

JEREMY HAUN | JASON A. HURLEY | JOHN RAUCH
THE BEAUTY
5
$3.50
image

ISSUE #5
Cover A
Jeremy Haun
& John Rauch

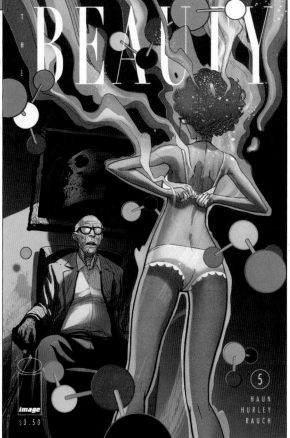

ISSUE #5
Cover B
Mike Huddleston

THE BEAUTY
5
HAUN
HURLEY
RAUCH
image
$3.50

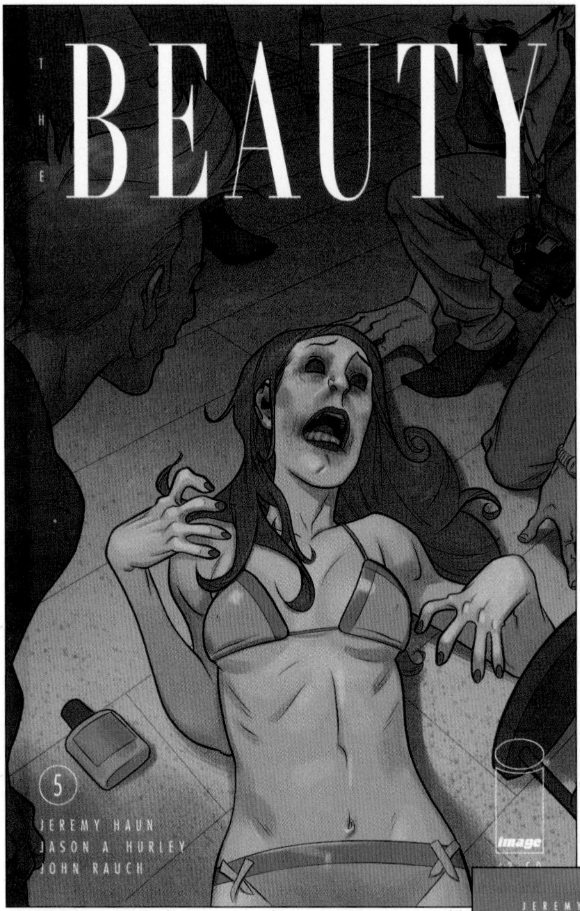
THE BEAUTY
5
JEREMY HAUN
JASON A. HURLEY
JOHN RAUCH
image

ISSUE #5
Cover C
Mike Tisserand

ISSUE #6
Cover A
Jeremy Haun
& John Rauch

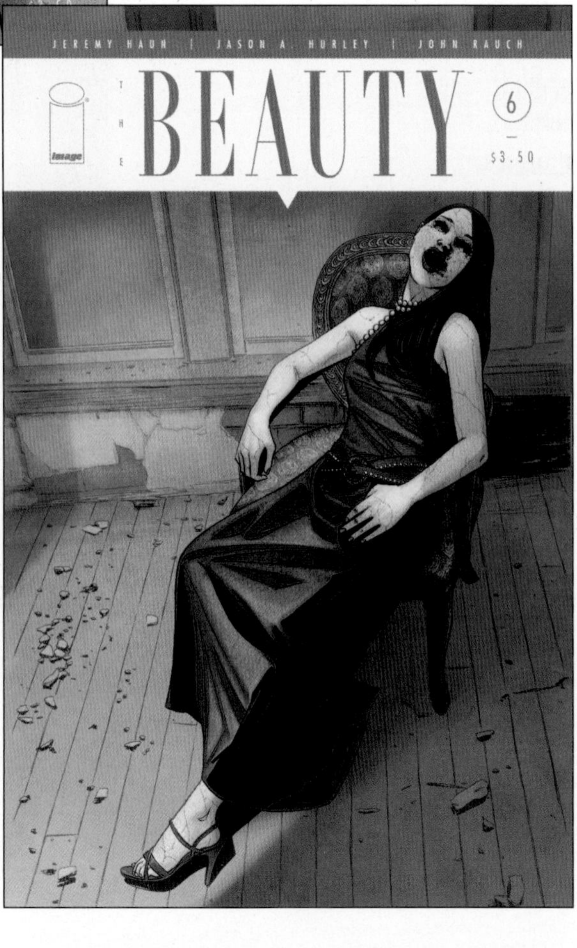
JEREMY HAUN | JASON A. HURLEY | JOHN RAUCH
image
THE BEAUTY
6
$3.50

THE BEAUTY
6
JEREMY HAUN
JASON A. HURLEY
image
$3.50

ISSUE #6
Cover B
Greg Hinkle

ISSUE #6
Cover C
Kate Sherron

THE BEAUTY
6
HAUN
HURLEY
RAUCH
image
$3.50

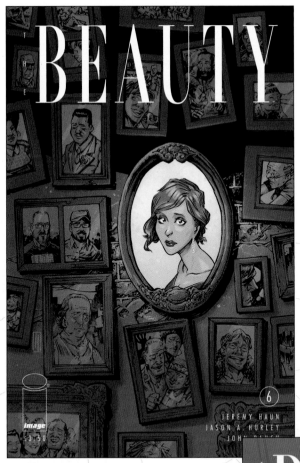

BIOGRAPHIES

Jeremy Haun, co-writer, co-creator, and often artist of THE BEAUTY, has also worked on *Wolf Moon* from Vertigo, and *Constantine* and *Batwoman* from DC. Over the past decade plus, along with wearing calluses on his fingers doing work for DC, Marvel, Image, and others, he has created and written several projects. Some you might know are the graphic novel *Narcoleptic Sunday, The Leading Man,* and *Dino Day.* He is a part of the Bad Karma Creative group, whose *Bad Karma Volume One* debuted at NYCC 2013, thanks to Kickstarter funding.

Jeremy resides in a crumbling mansion in Joplin, Missouri with his wife and two superheroes-in-training.

Jason A. Hurley has been in the comic book game for over fifteen years. However, none of you have ever heard of him because, until recently, he's been almost completely exclusive to the retail sector. In addition to comic books, he loves pro wrestling, bad horror movies, Freddy Mercury, hummingbirds, his parents, and pizza. While he's never actually tried it, he also thinks curling looks like a hell of a lot of fun. Hurley claims his personal heroes are Earl Bassett and Valentine McKee, because they live a life of adventure on their own terms. He also claims that he would brain anyone who showed even the most remote signs of becoming a cannibalistic undead bastard, including his own brother, without a second thought. He's lived in Joplin, Missouri for most of his life, and never plans to leave.

John Rauch is an American comic book colorist whose credits include: THE DARKNESS, INVINCIBLE, *Teen Titans: Year One, Patsy Walker: Hellcat,* and a bunch of other stuff not worth bragging about. He enjoys speaking about himself in the third person and pretending he is more talented and relevant than he really is to fight off bouts of depression.

Fonografiks The banner name for the comics work of designer Steven Finch, "Fonografiks" has provided lettering and design to a number of Image Comics titles, including NOWHERE MEN, INJECTION, THEY'RE NOT LIKE US, TREES, WE STAND ON GUARD, the LUTHER STRODE trilogy, the Eisner Award winning anthology series POPGUN, and the multi-award winning SAGA.